DEAD IN THE SKIP

DEAD IN THE SKIP

A DETECTIVE INSPECTOR ROLAND BENITO THRILLER

INGER GAMMELGAARD MADSEN

Translated from Danish by Sinéad Quirke Køngerskov

This is a work of fiction. Names, characters, places, and incidents are either products of the author's imagination or used fictitiously. Any resemblance to actual events, locales, or persons, living, dead, or undead, is entirely coincidental.

Cover design by Podium Publishing

ISBN: 978-1-0394-2218-6

Published in 2023 by Podium Publishing, ULC
www.podiumaudio.com

DEAD IN THE SKIP

When he straightened up, the shiny new Lloyd shoes he really only wore for good wear sank into the muck, and he almost fell backwards. The sensation of something fragile being crushed between fingers lay quivering uncomfortably beneath his skin. At the same time, it evoked in him an exhilaration reminiscent of sexual arousal. The feeling surprised him—and yet it didn't.

It was the same as the time with the toads that lived in the vegetation around the little pond in the back garden of his childhood home. The ugly, repulsive toads with their warty backs, crawling clumsily and helplessly around on the garden tiles. Some had been as big as the soles of his child-size shoes. The little arms, with their four stubby fingers that appeared to have been amputated, waved helplessly under his shoe as he stepped on them. Their whimpering only gave reason to press his foot even harder, until he heard a crunch and there was silence. Some died in silence. Pain was obviously not something all toads expressed. Afterwards, he threw them in the garden pond. Mum wondered what disease the toads had suffered when they lay dead in the water, belly up, and began to smell. But she hadn't done anything about it, either.

He stood with his arms down by his sides, stretching and clenching his hands to make the feeling go away. His trousers had dirty knees. Desperately, he tried to brush the soil off. His breathing was strained, coming in heavy gasps, and he could feel the sticky film of sweat on his forehead. The stifling heat lay on the damp air like a heavy duvet. The smell of rotten leaves and mould filled his nostrils. Panic crept in and mingled with the frustration. He looked around. Thankfully, there was no one here. And luckily, it was raining. It kept people indoors. He looked up and let the rain hit his face. The little cold slaps of the drops against his skin made him shudder slightly. Another feeling he hadn't experienced since he was a child. With eyes closed, he tasted the water dripping down his lips. Suddenly, he looked down at her. The rainwater had begun to collect in her eye sockets. The body was surprisingly heavy as he lifted it up. One arm fell limply down to the side, dangling towards his hip as he began to walk in the rain. The water ran down her cheeks like tears. He felt the crying in his throat. Why had she screamed? He hated that whimpering. She should have done as he had said. The tears mingled with the rainwater and tasted salty in his mouth.

1

The newsreader's voice on the radio told of several riots and suicide bombers in the Middle East. She listened to the voice without registering what was being said. It was the same every time she heard the news on the radio or TV. But it was so far away. On another planet. *Denmark's come closer to a terrorist attack since we followed the Americans into war in Iraq,* her husband said often enough. The world was cruel. But that wasn't her world. She felt safe in Denmark, particularly in Jutland, and most especially here in Aarhus, where there was rarely more crime than the occasional assault or rape. That was bad enough, of course, but it didn't affect her little world in the house in Brabrand protected by the high privet hedge.

The news ended and dinner music took over. She hummed along to "Kære Lille Mormor" by Richard Ragnvald. Through the kitchen window, she saw her teenage daughter come running back. The rubbish bin at the front door had been overflowing; it hadn't been put out on the road the night before for the binmen to collect that morning, so she had asked Maria, who had only been hanging out in her room with her iPod, to run down to the skip with it. She didn't understand all the modern gear young girls needed today. It hadn't been like that with the other two, who had long since flown the coop. They hadn't meant to have more children, but then . . .

Her gaze slid up towards the sky. It was going to rain again soon. Where had the sun gone this summer?

Maria tumbled breathlessly into the kitchen without taking off her shoes.

"Mum, Mum! There's something in the skip!"

"What?"

She turned off the radio, where a journalist had begun a debate with a politician.

"A hand." Her voice shook.

My teenage daughter watches too many films. She smiled, continuing to butter the rye bread for lunch. *And she certainly doesn't lack imagination, either.*

"Is it not just a doll someone threw out?"

"No!"

The girl was breathing heavily.

She turned to her daughter, only now understanding something must be wrong. Maria's face was chalk white. Her eyes shone with a horror she hadn't seen before. She was still clutching the bag of rubbish, as if her hand had seized with cramp. Then she broke down in tears and dropped the bag onto the freshly washed kitchen floor.

Desperate, she wiped her hands on her apron. "Oh, sweetheart, really? It can't be!"

She quickly put on a jumper.

"Let's go down and find out what you think is a hand."

Maria's entire body began to shake. Her mother made her sit on a chair at the kitchen table. She got a glass of cold water from the tap and put it in front of her daughter. "Drink that; I'll be back in a moment."

"No, Mum, don't go down there. What if the killer's still there?"

She smiled affectionately. "Let's see what it is first."

Still, on the way down to the skip, she felt uneasy, and her legs began to shake. If it were true, what would she do? She shook her head at the thought. Of course there wasn't a hand in the skip. The air was stifling and humid. She pulled her blouse away from her skin to cool down. The worn clogs she had hurriedly put on were having a hard time keeping up with her.

The skip was a large, closed model. It was rusty now, but it had once been red. There were three hatches on the front. One was open. Maria had apparently fled without closing it again. She peered inside, and the lukewarm stink of decay greeted her. The flies buzzed. She caught sight of the hand between some black bin bags and an old, stained chair cushion. She held her breath, and her heart began to pound. It looked like a human hand. She looked around for something that could reach in there. She spotted a stick on the ground, which she picked up. It could just about reach the hand. She lifted it gently with the stick. With the movement, a black bag rolled over, revealing the entire arm, a shoulder, and part of a white neck. In the light falling through the hatch, she could see the colour of the thin neck went from chalk white to blue-black. She didn't know where she had gathered the courage from, and she still didn't understand what it was she was looking at. It had all happened in a trance. Slowly, she lifted the stick again and pushed the cardboard box covering the face. The box overturned. She watched it roll around a few times in a kind of slow motion, following it with her eyes before moving her gaze to the place it had been. She wanted to scream, but she couldn't. Her throat was constricted.

A face had appeared. The eyes stared dead and empty at the roof of the skip, the mouth was open, and the lips were blue-black. It was a child. A little girl.

She threw away the stick and ran to the nearest bush with her hand over her mouth. But she couldn't stop the convulsions of her diaphragm. The bitter taste rose, stinging her throat. She moved her hand when the hot liquid came and threw up between the bushes.

2

She heard the phone faintly through the bathroom door and the thick terry towel she had wrapped around her wet, freshly washed hair. She had only just got up, even though it was past noon. There was nothing to get up for. There were, of course, the dishes, cleaning, and laundry. The house looked as if she had been having a wild party until the early hours of the morning. Her head felt that way, too. But if that had been the reason, at least then she would probably have had fun. Instead, she had emptied a bottle of red wine on her own while staring at a mind-numbingly boring show on TV, without really watching or hearing it. Her thoughts had been in a completely different world. When her eyelids had started to get heavy, and she had realised she was napping in an awkward position that would no doubt result in both fluid retention and a crick in her neck, she had turned off the TV. She hadn't been bothered with cleaning up and had collapsed onto the bed, where she had immediately fallen into a restless sleep with dreams and nightmares she no longer remembered. They lingered in her soul as an uncomfortable feeling. Something she remembered in small glimpses, but immediately forgot again. Something she *wasn't* going to remember.

"Is this Kamilla Holm?" asked the voice in the handset.

"Yes."

"Freelance photographer Kamilla Holm?"

She hesitated. It sounded like work. "Yes," she replied anyway, thinking about how many times she had declined assignments in the last year or hadn't picked up the phone when it rang.

"Yes, that's me," she repeated in a firmer voice.

"You were recommended to me. I'm new," said the voice with a Copenhagen accent, now sounding a little more eager.

New where? She tied the belt of her dressing gown as she held the phone between her shoulder and chin.

"I'm on the editorial staff of the *Daily News*," the voice continued, as if Kamilla's thoughts had passed through the telephone cables.

It had to be a new journalist. All the old ones had probably left a long time ago, and the whole gang of well-known press she had worked with on so many assignments—from newly opened businesses to the Aarhus Festival and political events—had been replaced with new and unknown journalists. It had been over a year since she had last worked for the newspaper. Since she had worked at all. Her savings were also about to run dry. The bank had written to remind her overdraft had been exceeded, as if she didn't have internet banking and know that herself. But it couldn't continue; the bank had been understanding for a long time.

So there was someone left on the editorial staff who remembered her enough to recommend her. Someone who had been happy with her work. Thygesen, she concluded. It was guaranteed to be editor Ivan Thygesen. She had always guessed he would stay on until retirement. He was the type of boss the employees didn't think had a life outside his job. He would still be sitting behind his desk when the others went home in the evening and was there again—or, rather, still there—in the morning when they arrived. The only sign a change had taken place during the night was that he had changed his shirt.

"I have an assignment for you—if you'd like it?" The last bit came hesitantly. Thygesen had probably warned the journalist that she risked getting a negative answer, and she would absolutely have another number, if not more, to ring in her notebook. Apparently, the newspaper still hadn't hired a permanent photographer. There were plenty of freelance photographers, but the journalist had called her. It was a chance. She was going to start again.

"Of course," she heard herself say.

"Can we meet on Edwin Rahrs Vej in Brabrand as soon as possible? You'll see where I mean."

"Yes! I'm on the way."

"My name's Anne Larsen, by the way," said the journalist.

Kamilla had already pulled the wet towel off her head before she hung up the phone. As she went over her hair cursorily with the hairdryer and got dressed at the same time, she remembered she had forgotten to ask what it was about. What did the journalist mean by "you'll see where I mean?" The first assignment in over a year, and she had forgotten to ask the most important question. Maybe she had lost her touch?

3

Pathologist Henry Leander always arrived at a murder scene with the forensics team, before anyone else had the chance to trample on clues that could prove to be vital evidence. Even a single strand of hair could be crucial.

Despite being a seasoned medical examiner, he had to admit every new case gave him a sense of fear deep in his gut. He never knew what sight was going to greet him. At the same time, it was that sense of fear that drove him. It was also a sense of excitement, a desire to solve a riddle, find the killer's mistake and expose them. He loved his job, even though it was the reason he had given up hope of finding new love after Mary's death nine years before. She had been his good, faithful, and trusted partner for twenty-five years. She had died of lung cancer shortly after their silver wedding anniversary, after years of intense smoking. She hadn't minded him crawling into bed beside her when he came home late after he had been poking around in a rotten corpse. She had been a vet, poking around in a bit of everything in that regard herself. Three years after her death, he had met a young widow through some friends. She was of English descent, like he was—and also Mary had been. He had figured they must have something in common. But she couldn't bear the thought of his dead "clients," as she had called them. She had claimed he stank of them and pulled away from him when he had tried to hold her. He had tried to explain to her that he wore sterile gloves whenever he touched a corpse and showered before coming home to her, but it hadn't helped. Of course, that couldn't continue long term. Also taking into account his fifty-nine summers, he had decided to give up his pursuit of women. He had bought an English setter, who he called Bruce—because something about it reminded him of Bruce Willis—joined the English Setter Club, and started going on a different kind of hunt. The latter two mostly for the sake of being social. Hunting also suited his English aristocratic exterior, and he thought he looked perfect in his khaki-coloured hunting gear and hat. At the same time, he had ample opportunity to move around in the vast woods early in the morning, when the dew was still sitting in cobwebs and the morning frost lay like cool bluish banks between the tree trunks. Fair enough, not many women went hunting, so his hobby hadn't improved his prospects in that area, but Bruce had found a mate and had fathered a litter of puppies, so a few additions to the family had come of it.

Inspector Roland Benito arrived and greeted him with a nod when he reached the skip. They hadn't seen each other for a long time, but this wasn't the time for anything other than a formal nod.

"It's a little girl," said Roland. It sounded like a warning.

A technician from forensics in a white protective suit and shoe covers crawled into the waste container with a camera. The flash flared in the darkness. The skip was so cramped they couldn't all fit in at once. At long last, the technician clambered out with a nod to indicate he had finished. Leander crawled awkwardly into the large bin. The hatch sat about a metre above the ground, and his foot sank into the rubbish when he stepped inside. Something damp penetrated one of his socks. He immediately smelled the decay and thought of rats. If there was one thing he hated more than anything else, it was rats. Rats could disfigure a corpse, rendering it unidentifiable and delaying proceedings. Not a pretty sight.

He turned on the torch. The girl had been laid carefully on a bed of black bin bags. Her eyes stared up at the roof of the skip, as if something up there had hardened her gaze. Reluctantly, he looked up, slamming his neck against the container's roof. "Ouch, damn it!"

"What happened?" asked Roland, sticking his head in through the hatch.

Leander had dropped the torch. The cone of light shone obliquely on the face of the dead girl, making grotesque shadows, like when children try to scare each other in the dark by shining torches under their chins.

He picked up the torch and squatted down next to the girl, as he had now painfully learned it wasn't possible to stand upright. Carefully, he stroked the muddy hair away from her cheek, almost dropping the torch again when a black beetle hurried from her ear and hid among the rotten leaves. A grimace slid over his face as he recognised it as *Necrodes littoralis*—aka the grave robber. Insects had been his great hobby for many years. Most women had found that bizarre, too. In a nook in his basement, he had decorated a little room with shelves and racks filled with jars and larger showcases of insects. Some he had collected himself from the wild; others had been hatched in the basement, never knowing life outdoors. But they retained their instincts and way of life, and that's what interested him. An insect could reveal much about the age of a corpse. Eggs and pupae develop into insects within a strict time schedule, which he had memorised through intense study—although their development also depended on temperature and humidity conditions at the site the body had been placed. He shone the torch around the inside of the container. The humidity conditions weren't that difficult to determine here. Moisture dribbled down the sides of the container. The wet and balmy summer outside gave the inside its own microclimate.

"How long's she been dead?" asked Roland from outside, making Leander look up.

"Rigor mortis has set in. Stiffness develops about two to four hours after death's occurred. The whole body's stiff, so we're talking over eight hours. It's a small body, so it's hard to judge. But I can give a more accurate time once I get her in. She's about ten years old. Choked with bare hands." He raised the girl's hand and turned it in the light of the torch. "She's been tied up, it seems," he mumbled, pointing to the red marks around both of the girl's wrists.

Roland looked the other way.

Leander was in the skip for a while without making a sound. Roland knew his old friend. They had worked together for years, and he knew the forensic pathologist was now examining the dead girl like a tracker dog, despite knowing this wasn't the best environment to do so in. Leander crawled out of the skip with an expression of discomfort on his face. Roland gave him his arm for support.

"Bloody hell, what a place to leave a child!"

Roland didn't respond. They had both seen a bit of everything, especially in their time together in Copenhagen. Fortunately, it had been a long time since a case like this had ended up on their desks.

The red-and-white striped police tape fluttered in the wind around the skip. They started walking. Leander took off his white latex gloves and pulled his facemask down under his chin. Both men were silent, thinking about what they had just seen inside the container.

Roland lit a cigarette as soon as they were away from the site of the grim discovery. He looked at Leander as he squinted at the smoke. A dead child was, in his opinion, the worst sight to behold.

"Did you find anything significant?" he asked.

"There's so much dirt, garden waste, and all sorts of other shit. We'll have to review the skip once the girl's removed."

Roland nodded. "Of course." He took a puff of the cigarette. People had started parking illegally along Edwin Rahrs Vej, staring out of their car windows or standing by their cars, watching the scene by the waste container. He was aware the murder wouldn't be kept secret for long.

"I'm afraid it might be a sex crime," he said, keeping a firm eye on whether people were starting to step inside the cordoned-off zone. He feared the reactions in the city. A child murder in Zealand could shake the population in Aarhus to its core. What would the murder of a child in their own city—the City of Smiles, for God's sake—bring about?

He could already see the bold headlines on the front page of the daily papers. "Child Murder in the City of Smiles. Girl Found Strangled in Skip." And why exactly in a waste container in the Gellerup area? No doubt many would take the opportunity to link the event to the immigrants, violence, and crime in the region. Not exactly the best thing to happen to the already burdened area.

"The girl's fully clothed, but she only has white sandals on her feet," Leander replied.

That made Roland wonder. The weather wasn't exactly geared towards bare legs this summer. *Damn paedophiles* Even though he found it perverse, if they really wanted to look at naked children's bodies, they could go ahead, as long as they left them alone and weren't the reason children ended up on Leander's table at the morgue.

"No one's missing?" Leander asked, stepping over a puddle.

"No, no little girls in any case. Only the usual dementia sufferers getting lost, but luckily, we usually find them again. So you're not sure about the time of death?"

"No, but the autopsy will tell us. It might also give us a tip about the crime scene. The girl was placed in the skip after she was murdered."

"So we also have to find a crime scene?" Roland sighed.

Leander nodded. "The skip's only where she was found. The crime scene's of much greater significance to us. But that's your job to figure out, old friend." He patted him on the shoulder to soften his words.

Roland scratched his head. "Yes, that's where forensics will find irrefutable evidence—once we've located it."

"Well, I can give you a quick answer," Leander reassured him. "Her hair's matted with mud, and her clothes are soaked with water. That's a lead. It couldn't have happened in the rubbish bin."

"Mud! Water!" Roland threw out his arms in despair, sprinkling the ashes from his cigarette everywhere. "In this wet summer, it could be anywhere."

Leander looked up at the sky, which was gathering clouds again for the next rain shower. "It depends on what kind of mud the analyses show. Mud isn't just mud. I found blood on her skirt, too."

"Blood! Her own?" Roland feared the worst.

"It's difficult to say yet. Only a DNA analysis can determine that. But at first glance, she doesn't appear to have any wounds that may have bled so profusely."

"What about the marks from the ropes?"

"Skin abrasions—and they didn't bleed. I don't think she was tied up for very long, just long enough to leave marks."

They reached their cars. Leander opened the door to his used Volvo. Behind them, the press had begun to show up, too. The officers stationed at the scene dealt with the aggressive questioning—they had no comment—and made a diligent attempt to keep the herd at a distance from the waste container. The blue flashes had attracted people from miles around, as if they were magnets and the people were made of light metal being drawn towards them.

"The vultures have arrived. Let's get away from here," he said, then sighed.

4

As she drove along Edwin Rahrs Vej, Kamilla immediately saw the blue flashing lights of the squad cars in the rain and the red-and-white tape cordoning off the area on the other side of the road. Now she regretted not asking the journalist what the assignment was. An accident had happened here—or a crime. Not exactly what she needed most. She had hoped for the opening of a new factory somewhere in the industrial district out here, or an award ceremony for an unusually beautiful garden in the Brabrand Garden Association.

The journalist walking towards her evaluated her with grey eyes from under a red umbrella. The expression in them showed she knew what had happened in Kamilla's life. The sensation-driven editor Thygesen couldn't help but tell it in his own dramatic way, of course. Kamilla was tired of seeing all those eyes filled with pity, clearly saying "poor little you." She hated being pitied, because she herself felt strong. Or rather, because she had now learned she wasn't quite as strong as she had thought.

The young journalist held out a hand. "Anne Larsen," she introduced herself in a confident Nørrebro accent, followed by a question: "Kamilla, right?"

Kamilla had no doubt she came from Copenhagen. Her hand was thin and sinewy, fitting well with the rest of the body. She was small and slim. Despite her slender build, the journalist had a warm and firm handshake. She looked pale under her short, jet-black, boyish hairstyle. One eye appeared sad; it seemed to hang a little. Kamilla guessed she was in her mid-twenties. Her black hoodie was a little too long under the yellow raincoat, the pre-washed jeans had bleach stains and were turned up at the bottom, so you could see her bare ankles in a pair of white trainers dirty with grass and mud.

"Yes, that's me. Kamilla Holm. How did you recognise me?" she replied, hearing her own characteristic mixture of Horsens and Aarhus dialects, which suddenly sounded peasant-like in her ears. She had forgotten to ask that, too. *What do you look like? How will I find you?* She felt unprofessional and squinted in the rain. Of course she hadn't remembered an umbrella or raincoat, either.

"Thygesen showed me a picture of you," said Anne with a twinkle in her eye.

"What happened here?" She looked at the crowd of wet people and the few officers trying to keep them at a distance. Her voice sounded nervous.

"A dead girl was found in a skip."

"A girl? Dead?" Reluctantly, she followed the skinny journalist, who began to walk with long strides towards the herd in the wet grass.

"A child," she said, turning. The lust for sensation shone in her eyes. Kamilla's legs began to fail. Her knees were like heavy bricks.

"A child," she mumbled, automatically following Anne, as if the old habit of trailing behind a journalist had been reawakened without her even wanting it to be.

She watched Anne rig her equipment as she held her umbrella, taking the opportunity to get shelter from the weather. Anne vanished into the crowd, while she herself remained standing outside the flock with the umbrella in her hand and the camera bag over her shoulder. It was an unfamiliar situation for her. Before, she always knew what to do when she was on a job. It used to come instinctively. She caught sight of Anne, who had managed to get the microphone up under the nose of a young officer who was talking. Kamilla folded the umbrella as she sent the sky a careful glance. It seemed to be clearing up again; one of this summer's many thunderstorms was drifting over. The sun began to shine through the layer of clouds despite a few raindrops still falling. She took the camera out of her bag and snapped a series of photos of the officers and the crowd of journalists and curious people who had gathered around them. Even though she knew it wasn't exactly going to be a shot worthy of this year's press photo award, she had to do something.

The officers were in the process of shooing the crowd further away from the skip. Anne stood behind the container, making signs to her from under the police tape between the bushes. Kamilla scowled at the officers before walking over to her. They were so busy driving people away and rejecting questions that they didn't see them at all.

"Shit," Anne whispered to the side of Kamilla's face as she bent down to help her under the cordon. "They've already removed the girl."

Kamilla felt relieved. Could she handle the sight of another dead child? Why did that have to be the assignment she had agreed to? There had been so many others she could have accepted. Because she hadn't asked. That's why. Had she known what it was about, she would have said no. Again.

"Come here!" Anne waved her closer. The bushes hid them from the officers. She had discovered a hatch on the back of the skip. The police hadn't locked it. They probably hadn't even noticed it, hidden by the bushes. It was rusty like the rest of the back of the large container. Its hinges creaked when Anne opened it. A lukewarm stench hit them. Kamilla stepped into something slimy. It was vomit. She was about to vomit herself.

"It seems that hatch was opened recently," mumbled Anne. She waved Kamilla closer again. "Here, come on! Take a picture!" she said in a low voice.

"Into the skip? Are you serious?" She heard her own shrill and puzzled voice, despite feeling deaf in both ears, but she did as she was told. The flash lit up the inside of the dark container. She couldn't see anything on the LCD screen, not even in the viewfinder, and she took some pictures at will. When the flash flared, she caught brief glimpses of black bin bags, blue-striped Aldi bags crammed with rubbish, cardboard boxes, old furniture, leftover food, leaves, branches, and rotten plants.

"We have enough now." Anne suddenly pulled her by the sleeve. She had spotted an officer approaching from where she was keeping a lookout.

"Hey! What are you doing there?" he shouted as they ducked down under the striped tape back onto neutral ground. Anne showed him her press card.

"No comment," he said, pointing to the camera hanging on its strap around Kamilla's neck. "What did you photograph?"

"Just the skip. We have to bring something back to the paper, otherwise we'll be fired," said Anne defensively, pushing back her hair.

Kamilla wondered how Anne could look so innocent, even be on the offensive against the broad-shouldered officer towering in front of them. She was red-cheeked from the excitement and was hoping the officer wouldn't notice. She began wiping the vomit off her shoe on the wet grass.

The officer nodded, but he checked anyway to see whether the padlock on the front of the skip was still locked, and whether the tape showing the container had been seized by police was still intact. You never knew with reporters.

"Okay, off you go!" He turned his back on them and started walking. Tall, erect, and full of authority in his police uniform.

5

It had been over a year since he had last driven here. He had a lump stuck in his throat. He coughed to remove it. Why did he do this? He had taken his punishment. Sanne had left him, as she couldn't live with what he had done—or, rather, she couldn't live with his guilt. When he had been asked to take leave from his job—which he could no longer concentrate on—when he came out of prison, she had thought he had been fired. She had felt the income and the good life disappear, then she had disappeared, too. He had neither been able to support her, nor give her a child.

Being in prison, isolated from everyone and treated like a common criminal, had been directly contrary to his nature and upbringing. He had found it deeply unfair he had been convicted and locked up, until what he had done had slowly dawned on him. He was reassured by the fact his father was dead. If not, he probably wouldn't have survived that shame. His mother's senile brain wouldn't grasp it anyway, despite a nurse probably having told her what had happened and why her son wasn't coming for his usual weekly visits. She just wanted to smile and nod and fiddle with the top button of her blouse. She might not have even noticed his absence. Thinking of his mother hurt just as much as thinking about his own sufferings. She was in a kind of prison, too. Her own prison. Old age without memories. Only after his father had died and she had gone into a nursing home did he notice how spoiled he had been as a child. He had been used to being waited on by his mother. Sanne wouldn't put up with it. Her life hadn't been quite so easy. In a way, he was relieved to take a break from work. He couldn't bear the reproachful looks from his colleagues. They had driven home drunk that night, too, but it had gone alright for them. *That damn cat!* He couldn't help the thought popping into his head but felt ashamed afterwards. His director was also his friend, so he had shown understanding beyond all bounds. If he hadn't been a friend, he would undoubtedly have been fired.

It was the psychologist he had sought help from who had advised him to return to Jutland as a form of therapy. The best thing for all parties, the psychologist had said, was that he seek out the relatives and talk with them if they wished. But he knew he would never have the courage or conscience to do so.

He realised he was driving past the spot where the car had almost slid into the ditch a year before. Shortly afterwards, he passed the accident site itself. He instinctively pressed the brake when he saw a boy with a large sports bag cycling on the bike path. The image of a football rolling out onto the road flickered like a slow-motion film clip before his eyes. It rolled infinitely slowly, stopped, lay there for a moment, rocking back and forth, as if it couldn't decide whether to stay or roll on. A sight that haunted him like a curse. Suddenly, he knew what the psychologist had meant by his advice. He needed to revisit the site and to drive this stretch in a sober state. Maybe he was just hoping time would be rewound. That he had managed to see the cat and brake in time. Or that he had run the damn cat down instead of trying to avoid it. He regretted his thoughts again. The cursed thing was he hadn't stayed over that night; he had headed out to reach the Molslinjen ferry back to Zealand.

He also wanted to see the place where it had all begun. He only had to drive a few minutes before he saw the marina ahead, catching dazzling glimpses of its beautiful white ships on the blue water in the sunlight. When he spotted the sign for Restaurant Egå Marina, he drove into the car park and parked. It was here they had held the fateful reception to celebrate the end of the huge assignment they had been working on for so many months. He still wondered how an Aarhus company had chosen an advertising agency in Zealand, given all the good agencies in Aarhus, but it had probably been because of their reputation. They had won quite a few advertising awards over time. They had practically worked around the clock to meet the deadlines and make it all run smoothly with models, photos, and film footage. It was a campaign worth several million Danish kroner, one the advertising agency had reaped great rewards from—hadn't he deserved that last drink?

There was a smell of grilled fish and fresh dill in the restaurant. He remembered he hadn't eaten since his meagre breakfast. After hanging his jacket over the back of the chair, he sat down at a table already laid, overlooking the harbour. Despite there being many people, it didn't take long for a young waiter to hand him a menu. He quickly decided on warm smoked salmon and handed the menu back to the gracious server, who bowed just the way he had been taught at waiter school. The waiter handed him the wine list, but he waved it away with his hand and asked for a jug of cold water with ice.

While waiting for the salmon, he recalled the festive reception. They had all been so happy and carefree. Nothing could touch them.

Suddenly, a tall, thin man carrying a sandwich on a plate and a cold beer sat down in the chair opposite him. Only now did he notice there was a jacket on the chair opposite and he had sat down at a table that was already occupied. He apologised and was about to get up, but the thin man asked him to stay.

"I could do with a little company. Troels Mortensen," he introduced himself before launching into his sandwich.

"Danny Cramer. Are you sure I'm not disturbing you?"

The man muttered and nodded convincingly. "You're not from here, are you? Copenhagen?"

He explained he was from Zealand and on holiday here in Jutland. Shortly afterwards, the salmon was served.

"That looks good," Troels said, nodding at Danny's plate. "For those who can afford it. May I ask what you do for a living?"

"I'm an advertising manager," he replied, knowing the other man had no idea what that meant. Not many were aware of the goings-on in the advertising industry, he had learned. They just turn their noses up at the junk mail that comes in the post and throw it in the bin. Some without even looking. Without knowing all the hard work that lay behind the colourful pages.

"What about you?"

Troels shrugged, indifferent. "Military. Came home from Iraq a year ago. Having a shot at real soldier life was nice—not just lying in some field saying *bang-bang*." He laughed, his mouth full of food.

Danny drank from his glass. He was glad he hadn't chosen a career that risked him being sent to international service in Bosnia, Kosovo, Afghanistan, Iraq, and God knows where else. He had served his military conscription, and that was enough for him. He preferred a calmer and safer life, even though his present one verged in the direction of loneliness.

"What are you doing now? At home on leave?" he asked to make conversation.

"No, my military career's over. I'm in favour of fishing now. Fishing equipment and what have you. I opened a shop here in Egå." He said it with a certain pride in his voice.

After enjoying the perfect salmon, Danny sat for a moment taking in the view. He felt better now and began to believe revisiting the area might benefit him.

A tall, slender woman bent over the man at the table. Her hair had red tinges when the sun fell on it. Her perfume was delicate and discreet.

"Hey, Troels!" she said, looking questioningly at Danny with bright blue eyes.

"What the heck—are you here, too?" Troels got up, embarrassed. With his arm awkwardly around the woman's back, he introduced her to Danny, who felt obligated to get up as well.

"This is Majken," said Troels. "She's a doctor—and a shrink."

She extended a slender hand to him as she sent Troels a warning look. She had a warm and confident handshake.

"Would you like to sit?" said Troels, respectfully gesturing to a vacant chair at the table.

Danny felt he was intruding. Perhaps Troels had been waiting for her, and he had taken her seat.

"No, but thank you. I'm waiting for a friend," she said, glancing at her watch before looking at Danny again. Her eyes had a quizzical expression, as though analysing him.

"Copenhagener?" she said.

He thought it sounded more like a statement than a question. *Why do Jutlanders always think all Zealanders come from Copenhagen?*

"No, Klampenborg—Dyrehavsbakken, the racetrack," he said to emphasise it had nothing to do with The Little Mermaid, Istedgade's porn shops, or Christiania's Pusher Street.

"I see, where you play *galf* and the horses *gallap*." Troels laughed with an excessively wrinkled nose and a raised pinkie finger that made Danny laugh, too.

6

———

Kamilla threw the withered flowers in the bin at the graveyard. When she forced herself outside the four walls of her home, it was to this bench in Egå Cemetery. She didn't live that far from it. She sat opposite Rasmus's grave and stared at the round marble stone and the gold letters with his name and epitaph: brutally torn away—forever missed.

The cemetery was a beautiful, peaceful place, particularly at this time of year, and especially now the sun was shining again, and flowers had bloomed on the many graves.

Previously, she had only felt anxious around graveyards and had feared walking past them in the dark when she was a child. She had always been afraid of the dark. She had grown up in Horsens, which had three cemeteries. One, Nordre Kirkegård, was close to her school, and on dark mornings when the cold bit her cheeks, she had scowled at it as she ran past, feeling afraid of the dead. Or maybe it was a fear of death. Her father was buried there. She had been seven years old when he died, and she only faintly remembered them lowering his coffin into the ground. The thought of him lying deep in the ground in a wooden chest had given her claustrophobia. The doctor had thought she was suffering from asthma. She hadn't visited his grave that often, not even as an adult. She'd had her own life. Nor had she felt particularly attached to him when he was alive. Her memories consisted only of the stink of fish when he would come home, tired from working hard at a fish exporter in Snaptun, and absently stroke her cheek.

She didn't remember any shared experiences or warm embraces. Not from her mother, either. Her mother had grown up in a fishing family on the rugged west coast of Jutland, but she had rebelled against the Inner Mission evangelical movement and moved to the east coast as a young woman to study. Here she met the fishing worker, and they had married before starting her studies. But she was still marked by her childhood and strict upbringing. She saw her husband's sudden death, which had made her an early widow with a seven-year-old daughter, as a punishment from God for denying him. She became bitter and withdrawn and lived a life without joy. Kamilla's mother also saw the tragic death of her grandson as a punishment. It was God's curse that would haunt the entire family for the rest of their lives. *God takes those we love from us. It's his punishment for our sins,* she had intoned.

There were only Kamilla and an elderly man in the graveyard. He was laying flowers on a grave up by the dazzling white church. She found the church beautiful. The oldest part was built in Romanesque style, the tower and porch in the later Gothic style. There were traces of a walled door on the north side of the church, and several walled-up Romanesque windows. But otherwise, it was a modern church. When it came to both clergy and other church officials, the main emphasis was on employing women, which had almost caused her mother to leave the church when Rasmus was about to be buried. She had also been opposed to the abnormal method of burial, so she had left early without a word of comfort. There had been no reason to incur more wrath from on high.

Kamilla got up and brushed the soil off her worn jeans. She had dark, wet spots on both knees from tidying up the grave. She sat, speaking softly to Rasmus. The vomit was gone from her shoe, but the discomfort returned just by looking at it. It was good they had removed the little girl. "Ten years old," she had heard a journalist say to another. Only a year older than Rasmus. He had been murdered, too. Another human had mercilessly taken his life. *Isn't that murder?*

She walked home slowly in the sunshine. Her legs felt heavy, as if they couldn't carry her to the empty house. The nightmare of that night still gnawed painfully at her. After letting herself into the house, she caught sight of the cat. It stood meowing with its forepaws on the glass of the patio door. She couldn't hear any sound, just saw its mouth and pointed canines open silently. She opened the door, and the cat slipped quickly into the kitchen to the food bowl that was always ready for it. Smiling, she took off her jacket. Now there was some life in the house. Rasmus had pestered her constantly to get a cat, but she had always very definitively said no. The furniture wasn't to be destroyed by cat claws, nor would she be responsible when Rasmus lost interest, as had happened to both the hamster and the rabbit. But now she enjoyed having the little animal with her. It was sitting by her door one morning, and she had immediately seen it as a message from him. It looked like a black Norwegian forest cat and had no collar or other markings to identify its owner. The cat had stayed with her, and she had therefore given it the name Rasmus had joked about wanting to call his cat once he had persuaded her: Tarzan.

She took an apple from the fruit bowl on the kitchen table. She couldn't be bothered to cook even though her stomach felt hollow and empty—like the rest of her body. The fruit was nicely arranged in a glass bowl, as if for a photo shoot. It was a habit she couldn't give up even if she tried. An occupational hazard, you could call it. In the bathroom, the creams and perfumes were displayed on the shelf in front of the mirror, as if in a perfume catalogue presentation. Anyone could see she either had a sense of composition or was meticulous. And she wasn't the latter in any case. The house was living proof of that. Living in a mess wasn't her at all, but the powerlessness she had felt the past year hadn't given her the energy for much. Definitely not for cleaning.

She took the camera into her home office and turned on the computer. When the Mac OS X symbol appeared on the screen, she connected the camera and transferred the images from the memory card to the hard drive. Then she opened the image processing program and chose *browse* in the menu. It gave her an overview of all the photos she had taken by and in the skip. She ate the apple as she studied them with a frown. They were nothing special, but Anne had gone through them on the camera's LCD screen and thought they captured the utter depravity of someone who could murder a child and leave them there like that. Not to mention what he had done to her beforehand. Anne hadn't been given all the details when she had called the police station from her mobile. The girl hadn't been identified, and the police wouldn't comment on the case for the sake of the relatives, they had said.

Kamilla spent some time processing the best images. Some were dark due to the changing light, but with a little tweaking of levels and brightness/

contrast, they turned out quite good, so there was nothing wrong with the quality. She had taken a course in Photoshop and still had a good grasp of it. Satisfied, she sent all the pictures in an email to Anne at the editorial office.

The *Århus Stiftstidende* newspaper was lying on the coffee table in the living room. She sat down on the couch and quickly flipped through to the TV listings. Apparently, during the summer, TV stations didn't expect people to be sitting indoors watching the box, so the offerings were even worse than usual, just re-runs—pure déjà vu. She threw down the newspaper but turned on the TV anyway, changing it to TV 2 News with the remote control. She broke into the middle of the report on the child murder in Aarhus.

The motive for the murder is not yet known but is suspected to be of a sexual nature. She wondered where they had got that information when no one at the police station was willing to comment. *The girl has not yet been identified. Police are not commenting on any details until the family has been informed,* the voice continued. The images of the half-rusted skip with the Dannebrog-coloured police tape ran briefly across the screen. *We will return with news of the case later,* promised the newscaster.

They wanted to show the same thing again on TV 2 Headlines and TV 2 East Jutland, but she couldn't bear it and would rather forget it all. She still felt exhausted, but a spark of energy was simmering. It felt good to be working again, she had to admit. Maybe she should have listened to Majken when she had said she should force herself to do something other than visit the cemetery. Move on. Not just shut other people out. But it was so hard. She had never dreamed a filthy waste container in which a murdered girl had been dumped would be the reason she would begin taking photographs again.

Tarzan raised his head irritably in his sleep, pricking up his ears as her mobile chimed, buried in her bag out in the hall. She reached it just before the call disconnected.

"Kamilla, have you forgotten our dinner? Restaurant Egå Marina!"

"Majken! Oh my God, yes, I totally blanked on it. Sorry!" She looked resignedly at her dirty jeans. "I just need to change my clothes; I'll be as quick as I can."

Before heading to the bathroom, she glanced at the dishes, the coffee cups, and the empty glasses on the coffee table. So she wasn't going to clean up now, either. Majken had tried to pull her out of the darkness so often. She had agreed at last to go out to eat—and then she had forgotten! What had become of her usually streamlined life? Just as well Majken hadn't come to collect her. A superficial clean-up she could manage for a visitor, but she didn't like unexpected guests.

7

Roland would never get used to the premises pathologist Henry Leander apparently found himself so at home in. Every time he stepped through the door to the autopsy examination room, his bowels turned with a rolling motion that could be felt all the way up in his throat, along with the bitter taste of bile. And it wasn't because they were dirty or smelly. The premises were clinically clean and cold. His own office was much less sanitary. It was probably just the thought of everything he had seen on the sterile steel tables, and not least what awaited him now—the little girl lying there. Crimes against children gave him unbearable nausea.

The others were already there: Henry Leander, Chief Coroner Ole Albertsen accompanied by a doctor he didn't know, Superintendent Kurt Olsen, and forensic technician Steen Dahl, who was ready with his camera.

"Do we still have no missing person's report?" whispered Kurt Olsen.

The atmosphere was grave.

"No, not for a girl of this age. We have two fifteen-year-old female friends, but they're most likely just off gallivanting," Roland whispered back. Then they both turned their attention to Leander, who solemnly raised his head as he took the floor.

"The girl died of asphyxiation. You can see the finger marks here around the neck." He pointed to some blue-black and purple marks on the child's white neck. Steen Dahl took a few pictures.

"The dark blue-violet colour of the corpse also indicates signs of oxygen deficiency in the blood at the time of death." He moved his index finger to the girl's eyes, which were staring up at the ceiling.

"The classic signs of suffocation—small pinpoint bleeding in the eyes—are also evident. It's due to the blood vessels *from* the brain being closed, so blood can only be carried *to* the brain. When this happens, the veins become overfilled, and the small blood vessels burst from the pressure and form these blood effusions. They can also be seen on the skin on the face, behind the ears, and in the mouth."

Steen Dahl bent over the steel table to take a picture of the eyes, which took on a completely vivid expression when the light of the flash hit them.

"That wouldn't take a whole lot of strength, so we can't rule out that it could have been a woman," Leander continued.

"Is there anything else to suggest that?" Kurt Olsen asked, scratching his neck. His curly hair was getting too long. His shirt hung over his trousers on one side. His entire persona was, on the whole, marked by the fact his wife had recently left him. It wasn't easy to keep women in the police job. Roland congratulated himself for having chosen Irene, who had never complained about the many overtime hours and his disappearance into another world whenever he investigated a crime. He had met her at the police station in Copenhagen, where she had worked as a secretary back then. Maybe that's why she understood. She knew a little about what they were dealing with.

"No, nothing specific. I'm only mentioning it because you shouldn't ignore that possibility. There are no signs of sexual assault. No lesions, no semen."

"She didn't defend herself? Bitten, beaten, scratched. Did you do a full nail scraping?" asked Kurt Olsen.

Leander raised one of the girl's hands and turned her nails towards the superintendent. "As you can see, there's not much to scrape under. She bit her nails." The girl's nails had remnants of pink nail varnish that was peeling off. They were bitten all the way down.

"Death was immediate at around five o'clock yesterday afternoon." Leander looked affectionately at the girl. Roland guessed he had talked reassuringly to her while he had worked on her. Leander's white moustache, which hung slightly downwards with a handlebar-like turn upwards, gave him a sad expression that nevertheless hinted at a little smile. But his blue-green eyes weren't smiling now.

"Perhaps putting her in a waste container was a shrewd calculation. The conditions mean we can't use the traces of anything we found on the girl's clothes for much until we have the perpetrator and can compare DNA and other things found at the crime scene."

"Because of other people's dirt in the skip, right?" asked Ole Albertsen.

"Exactly. It can be difficult to prove what we find isn't from other people's waste. Skips contain traces of many different people. There's a lot to keep track of."

"Can you say something about the rope she was tied up with?" Roland asked, desperately needing a cigarette. Unfortunately, the urge always came with renewed intensity in places where he wasn't allowed to smoke. He dreaded the smoking ban politicians were threatening to soon impose.

"You can see from the location of the wear marks that her hands were tied behind her back." Leander took the girl's hands again and turned them slightly so everyone could see the bands of red skin abrasions around both wrists. Steen Dahl took another photo.

"It's most likely a rough natural rope or cable. Maybe a Manila rope like the type used by the Scouts, or in agriculture, fishing, and other crafts or industry."

"We used just that kind of rope when we built our new terrace, but it had added oil for impregnation. Are there any traces of oil?" asked Steen Dahl.

"No, unfortunately not. The rope may have been well worn. That would also explain why it left such vicious skin abrasions. Of course, the girl may have tried to wrestle herself free. Evidence indicates an eight-millimetre rope," Leander replied thoughtfully. He took the girl with his gloved hands and gently turned her onto her side so they could see her bare back. She had a small brown birthmark that resembled a miniature version of Zealand, just below her right shoulder blade.

Standing in the small group of middle-aged men, staring at the child's naked body, Roland felt disgusted. What drove paedophiles? His philosophy was to think like the killer to find him. It would be difficult in this case. The thought discouraged him.

Leander pointed to a mark on the girl's back. It was an imprint on the skin, like a depression in which blood had collected.

"I can find no explanation for this mark. It looks like an instrument of some kind with a leaf-shaped tip. How the imprint got on the girl's back is hard to say. Perhaps she was lying on something."

Leander eyed Roland and Kurt Olsen directly with a look that clearly said figuring out what it was, and where this object was, was now their problem.

For the rest of the autopsy—the worst part—he tried to block out all his senses. He was only aware of the voice of the coroner routinely commenting on the organs he had examined. The other sounds, he tried to ignore. He held his breath so as not to inhale the odours, and caught himself standing and staring at his hands, clinging to such an insignificant thing as black dirt under one of his thumbnails. He had helped Irene with the rose bed a little last night. The autopsy of a child was an unbearable experience.

"You'll get my report sometime tomorrow morning," Leander concluded. And with these words, he released the group into freedom.

It was a relief to get out of the building and breathe fresh air again. The sun briefly broke through the clouds and baked down on the roofs of the cars. The heat from Roland's black Fiat Stilo, which smelled of leather from the seats, intensified his nausea when he opened the car door. He stood for a moment, leaning against the car, with the doors open to air it as he smoked the much-needed cigarette. Superintendent Olsen came and stood next to him.

"Wretched case," he said, taking the famous polished Stanwell pipe out. It was his hallmark. He stuffed it carefully with fragrant Mac Baren tobacco and really seemed to enjoy the first puff. He was a man who understood pipes. Yet Roland had never heard him snorting the thick, sticky, dark fluid produced by so many who smoked pipes.

"I guess we have to call a press conference. The gossip has already started. The media can smell a corpse from miles away," muttered Roland.

"We're not going out to the press with anything as long as we haven't identified the girl and the parents haven't been notified. It's bad enough it's already out in the media." Annoyed, Kurt Olsen puffed on his pipe.

"We need a bloody DNA database of all residents—then she'd have been easy to identify. But why are there no reports of a missing little girl? We can't walk around ringing doorbells in Brabrand to ask whether people are missing a daughter," Roland said, tapping the ash off his cigarette. "Should we issue a missing person's report this early?"

Kurt Olsen nodded and took another puff of the pipe. "I'd like to wait a little and see if the family contacts us themselves. But if it doesn't happen by tonight, we'll have to." He looked at his watch. "I wouldn't have allowed my daughter to go missing for a whole night without reacting, would you? There has to be something, some circumstance, that means the girl isn't missed."

"Or maybe the parents have something to hide," mumbled Roland.

Kurt Olsen got into his car and was about to close the door when he suddenly opened it again and looked directly at Roland.

"I want to check out all paedophiles and anyone we know with a connection to child pornography. Bring in every single one. We have to find this guy."

8

———

Looking out at the sea and the white sailboats in the strong sunshine was stunning. Kamilla sipped the cool white wine Majken had ordered. She looked for her; she had gone to the toilet ten minutes ago. Maybe there was a queue. There were quite a few people in the restaurant. She scouted the crowd and spotted her. She was talking to some people further down the eatery.

She immersed herself absently in the beautiful view again. A couple of seagulls were trying to grab something on a boat outside the window. She was always amazed at how big and beautiful the birds were, with their chalk-white plumage glistening in the sun.

"Kamilla, I've invited these two gentlemen to join our table." Majken spoke suddenly, making her jump. The disappointment that Majken was already drawing strangers into their circle could be seen on her face. She had hoped to talk a little with her friend on their own. They were moving on to other social contact too fast. She didn't like it, and it surprised her Majken hadn't thought of it.

"Troels here is one of my patients. And this is Danny." Majken pulled the man forwards in front of Troels in the reverent way a magician pulls a white rabbit out a hat. Troels fetched a chair from one of the other tables so they could all sit together. He talked to a waiter. Immediately afterwards, he arrived with a dewy bottle of cold Riesling. Troels poured the wine, but when he reached Danny, he put a hand over his glass.

"No thanks; I'm driving."

"Well, what do you know—a holy man." Troels laughed.

It was clear Majken was interested in Danny. Kamilla had to reluctantly admit he radiated a certain charm. His hands were so neat and elegant. They lay relaxed on the white tablecloth. His eyes were brown and had a warmth that made staring into them very comfortable. She caught herself doing it.

The mood at the table quickly changed from embarrassing to lively. Many of the anecdotes were so funny she eventually had to surrender to the laughter. She felt like she hadn't had so much fun in such a long time. But then came the guilt and shame. How could she sit here having fun when she had lost her son?

"You should have brought your camera with you, Kamilla! Look at that!" Majken tore her from her thoughts. She pointed out the window. Two seagulls were fighting in the air over something. Their struggle brought them very close to the windows at times. It was the kind of situation she had always captured with her lens in the past. The camera had been her constant companion, like a shoulder bag she always remembered to take with her.

"Are you a photographer?" Danny sounded surprised, as if he had been trying to guess her profession and had reached a completely different conclusion.

"Yeah, but I'm taking a break—a sabbatical." She scowled at Majken, who pretended it was nothing. She knew Majken believed she should be much further along in her grieving process. She didn't want to talk about the day's assignment. Not now that two strangers were sitting at the table. Plus, she had a duty of confidentiality when working for the press.

"Do you have a developing room with a red light?" Troels looked at her curiously with his pale eyes. The wine was starting to affect him.

"Everything's digital these days, so there's no need for darkrooms anymore," she explained.

"Do you have your own photo studio?" asked Danny, interested.

"A little one. I work freelance for advertising agencies, newspapers, magazines, and what have you. So I'm mainly out with other people when I work." The words made her think of all the times she had been called in vain during the last year. In the beginning, there were many who called, and then fewer and fewer. Had she lost all her regular clients? And what was she supposed to live on then? But now she had an assignment with a journalist: the murder of a little girl.

9

There was no great welcome committee when Anne returned to the newspaper office. The smell of coffee, IT equipment, and old cigarettes from Thygesen's unemptied ashtray greeted her as she tossed her backpack down by the legs of the desk and hung her raincoat up on the coat-rack. On the conference room table stood an insulated whistling coffee pot next to used plastic cups. Half a stale bread roll covered with a thick layer of butter lay in a torn brown bag that looked like it had been ripped open by someone with ravenous hunger. Anne remembered she hadn't had lunch and suddenly felt the hole in her stomach. She sat down and turned on the computer.

"Here, this is yours!" A colleague, Britt, threw a cardboard plate with the dried bread roll onto the table in front of her. Anne caught a faint mist of her sickly perfume. "How did it go with the skip?" Britt added scornfully as she sat down at her computer again with her back to Anne.

She stared for a long time at the roll. The butter was turning dark yellow at the edges, and it was guaranteed to have absorbed the smoke of the room while the others had held their meeting without her. She took a bite anyway, out of both hunger and politeness, given they had saved it for her. She got up and picked up the coffee pot. There was some coffee left; she could hear it rippling.

"They'd removed the girl, so we didn't get any pictures of the body, but word has it she was strangled—probably raped first," she replied when she could make eye contact with Britt.

"Ugh! Doing that to a child's disgusting. And then to leave her in a skip like a piece of rubbish. Bloody hell! I hate paedophiles!" Britt's eyes showed she really meant it, but otherwise, the journalistic façade was in place. You should preferably not let it show that terrible things affect you, not as a professional journalist who has experienced so much over the years—and Britt had several years in the industry. She rarely made mistakes. It hadn't been easy for Anne to come from Copenhagen and start the new job in such a seasoned circle of journalists. The competition between her and Britt had been tough at first, but now they had each other's measure. Thygesen was good at assigning them jobs according to their strengths, so there was no competition in that sense, but Anne knew it annoyed Britt that she often got criminal cases because she had worked a few successfully in Copenhagen, while Britt got the boring local stuff. As always, Britt's little radio was playing unbearable modern pop music, and right now, she was tapping her foot to the notes of "Fly on the Wings of Love." Anne would rather have peace and quiet when she worked. They didn't exactly have the same taste in music. Anne was more into hard rock and modern rap.

"Where's Thygesen—and everyone else?" Anne asked, scowling into Thygesen's empty office as she poured coffee into a plastic cup. She could feel it was lukewarm through the cup—and it looked weak. The intern must have brewed it.

Britt started typing again; her clattering on the keyboard almost drowned out her voice. "Everyone's out in the field, and Thygesen has a meeting in the city. He should be back in half an hour." She paused and looked at Anne. "By the way, you should look at what he's put in your top tray." She said it as if it had just popped into her head, but Anne knew full well she had already snooped.

She missed her old colleagues in Copenhagen. They had been like a big family, without the jealousy and power struggles, and the assignments had been different than in this provincial hole. Thygesen's "staff" consisted of a small team of women. In the capital, it had been a fifty-fifty mix of both sexes. There was friction with one woman every so often, but that's obviously how Thygesen wanted it. *He's a bit of a dirty old man*, she thought, smiling. Actually, it surprised her she had been hired. With her boyish appearance, she wasn't exactly one of the babes Thygesen apparently preferred. In her eyes, Britt and the other two girls could have been in *Baywatch* in their younger days, no problem. But now it was slightly embarrassing they were still wearing low-cut blouses and short skirts. Only the student intern, Bertha, was under thirty.

In her teenage years, Anne had been one of the many young people in Nørrebro protesting everything and everyone, occupying empty houses, and believing she was helping to change the world and make a difference. Her nostrils, lower lip, and ears had little scars from piercings that seemed to be part of being a true rebel. But it was that early experience that had driven her to become a journalist. It had all started one warm evening in Nørrebro on 18 May 1993, after the second union vote. Despite a hard night spent in custody, it was that event that started her writing. From that, Ragnarök was born—an effective Nørrebro network and a local newspaper—and she had felt better able to express her opinions and attitudes as a journalist. Finally, after drifting around since leaving school, she knew what she wanted. Journalism college had been exciting, so she hadn't wanted to drop out early. During the first few years, as one of the editorial staff of a small youth newspaper, she had only written articles about unfair political interventions—there was always something to write about there. Then came her interest in crime. Though how, she didn't really know.

It had to be her audacity, the perpetual phone calls to Thygesen, and not least her honesty that had got her hired, more so than her looks. She had a disfiguring scar on her left eyebrow that made her eye hang a little. Luckily, she had got the job, so she could get away. Pack a suitcase and get in the car to head for Jutland in the gloom and darkness of the night, without anyone noticing and asking about it.

She had been looking forward to the new job in the provinces. There hadn't really been anything exciting to write about until now. Finally, something had happened that smelled a little of the tough assignments she enjoyed working on. The discovery of a mutilated corpse on the streets of Copenhagen had almost been too much for her, but it was the kind of story she loved writing about. She felt as if she became part of the investigation. Her contempt for the police was set aside. She needed them now and was more than happy to exploit their knowledge. It was exciting and kept her interest piqued.

"Oh my God, it's so late!" Britt jumped up from the chair and looked at her watch. "I'm supposed to be meeting a soldier who's returned from Iraq—I'd almost forgotten," she said, zipping up her windbreaker. "Thygesen asked me to do a story on the torment they go through as soldiers.

This guy saw a couple of children being blown into a thousand pieces by a bomb, and it's left him mentally scarred." Britt paused while looking at Anne's back. She didn't answer but sat in deep concentration on her computer. "Yeah, he'd never give you that kind of story, Anne. You wouldn't understand it," she said angrily before turning on her heels and slamming the door.

Anne had heard her but had pretended not to. All too often, she had heard her opinions were controversial, and she didn't want to make herself unpopular in her new workplace. But Britt was right. She didn't understand. All the demonstrations she had participated in were against the wars, no matter the weather. She didn't understand how it surprised trained soldiers that people were killed and maimed in war. They came back traumatised, needing psychological help because the enemy had shot at them, and they had seen people die. What had they thought would happen? Why did they even want to be soldiers? If no one wanted to be a soldier, no wars could be waged.

She got up, turned off Britt's transistor radio, and grabbed a new cup of coffee. The editorial department was completely silent. Only the sound of the computer's soft hum could be heard. She was all alone, in peace and quiet. Now she could work. Britt's phone rang a few times, but she didn't pick it up. She had a story to write.

A few emails had come in while she had been out, including an email from Kamilla. Anne quickly skimmed through the pictures. For want of a better expression, something *more substantial* was missing, but otherwise, she was satisfied. She selected the images for her article. It didn't take her long to write as she didn't have much concrete information yet. Afterwards, she briefly answered the emails that demanded a response. When she reached the last email, she froze. How had he already found her? Unconsciously, she touched the scar over her eye. Then she pulled herself together, deleted the email without reading it, and took Thygesen's assignment from the top drawer of her letter tray.

10

After the breakup with Sanne, Danny hadn't been that interested in the opposite sex. He observed her face as she spoke. Something in her blue-green eyes touched him. She had to be in her mid- or late thirties. Her face was marked by life's experiences, those joys and sorrows that signify a certain maturity. The fine little wrinkles around her eyes became clearer when she smiled. Her blond hair was piled on her head, secured with a clip in a quick, casual hairstyle. A tuft of hair had strayed onto her forehead. He caught himself staring at it with an intense urge to sweep it away with a gentle caress. She had charming little freckles on her nose. And she was a photographer. When he thought of photographers, he pictured men who salivated greedily as they photographed beautiful models in tight-fitting lingerie, who swilled tar-black coffee boiled dry on the bottom of a coffee machine's jug in the back room. Being a photographer obviously meant something else here in Jutland.

"So what's your next advertising project, Danny?" Majken asked, leaning invitingly towards him so he couldn't help looking down her cleavage. Meeting this Troels Mortensen had irritated him at first. He needed to be alone to think, but he had to admit the company the meeting had brought with it certainly wasn't doing him any harm.

"I'm taking a little holiday—a sabbatical—at the moment," he said, glancing at Kamilla.

"How do you and Troels know each other?" Majken asked curiously.

He drained the last drop of water in his glass. The ice cubes had melted, and it had become lukewarm in the sun shining in on their table. He explained they didn't know each other at all, and that he had come to sit at Troels's table without noticing it was taken.

"Fate," Troels said with a mysterious voice, big eyes, and ghost-like movements. Danny couldn't hold back a shudder. He didn't like what fate had already brought him. Who was this man he had shared a table with? He had smelled of liquor when he had sat down.

"Are you driving?" Majken asked Troels, as if she'd had the same thought.

"Of course." Troels emptied his glass and set it down hard on the table, as though unable to judge the distance.

"Would it not be a good idea to get a taxi?" Majken said reproachfully.

Danny heard the echo of his colleagues' words in half-drunken voices. In this very room. Why hadn't he listened to them? Then everything would have turned out differently.

Troels lifted his glass and toasted the air. "My doctor's talking!" he said, feigning solemnity. "But I bloody well drive best with the-e-e e-d-d-dge taken off," he continued with an excessively drunk voice, nodding triumphantly.

Kamilla took her small handbag, left the table, and went to the toilet. Troels's behaviour evoked disgust in her. She stared at herself in the mirror and was about to wash her hands when a woman came in, leading a little girl by the hand. She put on lip balm and secretly watched as the woman helped the little girl reach up to the sink to wash her hands while she spoke quietly and instructively to her. Exactly how she had once helped Rasmus. When they had gone and closed the door behind them, she took a deep breath to make the uncomfortable feeling in her chest go away.

The memory of the two police officers who had knocked on her door that night would always remain vivid, along with the crushing emptiness, and the hideous, wailing scream she didn't even realise had come from her. The hatred for the man who had been driving while intoxicated flared up again. She would never forgive him. He had taken what was best in her life. When she looked at her face in the mirror, she could see she had changed. Her eyes were deeper in their sockets, and the fine wrinkles on her forehead seemed to have come from worry. But the outside wasn't the worst. She could put up with that. It was inside that something was wrong. As if something had been destroyed by the officers' words and what had followed.

Majken had told her about the four phases of grief. The shock phase, where she refused to face reality, and everything was chaos. She didn't remember much from that period. The reaction phase, where what had happened slowly dawned on her. That she had lost Rasmus forever. She clearly remembered that period as the greatest pain she had ever experienced. According to Majken, she was supposed to be in the processing phase now. The last phase, which she called the reorientation phase, was where new interests would replace the loss of Rasmus. She felt she would never reach that phase. How was she supposed to get there?

On the way back to the table, she bumped into Danny. He was standing at the door, lighting a cigarette. They looked at each other without saying anything. She smelled the smoke from his cigarette; mixed with the subdued scent of his aftershave, it seemed pleasant. She didn't usually like cigarette smoke.

Danny broke the silence. "I'll drive Troels home. Then he can pick up his car tomorrow when he's sober."

"Good idea," she muttered.

The conversation halted. She looked at the table where Majken was saying goodbye to Troels. She felt uncomfortable being alone with the mysterious man. He wasn't handsome like the male models she had occasionally photographed for various fashion catalogues and commercials. They tended to be beautiful but without charm.

Danny took his jacket and threw it over his shoulder. He smiled. She wanted to say something but didn't know what. Troels's uncertain steps reached them, and he thumped Danny on the shoulder with a clenched fist.

"This is rubbish; I can easily drive," he said, putting on his jacket with difficulty. Then he gave Majken a clumsy embrace. His breath stank of alcohol. She discreetly withdrew from him.

Majken said goodbye to Danny. She held his hand a little too long as she looked him over flirtatiously. "I hope *we'll* see each other again," she said in a soft voice that did nothing to hide what she meant.

Kamilla put on her jacket and looked at them. This was how Majken had been in all the years they had known each other. Charming and correct. How her humorous and intelligent friend had apparently never had a man in her life amazed her. She thought about how long it had been since she herself had felt the aphrodisiac of infatuation sweeping her legs out from under her. Jan had been her first great love. They had met at high school in Horsens. She had often wondered whether he had just been her ticket away from her mother and her sad home, with all the self-blame and doomsday warnings that had become fixed in her brain like a mantra. They weren't meant for each other. Not even after they'd had Rasmus. Jan hadn't been ready to have children. She had felt it while she was expecting. And even though Jan loved his son, he couldn't live up to his responsibilities as a father. He left. And it was too late now. He would never get the chance again.

They stood in front of the restaurant, watching the cars.

"He did well with a man he doesn't even know," Majken said with a little smile. She put her arm around Kamilla's shoulder. "Do you want to go for a walk? The weather's so nice."

She nodded. Fresh air was exactly what she needed.

Mols was visible on the other side of the bay in the clear weather. They walked in silence, looking at the beautiful sailboats anchored in the harbour, where there was room for about six hundred boats and a hundred fishing dinghies. Due to the wet summer, there weren't as many sailing guests as usual. The owner of one of the boats had used the dry weather as an opportunity to paint the bow. On another, a woman was sweeping the deck. An elderly man, who looked like a hardened sailor, was sitting on a bench smoking his pipe, watching life on the boats. The evening sun had begun to colour the sky reddish, and the only sounds were the soothing lapping of the water against the pier and the blackbirds singing in the distance. The air was fragrant with tar and sea water. At the northern end of the marina, the recreational fishermen had their own pier and clubhouse. The shops in the brown wooden houses were closed, reminiscent of Skagen with their characteristic roofs that looked like they had been cut with a pair of serrated tailor scissors. The evening sun was shining on the Sailing Club's large glass façade facing the dock. They could smell food from the large, covered barbecue area between the Bar Grill and the harbour service building and hear the noise from the playground and the minigolf course. Kamilla had often taken Rasmus down here, where there were so many exciting things for a little boy to see.

Majken continued to walk and smile.

"You liked him—Danny—didn't you?" asked Kamilla. Majken looked at her with happy eyes. "He's the yummiest guy I've seen in a long time!"

Kamilla smiled at her friend's choice of words, as if men were something to be devoured.

"Weren't you also just a little bit attracted to him?" Majken took her by the arm, nudging her teasingly with her hip as if she wanted to knock her down.

Kamilla shrugged. Yes, it had been a long time since she had met such a sympathetic example of the opposite sex. "He was very handsome," she replied.

"*Very hand*—uh, stop it, Kamilla." Majken laughed, letting go of her. "I could murder for a man like that."

She suddenly looked like a teenager in love. Kamilla had never seen her like this before.

11

He took advantage of the chance to head home at a halfway decent time. Roland sensed there wouldn't be many opportunities for that in the near future. But for now, they couldn't really move on. An urgent plea for help in identifying the child's body had been issued to the press at day's end; now they could only hope someone would come forward with information, so they could go from there.

He felt the coolness of the sea and smelled the salt water and seaweed through the open car window on Strandvejen. A Unifeeder cargo ship heavily laden with multicoloured containers was moving slowly south. Some yachtsmen used the period of sunshine to get the boats in the water. The traffic flowed well enough, and if he didn't know better, it could have been a perfectly ordinary afternoon after work. But the picture of the girl in the skip ruined that illusion. He lit a cigarette and waited patiently in his lane, while the coolness of the forest replaced that of the sea as he drove along the main road.

His stomach rumbled with hunger. He wondered what Irene had decided to make for dinner. She was on a diet, which meant he was, too, but he would eat anything now. He briefly considered heading to Pizza & Burger for a slice of pizza with a thick layer of mozzarella cheese and a Coca-Cola, but he ate his words. He was already late for dinner. He couldn't do that to Irene.

The villa in Højbjerg was Irene's childhood home. It had been built in 1953, and they had bought it when Irene's parents retired and moved into a small apartment—without a troublesome garden and stairs—in the centre of Aarhus. He had loved the house from the moment he saw it. Last year, they had remortgaged and completely modernised the villa from top to bottom. There had even been enough for a new roof. He spotted the high gable and window of the first floor protruding above the trees when he turned onto the residential road. The driveway and terrace were covered in Italian tiles, flanked by Irene's terra-cotta pots filled with blue hydrangeas. They couldn't have found a better home. It wasn't far to the forest or Ballehage sea baths, which he used faithfully. He loved the water, summer and winter, and was an active winter bather. It probably wasn't usual for a southern European, but given he had chosen to be a Viking, why not go with the whole kit and caboodle? He met many people with the same chilly habit on early winter mornings, when snow crystals glistened and the cold bit into your skin. Many were getting on in years. A few of the lads were over ninety, and so Roland had convinced himself weathering the cold shock of crawling into two-degree ice water could prolong your life.

He cursed quietly and braked when he saw his car's usual spot was occupied. The in-laws' weathered 1998 blue Saab was parked defiantly in the shade under the copper beech. They had a habit of spending part of the summer at the campsite near Ørnereden, and they were frequent guests at the old villa when they did. Of course they were here this week, when they probably knew he and Irene were looking after their great-grandchild. But why tonight exactly, when what he needed most was to enjoy a glass of Barolo on the terrace with Irene as they discussed the day's events. The only good thing about the visit was that it was unlikely low-calorie food was being served.

Having parked he reluctantly got out of the car and took his jacket from the back seat. When he entered the hall, he could smell his father-in-law's sour cigars overpowering the smell of bacon and garlic. The smell from the cigars always gave him a migraine, despite him smoking cigarettes himself. But you had to forgive a poor father-in-law who didn't have many other pleasures in his life.

He opened the door to the living room and heard his mother-in-law's sharp voice penetrate from the kitchen. His father-in-law had made himself at home with the newspaper and cigar in Roland's favourite chair. He looked up reluctantly when Roland greeted him. Carl Ernst looked like a withered stick. His wife, Dagny, had the ability to suck all the power from the strongest of men. He had often asked himself how two such people had managed to create a daughter like Irene. Both Carl Ernst and Dagny were filled with prejudice. They'd had a very hard time accepting Roland's "swarthy" appearance when he had joined the family, and they saw the fact he had quickly risen through the ranks of the police as his only mitigating factor. They were the polar opposite of Irene, who would take all sorts of homeless creatures in for a bite to eat and some shelter. After working as a secretary for Copenhagen Police, Irene had become a social worker.

Suddenly, Dagny filled the doorway to the kitchen. She was a small woman, almost as wide as she was tall. An area of excess fat dangled under her chin. She had put on a few more kilos since last time and now resembled an overweight turkey. If losing weight meant Irene would never look like this woman, he would support her endeavour in every possible way.

"Good day, Roland. I thought that was you. You're just in time. The food's on the table," she said with a sweaty face from standing and directing Irene by the hot stove. They were magic words to the gaunt man in Roland's armchair, who put the cigar down in the ashtray and painstakingly folded the newspaper before sending Roland a satisfied laugh. He shuffled past him into the kitchen, where he sat down—again—in Roland's usual spot.

Irene was standing by the stove with her back to him, seasoning a pot of coq au vin. Her light floral summer dress revealed the round hips she was in the process of fighting. Her dark hair—not her natural hair colour—was piled up on her head with a hairpin, but some charming tufts had strayed down onto her perspiring neck. If they hadn't had guests, he would have hugged her and kissed her on the neck, but he restrained the urge. When she straightened up, he gave her a kiss on the cheek instead and looked into her tired eyes. She rolled them to the ceiling with a resigned expression. Her parents had probably been bothering her for a while. "Is Marianna sleeping?" he whispered. She nodded. He smiled encouragingly at her and opened the bottle of Barolo. *Not all plans should be ruined.* He hoped camping life without a TV had impeded his parents-in-law from following the news, but he wasn't so lucky.

"So have you found the killer?" Dagny cooed as soon as he sat down at the table. Irene passed the salad bowl around.

"We heard it on the radio as we drove out here. It's dreadful, a little girl—and raped. What's with men these days?" Dagny shook her head, affronted, so the fold of skin under her chin dangled.

"The girl wasn't raped. But it is dreadful," Roland replied. For once, he could agree with his mother-in-law on something.

"I'm sure it's one of those immigrant boys in Gellerup who's making trouble. Wasn't she found in Brabrand?" asked Carl with his mouth full of chicken. Dagny nodded in agreement and looked at Roland as if she thought they had settled the matter for him now. He felt Irene's hand squeeze his thigh soothingly under the table. He took it as a sign not to get upset and that she was next to him, standing by him.

"We're in the process of identifying the murderer. We'll find him," he said, trying to sound convincing. He lifted the glass and toasted his guests. The rest of the dinner passed without drama. After Dagny had helped Irene with the washing up, and Roland had tried to find something sensible to talk to Carl about in the living room, they drove back to Ørnereden to their little family tent.

Roland emptied the ashtray of stinking cigar butts, filled his wine glass, and sat down in his Stressless recliner with his feet comfortably placed on the footstool. Irene sat down on the armrest and fumbled with the dark hair at the nape of his neck.

"You'd rather have some peace and quiet on your own, wouldn't you, my darling?"

She knew his rhythm in a murder case, and she knew her parents' visit had been an unfortunate interruption. He nodded and kissed her hand.

"It's late, too. I'm going to go up and look in on Marianna. She has a cold, the poor little mite. And then I'm going to go to bed. We can talk in the morning. Shall I put some music on?"

He nodded again as he sent her a look and a smile filled with gratitude. Shortly afterwards, Luciano Pavarotti's voice resounded like gentle thunder in the semi-dark room. Roland closed his eyes and let the notes of "Nessun Dorma" fill his head. He tried to let himself be enveloped by the song, carried to his homeland by the imagined scent of orange and lemon groves, but each time he ended up in a foul skip with the girl's bright eyes staring at him.

He was just about to slip into sleep when the phone rang. It was the police station calling to report they had finally received a missing person's report of a girl answering to the description in the murder report. The parents were coming in to identify the body at the morgue at seven o'clock tomorrow morning.

12

Are you going already?"

Vera tried to ignore the reproach in his voice. "You know there's a meeting tonight, don't you, Troels? Where have you been? Who drove you home, and where's your car?"

She stopped in the doorway of the living room and hitched up her shoulder bag. He didn't look at her. The TV was turned up high on a sports channel, where the commentator screamed and behaved like an idiot every time the ball was near the goal. Apparently, he forgot he had a microphone. She hated his sports, too. It was a pain in the neck when he came home from the shop and turned on the box. It was even worse when he came home drunk and she didn't know where he had been, like now. His indifference meant she'd had to buy her own little used Ford. She could never count on when the car would be home.

"Well, bye. I won't be long." She slammed the front door to drown out the sound from the TV.

"Don't rush on my account," he muttered, but only once he had heard the door slam.

During half-time, he got a beer from the fridge. She had put food in front of him under a piece of foil, ready to put in the oven. He couldn't be bothered to see what it was. It was rarely exciting. "Career women don't have time to cook properly for their useless men." He snorted, opening the can of beer so it sprayed onto the kitchen floor. He wiped it up with a dishcloth before sitting down heavily on the couch again. Half-time was the worst. Sitting there, listening to the experts trying to predict what would happen in the second half was so annoying. Why not just start the bloody game? Experts always had to judge everything. Clever war experts even analysed the Iraq War. Or politicians more like, who had been day tourists down there, who thought they had seen everything and could tell everyone at home it was under control. He snorted loudly. They had no idea what soldiers were going through over there. It was so easy to stand on the outside and judge. It was the soldiers who had to stay. "Fighting for what you love, even dying for it" took on a completely different meaning for them. Roadside bombs, ambush attacks, suicide bombers. The military uniform they weren't allowed to change out for civilian clothes—not even in the evenings. *It's not a summer camp*, they had said. But no one was in doubt about that. He felt sick thinking about the heat and the stench, and the anxiety he wouldn't admit had been there. Not now he had returned home to safe little Denmark. But he couldn't hide it at night. His own loud howls at the horrible nightmares that awoke him almost every single night. Luckily, Vera had thrown him out of the bedroom years ago. But she could probably still hear him.

"Blah, blah, blah," he yelled at the so-called experts, zapping the remote to other channels. Ads—that's what the bloke from the restaurant did for a living. Persuade people through lies to spend money. Promise them longer and shinier hair—or just hair for that matter. He smiled crookedly. What a joke of a job. And then he was all holy, didn't drink, and had to act like a lifesaver for other people. He could easily have driven home himself; he had done it a thousand times before on much worse benders. Troels toasted the TV screen, clicked further, and ended up on a channel with dancers at a nightclub in Miami. He took a big sip from the beer can as he studied the girls' firm young bodies with their long, black, patent leather boots that reached all the way up to the knees. Like snakes, they wound themselves around the shiny steel poles on the stage as though in a little fire station. One of the girls squatted down in front of a customer and flirted openly and naughtily with him with her tongue. She was beautiful, brown and shapely. Troels felt the throb in his crotch as a pain. Then the dancer straightened up and pushed the excited customer away as she laughed. Troels's grip on the beer became so hard that the metal gave way.

He zapped back to the sports channel, where the starting whistle had just been blown for the second half.

It wasn't long before the beer can was empty. He got a bottle of Irish whiskey from the bar and looked lovingly at the golden liquid before pouring some.

The match ended in a draw. He went out into the kitchen and lifted the foil. Chops from yesterday that just needed to be heated. He wrinkled his nose. The meetings usually lasted a long time, and maybe she would go out to satisfy her desires afterwards, so there was no rush with the food. He sat back in his chair, feeling drunk after the wine at the restaurant, the beer, and the whiskey. Still, he poured more into his glass. The signature jingle of the late news nearly made him turn off the TV. He couldn't bear to see and hear about the Iraq War and suicide bombers. The horrors were still under his skin, but when the newscaster announced a murdered girl had been found in a waste container in Brabrand, his finger paused on the power button. The body hadn't yet been identified, so the police had no further information. The discomfort rippled down his spine. He emptied the glass in one gulp.

13

The sound of the doorbell echoed through the house. Tarzan lay rolled up like a furry black pillow on the couch. Kamilla had stormed around like a tornado cleaning up when she got had home from the restaurant. It gave her relief now, and she quickly admired the reasonably tidy living room before opening the door.

Jan had brought Nina, who handed her a bouquet of roses from their garden. Kamilla had planted the bushes herself in the garden by the house in Mårslet on a cool autumn evening. The sight of Nina made her heart race. The feeling of inadequacy always got stronger when she was near the woman Jan had chosen over her and Rasmus.

"We were out for a drive and thought we'd drop by to see how you're doing," said Jan.

Kamilla knew that wasn't the truth. She accepted the bouquet and hesitantly invited them inside.

"Are we disturbing you?" asked Nina considerately as they entered.

"No. Would you like a cup of coffee?"

"No thanks, we'll head off again soon."

Jan walked into the living room with the long confident strides she knew so well from ten years of marriage. Rasmus had got his red hair from him. He was dressed in his casual wear: jeans and a light blue shirt that enhanced the blue colour of his eyes—made them even deeper. Kamilla had always found him extra attractive in a blue shirt, and it irritated her she felt that way now.

Nina's attire was a stark contrast to Jan's. She always looked like someone on their way to a party, and her hair sat as if she had just come straight from the hairdresser. She had politely taken off her high-heeled shoes out in the hall so she wouldn't leave marks on the polished wooden floor. Kamilla felt like a grey mouse in pre-washed T-shirt and trousers, hair not completely dry yet after the shower. Neither did she have any make-up on, as she was planning on going to bed soon. She sat across from them on the sofa. They hadn't taken off their coats. Jan sat drumming his fingers on the coffee table, staring at the picture of Rasmus on the bookshelf. His little face radiated serious pride as he hugged the football to himself. The picture had been taken when he had started playing football. She remembered that night clearly. Jan had been so proud his son was going to play football. A father's pride, she had thought, despite him not having participated in neither the pre-natal preparations nor nappy changes. Kamilla shuddered when she saw the hatred in Jan's eyes. Did he still feel she hadn't taken good enough care of their son?

Nina lit a cigarette. It quivered slightly between her long, thin fingers with the well-groomed lacquered nails.

"That's a lie," Jan said.

"What's a lie?" she asked. Kamilla knew his lies. His lies about working overtime, about business trips, about late lunches—she had believed it all blindly back then. Luckily, Rasmus had been only five years old at the time and hadn't really realised his mother and father weren't together anymore. She had found it more difficult. Suddenly, she was alone with a little boy because his father had had a mid-life crisis and found a Lolita. Nina was much younger than her. Jan could have been Nina's father. Kamilla had been so sure that, in the end, Jan would choose his family—her and Rasmus. She had been wrong.

"We weren't just out for a drive," Jan admitted. "We were at the cemetery. It's the first time. I haven't been able to . . ." He fell silent as he ran a hand down over his face, as though to remove the sight of what he had seen in the graveyard.

Nina tapped the ash off the cigarette into the ashtray she had taken with her to the coffee table. "I drove him there," she interrupted. She took a long puff of the cigarette and blew the smoke out one corner of her mouth. "Otherwise, he'll never face reality. But now he wants to find the man who killed Rasmus." She looked at Jan as if she had revealed one of his biggest secrets.

"You want to do what now? Why, Jan? Why now?" asked Kamilla, trying to catch his eye. He leaned towards her. "Do you realise that pig got six to nine months in prison for killing our son? He's been out for ages now. Driving again. Drinking again. Having fun again! He should have got life!"

"No, the death penalty!" Nina knocked the cigarette ash off angrily, even though she had just done so.

"It's been over a year now, Jan! What do you want to say to him?" Kamilla hadn't had the energy to think about how the motorist had been punished, and certainly not to contact him. Jan sat back again, staring at the picture of Rasmus. Hatred shone out his eyes. He didn't answer.

"There's nothing more we can do, Jan," she tried again. "Even if you murder him, it won't bring Rasmus back . . ." Her voice cracked.

"He should have got a longer sentence! If he hadn't been drunk-driving that night, we'd still have our little Rasmus!" Nina tossed the cigarette butt into the ashtray with an aggressive motion and stood up. Jan did the same. Kamilla stood up, too, when she could see they were already walking off. She knew Nina had really liked Rasmus, and that Rasmus had adored her. It was for his sake she had felt compelled to accept Nina, though she had stung with jealousy when she would see them together. For a while, she had feared Jan and Nina would take Rasmus from her, but luckily that hadn't happened. They weren't the ones who had done that.

"I was hoping you'd support us in this," Jan said reproachfully as they stood in the hall.

"No. Forget it, Jan! Forget finding that man. What good will it do us? The best thing is to stay far away from him. Should I ask Majken to make you an appointment?"

"A psychologist! No thanks; I have Nina to talk to." He reached out for Nina's hand. She took it. Kamilla could see the way he clenched it.

She followed them to the door, watched the car turn out onto the road and disappear between the trees where she had last seen Rasmus on his bike, on the way to training with the big sports bag and the football on the luggage rack. The pain in her chest struck again. She had scolded him that night. First because he hadn't done his homework, then because he hadn't packed his sports bag, even though he was to meet Jonas in the hall at six o'clock, and because he hadn't eaten his dinner—he was so picky. All trifles he shouldn't have been reprimanded for.

She sat on the sofa where Jan had sat, looking at the photo of Rasmus for a long time. A strange feeling began to grow in her. "Six months," she repeated aloud. "Six to nine months for a child's life." Then she got up and emptied the ashtray of Nina's cigarette butt with the red lipstick on the filter.

14

Who the hell let this happen?"

His fist hit the newspaper, where the image of a skip's filthy interior filled most of the front page. The plastic cup with lukewarm coffee almost overturned. Roland was sitting in the briefing room and had asked the person in charge at the container to remain until the delayed morning briefing was over. The officer stood upright in front of his boss but wasn't radiating quite the same authority as he had at the container the day before.

"I didn't allow this. But something came out of it." The young officer tried to defend himself with a crooked, insecure smile.

Roland thawed a little. Raising his voice and banging his fist on the table had helped. He had always had a hard time controlling his temper. He blamed the southern Italian genes. He had only got a few hours' sleep the previous night. When he had finally tiptoed up to Irene in bed, their grandchild had started crying because of her cold. The headache from his father-in-law's cigar had pounded in his skull. The neighbour's dog had barked, too. But it wasn't only that. He hadn't been able to sleep anyway. The image of the dead girl with her dark curls caked in mud played like a slideshow in his mind's eye every time he closed his eyes. He saw her tied up somewhere sinister. But where was it? How would they find it? He couldn't get into the killer's mindset, even though he tried to force himself to do so. He felt weak and feeble as he waved the officer away.

"Alright, Dan. We'll talk about that later."

What had happened had happened. Reproaching DS Vang wouldn't help, even though he often wanted to give him a kick in the arse. The green copper seemed to think donning his fine uniform was all it took to be a police officer. But with time, he would learn it was much more than that. Plus, Roland always found it hard to scold a subordinate who admitted their mistake and didn't start offering all sorts of possible and impossible excuses or try passing the blame. He hated that. It made him furious. And the lad was right. Something had come out of it. If nothing else, proof they had really bungled it, he thought bitterly. Why hadn't they—the police— noticed the other hatch on the back of the skip? Or Henry Leander! His old friend Leander, with eyes like a trained hunting dog. Maybe the hunting dog was getting on in years. Maybe he was, too, he reasoned when he realised he was doing what he hated most—passing the blame.

But it was Leander who had discovered the doll. It had appeared in the forensic images, but not in what the journalist had published on the front page. The doll was gone. Four men had searched. Turned the contents of the stinking skip inside out, but the doll was gone. Someone must have removed it, but why, and how? They should have taken it with them before locking the skip, but they hadn't immediately associated it with the girl or the murder. There was so much other junk. But how could it be the girl's doll? Wouldn't she have lost it long before, given she had been tied up? He leaned in over the table, grabbed the thermos, and poured some more coffee. The table showed traces of the morning briefing. Mikkel had left a crumpled napkin with butter stains, and Kim had left his empty cup, despite being given a clear message to clear the table after meetings. No one had pushed in the chairs or wiped the table of coffee spills and breadcrumbs. Sometimes having employees who had mothers and wives to clean up after them on a daily basis was a nuisance.

The whole day had been thrown off by the early meeting at the morgue. He hadn't even said good morning to Irene. She had taken the week off to look after Marianna. He didn't need to attend the identification, but he couldn't help it. It had also been worth getting the measure of the parents. They hadn't reported the girl missing because they had thought she was staying with a school friend. She had been invited to a birthday party on Monday afternoon after school. Only later did they learn she had never shown up for the party and hadn't slept over at her friend's.

Gitte, her name was. Gitte Mikkelsen. The mother, the deeply despondent and shocked mother, who immediately recognised the girl under the white sheet at the morgue as her daughter and almost fainted, told them how her daughter had taken a doll with her when she left. Though not necessarily the doll they had spotted. But the fact the doll was gone now made him suspicious. The mother had to identify it. From pictures, of course. She was heavily pregnant. Roland feared she would go into labour at the sight of her daughter's corpse.

He looked up at the bulletin board on the wall with the pictures of the pale dead girl. Her eyes stared directly at him. Her lips were dry and cracked. If only those lips could talk. Tell him what had happened. What had the staring eyes seen before the light went out of them? There were close-ups of her abused wrists and the mark on her back. He got up with a sigh and added the picture of the doll to the sequence of photos.

Again, he concentrated on the picture on the front page of the newspaper and lit a cigarette. Anne Larsen was the name of the journalist. Probably not *that* Anne Larsen, he concluded, thinking of Irene's low-fat cookbooks at home in the kitchen. He would rather the lean meat was replaced with a real steak with its fatty edge, the thin sauce ousted by one dripping with fat, and cheese that could walk on its own instead of that dry 15 per cent fat stuff. But when he pictured his mother-in-law, he understood Irene.

He went back to his office with the half-empty plastic cup of coffee, picked up the phone, and dialled the number of the newspaper's editorial office. At the morning briefing, he had just said the press was to be kept out of the case for as long as possible. *The world has turned upside down,* he thought.

15

———

He gave his wife a quick kiss goodbye and tousled the boys' hair a little. As usual, they were playing Nintendo in their rooms. The weather wasn't exactly geared for outdoor activities this summer, but that wasn't what they spent most of their time on anyway. To his involuntary disgust, he had to admit they were starting to get tubby. It couldn't be their diet. His wife and he were quite good about that, so it had to be the lack of exercise. Sussi was beginning to bulge a bit, too. It wouldn't surprise him if they scoffed sweets and cakes when he wasn't home in the afternoons. Perhaps her job in the bakery offered too much temptation. The oldest boy jerked his head away from him to continue the engrossing game, not once removing his eyes from the screen. His experienced fingers worked fast on the controller. His daughter got a kiss on her porridge-covered face as she looked up at him from her highchair and gave a loud scream of joy, smashing the spoon into the porridge again so it sprayed all over the kitchen table. She was forgiven as she was only a year old.

He had been happy when he had left the house, but as he sat in the car in the garage and put the key in the ignition, the despondency returned. It was so bloody hard to do his job after *that*. He had even considered quitting and finding something else, but that would be difficult, too, and especially given he would rather work with children. That's what he was educated for. That was his vocation. Maybe it would just happen of its own accord. Politicians were talking about closing more after-school clubs to save millions of kroner—perhaps his workplace would be next—but what about the children then?

When he parked the car outside Søvejen After-School Centre and saw the children on the construction site, he forgot about his worries. There were light and dark faces. Many of the children at the club were from ethnically diverse backgrounds. A couple of the kids spotted him and waved. He went inside. The child and youth workers were something else. Only Ib, who was an assistant youth worker, said, "Hello, Jesper." He felt the conversation stop when he walked in, and an embarrassing silence weighed heavily in the air. No one asked him whether he had heard about Gitte's murder, that she had been found in a skip not far from where he lived. No one asked how he felt about such a case popping up now. He took the pot from the coffee machine and poured it into a thermos. The coffee smelled burnt. While his back was to the others, he found a cup in the cupboard. He could hear them breaking up and quietly leaving the room. Only Ib remained, reading the newspaper, but when Jesper sat down at the table with his coffee cup, it didn't take long before he closed the newspaper and walked away with an apologetic smile, which he hadn't needed to do at all. Jesper knew what they were thinking. He turned the newspaper around and read the article on the murder. It didn't contain anything other than what he had heard on the radio and seen on TV. Maybe he should expect to get a call from the police soon. They were probably looking at anyone who had been suspected of being or was registered as a paedophile. Even if they had been acquitted. When he had drunk his coffee, he got up and went out to the children. They were the only ones who didn't accuse him. Neither did his family, thankfully.

16

The police station was a large red building of composite square bricks with lots of windows. Kamilla had often driven by it, but she had only ever been in the passport office. Anne had called from the newspaper office and said an inspector had summoned them for an interview. About the pictures Kamilla had taken of the skip yesterday. Of course the police knew they had crawled under the barricade now that her photo filled most of the newspaper's front page. It wasn't with a clear conscience she had driven to Aarhus. Concentrating on the traffic was difficult. What did the police want with them? Were they going to be punished for breaching the police tape? Had they ruined the investigation?

Anne was waiting at the main entrance to the police station. She looked calm and smiled when she saw her. She threw away a piece of chewing gum. "Come on; let's find out what he wants. This is exciting," she said eagerly.

They had to wait a bit before being shown into a small office where a man starting to go grey at the temples was sitting behind a cluttered desk. He looked up with dark, burning eyes set in a tanned face. As he got up to greet them, he loosened his tie a little. He explained to them briefly why he had summoned them, then poured coffee into three plastic cups.

"Of course we're happy to show you the rest of the photos, Chief Inspector Benito," said Anne.

"Detective Inspector." He corrected her with a face that revealed he was annoyed he wasn't a chief inspector.

"But we need something in return, Detective Inspector Benito. Italian, right?" she added. He nodded without elaborating.

Kamilla would have given him all the pictures immediately, as a fine for crawling into a forbidden area under the police cordon, or just out of sheer respect for the authorities. But not Anne. She wanted something in return.

Roland Benito didn't seem surprised. Quite the reverse. It almost looked like he had expected that answer. He told them about the doll. The missing doll. Anne set a tape recorder on the table. "May I?" Roland nodded resignedly. Then she gave him the pictures. Quid pro quo. The mafia method, as Jan always called it. Apparently, they had plenty in the real estate industry.

Roland Benito went through all the images slowly and thoroughly, studying them carefully. Kamilla observed him over the plastic edge of the cup, between quick sips of the lukewarm coffee that tasted of old, bitter beans. She was drinking it out of pure reflex. Nervous reflex, it suddenly seemed to her. Maybe the detective inspector concluded it was that, too. She didn't want to look guilty, so she quickly put the cup down on the edge of the cluttered desk and looked at Anne. It seemed foolish they were sitting here watching the detective review her pictures of the skip filled with all sorts of crap. But Anne's eyes were alert and attentive as she took in all his movements.

"When did you take these photos?"

Anne looked at Kamilla. "About two o'clock, wasn't it?"

She thought about it. Everything from the day before ran through her head like a timeless carousel. Containers. Vomit on her shoe. The strangled girl who, fortunately, she hadn't seen, but who she nevertheless saw in her mind's eye. Jan's desire for revenge. Danny's eyes.

"Yeah, around then." Her voice sounded hoarse.

"The others were taken around half past one," muttered Roland, mostly to himself, but the words still disappeared into the little tape recorder on the desk and stuck to the spinning magnetic tapes.

"That means the doll was removed from the skip between half past one and two o'clock. Within half an hour," Anne concluded.

Roland looked at her as if she were interrupting him with the same thought.

"Exactly! Someone other than you two must have known about the other door on the container. Because you didn't remove the doll, did you?"

He leaned back in the chair and let his eyes slide from Anne to Kamilla and back again while he rubbed his chin and its black stubble pensively.

Kamilla swallowed the lump that had been sitting in her throat since she had sat down stiffly in the chair, opposite the man with the twinkle in his dark, intense eyes. The black eyebrows were fused over the bridge of his nose, giving him an angry expression. It was how Rasmus had always drawn angry men, she remembered. A powerful V right between the eyes. He had seen it in comics. It was clear the inspector was from southern Europe. His tanned skin couldn't be due to the Danish summer. But his Danish didn't have any accent, so she guessed he must have grown up in Denmark.

"Are we under suspicion?" Anne's voice had a tinge of insult. It seemed she didn't care much for the police.

"Of course not." He smiled for the first time. Not a warm, encouraging smile, but a smile nonetheless. It gave some relief.

"Did the girl's mother recognise the doll?" Anne was making sure to get her share of the cake while there was time. It wasn't every day she, as a journalist, was invited to the police station. Except for press conferences, of course. It usually took hard work to get a detective to speak on a case like this.

"Haven't you talked to the family?" Roland sounded astonished.

"It's on today's to-do list," Anne admitted.

So she wasn't one of those journalists who immediately threw herself at the bereaved. Kamilla remembered the journalists who had hounded her after the accident. She hadn't picked up the phone. When the doorbell rang, she knew it was them, too. For that reason, the article "Tragic fatal accident on Grenåvej" had only enough material to fill two columns on the front page, with a picture of the place where it had happened. A picture of withered grass with little bouquets and glowing tea lights schoolmates had laid. Happened and printed. New disasters occurred, and old ones were forgotten.

"Did you see anyone suspicious on the other side of the container? Or did you observe anything else?"

The detective inspector's voice pulled Kamilla from her memory, and she straightened up in her chair. Anne shook her head thoughtfully and looked at her questioningly again.

"I stepped in some vomit," she replied. "Someone had thrown up behind the container." Maybe it was the perpetrator. Perhaps he had felt such remorse at what he had done that his stomach had turned.

"DNA," she suggested without knowing much about it. The detective shook his head regretfully with a little indulgent smile as he reached for his packet of cigarettes. He offered it to Anne, who took one. Kamilla refused; she had never smoked.

"Cecilie Nordstrøm, who found the girl, told us she threw up in the bushes by the skip. Didn't you talk to her, either?" Now he sounded almost offended, as if he took them for bad examples of the press. He lit Anne's cigarette with his lighter, then lit his own.

"I tried to get hold of her, but she's not answering the phone, and no one opens the door when I call," Anne defended herself. "Maybe they're on holiday." She made it sound like a question for Roland to answer.

"I asked the family not to leave the country in case we need more information," he replied.

"When's the press conference?" asked Anne.

"We only confirmed the girl's identity this morning. I expect you to sit tight on that for now. But we'll probably call one later today."

"I very much hope so. We're looking for answers," said Anne reproachfully.

"So are we," he replied curtly. "We're still waiting on results from the DNA sent to Copenhagen." He took a hard puff of the cigarette to hide his annoyance at having revealed too much.

"DNA! I assume it's semen? Is there suspicion of rape?" said Anne.

Roland tapped the ash of the cigarette into the overflowing ashtray and pushed it over towards Anne. "That's enough for today! Unfortunately, there's no more I can tell you. The rest will have to wait until the press conference," he said, getting up to indicate the meeting was over, no matter what they thought.

"May I keep the photos?" he said a little too loudly as Kamilla reached for them. "We need to review them again and compare with our own and those from forensics. More items may be missing," he explained with a conciliatory smile.

"Spot the difference." Anne turned around and laughed despite the seriousness of the matter.

Roland Benito closed the door behind them with an indulgent smile, the cigarette held loosely in one corner of his mouth.

17

Ida Mikkelsen's entire body shook as her husband helped her into the kitchen and gently placed her on an uncomfortable dining chair. They hadn't spoken to each other on the way home from the morgue. A shuddering cry spontaneously overpowered her. "No, no, no," she cried, collapsing across the kitchen table, sobbing uncontrollably. Allan Mikkelsen sat down on the chair opposite her as though paralysed. With great exertion, he raised his hand and stroked her awkwardly on the back. It was unusual for him to see his wife cry and to have to comfort her. She was so strong.

"Take it easy, Ida. Think of the baby," he muttered hoarsely.

She instinctively laid a hand on her pregnant belly and tried to pull herself together. She wiped her nose on a piece of kitchen roll, still shaking.

"Why didn't we look for her earlier? Why didn't they phone to say she hadn't arrived at the birthday party? Why did we even force her to go to that party? She didn't want to." She sobbed.

Allan stared straight ahead. It looked as if he was staring at the pictures of Gitte stuck to the fridge door with magnets that resembled ladybirds. Yet his eyes stopped short and looked at nothing. He didn't cry, but his eyes were red-rimmed, and his chin quivered. He stiffened when Ida took his hand. She suddenly stopped crying but stared at him as though she were now the stronger of the two. The tears and sorrow made her face unrecognisable.

"Do you think they'll figure it out?" she said quietly, wiping her eyes with her free hand.

Allan leaned back against the wall and ran a hand over his face. His hands were large and rough. He was a bricklayer and should have been at work at seven o'clock. Most of all, he wanted to just leave. To escape from the hell he had now ended up in. If there were anywhere to flee to. He just shook his head in response to her question, but the uncertainty gnawed at him. Gitte had been the light of his life. His live wire. She had made Ida happy, too, and all the regrets and reproaches had stopped when they'd had her. Now she was gone. Could their new child give them that, too? Could one human being ever replace another?

Gitte had been a strange child. Certainly. Withdrawn and moody in recent years. Often difficult. Maybe it was just the onset of puberty. What did he know about that kind of thing? He was only a bricklayer. Through the fog, he watched Ida get up awkwardly and go out to the bathroom, where she took a pill. He wanted to protest—she was pregnant. But he remained silent. She knew what she was doing. She was a nurse. She didn't return to the kitchen, and he guessed she had gone to bed. He feared she would start turning her back to him again now. It was all so unreal.

Bertil, their wirehaired old Danish pointer, woke in her basket as if she had suddenly felt something was wrong. She got up and came to him. In the silence, the sound of claws against the linoleum floor was loud in his ears. Bertil laid her head on his thigh and looked up at him with those unfathomable dog eyes. He had never liked her eyes. Bertil was wiser than that, and *not* knowing what she was thinking frightened him. He patted her absently on the head. She didn't follow him when he went outside and sat in the Ford Transit, as if it were a completely ordinary morning and he was going to work. As if Gitte and Ida were still asleep and would do the usual chores while he was at work at the construction site in Skåde. As if they were going to sit around the table this evening and eat and talk about what had happened during the day—with his brick work, at the hospital, at school. He spotted Gitte's yellow hairclip lying on the floor of the car. It was in the shape of a butterfly. He picked it up and turned it in the light. A few dark curly hairs were stuck in the clip. She had lost it and had looked for it in vain. And now he had found it. He collapsed over the steering wheel, his broad shoulders shaking as he cried.

18

The press coverage worked!" said DS Mikkel Jensen as he sat down in the chair opposite Roland Benito, who had gathered his people for an update of the case. They had held a brief press conference at noon to share limited knowledge so they could have some peace and quiet to work. TV 2 News had already reported the new information.

"Have we heard anything? Witnesses?" asked Roland, a little hope sprouting. They hadn't yet received the DNA results, and he was losing patience with all the waiting that came with the analyses they couldn't carry out themselves. Witnesses would be a good start.

"Yep, we just got a call from a Gerda Poulsen in Brabrand. Her daughter, Louise, is in the same class as Gitte and is—eh, was—her friend. She told her mother she saw Gitte talking several times to a man in a dark car at the playground."

"Would the girl recognise the man or the car?"

"She didn't say anything other than it was a big dark car." Mikkel sighed.

"Do ten-year-olds know anything about makes and models of cars?" commented DS Niels Nyborg, who was practically lying down in his chair with his legs stretched out in front of him under the table.

"Maybe not girls," replied Roland. At least, it had never interested his daughters. Nor Irene for that matter.

"But Gerda Poulsen believes her daughter could probably identify the car if she saw a picture of it."

"We'll drive out there after the meeting, Mikkel." Roland threw a report on the table and tapped it with his fingertips.

"The autopsy report's in; I've just reviewed it with Kurt Olsen. Now we just need the results of the DNA and the analysis of the mud. We've also got a rough overview of Gitte Mikkelsen's movements on Monday," he said. He gave them a rundown of the autopsy report. Then he went through as much of Gitte's activities as he knew: "Gitte left school when she was finished at half past one on Monday afternoon. A teacher talked to her briefly in the schoolyard. Gitte said she was going to Mathilde Beck's birthday party, a school friend, and that she had to hurry home to change. She was back in her home in Brabrand about a quarter to two, changed into the clothes she was discovered in—including white tights, which still haven't been found—then left home on her bike with the doll in a backpack. We need to find the backpack and the bike. The backpack's pink with a Diddlina Ballerina motif. The bike's a red Winther. It has a worn black saddle. Her parents couldn't provide any further details. But she was wearing a red Etto bike helmet. Gitte was seen in Bazar Vest a bit before two, where she bought fruit. The autopsy shows the fruit was her last meal." Roland cleared his throat and took a mouthful of lukewarm coffee.

"The birthday party started at two o'clock, but Gitte never showed up, so after Bazar Vest, there are no more leads. No one saw her cycling from there, and no one saw her again until she was found dead in the skip the next day, almost twenty-four hours after she left home. Her parents didn't expect her home because she was due to sleep over at her friend's with a couple of other friends."

"Why didn't anyone at the party react to Gitte not turning up?" Niels dared to interrupt Roland's flow of speech while eagerly chewing a piece of gum.

"The birthday girl's parents didn't know how many children their daughter had invited," Roland continued with an annoyed frown. "When Mathilde eventually mentioned to her mother that Gitte hadn't come, her mother tried to ring Gitte's parents, but there was no answer, and then she forgot about it again. Gitte's described as a girl who could be wayward at times, she didn't always stick to what she'd agreed, so it came as no surprise she didn't turn up and stay overnight. She's described as a slightly withdrawn and timid girl. The fact her close friend, Louise, wasn't going to the birthday party could have been reason enough for her not to go." Roland looked up from the report. Everyone sat silent, listening, as if he had read aloud from a fairy tale. Mikkel had noted a few things down on his pad.

"So we've nothing to go on after two o'clock, when Gitte left Bazar Vest, and we have a bike, a backpack, a pair of white tights, and a bike helmet to find," Roland concluded his briefing.

Nobody said anything. The mood was as solemn as the rain hitting the windows outside.

"Any questions?" asked Roland, gathering the papers. No one had any, and they quietly left the briefing room. The case was affecting them. Roland sat silently staring at the photos of the dead girl on the blackboard. Then he realised Mikkel Jensen was still sitting there.

"Bloody hell, of course. The girl who saw the car," he exclaimed, embarrassed.

Mikkel drank the last bit of the Coca-Cola he had brought to the meeting. "If Louise was Gitte's close friend and could be the reason Gitte didn't show up for the birthday party, she's probably worth talking to," he said, getting up eagerly.

Roland nodded. "Do you have the address?"

Mikkel nodded.

"Then let's go to Brabrand."

Gerda Poulsen was a small, thin woman in her late thirties. She was wearing a loose purple knitted jumper with silver Lurex threads and a giant cowl neck, with a flowy delicately floral-patterned summer skirt. She smiled wearily as she opened the door and showed them into a living room where toys were scattered all over the floor. A boy of about two sat in the middle of it all, smacking two wooden blocks against each other. Saliva ran down his chin onto a pair of blue dungarees.

"Hello, little man," Roland said kindly as the child looked up at him with astonished big blue eyes and, puzzled, put a finger in his mouth. Then the boy howled. His mother picked him up, shushing him.

"It's terrible—what happened to Gitte—she used to come here often. They'd hide out in Louise's bedroom all giggly, chatting on the internet. She was such a sweet girl. It's unbelievable," she said loudly to drown out the child she was rocking in her arms. Gerda had tears in her eyes when she looked up at them, as though they had all the answers and could explain why such things happened.

"Is Louise home? We'd like to talk to her about the car she saw at the playground."

The child howled so loudly it grated at their ears.

"I asked Louise to stay home because you were coming, but she just had to go and get some schoolbooks from a friend. She'll be back soon. Would you like a cup of coffee?" she said on her way into the nursery with the boy, whose crying was calming down. His face was wet with tears and snot as he looked at them reproachfully over his mother's shoulder. She searched for something between the sheets in the cot. She found the dummy and stuck it into his wet mouth. Finally, they only heard the ticking of the living room clock and a few small, jerky hiccups from the child.

"No, thank you; we have to be going once we've spoken to Louise. I'm sorry the police have that effect on your son." Roland smiled. He knew he had a brusque appearance, but not that it was that bad. She laid the boy down in the bed and pulled the duvet with its teddy-bear pattern up under his chin.

"He's just overtired," she said. *Every mother's explanation of an impossible child*, thought Roland, sitting down next to DS Jensen on the black leather sofa. The leather felt cold through his trousers. "Is there anything else you'd like while you're waiting?"

She carefully closed the door to the nursery and removed a book about farm animals from the armchair before sitting across from them. They both declined her offer.

"Louise didn't go to her classmate's birthday party on Monday?" Roland asked.

Gerda looked sad. "No. We had to go to a funeral."

"My condolences. Was it someone close?" he asked sympathetically.

"It was Louise's grandfather. He lived in Skagen. We weren't very close to him. But still." She clasped her hands, visibly affected by being alone with two police officers. "I can call Louise's phone. It's strange she isn't here yet."

Roland was about to protest by reminding her she was talking about a ten-year-old child. He had a hard time getting used to the fact even kindergarten children were walking around with mobile phones nowadays but had no idea what a vinyl record was. At the same time, it struck him he hadn't thought Gitte Mikkelsen undoubtedly also had carried a mobile phone. He would have to address that when they got back.

"That's not necessary; we'll just wait," he said with a smile. But Gerda had already called and was listening expectantly. Suddenly, she seemed nervous. Such is the plight of being a parent when there's been a child murder in the neighbourhood. Fear creeps into everyday life, and things that used to be normal quickly become something frightening. Roland knew it all too well. They had to solve this murder soon so everyday life could return to normal.

"She's not answering," said Gerda almost to herself, quickly typing a new number on the keypad. This time she got up and stood with her back to them, looking out the window as the call went through. Mikkel Jensen sent Roland a worried look.

"Hi, Tina," her voice trembled slightly. "Is Louise on her way home? We're waiting for her." She listened, then sat down on the edge of the nearest chair. "She hasn't been there? Are you sure? She left about an hour ago. She just had to get some books from Lise. Is Lise there?" The conversation was cut short. Gerda's breathing was rapid when she hung up.

"She wasn't at Lise's at all. Where is she?" she said after a short pause, lost in her own thoughts.

Roland got up and stood behind the woman. He looked out the window, where the sun was hidden behind the buildings opposite, and threatening thunderclouds were coming up over the horizon. He laid a reassuring hand on her shoulder.

"Louise is probably just talking to a friend. Which way does she usually walk to Lise's?"

"She usually walks through the playground." The woman's eyes shone anxiously when she looked up at Roland.

"We'll look for her," said Mikkel, getting up from the sofa. He discreetly pulled the trouser material out from between his buttocks; it had got stuck while he had been sitting on the warmed-up leather.

Just then, the hall door opened. It wasn't Louise everyone's eyes turned towards, but a small man with his briefcase under his arm who looked like a sales rep of some kind. He entered the living room, surprised at seeing two strangers with his wife.

"Louise is missing!" Gerda threw herself, sobbing, into his arms. He hurriedly put the briefcase down on the corner of the dining table before embracing her, looking towards the officers for an explanation.

Roland introduced himself and DS Jensen.

"Calm down, Mrs. Poulsen; it's not certain Louise has disappeared. We'll take a look around before we drive back, but if we don't find her, you're very welcome to contact us when she shows up." She was crying on the man's shoulder. "Yes, and hold on to her," Mikkel added.

"She's not answering when I call her mobile. She does usually; you know that, Peter!" Gerda looked at him in despair.

"What's going on? Does it have anything to do with Gitte and the car Louise saw?" Peter Poulsen asked, stroking his wife lightly on the back, interspersed with little soothing pats.

"Yes, we'd like to talk to your daughter. We hoped she could give a description of the man she saw talking to Gitte at the playground."

In the nursery, the child began to cry loudly again. Gerda went in, wiping her eyes as she walked.

"I have girls myself. They were once Louise's age. They don't always think they're missing if they don't come home on time. It doesn't mean something's happened to Louise," Roland said gently. He signalled to Jensen to follow.

"If you're going to look for Louise, then I'm coming, too." Louise's father said it so firmly Roland could hear it wasn't up for debate.

They followed him down the stairs and out into an area with bike racks and a mountain of bikes. The blackbird's song resounded between the concrete blocks. They walked on to a playground that would almost certainly be deserted by this time—most children were probably at home for dinner, if things were the same as when Roland was a child. Without warning, the thundercloud broke. The rain fell as though from a giant showerhead and drummed on the sheet-metal roof over the bike racks. *Bloody summer*, Roland thought.

19

—————

Tarzan jumped up to her on the couch. The cat purred softly as Kamilla scratched it on the neck, lost in her own thoughts. It was strange to think the bad photos from the skip had really given the police a lead. The images showed the doll had been removed from the waste container, which may prove it had something to do with the crime.

She took the photo album from the shelf—she could just reach it without waking Tarzan. Slowly, she flipped through the first few pages without really seeing the pictures of her and Jan on their first trip to Paris and at parties they had attended together. Then she stopped. She sat for a long time looking at the picture of Jan and her with newborn Rasmus, who she was holding in her arms, then she quickly flipped on. Now came all the pictures of Rasmus she had once taken. She looked at a close-up for a long time and lovingly slid a finger down over his face. The hopelessness and longing returned with renewed strength. She should hide this album. Maybe even burn it. Nothing in it existed anymore.

She had reached the last pictures of Rasmus when she heard the doorbell. Tarzan sat up, his ears pricked towards the entrance. She couldn't see anyone through the peephole, but then the bell rang again, so she opened the door. She hadn't been able to see the boy because he wasn't very tall. Jonas had always been a lot smaller than Rasmus, despite them being peers. He stood with the large sports bag over his shoulder. It seemed to want to pull him over. His white Adidas sports shirt with the logo on the chest was green with grass stains, and his shorts were marked by the fact he'd had a few tackles.

"Hi, Jonas!" she said. "Would you like a cup of hot chocolate?"

Jonas smiled happily and stepped inside. He dumped the sports bag with a thump in the corner of the hall, as he and Rasmus had always done when they had come back from football together, anticipating the traditional hot chocolate at Rasmus's mum's house.

Initially, after the accident, Jonas hadn't come, but now he came every so often because his parents usually worked late on the days he had football training, and he didn't like being alone in the big house. Not seeing that much of him suited Kamilla well. Even now, it was hard to look at a boy she had been accustomed to seeing with her son. She didn't like the feelings it evoked in her. The first time she had asked herself why it hadn't been Jonas who had been killed, instead of Rasmus, she had hated herself for it, but the thought had returned again and again. Majken said it was natural.

"Tarzan's here!" cheered Jonas as he spotted the cat still lying on the sofa, licking his forepaw with the superior expression only a cat has. Kamilla went out into the kitchen and heated a carton of Matilde chocolate milk. She put the container on the table along with two mugs. She needed something warm herself. Jonas was so occupied with Tarzan that he hadn't noticed the photo album open on a big picture of a laughing Rasmus on his first bike. But before she could close it and put it back on the shelf, Jonas caught sight of it. His lower lip began to tremble. His eyes filled with tears. She reproached herself for not putting the album away before she had opened the door. She squatted in front of the boy. Tears flowed down his dirty cheeks, leaving light trails all the way down to the quivering lips. Instinctively, she pulled him to her and stroked his hair.

"I miss him so much," he sobbed into her neck. She couldn't answer. The boy smelled of sweat and fresh grass after the football game. The smell reminded her of Rasmus. She struggled with her own tears.

"Let's have some hot chocolate while it's warm," she said, her voice cracking.

They sat drinking in silence.

"I saw the car yesterday," Jonas said suddenly.

"What car?"

"The car! The one that killed Rasmus."

"Where did you see it? What kind of a car? How did you recognise it?" The questions all came at once, but she sensed there was something he hadn't told her.

Jonas sat looking down at his socks. "When Rasmus didn't come to the sports hall like we'd agreed that night, I went out to look for him," he began hesitantly. "I saw the car that knocked him down. It was parked next to the ambulances and police cars when I got there."

Jonas and Rasmus both loved cars and knew almost every make by heart after studying car magazines and countless car ads in newspapers. Kamilla had often admired the two little boys for their extensive knowledge of the subject.

"What make was it?"

"An Opel Vectra GTS, a dark blue one."

"Are you sure?" It's been over a year since you saw it."

By wiping the tears away with his filthy hands, he had smeared the dirt all over his face. His nose was running. The blue eyes under his light curls became defiant. "I'm certain! I saw it drive by. I hate that car!"

Kamilla looked at the boy's dirty face. The desire for revenge shone in his eyes. Was she the only one who didn't want to avenge Rasmus's death? Or did she want it deep down? She gathered her jumper closer around her, suddenly freezing, and considered whether to tell Jan. Should she support him in searching for and further punishing the man he referred to as their "son's murderer?" She pulled herself together. It was all a coincidence. A car that just looked like the one that had hit Rasmus.

Kamilla persuaded Jonas to go to the bathroom and wash his face before going home. He told her he was home alone and was supposed to go over to his boring neighbours', but that he would rather be with her. She was moved by his statement and called the neighbours to tell them she had Jonas. After the conversation with the elderly neighbour couple, she felt hungry. Another day would soon have passed where she hadn't had much to eat. Jonas had to be hungry, too, after the football match, but she hadn't taken anything out of the freezer.

"Do you want to go out to eat?" she asked.

Jonas's face lit up with a big smile. "Like in a real restaurant with waiters and stuff?" he asked a little suspiciously. It didn't sound like he was used to being taken to such places.

"We can drive down to Egå Marina. It's a very nice restaurant," she said, wondering why she had chosen *that* particular restaurant.

There weren't many people in the restaurant, so it was easy to find a table. She ordered a fish fillet with remoulade and a Coca-Cola for Jonas, and a fish soup with a baguette for herself. While waiting for the soup, she watched Jonas eat his fish without saying a word. He reminded her so much of Rasmus. Except Rasmus wouldn't have sat there chewing in silence. He would have filled the space between them with endless chatter and laughter. She looked at the other patrons. Then she spotted them. When Majken leaned back a little, Kamilla saw who she was with—Danny. The waiter blocked her view for a moment when he came and placed the hot soup in front of her. She took a spoonful and watched the couple by the window again. They didn't seem to notice anyone other than each other. She could go and say hi, but something held her back. Maybe it was the crippling feeling of jealousy. *It's Majken's turn now.* That fact shouldn't pain her. Quite the opposite.

Jonas had finished his fish fillet. She took the last spoonful of soup, and he drank the last of his Coca-Cola.

"Let's go," she said, getting up. She paid a waiter who happened to pass by. Jonas ran out to the car. At the door, she turned around. She just wanted to see him again. Right then, he looked at her. She quickly closed the door.

20

———————

Simon and Tue were hanging out on a bench outside the supermarket. They were waiting for Benjamin and Johnny, who had promised to get a crate of Tuborg Green beer in SuperBrugsen.

"Where the hell are they?" Simon asked angrily, stubbing his cigarette out on the wooden bench. Tue didn't answer; he sat chewing on a blade of grass.

None of them had anything special to do during the summer holidays. They were waiting for the Green Concert festival and had agreed to get the party started now. Benjamin had laughed when Johnny had suggested it. There was a long wait ahead. Johnny had something to celebrate, he had said. He had dropped out of Year 12; he was done with school. That was it, he had pointed out defiantly. The three slightly younger comrades had another year before they could do the same thing. And what then? None of them had any idea. They had that in common, too.

Finally, they saw Benjamin and Johnny strolling slowly through the wet grass towards the playground with a crate of Tuborg Green between them. They set it down hard on the edge of the sandbox, so the bottles clinked.

"Did you need a map?" said Simon, taking one out of the crate, knocking the cap off against the bench and drinking as if he had been in the desert for several days without water.

"Where were you?" asked Tue, accepting the bottle Benjamin handed him. He opened it with his pocketknife.

"That kid Abdul was on the checkout, so we had to tease him just a little bit," Johnny replied, laughing. The others laughed, too, despite all knowing it wasn't true. Abdul was in Tue's class. He was kind of a nice guy, but when someone had to be picked on, it used to be him. That had changed when Abdul became a member of the gang that always hung out at the garage. There were rumours of dog fights, too, and one evening, Benjamin saw Abdul walking a fighting dog. That earned respect.

"What about going to the youth club afterwards?" asked Simon. "There's supposed to be a little party there tonight." The others wrinkled their noses but didn't respond.

"By the way, who's the girl I saw you with the other day?" Benjamin suddenly asked Tue, who winced at the question.

"I wasn't with any girl," he shot back, looking for the pack of cigarettes in his pocket. Tue thought he had found himself a girlfriend. But he hadn't told the others about it. They would only laugh at him.

"Yes, you were. You had your arm around her. Tue has a girlfriend," jeered Benjamin. "Isn't she a little young for you?"

"That's not true! What do I want a girl for?"

"Yeaahhh, what do we want girls for?" Johnny winked at the others, and Tue turned red in the face.

"Hey—did you hear about that girl they found strangled in a skip here? It's creepy," said Benjamin.

"Yeah. Imagine, a psycho like that's walking around the neighbourhood."

Tue swept his long fringe away, clearly pleased the subject had changed. "I'm sure the girl who's been kidnapped is dead now, too." They got serious and drank their beer.

"Do you want to go back to mine? I've got the place to myself. The fogies are in a summer house," said Simon, as though just now remembering this was where the girl had disappeared and feeling unsafe sitting on the bench in the playground.

"We can get into trouble for sitting here and drinking, too," Johnny contributed.

They got up and gathered the empty beer bottles. All four were wearing jeans with hanging crotches that seemed to have been worn for years even though they were brand new. They began to walk back through the tall wet grass. Simon stopped, staring at something lying in the grass. It almost made the others drop the beer crate. Simon bent down and picked up his find.

"What the hell! It's a mobile phone!" exclaimed Benjamin.

Simon laughed excitedly. "Cooool!"

They put the crate down in the grass and crowded around him.

"The battery's dead, but it can be charged." Simon smiled crookedly.

"You can't keep it," Tue said sceptically.

"Why not? It's practically brand new. If someone's going to throw it away, they probably don't need it," Simon defended.

"Is it not a bit girly for you? Pink?" Benjamin sneered, clearly envious of the find.

"Tue can give it to his girl," Johnny teased, earning him a hard blow on the arm from Tue, who smiled this time.

"It just needs a new cover; they don't cost much." Simon put the phone in his pocket, and they started walking again.

"You know a phone can be tracked, right?" said Tue. "You could be done for theft."

"Not if I get a new SIM card," Simon argued.

Benjamin shook his head. "The police can easily get the phone's IMEI number. It's *that* phone's, like, civil registration number, and then they can find you," he warned.

"Rubbish," Simon muttered.

21

Danny didn't know what to say to the unpredictable woman sitting across from him, but he couldn't help but laugh. She had just cheerfully suggested breakfast, implying they should spend the night together. It was hard not to feel flattered and attracted to her boldness. He had met her by chance again at the ARoS Art Museum, which he had long ago decided to visit, now he was in Aarhus anyway. They went for a coffee afterwards at Café Jorden, and she had lured him out to eat in the evening, "where we met," as she put it. He enjoyed her company, though the thought of her friend Kamilla hadn't left him.

The golden white wine cast a yellow shadow on the white tablecloth. Red reflections shone in Majken's hair as the evening sun hit it through the window they were sitting by, and her blue eyes were so vivid and challenging. But she didn't turn him on sexually. It amazed him that, after he had grown up, he could meet beautiful women who didn't turn him on. As though he sought other values now.

As he leaned back, he caught sight of her. She was standing in the doorway with her son. His stomach sank at the sight of the boy. He had been right. She was married with children.

"Your friend's here," he said to Majken, who looked up from her plate at him in astonishment before turning her eyes in the direction he was looking. But Kamilla was gone. He wanted to get up and run after her.

"Kamilla? Where?" Majken's voice pulled him away from the thought.

"She's gone—with her son."

"That wasn't her!" Majken's voice sounded sure. "Kamilla doesn't venture out into the big dangerous world! Besides, her son's . . ." She caught sight of the waiter and waved him to the table.

"What's Kamilla's son?"

They were interrupted by the waiter standing in front of them, listening expectantly. She ordered two coffees. She didn't bother to ask him whether he wanted one. She was beginning to annoy him. He had never been a fan of dominant women. Sanne had often called him an old-fashioned male chauvinist, but that's not how he felt now. He was happy to help with the washing up, and he could even cook a few light dishes. He was forced to do so after Sanne had left him. Yes, it had been hard. In the beginning, McDonald's had been his ultimate rescue from starvation. But the weight gain and the film *Super Size Me* had changed his mind on that. Despite the first tour of the supermarket with the trolley feeling unfamiliar and silly, it was now a daily habit he didn't have to think about. The little one-bedroom apartment he had found for rent in a property on Christiansholms Parkvej in Klampenborg, with a view of the lake, suited him fine. He had renovated a little. Though he certainly wasn't a handyman, he had taken pride in being able to replace the kitchen counter himself. But there had been no women to praise his skill or comfort him when he wounded himself with the hammer or saw as he went about the unfamiliar work.

They sat in silence, drinking the coffee. He wondered why he hadn't seen Kamilla before. If it had been her with her son.

"Are you sure you don't want to come home with me and have morning coffee?" lured Majken again. But his good humour had gone. They were standing in front of the restaurant. The blackbird was no longer singing. Only the splashing of the water could be heard in the dusk.

"No, thank you, Majken."

She shrugged, trying to pretend she wasn't disappointed. "It's been a nice day," she said.

He nodded and lit the cigarette he had tapped out of the packet and caught with his lips. "Shall I drive you home?"

She shook her head. "I don't live that far from here, and I need some fresh air." The conversation stopped. She started walking.

"Can we do it again?" she shouted after him as he got into his car.

"I don't know how long I'm staying. Let's see how it goes."

He started the car and saw her waving. He felt tired and discouraged, and a lot of other unfamiliar emotions.

22

———————

The evening was warm, and even though it was getting dark, Majken took a shortcut down to the beach. Giggling, she took off her sandals and walked barefoot in the sand. It was cold and damp after soaking up the day's many rain showers, but it was cooling and pleasant against her hot feet, which had been squeezed into tight sandals. Fashion wasn't always practical.

She felt a little drunk from the wine—and the heady feeling of falling in love. After so, so long, she felt the sensation bubble inside again.

As no one could see her, she spread her arms out and spun around. Her dress danced around her bare legs and the little shoulder bag swung around her on its strap, as if she were the centre of the universe. It was important no one could see her. That was how she had been raised. As a doctor, you couldn't afford that kind of behaviour. Her parents would no doubt also have reproached her for inviting a patient to dinner. But really? It was just Troels. Besides, it was Danny she was interested in, and she couldn't invite just him when he was sitting with Troels. Kamilla needed the company, too. She needed to meet other people and forget.

She stopped dancing and walked on quietly, carrying the sandals by the straps in one hand, listening to the sea. Seeing Kamilla in the condition she had been in for the past year tormented her. Kamilla, who faced everything head-on. Jan leaving her. She had even accepted Nina, almost as if she were one of the family. But losing her son, on top of everything else, had been a death knell. She was sure Kamilla was suffering from severe depression. But Kamilla didn't want help. Never. So what could be done, other than what she was trying to do?

Despite it being nearly midnight, it wasn't quite dark yet. It was one of those bright evenings that hadn't been spoiled by this summer, when dark rain clouds had commanded the sky. The longest day of the year had passed; it wouldn't be long before darkness slowly began to dominate again. But now it was so bright she could see a good distance out to sea and the lights from the ships passing on the horizon. She wished Danny had joined her. It had been so long since she'd had a man that she probably would have ripped his clothes off here at the water's edge. She stopped and let the icy seawater reach her feet. She shuddered every time it hit them. She stared down into the water, which quickly retreated and disappeared into the darkness again, only to soon return. She imagined them lying in a hot embrace in the cold water and felt a warm stream flow through her body.

That's not how a doctor thinks. She heard her mother's voice. *Remember, you come from a nice family of doctors; you can't just do what suits you. Your title comes with obligations and duties.* She had heard those words so often they were branded into her brain. She had always admired her father's work and knowledge. The family had been doctors for as far back as she could remember, and now the title and responsibility had been passed on to her. But the duty wasn't mandatory. She should have been a boy. *Real* doctors were men, after all, and there was no doubt Doctor Ove Thorup had wished his son had taken over. But those plans weren't a part of Tobias's life, and this had caused many quarrels at home, that is, until her brother had moved away in protest. He would rather work with computers and programming. And her sister had neither the desire nor the ability to become a doctor. She had quickly dropped out of her studies. But Majken had passed all the exams with flying colours. She now knew as much as her wise father and had even specialised in child psychiatry, as both the mind and children interested her.

She hung her head. The thought of her sister and children was starting to spoil her mood. The wine was also beginning to make her head thud. Her self-confidence had waned. But maybe it wasn't too late. Maybe all hope wasn't lost. Danny had seemed interested in her yesterday when they had first met, and again tonight. But then he claimed to have seen Kamilla. It couldn't have been her, could it? Had she really started to pull herself together and get out among other people? But with a little boy—that couldn't be right. She stood still again and stared out at the sea. A cold breeze crept in over the water, making her dress blow up. Rasmus had been an open boy. Easy to talk to. Their many conversations after Kamilla and Jan's divorce had brought them close.

He had only been five years old at the time. Helping him had felt good, the same way she had helped so many other children with problems since then. Rasmus was a sweet and suitably naughty little kid, like her own son would have been if she'd had one. She still could if she hurried. She should make it. *You haven't lived if you don't have children. You're not a real woman.*—another of her mother's many philosophies. Who else was to carry on the Thorup medical family name? The bitterness returned. She felt something wet on her cheeks and realised it wasn't seawater. She wiped the tears away and saw her mascara had run. It had to be the wine. Wine always made her overly sentimental. She was beginning to freeze so found the path back to the road. Home wasn't far.

23

D S Kim Ansager knocked gently on the door before entering the office without waiting for an answer, but Roland was expecting him. He straightened up in his chair and asked the nervous officer, who had already sniffled and pushed his glasses up on the ridge of his nose twice, to sit down. Roland had often wanted to ask him to fix the glasses, but they didn't seem to bother Kim.

"Did you get anything out of tracking the mobile phones?" he asked.

"Nothing. If the phones are switched off or the batteries are dead, which they probably are now, then they can't be traced." Kim pulled a chair in front of Roland's desk and sat down. "But I contacted TDC and received a transcript of both Gitte Mikkelsen's and Louise Poulsen's telephone conversations based on the phone numbers. I also got the phones' IMEI numbers, so both phones are cancelled."

"Hmm," muttered Roland. "What did you get from the phone calls?"

"Unfortunately, there's nothing we can use. The conversations were to and from the parents, Louise called Gitte once and vice versa. The last call from Gitte to Louise was at three o'clock on Sunday afternoon. The day before she was murdered. A number of text messages were also sent, but none significant."

"Damn." Roland leaned back in his chair as he looked inquisitively at Kim.

"But you said this morning that you noticed something important last night?" The question hung in the air until Kim had poured a mug of coffee from the insulated coffee pot Roland had handed him.

"Yes, Trille—my daughter." Kim glanced at his boss to make sure he knew who Trille was. Roland's nod encouraged him to continue. Kim took a sip of the coffee. "I've told her she has to stop; you hear so much about bullying, harassment, and much, much worse. But it's so popular with kids and teenagers. It's impossible to ban. Even if we were to take her computer away, she'd just go to her friend's, and then we'd have absolutely no control."

"What are we actually talking about here?" Roland could make neither head nor tail of the officer's rambling explanation.

"Chat rooms! Chatting on the internet. A children's website!" Kim Ansager took off his glasses and massaged the bridge of his nose with his thumb and forefinger. "But they're not just writing emails to each other," he explained. "They log in to a website with a username, a picture, information about their age and everything. There's a picture gallery that looks like a bloody porn site. Some of the girls pose in low-cut blouses with seductive looks well beyond their years. Well, not Trille, of course, I won't allow it. They chat about everything from how crazy their parents are to sexual abuses and who they fancy."

Roland placed his elbows on the desk and leaned in towards the officer. "Where are you going with all this?"

Kim cleared this throat nervously. "Well, last night, Trille told me she'd seen pictures of the two girls from the newspapers and TV on a chat site. I followed her into her room and saw the profile pictures on the computer screen." He straightened his glasses and drank some coffee, though he didn't seem to enjoy it.

"It was them. Both Gitte Mikkelsen and Louise Poulsen are—uh, were—active users of the website. They must have lied about their age because members have to be at least twelve years old."

"Are you absolutely sure it was them?" Roland's interest was piqued.

"Sure. They didn't use their real names. I can't remember what Louise called herself, but Gitte's username was Doll Child."

"Doll Child?" Roland felt discomfort somewhere between his shoulder blades, and the little hairs on the back of his neck rose. He thought of the doll that had disappeared from the skip.

"Is there a connection, do you think?" he pondered.

"It's an encyclopaedia, Roland. An encyclopaedia for offenders with a penchant for children. Maybe the murderer found the girls there and arranged to meet them. It's not uncommon for children to meet their contact outside of cyberspace. Fortunately, things often turn out fine. Do you think the website would help the investigation?"

"This is about grooming. Maybe we should contact the Cyber Investigation Unit. Did you spot any older men among the profiles?"

"I have to admit, I wasn't looking for them." Kim made an apologetic grimace that sent the glasses sliding down his nose yet again. "It's not certain he'd have a profile picture if he is a user. Not everyone has one, and wouldn't an older man with that intention avoid putting his photo up?" Kim looked at Roland quizzically.

"I don't suppose it could be a teenager. Can we rule that out?" Roland asked slowly, considering the possibility. After all, sexual offenders weren't always, as many people assumed, old men in long camel-coloured trench coats and glasses with thick lenses. They could come off like the sort of nice people who easily win the trust of both children and adults. They could have a well-functioning and happy family life—even have children themselves. They could take advantage of a child's natural curiosity once trust was aroused through chats on the internet. A child's lack of experience and maturity meant they couldn't always see the consequences until it was too late. Roland shook his head and reached for the thermos. From its weight, he realised it was empty and put it back on the table.

"It could be an older user pretending to be much younger than he is. Yeah, maybe a teenager. But if the dark car's linked to the case, we have to assume it's someone over eighteen, who has a driving licence. Given the description, it sounds like a slightly too big and heavy car for a young man," said Kim.

"Borrowed from daddy?" suggested Roland.

"Maybe. What about the girls' private emails? Could they have been contacted there, too? Trille often receives emails from outside that website." Kim had a thought. "If it were done anonymously, which is probably what a criminal would prefer, do you think we could find something on the girls' computers?" He had all the demeanour of someone who had invented the wheel.

Roland nodded. Again, he thought about the context in which they were discussing ten-year-old girls. When his girls were ten, they had played with Barbie dolls. Today, children were chatting about sex and boyfriends online—and he was still learning how to use the internet.

"It's worth a try. Will you do it? You can take Mikkel with you. He knows all about computers," said Roland, concentrating on the computer again with narrowed eyes. A larger screen would do wonders.

"What does Mikkel *not* know about," Kim mumbled. "By the way, did the dog unit find anything on Louise Poulsen?"

Roland sighed. "Unfortunately not. They sniffed their way to a couple of tyre tracks on the playground that forensics are currently working on. It'll be exciting to see if there's a match with the tyre print in front of the skip, so we can establish whether it's the same car."

He was cut short by the phone ringing. As he listened, he raised his dark eyebrows higher and higher in interest. Kim looked at him curiously from the other side of the desk. Roland breathed out as soon as he hung up.

"We've received a report we have to look into," he said grimly.

*

There came a day when stepping on toads was no longer enough; he wanted to feel the life disappear from their bodies between his childish hands. Make them stop whining while he looked them in the eye. The protruding eyes staring at him until they became dull and lost all signs of life. It wasn't the same crunching sound as when he stepped on them, but the sensation in his fingers gave him a better feeling. His little sister didn't like the toads in the garden, either. But when she had seen him stepping on a toad one day, she had lunged at him from behind, put her small arms around his neck, and nearly suffocated him as she kicked at him with her legs. You idiot! You idiot! Hear how they scream! she had shouted. He had grown angry because she had exposed him. Toads don't scream; they whine. They whine like you! he had answered nastily, and she had started to cry loudly. He had warned her not to say anything to Father. Mother wasn't around anymore. Mother was a coward. She had just run away.

Her skin was so soft. Like the bellies of the toads, which, in contrast to the roughly knobbled backs, were as soft as silk. And yet her skin was soft in another way. She was prettier, too. They are at that age. Firm and tight in body. Unspoiled was the right word. They hadn't tried it before. Had no comparisons to throw mockingly in his face. But she had lied about her age, too. So it was her own fault. It didn't matter to him; the younger the better. Though there were limits. They had to know a little about what was happening, otherwise he couldn't see it in their eyes. First naïve curiosity about something forbidden and exciting, then pain, and, finally, fear. If he couldn't see it, he couldn't feel power. A power in direct opposition to the powerlessness he felt towards women. But she knew too much. He would have to get rid of her soon. It needed to be soon. He repeated that aloud to himself several times before reaching the hiding place.

24

After some interesting sightseeing in Aarhus, Danny drove along Marienlundsvej surrounded by Risskov's tall trees. He parked in front of Danhostel Aarhus, the city's only youth hostel, where he was staying in a single en suite room. Yet again, the beauty and location of the hostel captivated him, just as when he had arrived. He stood for a moment looking at the building. It was reminiscent of a beautiful, oversized gazebo with its eight-sided main building, many white lattice windows, and Swedish-red woodwork against light blue painted carvings matching the blue flag waving on the black octagonal pointed roof. An unusual building with a unique location in the middle of Risskov, and only minutes from the beach. A colleague from the advertising agency had once mentioned the place, praising it warmly, so he had no doubt this was where he should stay on his trip. Not to mention it was cheap and had a relaxed atmosphere. A busy, overcrowded hotel in the holiday season wasn't exactly what he needed.

He quickly took off his clothes, wet from the rain, and stepped into the hot shower. The rain had prevented him from visiting Den Gamle By again. So it had turned into a couple of lonely café visits and a peek at the Music House to see what they had to offer. He didn't buy tickets. He found going to a concert on his own foolish. A concert was something to be shared. A stab of guilty conscience had hit him, too. He was behaving like a simple tourist, enjoying himself with amusements and pleasures. Shouldn't he be seeking out the family he had destroyed?

He wrapped the thick freshly laundered white terry towel around him and styled his wet dark hair. When it was wet, you couldn't see the greying hairs at his temples. He thought he looked a little younger than he was. The comb couldn't tame the hairs curling around his neck. They always appeared whenever his hair was wet. Sanne had loved those curls. Once. The letter he had received from her while he was serving his sentence had ruined everything. Though it had started out well. The first letter in Sanne's small, clipped handwriting had told him she had taken a pregnancy test. It was positive. They were going to have a child. The doctor had confirmed it. She was in her third month. Their hard work had finally borne fruit. He was so happy. The time before he was to be released no longer seemed so bleak. He didn't hear from her for a long time after that. He wrote and called in vain. He panicked. Then came the second letter. She had miscarried and blamed him. Sanne had never been particularly strong, and she lived in a very self-righteous world. He had cried without sound and crumpled the letter in his clenched hand. Later, he had wondered if it really had been his fault they had lost their child. Sanne had been shocked at what he had done, and having her husband in prison didn't fit her concept of a perfect life. Having to tell her friends he had been convicted of negligent manslaughter under Section 241 of the Danish Penal Code, had his driving licence conditionally revoked, and had been sentenced to nine months in prison didn't suit her. Nine months he avoided thinking back on. The worst months of his life. He cringed at the thought and felt the unreal sensation that he had dreamed it all again. He had attended a course on alcohol and driving and passed a new driving test, although he had found it more difficult than the one he had passed as an eighteen-year-old.

He took a deep breath and pulled himself together. As he ran a hand down over his face, he realised he needed to shave.

Should he call Majken? The thought popped up again and again, along with his guilty conscience at having been so cool to her last night. Good God, he had just learned the woman he thought he was falling in love with wasn't available. So what! Hadn't he experienced this a thousand times before? That was life as a single man in his early forties. And what was it Majken had wanted to tell him about Kamilla's son when the waiter had interrupted her?

He counted the buttons as he fastened the new shirt he had bought in

Jack & Jones in Bruuns Galleri. When he finally called and heard Majken's voice on the phone, he was no longer in doubt.

"Danny! I'm delighted you called. Have you seen the newspaper? Kamilla's started working again. Her photo's on the front page. It's about the murder of a little girl found in a skip. Isn't it awful? Here, in Aarhus! This kind of thing might happen in your Copenhagen, but not here."

"No, I haven't seen the paper, but it sounds dreadful." He shuddered at the thought of a little girl lying dead in a waste container.

"Are you coming over? It's my day off," she replied. She gave him the address in Risskov.

The house was nice. Three blocks from the water. He wondered how she could afford it on her own. Doctors must do well for themselves. More than advertising managers, obviously. The sun was shining again. The weather was more changeable here in Jutland than in Zealand, it seemed. The house was nicely decorated with mid-priced furniture. Ikea, he guessed. Even on a doctor's salary, there wasn't enough for everything.

"Sit down—wherever you like," she added when she saw him hesitate.

"Would you like a drink? After our dinner yesterday, I know you're not a teetotaller."

There was a twinkle in her eye, but the words still hit him like a slap.

"A little one, then," he replied.

She fetched some slices of lime from the kitchen like a TV chef who had prepared a little in advance. She poured gin into two glasses and dropped the slices in. He understood the plan was obviously for him to have that drink.

She sat down in the chair opposite him and carefully crossed her long bare legs—in slow motion.

"It's lovely to see you again!"

"It was only yesterday," he reminded her, amused by the tone of her voice, which sounded as if they hadn't seen each other for years.

"That's a long time for me," she said, flirting.

They talked about ordinary everyday things. Her work and his work. What it was like in Zealand, "over there," as she jokingly called it. A relaxed mood fell over him again. Or was it the second gin and lime he should have politely declined?

"Coffee?" she asked and got up, almost in answer to his thoughts.

"Yes, please. Thanks."

There were a few flyers on the coffee table. He started flipping through them while she was in the kitchen. He didn't look at the offers and prices, only the images, the models, the photo set-ups, and the lighting. He shook his head at the far-too-posed lingerie models. He well knew it was hard to look natural when there were safety pins and tape on your back, all so the bra would fit and sit in a way that it didn't fit and sit in reality. And when the photographer demanded a pose to enhance a bosom, the pins stabbed you in the back. He loved the advertising industry, although he had to admit certain parts of it might seem repulsive. It was about selling dreams and illusions, and the ends didn't always justify the means.

The newspaper landed hard on top of the colourful pages. Majken had thrown it down as she threaded her way to the coffee table, balancing a tray of clinking coffee cups.

"There, you can see the photo Kamilla took. And the article. It's not nice to think about. A child murder here in Aarhus." She set down the tray and gave them each a cup. She placed them next to each other, he noticed out of the corner of his eye as he looked at the front page of the news-paper. So she had decided they were to sit close together on the sofa. His stomach sank a little. Still, she wasn't the worst person to have to sit close to. Although . . . He read the photographer's name again. It was printed in small italic letters under the picture. "Photo: Kamilla Holm." Wife: Kamilla Holm. Wife and mother: Kamilla Holm. One thought followed the other. He read the article. There wasn't much substance. Majken sat quietly next to him. She had kicked off her shoes, pulled her legs up under her on the sofa, and was studying him with both hands around her cup, as if warming them, her chin resting on the edge of it.

"Isn't it creepy?" she whispered when she could see he had finished reading. Her voice sounded close; he felt her warm breath on his neck.

"Sick," he answered.

25

As usual, the day ended with a little overtime while they waited for the last of the children to finish their chores and be collected. Most of his colleagues had thawed a bit and had spoken to him during the day, albeit with a touch of reservation. But it was progress. Maybe it would all work out in the end, once it dawned on them there were no grounds for the accusations. Children had active imaginations, and when a psychologist asked just the "right" questions, a conversation about touching "secret" places could easily be misinterpreted.

As he walked towards his car, which was parked in the shade of the trees around Søvejen After-School Centre, he was close to resuming the usual cheerful whistle that hadn't come out of his mouth for a long time. A light breeze made his blond hair fly down onto his forehead. It had been combed back to hide a developing bald spot. He pulled the steel comb out his back pocket and brought the hair into place with a single backwards movement.

He hadn't even reached the car before he saw something was wrong. His old white Opel Astra looked different, even from this distance. Puzzled, he stared at the black paint scrawled along the side of the car. Only when he got closer could he see the scrawl was words. He couldn't make them out; neither did he want to. Nausea burned in his throat, and he quickly looked around the car park. Ib was getting into his Toyota a few metres away. He looked at him as he fastened his seat belt, still pretending not to see him, started his car, and drove away. Jesper was left alone by the vandalised car. When he opened the driver's door, his fingers became sticky with black paint. Some of a *P* and an *A* and *E* had been smudged. By one of the front wheels was an empty canister—the kind of paint used for graffiti. Desperate, he tried to remove the worst of the words with his sleeve, but the paint was relentless. "Shit. Shit," he muttered. Tears blurred his vision. He couldn't drive home with those horrible words on his car. He was meant to pick up Sussi from the bakery. It would be the final straw for his otherwise loyal family. First the scratches on the car, then the slashed tyres, and now . . .

How was he supposed to remove it all without the car having to go to a garage to be repainted? Without everyone hearing about it?

He heard someone sobbing pleadingly and realised it was him. He stood up stiffly by the car, his arms hanging down by his sides. His body shook from the tears he was holding back. The hair blew down onto his forehead again, but he didn't notice it. His vision cloudy, he saw a mother walking across the car park holding a little boy by the hand. It was Nick from the after-school centre. He shouted happily at Jesper and waved, but he couldn't read yet. His mother pulled the boy away angrily as she shot Jesper a look that radiated disgust.

He had been standing by the car for a long time, his shoulders sinking more and more, when a shiny dark blue Ford pulled into the car park and stopped in front of him. He was in no doubt as to the identity of the two gentlemen, who seemed to step out of the car as if in foggy slow motion. They didn't need to bother showing him their badges.

26

Kamilla hadn't seen Jan go and lay flowers at Rasmus's headstone. Only when he sat down on the bench next to her did she return to the present.

"You were lost in your thoughts," he said.

She nodded absently. She had been. Anne had driven her home after the interview with the murdered girl's parents. She had been thinking about them, Ida and Allan Mikkelsen. Their house was a fairly ordinary home. They had seemed quite ordinary, too. Ida Mikkelsen was heavily pregnant and could give birth at any time, it seemed. They had no other children, only a dog and a ten-year-old girl. Gitte was her name. As always, the murder case was named after the victim, so it was now called the Gitte murder. Kamilla had seen Anne writing that in her pad. The family hadn't wanted Anne's tape recorder turned on or any photos taken. If Anne hadn't given her a lift, she would have been home a long time ago, but she'd had to stay until Anne had finished the interview.

It was hard to see parents who had lost their little girl so inhumanely. To see their despair and powerlessness. But she couldn't comfort them and tell how she knew exactly what they were feeling. That it wouldn't be like it once was. The emptiness. The grief and the longing. She hoped their marriage could cope with the trauma. They would either come out more strongly attached to each other, or the opposite. Gitte's father had pulled himself together, but he couldn't conceal his anger or desire to take revenge on the killer. The haunted expression in his eyes had been frightening as he mentioned the teenager with developmental disabilities another family in the neighbourhood cared for.

You're welcome to write that, he had said. *That kind of maniac shouldn't be walking around freely.*

Do you think he has anything to do with the murder? Anne had asked in a journalistic voice.

Him, or one of the Pakis in Gellerup Park, he had replied.

Kamilla didn't like him. She didn't care at all for people with the kind of prejudices that usually came from ignorance or a lack of interest in foreigners and those who were afflicted. But she also knew this kind of crime could cause all sorts of prejudices and hidden hatred to flare up in even the best person when they needed a scapegoat. Someone who could be punished, so they could put it behind them and continue with their lives. *Move on,* she thought bitterly.

Gitte's mother hadn't said much; she had seemed completely numb. She was a nurse at Aarhus Hospital. Kamilla had wondered whether she was taking something for her nerves, despite being pregnant. She had recognised the dullness in her eyes.

Jan didn't look at her but stared at the grave with a lost expression on his face.

"I saw your photo in the paper," he said, breaking the silence, tearing her from her thoughts. He leaned back on the bench. "It's good you've started working again, Kamilla. We've all been waiting a long time for that. But not that kind of assignment. What the hell were you thinking?"

She couldn't hide her anger. Who was he to interfere in her life? She wasn't about to admit to him that she *hadn't* thought. That she had been so unprofessional she hadn't thought to ask what the assignment was.

"What's Nina doing?" she asked, changing the subject to avoid starting one of their usual quarrels.

"Nina's at home. I was showing a house in Egå but decided to stop here."

The conversation stopped, as if they had said everything there was to be said during their ten years of marriage.

"There's something I think you should hear from us," he said, but fell silent again, as if he doubted whether he was going to tell her the rest of it, too.

She sat waiting.

"Nina's expecting." He looked at her to see her reaction.

She just opened her mouth in astonishment without saying a word. What she wanted to say didn't come out. She couldn't imagine Nina as a mother, and she'd had no idea they wanted to have children.

"We didn't tell you the other night. Nina wasn't entirely sure," he explained, almost apologetically. "We hope it's a new little Rasmus."

She exhaled when she realised she had been holding her breath. Did Gitte's father think the same thing? Never mind, we're having a *new* baby. As though it were a kitten.

"How can you say that in front of Rasmus!" she exclaimed, louder and more angrily than she had expected. The thought of their agreement to never quarrel when Rasmus was in earshot gave her a sense of remorse.

He looked at her in surprise. "Dear God; he can't hear us." There was humour in his voice, but his smile faded when he saw her anger.

She got up quickly and walked with angry steps along the gravel path between the graves, towards the gate at the exit. She wanted to scream.

By the time she reached home, her anger still hadn't evaporated. She slammed the front door. How could he say that! How could he think of having a child with Nina? Why had the news turned her world to rubble? It scared her. Was this news the definitive rejection? Had she secretly hoped Jan would come back to her when everyday life had returned to normal? Could she even think that after five years? No, that wasn't it. She didn't want him back. Not him. She breathed anxiously as she picked up the phone ringing in her jacket pocket. Anne's number was displayed on the screen.

"We're going to Brabrand," she said briefly without introducing herself.

"Now? It's late, Anne!"

"I know that, but I finally got hold of the Nordstrøm family."

"They've agreed to an interview. Maybe they'll regret it tomorrow. And the daughter's due to start an internship in Svendborg tomorrow."

"The daughter? What does she have to do with anything?"

"It was their teenage daughter who actually found the girl. Not the mother. And while we're in Brabrand, we have to follow up on another case that's come up, too. A witness in the Gitte murder has disappeared. In the same neighbourhood."

"Was there a witness?"

"Yeah—one of Gitte's friends. Haven't you heard the appeal for information regarding a missing person on the radio?"

27

The man sitting in the chair opposite Roland had beads of sweat on his upper lip. It couldn't have been fun seeing his car painted with abusive insults. It would be expensive to have it removed. He could well offer the man a little compassion.

"Do you have any idea who'd vandalise your car like that?" he asked by way of introduction. The man in front of him stared silently down at the table, shaking his head absently.

It wasn't Jesper Ingemann's first time sitting here. He was known to the police from several paedophile cases, but they had never been able to pin anything on him to put him away—to Roland's great annoyance. Unfortunately, it was often difficult in such cases, despite East Jutland Police having their own small specially trained unit, which was considered one of the best in the country in investigating paedophilia cases. Many children, some as young as three, had been video-interviewed during the many sexual assault cases against children that had gradually come to light in East Jutland after-school centres and kindergartens. He was happy psychologists and trained staff had led those conversations, which had taken place at the Centre for Children at Skejby Hospital. The interviewer often used dolls and teddy bears as props for the child to indicate the answers to some of their questions. The child and the interviewer sat in a nicely decorated room in safe surroundings, while in another room sat a legal representative, someone from social welfare, and a case officer from the police. Public prosecutors and defence counsel often attended these sessions, too, in case anything should come from the interviews that could be used in court.

Roland wiped his forehead with his handkerchief. Could that sun not just decide once and for all whether it was going to stay in the sky or not? The humid climate that reminded him of the temperature in his greenhouse was unbearable. His hair stuck to his head. Most of all, he wanted to sit in the shade under the copper beech on the terrace at home in the garden in Højbjerg, wearing only his shorts.

Mikkel Jensen came in with the requested cold Fantas. He opened one with a bottle opener and handed it to the sweating man, who poured it into his glass with a slightly shaking hand. Roland poured his out, too, and felt the tingling sensation of the carbon dioxide as he took the first cold sip. Jensen stood against the wall, as if in a TV crime series, drinking directly from the bottle.

"Jesper Ingemann," Roland said kindly. He had to assume initially that the man was innocent. They didn't always bring in people who were reported anonymously, but the fact he had been accused in similar cases before meant they had to. Most others of his kind in the city had already been investigated—the ones they knew, at least. And although Jesper had never been convicted in any of the cases, it didn't mean he was innocent. They'd had to investigate him further before approaching him. Jesper stirred uneasily and drank from the glass in small quick sips. His gaze flickered. Roland continued in the same friendly tone, "You've been in that chair before. Of course, it hasn't *only* been about accusations of child molestation." He took a short pause. "How has it come to murder and kidnapping, Jesper?" he continued in a penetrating tone.

"It wasn't me. I didn't do anything," he said weakly. "I haven't done any of the things I've been accused of. I love kids!" He finished almost sobbing.

"We know you *love* kids," came the accusation from Jensen, triggering a warning look from Roland.

"Gitte Mikkelsen attended Søvejen After-School Centre, where you work. Naturally, we've checked. So you knew her?"

Jesper looked down at the table again and turned the glass between his hands, which had stopped shaking. He seemed calmer, as if he had mastered the situation. It had been the same every time they had brought him in, Roland remembered.

"Yeah, I knew her," he admitted. "But not very well," he added hurriedly, looking quickly at Roland. "Gitte was very withdrawn and difficult to reach, you know. And she didn't actually attend the after-school centre for that long."

"You have to tell us where you were on Monday and Wednesday." Roland stubbornly held his gaze, which no longer flickered.

"I don't have a problem with that. I was in the after-school club both days." He hesitated, then added, "My colleagues can confirm that."

"You finished work at some point, didn't you?"

"Of course. But both days were long. We always stay until all the little ones have been collected, and in case any of the children need to talk."

"So at no time did you leave your workplace? Remember: both the children and your colleagues can attest to your movements."

Jesper took his eyes off Roland and seemed to be thinking as he watched the last swig of orange Fanta in his glass. It was practically flat.

"Now that I think about it, I had a dentist appointment on Monday at the end of the day. You can ask my dentist. I went home immediately afterwards. My wife and children can confirm that."

Again, it seemed Jesper Ingemann was going to walk free. What was he up to? Roland emptied his glass and glanced at Jensen, who shook his head slightly. He had nothing to add. Roland got up.

"You can go now, Jesper. If we can't confirm your statement, we'll bring you in again, but you know that already."

A small dry smile appeared on Jesper's narrow mouth. There was a slight triumph in his eyes, and Roland clenched his sweaty toes in his shoes, frustrated they apparently weren't going to get him this time, either.

"Maybe you should take a look at Gitte's own family, instead of wasting your time on me," he said, walking out of the door.

"What do you mean by that?" Roland asked coldly.

Jesper stopped and turned towards him. "It's my impression the family had huge problems," he said condescendingly.

Roland frowned and looked him straight in the eye. He had nice eyes, he had to admit reluctantly. Nice and friendly. Eyes that evoked confidence.

Eyes are the mirror of the soul, Irene always said. Was there anything to that, or could a man with those eyes still be a murderer?

"What huge problems?"

Jesper shrugged indifferently.

"As youth leaders, we can't just interfere like that in the lives of families and children, so I can't answer exactly. But it was my understanding the girl was a bit psychotic."

28

The apartment was empty and quiet when Amalie came home from school. The kitchen smelled of coffee and toast from the morning. She was soaked from cycling home in the rain, so she changed her wet jeans for a pair of red tracksuit bottoms. Her mum and dad were still at work. Her brother was at work, too, in his new apprenticeship at the auto repair shop. It probably wouldn't be long before he moved out, then she could get his big room. Her twin sisters, Sofie and Line, weren't home, either. They had been so angry and irritable recently. Stress, Mum had said, because they were preparing for their end-of-school exams. Amalie threw her schoolbag in the corner of her own little room and turned on the computer. She was happy she was only in Year 5 and didn't have to go to work or deal with exams or have an apprenticeship that meant she wasn't home until late in the afternoon. Sometimes Dad didn't get home until it was late evening. He was working overtime, he said. Whatever that meant.

In the kitchen, she spread a slice of bread with butter and jam and took it over to the computer along with a glass of cold milk. When she was home alone in the afternoons, she could do that without being scolded by Mum.

The horses looked down at her with their brown velvet eyes from the posters on the walls. On the table was a book she was reading about horse riding. It was exciting and she was looking forward to reading on. But first she wanted to see what they were talking about on the chat site. It was best to do that, too, when Mum and Dad weren't home. Mum would have a conniption if she discovered she was chatting with other kids about sex. Talking about sex was exciting. It was forbidden. She had heard Sofie and Line whispering and giggling about it. Even though they whispered, she still sometimes heard a little. And chatting online with kids her own age about everything else that happened to your body was nice. If they felt the same thing. If they were getting fluff down there, too. One day, when she had crept into Sebastian's room, despite her knowing he didn't like it, she had found some magazines. She had looked at one. It was naked men and women doing disgusting things to each other, so she had thrown it away again immediately, as if hot to the touch. But those ladies hadn't had any hair down there, so was it normal to have it? She didn't dare ask Mum. She always got so angry. There was no way she could ask Dad about that kind of thing—or Sebastian. Sofie and Line just laughed. She tried to sneak a peek when they changed clothes and took showers, but they always screamed and slammed the door in her face.

There was nothing she wanted to talk about in the chat forum, so she opened the email program instead. She smiled when she saw there was an email from *him*. He was so sweet. She could talk to him about everything. Fluff, too. He had even asked her about it. But the best part was that he had what she dreamed of most in the whole world—a horse. Mum and Dad didn't have to be so adamant about it being impossible to have a horse in an apartment on the second floor; she could see that. But they could move. To the country. Live like Grandma. A few of the kids in her class lived in the country, and it sounded so cool. He probably lived in the country, too, and he wanted to teach her how to ride. She would even be allowed to borrow his horse when he wasn't riding it himself. One day she would go and see it. She looked forward to patting its soft muzzle and sitting up on it. She had only been horse riding once, and it had been the best experience she had ever had. Amalie put the empty glass in the kitchen sink before sitting down in front of the computer again to reply to him.

29

Kamilla was on her way to Brabrand again, not completely wanting to be. Anne's yellow Lada was already waiting in front of the Nordstrøm house, a quite ordinary detached house. Everything was so ordinary. The only uncommon thing was that it was all about the murder of an innocent little girl. Perhaps two girls now.

She took the camera bag from the back seat and walked up to the house with slightly reluctant steps. Still, it probably wouldn't be as unpleasant as the visit to Gitte's parents, she reassured herself.

"Here comes my photographer!" Anne quickly laid a piece of greasy pastry on a plate and wiped her fingers on the legs of her pre-washed jeans. The recording device on the coffee table was still on. So they weren't dealing with people quite as press-shy this time. Anne reached for it, turned it off, and put it back in her backpack. Kamilla realised the interview was already over. Anne had probably been there a long time.

Cecilie Nordstrøm welcomed Kamilla. She was solid and in her mid-fifties. Her hair was a dull mousey brown with hints of grey, tied at the nape of her neck with a large hairclip. Her eyes were happy and lively in her round face with hints of apple red cheeks. She held out the plate with the pastry to Kamilla. There was just one piece left, probably left for her. But she didn't feel like it and declined.

"A cup of coffee?"

Kamilla shook her head apologetically again. "No, thanks. I just . . ."

"We'd better get those pictures taken." Anne saved her.

The teenage girl, who was chomping loudly on a piece of chewing gum, got up eagerly from the couch. She was wearing a short summer blouse cropped at the navel, and a ridiculously wide black belt with metal studs fastened around a pair of jeans; they sat so low on her hips, you could glimpse the top of her buttocks when she turned to walk out of the living room. She was one of those young girls who was going to follow fashion, despite not having the typical figure for it. She had a solid build, and a soft muffin top hung over the top of her trousers. Kamilla guessed she was wearing a G-string, too.

"Do I need to take the bin bag with me?" The girl chewed with an overly distorted face.

"We talked about having a photo of Maria throwing a bag into the skip. To give it a slightly more natural and everyday feel. What do you think?" asked Anne.

Kamilla thought it a bit set up, but it wouldn't matter what they did. No one would be in any doubt the picture hadn't been taken at the exact time it had happened. Snapped in the same second the body had been found. She shuddered at the thought.

Cecilie Nordstrøm started to take the cups off the table. "Do I need to come, too? I don't really think . . ."

"No, that's alright. We just need Maria. Nothing will happen to her. She's not the type of witness who can reveal the murderer's identity," reassured Anne, throwing the backpack over her shoulder and signalling for Kamilla and Maria to follow her. Mr. Nordstrøm, presumably, was in the garden behind the house, rummaging in a flower bed. He looked shyly after them. Apparently not everyone in the family wanted the attention of the press.

Kamilla found the cropped photo of the teenage girl on the LCD screen. "You probably shouldn't smile so much," she said. The girl was standing by the skip with a big smile as though for a family photo. She had apparently recovered from the shock of the gruesome discovery. *Carefree youth.* Or it was the exact opposite. Adolescents today were supposed to be so cool, they weren't allowed to show they were afraid of anything. Maybe films, TV, and the internet had hardened them. Nothing shocked them anymore. Except perhaps a strangled girl in a local waste container.

"No," Anne supported her. "Look a little more scared, Maria!" Anne walked over and opened the lid of the skip. The contents from the day of the murder had been seized by the police and the container was reopen for public use.

"Go back in time; imagine the hand again. Pretend you're throwing in the rubbish bag the way you did that day," instructed Anne.

As the girl stared into the half-empty skip, she suddenly turned pale. Horror appeared in her eyes.

"Good, good—that's it!" Kamilla heard Anne shout excitedly behind her as she pressed the shutter button again and again. She started to feel nauseated.

Afterwards, they drove to the playground Louise would have walked through after leaving her friend Lise's house. The tyres of the swing set were wet from the rain. A young boy sat on one, eating sweets. A woman was sitting on a nearby bench with three girls, whose eyes watched them intently while they licked ice cream. The woman offered her own ice cream cone to a child in a stroller in front of her and let him taste, so half the child's face was smeared in ice cream and chocolate. There was no one else at the playground. Murder and kidnapping made people keep their children indoors.

Anne wiped the rainwater off the other tyre of the swing set with her sleeve and sat down next to the boy.

"Would you like a push?" she asked. He scowled at her without answering and continued to eat his sweets. He fished a wine gum out a bag of Tom's TV Mix, one of the big family bags.

"Do you come here often?"

No answer.

"What's your name?" Anne tried again.

"Bjarne. I'm not allowed to talk to strangers," the boy said sharply and dismissively.

"No, I can understand that after what's happened. Did you know Gitte and Louise?"

Kamilla leaned up against the post of the climbing frame and thought Anne herself looked like a boy, sitting there on the swing next to Bjarne, who now quickly looked up at her. His eyes rested for a moment on her camera bag, hanging by its strap over one shoulder.

"I'm a photographer," she explained to reassure him. His eyes shone with suspicion and scepticism. She wondered how parents' warnings affect a child's understanding of a safe life With panicked anxiety over every stranger?

"We work for a newspaper, and we're helping the police find Louise," Anne half lied, regaining the boy's attention. "Did you see Louise the day she disappeared?"

The boy shook his head, jumped down heavily from the swing, and scurried clumsily towards the block of flats next to the playground. Kamilla caught the dangling car tyre he had left behind and sat down.

"I don't think it's going to be easy to get children to talk these days." She smiled.

"Maybe not. But how the hell are they being kidnapped and murdered when they're so shy?" Anne kicked the ground under the swing and looked up at the cloudy sky and on over towards the block opposite.

"We could go around the flats; someone bloody well must have seen or heard something."

"The police were here today, too." The voice came from the woman on the bench. She had lifted the baby from the buggy onto her lap and was in the process of wiping the sticky cream off his chin with a paper napkin. They got up and walked over to the bench.

"Go and play on the swings, girls. The boy's gone now," the woman said to the three girls, who immediately ran in that direction. Two of them threw themselves into their respective car tyres, while the largest girl pushed them from behind. Their summer dresses blew up in the wind, revealing the children's brown legs that stretched out in front and bent back again to gain more speed.

"Was there anyone who was able to tell the police anything?" Anne sat down on the bench next to the woman and made eyes at the child, who immediately began to laugh, showing a tooth emerging from his lower gums.

"You're from the press, right?"

Anne nodded. "Yeah, we're working on an article about Louise's disappearance."

The woman looked at Kamilla and her shoulder bag.

"I'm a photographer," she explained again, sitting down as well. She held out a finger to the child, and a warm feeling slid through her as the sticky baby fingers squeezed it. The image of Rasmus at that age was crystal-clear to her. "How old is he?" she asked.

"Christian here—he's barely a year old." The boy writhed affectionately on her lap, enjoying the attention.

"We call him Prince Christian. Children are lovely," said the woman, showing her motherly feelings as she lovingly shook the child and made him gargle with laughter.

"I love taking care of them. I'm a childminder, but I wanted to be a journalist once," she said, looking sadly at Anne.

"Then why didn't you become one?"

The woman nodded her head in the direction of the girls at the swings. "Two of them are my own."

Kamilla and Anne both nodded in understanding. The story of so many women. Children came, and all other plans went out of the window, then suddenly it was too late. Kamilla was glad she had trained as a photographer before she'd had Rasmus.

"Do you come here often with the children?" asked Anne.

"Every day. They need to get out, get some fresh air and move around, even if the weather's been miserable this summer. And given what else happened."

"Do you know Louise?"

The woman shook her head, and her eyes grew serious. "No, nor the other girl. The one who was murdered." She cast a quick glance at her own girls.

"I always keep an eye on them. They're never allowed to be alone out here," she said, starting to gather up the girls' jackets, which they had left on the bench.

"I'd better get home. The children will be collected in a little while. I was just looking after them a little longer today. Being a childminder isn't a nine-to-five job." She smiled wearily.

"Did you talk to the police?" asked Anne.

"No, I didn't see anything. But my neighbour told me someone in the flats behind here saw a large dark car drive away from here at full speed that day. She thinks it was a woman behind the wheel."

The girls came running back and interrupted them, breathless from play and talking over each other.

30

"Can't you for once get a tea towel and help me with the dishes, Dennis?" Vivi Hansen shouted from the kitchen but got no answer. At times, it annoyed her that he just sat there in his room, in front of that computer. A twenty-year-old kid should have hobbies, play football and what have you. She saw them on TV—young men who had become something within some sport or other, or who had started their own IT business and were now multimillionaires. Given the computer interested him so much, why hadn't he gone down that route? No, he was unemployed because no job had been good enough for him after he got out of secondary school. He would prefer not to exert himself too much. Getting him to continue in secondary school had been such a struggle. His grades hadn't been too good, either; there had been too many pranks and drunken binges with his friends.

Annoyed, she put the used dishes from breakfast in the hot soapy water. Jam had dried onto a plate, so she had to scrub hard to get it off. He obviously couldn't be bothered to answer her, either.

Sometimes she enjoyed being able to close the door to his room and not even feel she had a son, enjoy the silence, read her weekly magazines, and relax. Almost as if she were alone, as if Karl wouldn't be standing in the door at precisely six o'clock, looking annoyed at the dining table if she hadn't managed to set it, or if she had got behind with the cooking. But he provided for the family. It was hard in the factory, doing the same thing day in, day out. Every so often, she felt sorry for him.

"Didn't you hear me?" She leaned against the doorframe of his room with the tea towel over her shoulder and her arms crossed. Today was one of those days when he annoyed her.

"Mum, I'm chatting here!" He detached his gaze from the computer screen and looked up at her. She never could judge whether it was contempt or pity she saw in his eyes. Maybe she was a despicable sight in the tracksuit with its saggy knees and her messy hair with several inches of grey roots because the colour needed to be done. But the hairdresser was something she absolutely didn't want to spend money on, so she dyed it herself, and lately, there hadn't been any money to buy hair dye in the supermarket. It had become so expensive and there were so many other things they needed the money for. Her son didn't look much better. He was wearing a tracksuit, too, though a slightly newer and more modern version than her own. What was called a leisure suit nowadays, instead of a tracksuit.

"You live here scot-free. You could help out a little from time to time. Can you not come and 'chat' a little to the dishes instead?"

It wasn't meant to be funny, but he laughed at her, so his long, greasy fringe fell down over his pimpled face and hung over one eye. He did nothing to remove it.

"It's not as much fun as chatting here, Mum. Just come and see this babe."

Reluctantly, she walked over behind him and looked at the screen. Curiosity took over. She had never dared ask him what he did on that computer for fear of being called ignorant.

"Look. She's only fourteen. And look at those jugs."

The boy grunted as he laughed and took a swig of the Coca-Cola bottle that always stood next to the screen, beside a bag of crisps. She didn't understand how he didn't get fat, but he was thin and lanky. Probably took after her.

"What kind of website are you on? You're not staring at porn all day, are you?"

"No." He sounded indignant as he set the bottle down hard.

"We just talk to each other online. Not everything's about sex, but you probably know all about that already, given you and Dad have your own bedrooms."

It was one of the things she feared about him. His ability to hurt her and evoke memories of the past. He knew sex was a subject she couldn't bear to touch upon in either thoughts or words. And certainly not in action. She knew where the boy was coming from.

"Aren't you supposed to go to the psychiatrist today? He's probably the only one who can . . ."

She couldn't stand it today; he was annoying her. She raised the tea towel and swung it with all the force she could. The damp fabric swept over his mouth. He got up angrily with a roar and both hands to his face.

"What are you doing, bitch! I'm bloody well moving out of here soon."

"So do it then! Do it!" she shouted at him as she heard the front door slam. She sat down on his chair, which was warm from his behind, and looked at the pictures of the girls on the screen. There were all sorts of faces of various ages. Some challenging, some shy, some downright vulgar. There were girls and boys, beautiful and ugly. Profile pictures were positioned above the gallery. Inexperienced, she tried to take the mouse and click on one of the pictures like she had seen Dennis do. A lot of information about the girl popped up on the screen. Her username was "Naughty Belinda." She was only twelve. What was he doing on the computer? Some of the girls were the same age as she had been, back then . . .

She let go of the mouse and got up quickly. Hopefully Dennis wouldn't see she had touched it. She felt unwell again. She wasn't going to the psychiatrist today, so she took a few tablets. They usually never spoke about the psychiatrist in the family. It was only when Dennis wanted to hurt her that it was brought up, without him having any clue as to what was behind it. She didn't talk about what had happened back then, either. She had loved her father. Loved him and feared him. And didn't the fact he had taken his own life show he deeply regretted the anxiety he had filled her with each time she heard his footsteps in the hall at night, and the pain he had caused her when he closed the door to her room and lay with her? When she had heard he was dead, she had loved him unconditionally.

She went back to the kitchen and continued with the dishes on her own. As long as Dennis wasn't in trouble again. Maybe she should get his dad to have a little talk with him when Dennis was home again. She knew he would come back when he got hungry enough.

31

The coffee machine sputtered, signalling the three cups of morning coffee were finally brewed. And that it needed to be descaled soon. Kamilla had just got the newspaper from the letterbox, still wearing her dressing gown. She read the headlines on the front page as she walked back to the kitchen.

"Gitte's Father Suspects 'Immigrant or Developmentally Disabled Teen' of Daughter's Murder" headlined Anne's article. Kamilla's photo was positioned nicely above it. It hadn't turned out too bad. She had captured the horror in the girl's eyes. She cringed at how she had asked the girl not to smile. That the whole thing was in fact a set-up, an artificial photo, probably the same as most other photos taken in similar situations. She had even heard of journalists cutting onions to bring tears to the eyes of those they interviewed if they weren't showing the right emotion. Maybe it wasn't true, but she knew if she ever experienced that, she would refuse to take the photo.

But why had Anne written this? After all, there was nothing to suggest an immigrant had anything to do with the murder, and the boy with developmental difficulties wasn't under suspicion at all. Wouldn't it just evoke unnecessary feelings that would affect the innocent parties?

She took the jug from the coffee machine, poured the dark liquid into a mug, and sat down. As she read on, she saw the connection. The headline was a sort of quote from Gitte's father's statements. Not facts. The headline was to attract readers. Make them believe there was news on the case. Get them to buy the newspaper. The same method used by gossip magazines. Enticing headlines that reflected neither the truth nor the content of the article at all. Many people only read the headlines and look at the pictures, she thought, leading to false rumours often being spread by people who claim they read them in the newspaper, so "they must be true."

Further on in the newspaper, she found Anne's article from the playground. That image had turned out well, too. The childminder sitting with the little boy on her lap and the three girls next to her on the bench. When she had started getting the camera ready, the girls had just wanted to be in the picture. "Fear in the Playground" said the headline in bold. In the text, the childminder, Bente Kristensen, spoke of how such crimes taking place locally affected her everyday life with the children. One of her quotes was pulled out and highlighted on the page: "We never thought about the danger before—it's always been safe for children to play here—but now!" Anne had also mentioned the dark car and encouraged readers to contact East Jutland Police if they had seen anything.

The scrape of paws and claws against glass pulled her away from her reading. Tarzan had climbed up onto the ledge and was trying to get in through the kitchen window, which was on the latch. She let him in. "Well, little Tarzan, why are you coming in that way?"

The cat jumped in onto the kitchen counter. It stood for a moment in the kitchen sink between the dirty cups and glasses, drinking water from the dripping tap, before jumping elegantly down onto the floor. When she closed the window, she noticed the sun was still shining from a cloudless sky. Perfect weather for her second assignment. They had called her mobile just as she was turning into the driveway after the trip to Brabrand the day before. Aarhus Tourist Office had asked if she would take some up-to-date photos in Den Gamle By when the weather was good. They were for a new tourist brochure. Just her kind of job. Nothing with skips, dead or kidnapped children, or posed teenagers.

32

Why the hell did she write that?"

His fist hit the day's newspaper, startling Leander, who was sitting in the chair opposite. But the forensic pathologist knew his old friend's temperament. He had always had it. Ever since he himself had come from England, all those years ago, and met the young Roland Benito, who had just started as a fledging police officer in Copenhagen. It was probably due to his Mediterranean roots, he had often thought. Roland's parents were Italians of the warm-blooded kind. From Naples. His real name was Rolando, but it was quickly replaced by the more Danish-sounding Roland. As far as he knew, police work had always run in the family. Roland's father had been employed by the Carabinieri Corps, the Italian military and security police, but had been killed by the Camorra in a mafia showdown, after which his mother had fled to Denmark with the then four-year-old Rolando. Her sister was married to a Dane. But Leander hadn't got all that from Roland—he never talked about his Italian family or his past. The question was how much Roland could remember.

"That's not what's annoying you." Leander pointed to the photo lying next to the newspaper. It was a magnified, pixelated image of a boy with a haunted expression in his slightly squinting eyes. "Be glad it wasn't an immigrant," he reassured him. "That could have caused a lot more trouble."

Roland stubbed his cigarette out in the ashtray that had already been filled up before lunch.

"We have to do something. The phone's been ringing most of the morning. People are calling, because of the newspaper article, to say they saw the developmentally disabled boy that day at the skip. The press usually uses us, not the other way around."

Leander knew the press was always getting on Roland's nerves. Especially in serious cases like this one. It was hard for him to admit they could be of help, too.

"Take it easy, Roland. Just because he was seen behind the skip doesn't mean he's the murderer. And it was hardly him who abducted the other girl. What about the dark car seen in connection with both crimes? He doesn't drive, does he?"

Roland pointed hard at the picture with his index finger. "We found it by reviewing all the photographer's photos." He snorted.

The photo was taken over the crowd of journalists, police, and spectators at the waste container. And there, furthest out in the right corner of the image, the boy was standing half-hidden behind the bushes near the other hatch they had overlooked. Taken during the half hour the doll had disappeared.

"He knew about the door in the skip, I'm sure," Roland grumbled.

"What's wrong with him? Developmentally disabled means so many things." Leander leaned back in his chair and put his folded hands behind his neck as he looked at the inspector, who was red-faced with excitement. His complexion was reminiscent of mahogany. Leander's routine was to pay a visit to the police station and look in on Roland whenever they worked together on a case. There were always loose ends to follow up on. Besides, they enjoyed each other's company. The fact they were both "foreign workers" gave them a certain commonality.

"Fetal alcohol syndrome. The boy's mother was both a drug addict and an alcoholic, and she drank herself half to death when she was expecting him. But the foster parents claim he wouldn't harm a fly. His name's Kristoffer, by the way. Kristoffer Kjær."

"Sad fate. Can he even use a computer? Have you found anything on the girls?" He rolled the tip of his little white handlebar moustache between two fingers, which he was in the habit of doing when his hands were at rest and not using their skills on dead bodies. Unlike Roland, he didn't smoke.

"We've gone through every email but didn't find anything suspicious. Jensen's investigating the deleted emails. It's not unlikely the girls would hide or even delete those kinds of emails. It's a little against the law to lie about your age like that."

Leander nodded. "You hear about children being offered sex on the internet. Girls want to grow up too fast today. They don't think about the dangers." He sighed. "But is it possible to recover deleted emails?"

Roland sat, turning his pen around and around while looking at him. Technology-wise, they were probably at the same point in the investigation.

"Mikkel Jensen says you can. He has a program that should work, but sometimes only a small percentage of the deleted emails can be recovered, he says. He wants to try it before we pass the case on to the Regional Cyber Unit. They're so busy, and as long as we don't have reasonable suspicion the emails are linked to the murder, it'll be difficult to get a rush on it. But don't let any of this leak to the press. The more peace and quiet we have to investigate that website, the better," he added confidentially.

Leander nodded absently, keeping an eye on a greenbottle fly on the latch of Roland's window. From its greenish metallic body, he recognised it as the *Lucilia sericata* species, one of the smaller blowflies that searches indoors to find a suitable place to lay their eggs. Roland followed his gaze and smiled crookedly.

Leander knew his weakness for insects had always amused Roland.

"What do you call it—the forensic pathologist's little helper?" he joked.

"Yes, their larvae, the maggots, can help us a lot. Their eggs hatch in about a day, so if you have a body with maggots, you know it's been dead for a day. Based on the larval development, we can determine the time of death more precisely."

Leander again watched the greenbottle fighting its brave battle to escape through the glass window with an aggressive buzzing that sounded bee-like.

"Did you know the maggots are also little doctors and can be used by medical science in contexts other than forensic entomology—as wound healers?" he continued.

Roland made a face. "I've heard of it. But isn't it just an old wives' tale? Old soldier stories?"

"No, no. It's true. The method's been used since ancient times and was practised in many hospitals right up until antibiotics were discovered. During World War I, maggot therapy was widely used to heal open wounds in war veterans. The maggots secrete proteolytic enzymes and antibacterial substances that stimulate wound healing. Very effective. Of course, the maggots had to be sterile."

Roland shuddered visibly. Personally, he wasn't enthusiastic about the idea of having maggots crawling around an open wound. Fortunately, Gitte Mikkelsen hadn't been in the skip long enough for maggots to have made their appearance.

"Have you heard anything about the analyses of the mud from Gitte's hair and clothes?" asked Roland, changing the subject.

"Not yet. Maybe today. I've sent another reminder to Copenhagen." He brushed invisible fluff off a trouser leg.

"The skip's emptied on Tuesday afternoons. Maybe the murderer knew that?" muttered Roland.

Leander nodded thoughtfully. "And would a developmentally disabled boy have that knowledge?"

"Hmm." Roland shrugged. "Good she was found so quickly. God only knows if she'd ever have been found otherwise."

"Did you find her bike and backpack? And what about the tights? And the strange object that made the mark on her back?"

"Unfortunately, no. The entire area around Bazar Vest and where we believe Gitte was on Monday have been searched. No bike, no backpack, and no white tights—or mobile phone. We probably won't find more until the actual scene of the murder's found."

Roland shook his head resignedly and looked out through the window at the blue sky. The fly had apparently found its way through the crack, or it was somewhere in the room, searching for a suitable place to lay its eggs. Leander chuckled to himself when Roland cast an inquisitive glance at the cardboard box with the remains of his pizza from lunch. He had obviously had the same thought.

"You'd better throw it out," he said with a twinkle in his eye. "Well, I'd better be getting a move on, too. I hope the young man has his alibi in order." He put both hands on the armrests of the chair, about to get up.

"We have no other suspects. The girl's father was the obvious one initially, but he was at work and has a perfect alibi." Roland got up and took his tweed jacket from the back of the chair.

Leander got up, too. "While I think of it, the results of the DNA test are to come from Copenhagen today," he said.

"About bloody time, too," Roland growled.

"That's an improvement, if you can believe it. Things don't usually go that fast—and certainly not during the summer holidays. But let's hope they've found something. It wasn't the best of conditions. Moisture, pollution, and decay are the forensic pathologist's worst enemies. It can break down DNA. The rubbish from the container may have destroyed some traces," he explained.

Roland sighed heavily.

"Lucky the girl was found so quickly; had she been in the skip for a long time, all traces could have been destroyed," reassured Leander.

"I just don't understand what the motive is," Roland said.

"An orgasm lasts only a short second, yet people are murdered, raped, and sold for that brief pleasure," he replied bitterly.

"That's just it. There's no evidence of a sex crime, no semen, or signs of attack. So what's the motive? Does it mean the murderer may be a woman, as you mentioned during the autopsy?" At long last, Roland opened the door and he followed him out of the office.

"I know you face a lot of questions. But maybe Kristoffer Kjær can answer some of them."

"But the circumstances make me wonder," continued Roland, as if thinking aloud. "Why wasn't she wearing her tights anymore? It suggests she was undressed—and doesn't that imply a sexual motive?"

"Yes. Or a pervert. The murderer put her sandals on again. Maybe as a sign of regret? Did Gitte know her killer?"

"Yes, that's an interesting thought. Shit, there were no fingerprints on the sandals. Perhaps the water and mud destroyed whatever prints there were." Roland took out his car keys.

"Are you going to interview the boy? Can he be interviewed?"

"We have to do something. Maybe he's worth a visit?" Roland stuffed the photo of the boy behind the skip in his jacket pocket.

33

Today was the day she was going to see the horse. It had been hard to wait until school was over. Amalie had packed her backpack long before the bell, so she was ready to run out to her bike as soon as it rang. She had hurried home so rapidly she had nearly gone through a red light. As soon as she was inside, she quickly changed into a tatty old tracksuit she hadn't worn for a long time, but as she didn't have horse riding clothes, it was the best she could find. She took biscuits from the cake tin, filled an empty bottle with water, screwed on the lid, and stuffed it all in her backpack—then headed off. Luckily, it wasn't raining. He practically lived in the country. True Forest was close by. He had written it was a great place to go horse riding.

The wind made her shoulder-length fair hair dance around her ears. A smile broke out on her face. She was growing up. Just as grown up as Sofie and Line. They did loads their mum and dad didn't know about, either.

She could have taken the bus, but when the weather was good, she would rather cycle; it wasn't that far, and there was a bike path most of the way. As long as she remembered to turn right at the roundabout, she would find it.

It was further than she had thought. The sweat made the sweatshirt of the tracksuit stick to her back under the backpack, so she pulled over to the side and took the sweatshirt off. It was better to cycle in the sleeveless top now that the sun was in the sky. She took a few sips of lukewarm water from the bottle, stuffed the sweatshirt under the pannier rack, and got back on the bike. That was better.

Her mood rose when, in an instant, fields were all around her. She caught sight of the brook. A little further along, she glimpsed the forest on the horizon. She would be there soon. It felt like she had been cycling for hours and hours. Her thigh muscles hurt, and she began to regret not taking the bus. That would have meant getting home quicker—before Mum and Dad got home. But she would be at her destination soon.

When she spotted the house, which he had described in the email, she increased her speed. But where was the stable? There was a large pasture behind the house, but there were no grazing horses. Maybe it wasn't the right house. She tapped down the kickstand, set the bike on the gravel in the yard in front of the house, and walked to the front door. Then she hesitated. Maybe it would be a good idea to look around a bit first.

Behind the house was a small garden that looked like it had never been kept. The grass was long and full of weeds. There was a greenhouse, too, like the one her grandma had, but all the plants were dead. A pile of old manure that was attracting a swarm of buzzing flies stank. The house looked empty. She must have taken a wrong turn, so there was nothing to do but to get back on the bike again and find the right house. A kitten that had emerged from the bushes made her think differently. It meowed affectionately and seemed to be hungry. She squatted down and petted it. Her mobile pressed against her thigh in her trouser pocket. If she had just got his phone number, she could have called or texted him. *Stupid*, she thought, patting the kitten, who tensed and affectionately nuzzled her hand. She was about to pick it up and get up when she heard a voice behind her.

"Amalie?"

She looked up. He was standing with his back to the sun—a dark shadow.

"Yeah," she said, getting up. When she stood up, she could see his face. He was old, older than she had imagined. The dark sunglasses meant she couldn't see if he had brown eyes like the horses as he had written in the email. The wind blew his hair down over his forehead. She could see he was going bald. He held out his hand, but she didn't take it. The kitten was rubbing against her legs.

"Where's the horse?" she asked.

34

Danny paid and walked through the entrance onto the cobbled streets of Den Gamle By, the old town of Aarhus. It was like landing in a completely different world. It smelled of old houses and horses. He heard sounds that brought him back in time, and he sensed what it must have been like to live back in the nineteenth century. He peered in through the windows and felt like a peeping Tom glaring into people's homes. It was all brought even more to life by the working women clad in old clothes and wearing bonnets, who he spotted through the kitchen windows, and the baker's wife standing behind the counter in the bakery wearing her apron and brooch, as was the fashion over a century ago.

He sat for a moment on the low wall over the river, enjoying the sun, which was now beating down on him from a blue sky. He inhaled the atmosphere. It stank of stagnant water. The water was green and muddy and filled with ice lolly wrappers and cigarette butts. Probably not how it was back then, he thought, lighting a cigarette for himself. The sound of horses' hooves mingled with children's shouts and laughter. A horse pulling a rickety carriage with a young couple on board passed him slowly on the cobblestones. He followed the coach and the couple with his eyes. Saw them kissing each other, how she laid her head on his shoulder before they turned the corner, and he couldn't see them any-more. He sighed and flicked the ashes of the cigarette against the wall as he continued to listen to the sound of horseshoes on cobblestones, which grew slowly weaker and was eventually drowned out by the children's roars and screams.

He felt tired. Throughout the night, he had woken up bathed in sweat from nightmares. It had been a long time since he'd had those nightmares; last night he hadn't slept much. Maybe it was seeing this place again. Maybe the psychologist was wrong about it being good for him.

He bought an old-fashioned ice cream cone and ate it as he wandered, lost in his own thoughts, between the yellow and red timber-framed houses. A little girl ran into his legs and almost fell over. He managed to grab her by the arm and set her on her feet again. She had run after one of the geese drinking at the water pump. Women walked around in clothes from bygone eras, fetching water in heavy wooden buckets. Though they seemed to be of a slightly more modern appearance.

Then he caught sight of her. She was standing with her camera, taking pictures on the other side of the water pump. Only when she took the camera away from her face and let her eyes glide around in search of new subjects was he sure it really was her. A white jumper was carelessly tossed around her shoulders and tied by the sleeves in front of her chest. Like himself, she resembled a relaxed tourist. When she caught sight of him, she stood looking at him as if he, too, were part of the scene. She put a hand in the pocket of her bright trousers, lifted the camera again with the other, and focused on him. He smiled and saw her press the shutter button. She slowly lowered the camera again while still staring, seeming to measure him up. He hesitated. Then he walked over to her.

"Hi."

"Hi."

Her response was almost inaudible, but she smiled. He loved that smile, he realised.

"New assignment?"

"Yes, fortunately," she replied, "this is a little more me."

The sun shone in her eyes, making her close one a little as she looked at him. "Playing tourist?" she asked with a mischievous smile.

"I *am* a tourist!" He gestured with his arms to emphasise it and ended up hitting an well-dressed elderly gentleman in the back. "Oh, sorry!"

The old man waved his hand in a manner indicating it wasn't a problem and walked on. She laughed and started walking. Danny followed her.

"Who are you working for now? Still the newspaper?"

"No, Aarhus Tourist Office. They needed some new pictures for a tourist brochure. I'd say I have enough now."

"Am I in them?" he asked happily, pointing to the camera. She looked a little puzzled at first, but then remembered the photo she had just taken of him.

"Maybe. A relic from the old days," she teased.

The girl has humour, too. But the notion she thought he was old caught him for a brief second. They laughed again.

They went into the bakery with a beautiful sign in the same pretzel shape as a characteristic Danish pastry hanging out from yellow timberwork and arched windows. They bought two pastries and strolled on through the old town in the sunshine as they ate them. They saw the mayor's house. Visited the many booths. Stood by the railing of the watermill and watched the water cascading into the green liquid, splashing small cold drops onto their faces. Every so often, Kamilla put the camera up to her eye and took a series of pictures. Behind them, The Prism office building seemed to merge with the firmament as its glass panes reflected the blue sky and the little white clouds. A stark contrast to the antiquated buildings and the modern world whizzing past, out there at the Ceres junction.

"Do you feel like getting something to eat? I saw a restaurant next door." He suddenly had the courage to ask. He feared she was about to walk away from him now.

"Prins Ferdinand? No, it's way too expensive," she said, still looking at him expectantly.

"We're tourists. Come on!" he urged.

She hesitated. "I'm not dressed for it," she said, trying to get out of it again.

"It's my second-last day in Aarhus. Come on, Kamilla!" He made his most persuasive face.

She followed, resignedly, as he pulled her with him.

35

Before Roland turned right and drove along Sønder Allé, he lit a cigarette. It smoked up between his fingers resting on the steering wheel as he deftly steered the car through the dense downtown traffic. There was a traffic jam on Amaliegade and towards Salling Car Park. He took another puff of the cigarette while he waited. A woman pushed a pram out onto the roadway, taking advantage of the traffic jam to get over to the other side, so she was free to walk down to the pedestrian area on Fredensgade. "You probably wouldn't have done that, little lady, if I were driving a squad car," he said, tapping the ashes off in the car's already overflowing ashtray. He wondered about the pram behaviour of mums. Mothers should go first and pull the pram after them. Especially when it comes to assessing whether it's safe to cross, he thought. He followed the woman with eyes narrowed due to the smoke from the cigarette. She ran the last stretch and reached the footpath on the other side just before the traffic started moving again.

The traffic accelerated slowly. He quickly shifted gears and followed the line of cars up to the Regina junction, where he had to stop again for a red light. A cyclist with earphones in didn't see the red light and was about to run down a couple of pedestrians before it dawned on him he wasn't in the world of music. Roland shook his head and rolled his eyes. He knew how to easily disappear into another world by immersing himself in music, even though it probably wasn't Pavarotti the long-haired guy was listening to.

He shook a new cigarette out of the pack and rested it between his lips as he searched for the lighter in his jacket pocket. He felt bad about it. He knew it wasn't healthy. But this case was getting on his nerves. He had spent most of the night by Marianna's cot, looking at her little sleeping face. Such innocence. Carefully, so as not to wake her, he had wiped her nose. The cold had made it run. *What if it had been her?*

He turned off onto Edwin Rahrs Vej and back onto Bentesvej. The foster family lived on the third floor. The stairwell smelled of minced beef with onions and garlic. Behind one of the doors, a child cried heartbreakingly. A woman scolded in Arabic. Roland was slightly out of breath when he reached the door. MIE AND JOHN THORSEN it said on the door sign. The boy wasn't mentioned. He had already taken his police badge out his pocket when a woman in her mid-thirties slowly opened the door after he had pressed the doorbell a few times. She only glanced briefly at his ID.

"I've been expecting you," she said, gesturing for him to come in. When he saw the day's paper on the table, he knew why.

"Coffee?"

"Yes, please. Thank you." It was part of the ritual, as he had learned after countless visits to all kinds of homes. Danes gathered around coffee when beer couldn't be offered.

She placed two cups and a plate of biscuits on the table in the kitchen. He looked around the living room; it was nicely decorated with a mixture of new and old things that looked like they had been bought at a flea market.

Roland sat down on one of the chairs at the table in the kitchen's dining nook. She sat on the chair opposite and poured the coffee. It looked thinner than the coffee at the police station, but he was used to drinking various strengths. Out of courtesy, he took a biscuit when she offered him the plate. He wasn't particularly hungry, not even for something sweet—one of his weaknesses.

"Unfortunately, Kristoffer won't be home until three o'clock," she said. "He's with my husband in his lorry; he loves it. John's a truck driver," she explained, taking a bite of a biscuit, which crumbed into her lap. She had dark frizzy hair, which could well have been a failed perm, and wore modern glasses with a light titanium frame. They suited her narrow face. Her grey eyes looked out at him through the lenses. "You should have called first," she said with crumbs in the corner of her mouth. It was a reproach.

He heard the tone, but the police didn't call to give advance warning. He looked at his watch.

"Well, I'll just wait the fifteen minutes. Can you tell me a little about Kristoffer in the meantime?"

"You can't arrest him. He hasn't done anything." She crumbled the biscuit on the plate nervously as she looked at him with eyes that had a touch of uncertainty. Maybe she was one of those foster mothers who had bitten off more than she could chew, caring for a developmentally disabled teenager without fully knowing the responsibilities that came with it. It wasn't just about food, a warm bed, and a few goodnight kisses. Maybe they had taken him in for the money. You heard about that, too.

"We don't think so, either. But we know he was near the skip at the time Gitte's doll disappeared, which you probably read about in the newspaper." He pulled the enlarged image of Kristoffer behind the waste container out his jacket pocket and placed it in front of her. She looked at it without much interest as she brushed the crumbs she had just discovered off her lap.

"That's why we'd very much like to talk to him. Is it normal for Kristoffer to go out on his own, without supervision? "

"He can easily do so. On his good days, there's no problem."

"And on his bad days?" Roland drank from his cup and looked at her over the edge with a raised eyebrow.

"I'm usually with him," she said meekly. She broke the biscuit into smaller pieces. "But he loves to go down to the playground and watch the other children. He can easily do that on his own."

"Hmm. Does he happen to have a computer?"

Mie Thorsen shook her head. "He's not able to use a computer. Not even computer games." She sighed.

"Does Kristoffer have a doll?"

"No, he doesn't!" She looked at him in surprise, but then changed her mind. "I don't know. We don't go into his room very often." She pulled the worn blue cardigan around her more tightly, as if she were suddenly freezing. "We've agreed it's his own private place where we don't interfere. He's a boy who's nearly fifteen. He doesn't play with dolls," she muttered, mostly to convince herself.

Roland crunched the last of the biscuit and rinsed it down with a sip of coffee. "Do you mind if I look around his room a little?"

She hesitated again. "What if he comes home?"

"Then we'll talk to him." Roland smiled convincingly.

He was allowed to walk around Kristoffer's room by himself. He had read in the report that the boy was a little immature. His room reflected that. It wasn't the room of an ordinary fifteen-year-old boy, where he would expect to see posters of Britney Spears and Pamela Anderson—or whoever the scantily clad young ladies were he occasionally caught a glimpse of on TV nowadays. Instead, posters of Disney's *The Lion King* and *The Little Mermaid* adorned Kristoffer's walls. By the bed hung an old Hans Christian Andersen *Ole Lukøje* lamp with a red umbrella adorned with gold stars as its shade. Probably found at a flea market. He walked around, carefully moving things without touching them with his hands. Instead, he used a pen he had in his pocket. On a shelf in the bookcase stood a large Homer Simpson figure. He smiled wryly as he remembered watching the cult cartoon with his daughters. They had teased him that he would end up looking like Chief Wiggum if he didn't keep an eye on how much cake he had with his coffee. He shook his head slightly at the memory. As he moved the Homer figure, the row of books overturned. He hadn't noticed it was being used as a bookend.

A *D'oh!* as Homer would have said was about to escape from his lips, but then he spotted it. Stained with mud and staring out at him with expressionless glassy eyes from the darkness behind the books. It was missing its right hand. The doll!

36

It was getting late in the day, and the waiting room had thinned out. The last patient wouldn't arrive for another hour, so it gave her the chance for a short coffee break. A rare occurrence. Normally, she was running behind because some consultations took longer than intended. She had just let her second-last patient out of the clinic with some reassuring words when she spotted him in the waiting room.

"Your secretary said I could wait. I don't have an appointment." He stood up in the empty waiting room and cleared his throat, embarrassed.

"It's been a long time since you've been here!" she exclaimed. His lean body showed he certainly didn't like being back here, either.

"Come in, Troels. My last appointment ended earlier than intended. Have you been waiting long?"

"Not too long. I read some of your ancient magazines. Thanks for the other day, by the way."

Majken held the door and let him walk past her into the surgery. She smiled indulgently at his critique of the magazines; she had heard it many times before. She looked completely different in the white doctor's coat, with her hair up and wearing glasses, but that didn't deter Troels. And yet he looked frightened and unsure. Maybe it had been wrong to invite him to the table the other day. Maybe he felt uncomfortable about having a closer relationship with his doctor. Intimate questions took on a different slant when patients were also personal friends. They generally chose another doctor. A patient shouldn't really say "thanks for the other day" to their doctor, should they? That's what her father would say, in any case. Doctors should remain separate from "the rabble."

"Is there something wrong?" she asked.

"It's my pulse again. I think my heart's going to bloody well stop soon." The bright, almost invisible, eyebrows on his pale face contracted in a worried frown over his narrow straight nose.

"Sit down, and let's take a look at you."

"Can't you give me some sleeping tablets? I can't sleep at night."

She took his file from the cabinet. She found it easier to work from the folder in the filing cabinet than to find the information on the computer, even though everything was entered in the electronic patient record. Old habit. She knew full well she had to get used to using the digital system.

There were no signs of arrhythmia when she listened to his heart with the stethoscope. A cardiogram didn't show anything abnormal, either.

"It all looks fine. I'll take some blood, too, just to check everything. But what you mention sounds more like symptoms of anxiety. Is there anything you're worried about at the moment?"

"Things aren't great with Vera and me."

It erupted from him, as if that were the actual reason he had come.

"There have been problems before. But you always get through them. Did you talk to the marriage counsellor I suggested last time we talked about it?"

"It's no use. The problem is—you know I . . ."

Majken nodded to spare him from having to say more.

"You're not the only one. Your wife knows that and likes you the way you are, doesn't she?"

He nodded vaguely, buttoning his shirt, which he had left open after the examination. His chest was white with only a few blond hairs.

"A marriage of convenience," he said dryly, "for the sake of her career. Suppose she lost her position as a solicitor or her seat on the city council. My wife, a bloody politician!" He grimaced.

"Well, she probably didn't do it because of that." Majken put her pen back in her breast pocket and smiled.

"Vera has decorum. There are things you don't talk about. Like *that*," he mumbled.

Through the cracks in the blinds, the sun fell on his pale face and cast stripes across the desk. Majken wanted to suggest he go on a sun-filled holiday to get some colour, some meat on his bones, and have a good time with his wife.

"I'm sure you'll work it out, Troels," she encouraged.

"What about those sleeping tablets? Will you write a prescription for me? Or for something to calm me down so my heartbeat can return to normal!"

He got up quickly and rolled down his sleeve. He seemed annoyed. The cotton wool she had put over the spot where she had taken blood was still on his arm.

"I don't think we should talk about medicine until we know the results of your blood test. You can call in a few days to find out." She wrote a few notes in his journal. "What about alcohol? Are you managing to take it easy? Last Tuesday, you were . . ." She fell silent. That was precisely what was wrong with seeing your patients in private. It was too easy to judge them.

"Shit, Majken! What else am I supposed to do to calm my nerves when you won't give me anything?" He was red in the face now, a transparent rose colour.

"And your temper. Your blood pressure's fine, but you should be careful anyway."

"If you're not going to help me, why the hell do I need a doctor?"

The door slammed shut behind him.

Majken leaned back in her chair in exasperation and took off her glasses. Was she really going to admit her parents were right? Did Troels think she was going to give him medicine like that just for the sake of their "personal" friendship?

She flicked quickly between the archive's tabs looking for his name to replace the file. When she put the folder down in its place under *M*, a name on a nearby tab caught her eye. Why hadn't she been aware of that? She tried to think back. But she had so many patients that names didn't always ring a bell before she looked at their medical records. She was interrupted by a gentle knock on the door. Her secretary stuck her head around the door to apologetically announce the last patient was sitting in the waiting room.

37

I really have to go now!" Kamilla's voice didn't quite have the strength of will she had hoped to show.

He poured more red wine into her glass. "You don't walk away from a full glass in a nice restaurant."

"Danny!" She sent him a pretend hurt look but couldn't be seriously angry at him. The wine relaxed her and warmed her cheeks.

It had been a delicious lunch. One she wouldn't have been able to conjure up in her own kitchen. It had been beautifully served, so much so, they had both sat for a while staring at the food on the big white plates, not wanting to ruin the beautiful creation with a knife and fork. There was something about going out to eat.

They had started with coffee on the terrace of Restaurant Prins Ferdinand, with the din from Den Gamle By in the background. When it had begun to rain, they had moved inside the restaurant, where they sat at a table overlooking the entrance to Helsingør Theatre. She had been there a few times with Majken to see the summer concert with Den Jyske Opera. Danny had suggested they stay and have lunch together, which she had agreed to hesitantly. She needed it. Jan had never invited her out to eat after they had got married. It had become her duty to always come up with exciting dishes for dinner, which hadn't always been easy with a picky eater like Rasmus. Jan didn't exactly eat just anything, either. Today had been so unexpected and impulsive, everything that had happened.

She had learned the happiest moments were often so because they came unburdened by the huge expectations that always accompanied planned events.

"So what's happening in the murder case?" Danny asked, pouring another glass of red wine for himself.

"Not much."

"I'd imagine the police probably aren't saying much for the sake of the investigation, either," he said, lifting his glass towards hers.

Kamilla shook her head, clinked his glass, and drank the wine. The last glass. She had to drive home.

"Nah. I have the feeling they're hiding something from the press."

"It must be terrible for the parents. Parents always expect to die before their children." All at once, he fell silent, as if his own words were stopping him. "Is there someone waiting for you at home—since you say you have to go?" He hurried to change the subject.

They had mostly chatted about work. Both had avoided talking about themselves and their personal lives. Kamilla shook her head. She was going to the graveyard soon. She had to remember that.

"Me neither. So let's enjoy the afternoon." He looked at her persuasively.

There was something about his eyes that made her go soft inside. He made her feel pampered. New emotions she hadn't felt for a long time began to spread like ripples in still water.

He gazed at her as if he didn't know what to say, then it came hesitantly. "Kamilla. I know you're probably married and not at all interested in me that way . . ." He cleared his throat. "But you're the nicest woman I've ever met, so . . ." He fell silent again as he looked at her embarrassed, as though waiting for an answer.

Who is he? A real playboy. Someone who can get all the girls without blinking, or by doing exactly that. Maybe he was married with children. She hated infidelity. That was how Jan had found Nina—behind her back. It might have been going on for years without her knowing it. Had Jan said the same thing to Nina at their first meeting? She hated Nina. Majken must never feel like that towards her. Majken, the only one she hadn't excluded in the despair of grief, and who hadn't turned her back on her because she didn't know what to say to a single mother who had lost her son. The friend who was there whenever she needed her, whatever her mood.

"Say something. You're so quiet." He tried to take her hand, but she instinctively pulled it away so violently that she overturned her empty water glass. Danny picked it up, maintaining eye contact.

"I don't know you. I don't even know if you're married. And what about Majken?" she said, trying to assess what was happening in his eyes. But she only saw confusion in them.

"I'm not married anymore. And what about Majken?" He sat for a while thinking about it, then he started to laugh. "Do you think we . . . ?" He shook his head. "Majken would like to, but . . . you're not jealous, are you?" His voice sounded as if he was having fun.

"Are you just playing with her?" Kamilla's cheeks flared with anger and her voice trembled.

"Playing! No, of course not! More like Majken's playing with me." He became serious.

She got up and waved the waiter over to pay.

"Stop it, Kamilla!" he said angrily, standing up, too.

As she still couldn't open her bag because of the stupid clasp and because her hands were shaking, she let him take over. He paid and apologised to the confused waiter. Kamilla disappeared out of the door and walked with rapid steps down towards her car. He caught up with her.

"You have to explain to me what's going on!"

She was confused by her own behaviour, refusing to respond. With her back to the car, she looked up into his eyes, which had now darkened. She could feel the weight of his body as he leaned against her, and the car's wet and cold metal penetrating her clothes as she pressed herself closer to it to avoid him.

"I don't have anything to do with Majken," he said. "And I'm not married. And I don't have children, either. I'm completely free and on the market!" He smiled and stood so close to her that she felt his breath with its faint scent of red wine. His lips came closer. She wanted to just surrender, but the anger had grown in her. Just because he was free and on the market didn't mean she was interested. Men could be so conceited. Her mobile rang in her bag. She hurried to answer it, like a drowning woman who had been thrown a lifeline.

"Kamilla? It's Anne. They've found him!"

"Who?" Dazed and disoriented, she turned away from Danny.

"The killer, damn it! Gitte's murderer."

38

Jesper had stayed home. The car was in the garage, and the suspicion it was one of his colleagues who had written the cruel words couldn't be erased from his tormented brain. He knew he would look at them accusingly, maybe even attack them verbally given the opportunity. Spit on them and call them traitors. It wouldn't help him. Only do the opposite. The best thing was to stay at home. The hatred he felt was going to come out somehow. Now he had taken it out on the garden, where he had attacked the flower bed like a mad man to create a trench. Then he had cut the grass until sweat dripped off him. It had to be one of them who had called the police anonymously. Why would they ruin his career? He couldn't do anything else.

He got up from the chair he had been sitting on since coming in from the garden and put a coffee filter in the funnel. Where had she put the coffee now? He opened all the cupboards and drawers and finally found it in the very top cupboard. *What a place to put coffee!* He spooned it into the filter and put the can in the cupboard above the coffee machine; logically, it belonged in there. Shortly afterwards, the kitchen was filled with an aromatic smell and the sound of gentle gurgling. Sussi would be home with the kids in a little while. Probably with cakes. They needed to talk about all the cake. He hated chubby kids, and both boys were starting to develop disgustingly thick, round cheeks, double chins, and muffin tops like little old men. They might end up being teased at school, just like he had been as a boy. But he had pulled himself together and lost the weight. If *he* could, so could they. But the boys seemed happy enough. Neither cried when they came in from school, where, contrary to his own childhood, there was someone to offer comfort. They didn't wake up with nightmares, either, so maybe everything was fine. He put cups on the table and poured the coffee into a thermos.

"Yoo-hoo, we're home!" Sussi's voice sounded in the hall, along with the noises of boots being kicked off, rainwear being shaken, and a little girl crying unhappily. Sussi came out into the kitchen with the little one on her hip. She hadn't taken off her jacket yet. She handed him the bakery bag. "Will you take that—and her?" She tried to pass the girl over to him, but she turned away, clung to her mother, hiding her head in her mum's neck as she howled and kicked.

"Okay, sweetheart, I won't let you go." Sussi sighed, annoyed.

She took the child out into the hall again. Jesper heard her murmur to calm the girl and get the jackets off.

Reluctantly, he took the bag and poured its contents onto a plate. There were lots of different kinds of cakes and breakfast rolls all mixed together. Things they hadn't sold in the shop.

"Hi, Dad!" The two boys came running into the kitchen in stockinged feet and threw themselves at the plate of cakes. They took as many as they could in each hand and ran off to their rooms. Jesper sat down resignedly on a chair and poured the coffee. His parenting plans always went out the window at home. *Why is raising other people's children so different? Why do other people's children seem so different?*

Sussi placed the girl in the highchair and sat down wearily on a chair next to him. She took a cinnamon swirl dripping with grease. He watched in disgust as it quickly disappeared into her mouth.

"How's your day been? Did you stay at home?" she asked before she had finished chewing, pouring coffee into her cup.

"Yeah, I stayed at home. The car's in the garage."

"Well, yeah, but you could have taken the bus." She sucked cinnamon and grease off her fingers. "Have you heard anything more from the police?"

"No, of course I haven't. Why would I? I haven't done anything." He drank the coffee but stayed away from the cakes. The little girl tried to grab one from the highchair and started complaining when she couldn't reach it.

"No, of course you haven't." Sussi took a raspberry slice and broke it down the middle. She handed half to the child.

"Don't you want to even taste it?" she said to him. He shook his head. The little girl gnawed contentedly on the raspberry slice and soon had raspberries and white icing all over her face, her fingers, and her clothes. Sussi laughed as if the girl was a little clown putting on a show.

"Did the police talk to you?" he asked cautiously.

"No; should they?"

"They wanted to know where I was on Monday and Wednesday afternoons, so they'll probably ask you that, too."

"Why?" She didn't look at him, only at the child, who continued to clown around with her raspberry slice.

"Have they really not contacted you?" He tried to assess whether she was lying. It wasn't like Roland Benito to dawdle with that kind of thing.

"Just look at this little mucky pup here. I think she needs a bath. Should Dad put you in the bath?" she asked in a childish voice.

The girl wriggled in the chair and held out her sugar-sticky arms towards her father. When Jesper picked her up from the chair and carried her out to the bathroom, where he undressed her, he knew Sussi wasn't lying.

39

She mimed pouring more coffee into Anne's cup. Anne nodded and pushed the cup closer. Kamilla had another cup, too. The wine from lunch with Danny was still making her cheeks burn. It was a relief it was already over. Both the meeting with Danny and the case of the murdered girl, despite them not really seeming to get off to a good start.

"Is it all over now?" she asked.

"As good as. Kristoffer's in custody, but they won't know anything until the results of the DNA test come in. I think they're due today."

"Has the boy confessed?" Kamilla still couldn't believe a boy with developmental disabilities was a child-killer. He was only a child himself.

"Nope. He's refusing to talk to the police, or else he just comes out with nonsense no one understands."

Anne tucked her legs up under her on the couch. She had kicked her shoes off under the table. It was her first visit to Kamilla's. Kamilla wasn't so free and easy. Her strict mother had taught her not to do that in a stranger's home. It hadn't even been allowed on the sofa at home in the living room. Anne didn't have the same inhibitions. She didn't seem like the kind of person someone could push around and tell what to do. Kamilla liked her. Maybe because she was so different to herself. She found the scar on her left eyebrow, which made the eye hang a little, more charming than ugly. She wanted to ask what had happened but didn't dare.

"He's admitted to knowing Gitte, but not that he murdered her. But he doesn't have an alibi for the time of the murder," Anne continued, blowing into the cup to cool the hot coffee.

"Does he know Louise, too?"

"It doesn't look like it, but there's nothing to say there's not a connection between the two cases."

"No, there isn't, but it's still a little strange Louise disappears just as she's about to tell the police about the car."

"It could have been anyone in that car. But it certainly wasn't Kristoffer."

"Why did he take Gitte's doll from the skip?" Kamilla wondered.

"He couldn't answer that, either, according to the police."

"The poor boy!" The words came out almost silently, but Anne heard them anyway. Journalists probably had extra sensitive ears.

"Do you mean that?" Anne sounded indignant. "If he really *is* the murderer?"

"He's developmentally disabled." Kamilla clung to the view the weak should be protected. She would always insist neither the developmentally disabled boy nor an immigrant could be the guilty party in Gitte's murder. She was of the clear view it was people's prejudices that made them appear so. But she sometimes wondered whether she was too naïve. Now the cards were on the table. Kristoffer was in custody. Yet she kept defending him as if she *wanted* him to be innocent.

"Then he'll get a milder sentence and will be free again soon," Anne replied sourly. Bristles stuck out of her short dark hair, as though it hadn't been styled that morning.

"Who's the little boy in the photo? Is that your son?" she asked out of the blue.

"Yes, that's Rasmus."

"Don't you hate him? The guy who did it?" Anne looked at her in the serious professional journalistic way she had also employed when interviewing the murdered girl's parents. The question surprised Kamilla.

"So you know, then?"

"They told me at the newspaper. I was very sorry to hear about it," Anne replied, looking at the picture of Rasmus again. "He looks like he was a sweet boy."

So Thygesen had told her. She was relieved; it meant she didn't have to share what had happened. She didn't know how to answer Anne's questions and searched for an emotion. "I don't actually know how I'd react if I came face-to-face with him," she replied honestly. *And what will Jan do if he finds him?*

"I'd want to kill him," Anne assured her. "In cold blood!"

Kamilla noticed a dark shadow fall over her face as she said it, but she couldn't tell if it was fear or hatred. It was gone again immediately.

"Do you have children?" she asked gently. It dawned on her she knew very little about the young woman she was now working with.

Anne shook her head.

"A boyfriend, then?" Kamilla continued.

"No, that's over. All over!" Fear returned to her eyes for a split second, but it disappeared when her mobile, which was lying on the coffee table in front of her, started vibrating and playing Mozart's Symphony No. 40.

"Duty calls," she announced regretfully, putting the phone to her ear. She looked out into the garden through the patio door when she answered.

"Yes, Thygesen. Okay, we'll leave right away." She hung up and put the phone in her backpack. Kamilla remembered Thygesen's short messages that sounded more like brief commands.

"Press conference at the police station. Probably the results of the DNA test. Now we're getting somewhere. Come on!"

Kamilla left the cups and rushed after Anne, who had already reached the car. The air was warm and seemed almost thick from the humidity after the rainstorm that had come from nowhere, despite the sunny start to the day. The sun was behind the clouds, making the droplets of water on the leaves of the hedge shine.

The heat was stifling in the packed press room at the police station. The journalists were squeezed together like sardines. Roland Benito and Superintendent Kurt Olsen sat at the table in front of the chatting and restless crowd of journalists and photographers noisily finding their seats. The tar-like coffee was replaced with Ramlösa sparkling water with a touch of lemon. Either out of thirst or for the sake of image; it looked a little better. Drinking mineral water cleared the brain. *You are what you drink.*

Roland looked like someone who wanted to get this over with quickly. He looked even more tired than when Kamilla had last seen him. He was pale under the tanned skin. Cornered—literally. The superintendent looked rather unkempt, too. He had obviously tried to do something more with his attire than usual, but the female touch was missing. A polished pipe lay barren in an ashtray in front of him, next to a flat packet of Mac Baren tobacco.

The scraping of chairs, cameras being made ready, and the buzzing sound of voices stopped abruptly as the superintendent tapped a pen hard on his glass, which replaced the usual plastic cup for the occasion. He took the floor with a powerful, authoritative voice.

"Welcome, everybody! Have you found your seats?"

Kamilla lined up near the other photographers so there was a good view of the officers at the table. It was her first police press conference.

"We've convened a press conference today as we've received the result of the DNA test in the murder of Gitte Mikkelsen."

There was complete silence in the room as Kurt paused for effect while looking out over the herd of impatiently waiting press. A few flashes flared.

"We can now state the DNA does not match that of Kristoffer Kjær. Nor is there any other evidence to suggest he's connected to the murder or the kidnapping. Therefore, we're ruling him out as a suspect."

There was silence again. Everyone sat waiting, but Kurt said no more. A large journalist in a checked shirt and rolled-up sleeves held up a hairy arm at the back of the room. There was a distinct sweat patch on the fabric under his arm.

"Has he been released from custody?" he asked breathlessly.

Roland and Kurt both nodded in the affirmative. "We can't hold him without evidence."

"Does that mean you're back where you started?" Anne stood up to be better heard. She wasn't very tall, and when she sat down, she disappeared into the crowd.

Kurt coughed and glanced quickly at Roland, who recognised Anne and replied, "We have some other leads that are being further investigated."

"What leads?"

"We won't reveal any more details of that now." Kurt came to his subordinate's aid.

"What about the father?" said a male voice. "Child murders are often committed by a family member. Could incest have led to murder?"

Kurt answered. Roland took a sip of Ramlösa.

"The father's DNA doesn't match, either. And, incidentally, there are no signs this was sexually motivated," the superintendent emphasised with a dry smile to the well-informed journalist. *There's always at least one.*

Unrest in the form of whispers and coughs broke out in the room. Kamilla looked over at Anne to see her reaction. But she sat unfazed, writing eagerly on her pad.

"There have been rumours a paedophile from an after-school club in Brabrand was brought in for questioning; is that correct?" asked a hoarse female voice.

"It wasn't a paedophile. The youth leader in question was only under suspicion," reprimanded Roland. "But it's correct he was questioned. However, we found no evidence to hold him." Roland turned his glass nervously.

"What role does the doll play in the case?" A tall and thin young journalist, who apparently was quite green, asked the question.

"Kristoffer Kjær has explained to us he took it from the waste container to give it back to Gitte Mikkelsen. Unfortunately, he can't remember how he knew it was there. He suffers from blackouts, and there are many gaps in his statement," replied Kurt, looking at his watch. It looked like he wanted time to move faster so it would be over sooner.

"Where was the girl murdered?" asked a reporter from one of the free newspapers.

"So far, we've not identified the scene of the murder. We're still waiting for the analyses of the mud found on the victim," replied Kurt.

"And the kidnapped girl—do you have any leads on her?" The questions came relentlessly from the flock of journalists.

"We've talked to the residents in the area where Louise Poulsen disappeared, and an investigation's currently underway."

"Could there be a reason to suspect a serial killer?"

"This is not a serial killer!" said Roland angrily. That would be the worst thing to state publicly. There was no reason to scare people more than they already were. "We're talking about a single murder," he continued in a more conciliatory way.

"Given the amount of time that's passed, is it not reasonable to suspect Louise has also been murdered?" continued the annoying journalist. He was no doubt looking for a sensational headline to help sell his likely ailing newspaper.

"Naturally, we can't say anything about that now. But as I said, an investigation's underway."

"An investigation into what?"

Kurt cleared his throat. "Unfortunately, we can't expand on that at the moment for the sake of the investigation." He sighed.

"I thought the police called a press conference when there was something of interest. You're not telling us anything we don't already know," came a clearly dissatisfied voice from the front row.

Kurt accepted the criticism with great composure. "We convened a press conference to announce the news to you as a group, given information had come to light that a teenager was under suspicion."

Roland sent a reproachful glance down to Anne in the middle of the room. She didn't seem to notice. She was still sitting and taking notes.

"Have no witnesses come forward in any of the cases?"

"Louise Poulsen was a witness we, unfortunately, didn't get to talk to, but we've received information from a woman who thinks she may have seen a car parked by the waste container for a suspiciously long time on Monday evening around six o'clock. This may be the same car seen at the playground on Wednesday afternoon when Louise disappeared. It's unknown whether the driver was a man or a woman. We've received conflicting information on this." Kurt took a deep breath. "We therefore ask you to appeal to your readers to help as much as possible. Someone else may have seen the car by the skip on Edwin Rahrs Vej or at the playground in Brabrand." He took a sip of his sparkling water.

"What kind of car is it?" Anne got ready to take notes again.

"Unfortunately, none of the witnesses recognised the make of the car, so we know only it was a dark car of a larger model. Probably an Opel or a Honda. Perhaps navy or black. If anyone's seen a red girl's bike, a pair of white tights, or a pink backpack, that would help us, too. We're also looking for two mobile phones. We can give you some images afterwards."

Anne changed the subject. "What type of DNA did you find? It's not semen, I understand."

Kamilla had been waiting a long time for that question.

"Blood," replied Olsen. "The perpetrator may have cut himself on the edge of the waste container."

*

Gasping, he stopped running and struggled to catch his breath. The old woman was dead. The tenacious old harpy was finally out of the picture. An exultant laugh bubbled in his throat, but he stopped it. That was too inappropriate. This time he hadn't felt anything. The lovely feeling was absent. That annoyed him, and it dawned on him this was what he was seeking. Was it the crunchy sound that had been missing? Was it the non-existent whining? It had been like that, too, with the toads. They hadn't given him any satisfaction, either. She had died like them—in silence. She looked like them, too. Not warty, but wrinkled. Old and wrinkled and just as helpless. An old crone who snooped. She had come too close. Why had she done it, though? She should have kept her nose out.

Calmly, he walked on, trying to think of something else. Darkness was falling. He heard the noise of loud pop music from a residential street nearby. Probably one of the usual middle-class street parties behind the privet hedges, with coloured lamps, drinks, and a table of homemade potluck dishes from the neighbours. A couple of festively dressed kids took the opportunity to stay up past bedtime and play on the pavement. A yellow ball with red spots rolled towards him and came to rest by his freshly polished Lloyd shoes. A little girl in a short summer dress came running after it and stopped abruptly. She looked up at him fearfully, as if she didn't dare take the ball that was so close to his shoes. He squatted down and picked it up. When he handed it to her, he inhaled her sweet, fresh scent.

40

She ran across the yard and up to the yellow-painted house. There was still a light on in the living room, thank God. She looked at her watch. Thunderclouds threatened on the horizon, making the evening darker than usual at this time. She was hours late. It hadn't happened before, but things with the old man who had fallen in the bathroom and needed medical attention had dragged out. She'd had to stay until the ambulance came. Poor Olga Halgren had been waiting for her medicine. And she was only just home from hospital after breaking her leg. Maybe that was why she hadn't answered the phone. Her leg probably couldn't support her yet. She rang the doorbell several times without hearing any sounds of life from within the house.

"Olga, it's me, Gitta—Gitta Kofoed, the home help." She knocked hard on the door. "I'm coming in. It's just me," she shouted.

She took the extra key out of the bag and put it in the lock. The door creaked as she pushed it open and stepped into the narrow hall with its worn coconut fibre rug. A ball belonging to the cat rolled out. She picked it up. As long as that creature wasn't inside. She was allergic to cats. Luckily, it hadn't been there the last few times.

"Olga, are you asleep? I'm here to give you your medicine. Sorry I'm so late."

She sniffed as soon as she entered the living room. The presence of the cat, or even cat hair on the carpet, was enough to trigger her allergy symptoms. The lamp next to the armchair was on, but there was no one in the chair. The house was eerily quiet.

"Mrs. Halgren?" she called again without getting an answer.

There was an empty plate on the coffee table. Someone had made food. Fried eggs, it looked like. She must have had visitors. She sensed a strange smell mingling with the smell of fried eggs. Cigarettes and perfume. So Olga had eaten, thankfully—she didn't need to feel guilty. She felt guilty enough already. She wanted to be much more involved in the lives of the elderly and sick she looked in on, but there weren't enough hours in the day. Only for what took priority. Her body always felt stressed. The salary wasn't great, either, so she often asked herself why she kept doing it. The question was whether she could even hold out until retirement. Her back often plagued her. Viggo had also said she was starting to look hunched and worn out.

She took the empty plate out into the kitchen. On the way out, she glanced into the bedroom. There lay Olga Halgren, sleeping soundly with the duvet pulled up over her head. Gitta smiled. Therein lay the reason she kept doing what she did. She had cared for her mother until her death four years before. Good care, nursing, and help for the weakest had then become her favourite cause, despite the conditions of the job not being the best, even deteriorating in recent years.

While Gitta rinsed off the plate and did what little washing up there was, she smiled again, relieved. Everything had gone smoothly. There would be no complaints about her tardiness. Olga had eaten food and been put to bed. She began to hum happily. The crutches stood against the wall by the armchair. She straightened the pillows on the sofa and found the medicine. It was a shame to have to wake her up to give it to her, but it was necessary.

"Olga," she called gently, knocking lightly on the doorframe before slipping into the semi-dark bedroom. The woman in the bed didn't move. Gitta squatted down and turned on the lamp on the bedside table.

"Olga, I have your medicine with me. You have to take it." The duvet was pulled up all the way over her head. She never usually slept like that. Gitta gently pulled the duvet down so her face became visible. She quickly straightened up and took a step back with a loud gasp, dropping the jar of tablets. She heard the tablets rolling across the wooden floor and under the bed.

It wasn't the first time she had seen a dead body. Not at all. It was a sight she was gradually becoming used to in her job, but the expression on Olga's face made her swallow hard a few times. Her toothless mouth hung open, gaping like an open wound. With a quick side glance, she saw the teeth in the glass on the bedside table, an incongruous sight next to the dead woman's empty mouth. Her dull milky-white eyes were puffy and had a terrified or startled expression. As if she had seen a ghost. What had she died of? Gitta was used to natural causes of death. This didn't look like that at all.

Panic set in. The bedroom was so quiet. She could hear only the ticking of the alarm clock, her own rapid breathing, and, somewhere out in the dusk, music from a street party. The dim light from the bedside table cast long dark shadows on the ceiling. She ran out of the house with her heart pounding in her throat. Only when she had reached her car did she stop. What was she supposed to do? She couldn't just leave the woman lying there. Should she call the police? Was calling the police not a bit drastic? While she kept an eye on the house that was almost hidden in the dark shadows of the trees, she rummaged in her bag and found her mobile. The lights were on in the living room and the kitchen, making the windows look like two glowing eyes in a sinister face. With trembling hands, she dialled 112.

41

Mikkel Jensen entered the smoky office. The door was open just enough to let some of the smoke out. A cigarette burned in the ashtray next to Roland. A half-eaten burger from McDonald's lay on a cardboard plate between large piles of paper. Roland would have preferred pizza. It was in his genes, he always said.

"Come in, Jensen. Do you want a cup of coffee?" Roland offered him the inviting thermos and shook it so it slopped, before pouring some for himself and handing it over. Mikkel sat down opposite his superior.

"There's nothing on Louise's computer we can use. But I saved a bit of an email sent from Gitte Mikkelsen's account." He handed a printout across the desk, and Roland quickly snatched it out of his hand.

"Only a bit?"

"Yeah, I don't know how much sense it makes. It was the only suspicious thing I could find. It looks like they've corresponded before. Someone her own age, I'd say. There could be several emails the program wasn't able to recover. If she had deleted an email before the recovered email saved, then the program can't recover that one."

"Someone her own age? That doesn't make sense," said Roland, studying the note:

. . . whÃ¥rn I get home from school . . . my dad . . . will mÃet . . . to you as promised . . . reply to the address . . . t . . . @ . . . com

"Well, that's not much to go on! What are the strange characters?"

"It happens if there's a character the program doesn't recognise. It replaces those letters or characters with other characters. It'd be great if the email address was as easy to salvage," Mikkel admitted annoyingly, putting the thermos back on the desk without taking anything. His coffee ration had long since run out.

"Did you talk to Cyber about it?" Roland asked worriedly.

"They don't really have time for more at the moment. There are so many internet scams. It's taking all their time. Debit and credit card fraud and what have you. They're also reviewing some computers for a child pornography case. They don't really view this as a cybercrime for them, either, they said." Mikkel sighed.

"A murder—and a kidnapping!" exclaimed Roland indignantly.

"We don't know if the emails have anything to do with the murderer or the kidnapper yet. But I told Cyber we'd like to hear more about whoever had child pornography on their computer," said Mikkel, just as he was interrupted by DS Kim Ansager, who burst in and handed some papers to Roland.

"Well, welcome. You're here, too, then?" exclaimed Mikkel with a beaming smile.

Kim's hair was bristled as if he had messed it in frustration. He was an expert in the type of information that required deep research into databases and *non*-public data lists. His patience gave him the ability both to convince the public authorities of the importance of the police getting the knowledge he was looking for, and to meticulously go through every list. It was very time-consuming. Of all his assignments, he was in the process of finding out who sold the ropes forensics had mentioned as possible evidence. It was difficult, as the rope could have been bought online or locally.

"Louise's phone's been tracked. Simon Agger claims he found it in the grass at the playground. We're bringing him in."

"Good, Kim. You'll deal with it, won't you?"

Kim nodded and spotted the printout in front of Roland. "Are these the deleted emails?" he asked, turning to Mikkel.

"What I could recover of them, yeah. I couldn't recover it all. I'm not an IT expert, am I?"

"Have you tried Properties? On the menu, go to Files, then Properties, and Details in the tab." Kim couldn't hide his instructive tone. "Come with me!" He gestured to Mikkel, who rolled his eyes at Roland before following.

Roland looked at the two young officers, confused. They might as well have spoken Russian. He concentrated on his work again and heard his stomach growl. A burger wasn't enough food to keep you sated.

It wasn't long before Mikkel appeared in his office again.

"Kim was bloody well right. He knows a bit about computers. Maybe they could use him in Cyber?"

His cheeks were red, and Roland wondered if reproachful words had been exchanged between the two officers, as it was something Mikkel had difficulty grasping. He had noticed the two tended to fight over who was best. That Mikkel wanted Kim moved to another unit was probably a fresh attempt to remove a competitor from the field.

"Honestly, I hadn't expected you could do this with a recovered email. Or maybe it's just pure luck. Computers have a mind of their own." Mikkel laughed.

"So what did you find?"

"An email address! And even better—a date." Mikkel stuck a handwritten yellow Post-it to Roland's computer screen:

X-From_: ted.dybear@hotmail.com Sun Jun 20 18:05:46
Return-Path: <ted.dybear@hotmail.com>
X-Original-To: gitte.mik@hotmail.com
Delivered-To: gitte.mik@hotmail.com

"What does that mean?" Roland said, annoyed at his ignorance as he searched for his lighter in his trouser pocket. A fresh cigarette hung from his lips.

"It means the email was sent to Gitte Mikkelsen's email address on Sunday evening, a little after six o'clock, from the email address ted.dybear@hotmail.com," Mikkel explained knowingly.

"Ted.dybear? Teddy bear! Talk about contrived." Roland snorted, lighting the cigarette.

"Genius for contacting children, right?" commented Mikkel sourly. "Gitte Mikkelsen was killed the next day. There's definitely a connection. I'm sure Doll Child accepted Teddy Bear's invitation."

"But it could be someone her age—look at how they use words like *school* and *dad*. Can we find out whose email address it is?"

"Anyone can hide behind an email address, and I don't believe it's someone the girls' own age," said Mikkel. "Hotmail's difficult to track, but I'm going to start investigating immediately. We should be able to get some help to track the IP address from our so-called experts now."

Mikkel took the thermos and poured coffee into a plastic cup anyway, which he put in front of him after moving a pile of Roland's papers a little.

"Did you talk to Jesper Ingemann's wife?" he asked as he sat down and looked at the distracted inspector. Distracted probably wasn't the right word, but Roland's concentration was directed towards the computer keyboard, where he was typing slowly with one finger, as if aiming at each key he had to hit. Afterwards, he carefully checked the screen with narrowed eyes to see if he had hit correctly. Mikkel hid a small smile as he drank from the plastic cup.

"I didn't have time today, but my gut tells me it's not him. Sure, he's fond of children, but I still don't think he's a murderer," Roland replied. "Besides, neither his DNA nor the car matches. Jesper Ingemann drives a white Opel."

"I heard it'd just been painted black." Mikkel tried to be funny, but Roland didn't laugh. He didn't even answer.

"I don't trust those kinds of people at all. Should I check it out tomorrow?" Mikkel asked helpfully.

Roland grumbled something incomprehensible from behind the screen. Mikkel took it as approval.

"But what if the blood on the hatch isn't the killer's at all? Aren't we going after a completely wrong lead, then? Have you thought of that?"

Surprised, Roland looked at Mikkel with a raised eyebrow and the frown that always appeared when someone questioned his approach.

"I'm sure of our lead. Blood was also found on Gitte Mikkelsen's skirt, and it's not come from her. Therefore, we ruled out Jesper Ingemann. We can't waste time on a perpetrator who's already been ruled out."

"It'd be bloody nice to put him away, regardless of whether he's a murderer or not. It'd save a few children from getting groped. How did the press conference go, by the way?"

Roland growled again. "Fine. Now we just have to hope the press can get people to come forward. It's been almost a week since Gitte was murdered. If nothing happens in the case, we'll be called to account, I can assure you."

"Has the Special Operations Unit been called?"

Roland shook his head. "Not yet, but that's probably the next step."

"Has no one come forward after the feature on the news?"

"The usual." Roland sighed, not needing to explain further to Mikkel. It infuriated him that people could make prank calls even in such serious cases as child murder and kidnapping. Still, something had landed on his desk for further investigation.

"Aren't you heading home for the weekend soon? Isn't Irene waiting for you on a Friday night like this?" Mikkel moved to get up.

Roland looked at his watch. He had been on standby since the news. It was so late now, it was unlikely there would be more calls.

"Are you heading home?"

Mikkel nodded. "I have a date." He winked tellingly in his most charming way. DS Mikkel Jensen *was* charming, despite the shaved head, which he had the face to pull off. A young, modern, popular style that didn't suit everyone. *Some ended up looking like hardened criminals*, he thought. But not Jensen.

Mikkel stood up and emptied the plastic cup in one mouthful, followed by a grimace, then he threw it in the bin and set the chair in place in a corner of Roland's office. He looked wonderingly at it for a moment. The girlfriend was obviously working on teaching the lad some manners.

Roland took his jacket, which hung, as always, on the back of the chair in case of emergency, turned off his computer and then the light. He was about to close the door when he heard the phone ring. He turned on the light again, took it, and listened with a raised eyebrow. Mikkel stood in the doorway, looking at him questioningly.

He hung up and looked wearily at Mikkel.

"We have another murder," he said.

42

He drove at full speed along a wide, straight country road that stretched as far as the eye could see. The asphalt was rough, dark, almost black, and the hot air flickered out on the horizon. The sky was a crystal-clear surreal blue with not a single cloud. He felt happy and uplifted. Then a fierce wind came. It shook the car, and the darkness began to descend. He no longer drove on asphalt, but on pitch-black rough water. The speed grew faster and faster. It hissed in his ears, and he no longer had power over the car. Out in the dark, he could sense them. A pair of eyes. Green and luminous. They resembled a reptile's with their narrow pupils with slits in the middle. Or a cat's. They came closer and closer. They were right in front of the windshield, filling it completely so he couldn't see anything but its big mouth. Sharp canines bordering a smelly, slimy, and glistening throat. The windshield burst, and the monster lunged at his throat between shattered shards of glass that pierced his skin.

Danny woke with a start and a loud roar. At first, he didn't know where he was. His shirt was wet with sweat, and his heart was pounding fiercely as it always did when he woke up from those nightmares. His suitcases were on the floor next to the bed. Then he remembered where he was and tried to calm down.

It wasn't normal for him to sleep at this time of day. But he had slept so badly last night, full of unrest since his meeting with Kamilla in Den

Gamle By. She had disappeared so quickly. A kiss would have been inevitable if her phone hadn't rung. It had been the journalist, he figured.

Maybe it's good I'm going home early tomorrow. The essentials were packed in a little bag in the bathroom—toothbrush, soap, razor. Now he had to find a clean shirt.

The humid evening air hit his face when he opened the window, and his heart beat at a more normal pace. The nightmare was over. Those cursed nightmares. He needed a shower.

He nearly fell when he put the wrong leg into his trousers, jumping around on one foot, trying to pull them on. He imagined Sanne's large green eyes with their unusually long doll-like lashes and her narrow mouth with the fine little wrinkles in the corners when she smiled. Why had it gone so wrong? They had loved each other once. Now it seemed as if she hated him. As though she believed he had killed the boy on purpose. Would Kamilla hate him, too, if he confided in her? The comb slid through his wet hair as he pondered the question. Would she be able to see it had been an accident? That it was the cat's fault. That when he had swerved to avoid it, he had hit the boy in the cycle lane. His blood-alcohol level had, naturally, reduced his reactions. He shouldn't have driven, should have stayed overnight in Jutland. Sanne had blamed him for all that, too. As if it wasn't enough that he blamed himself.

He lit a cigarette and let it hang between his lips while he put on his socks. Majken had invited him over for dinner, but he had declined, which he now regretted. What was he going to do on his last night in Jutland? He had promised to call her before leaving. And what about Kamilla?

He ate his last meal in Jutland in the cosy restaurant at Sjette Frederiks Kro. Yet another beautiful building, this one built in 1826, which he stood and admired for a long time in the evening sun. The atmosphere inside, and the food, were just as fantastic, and he was quietly annoyed to be sitting there alone. But time passed when he fell into conversation with a married couple who also came from Zealand.

It was almost ten o'clock when he let himself into the room again and considered whether it was too late to call Majken. It wouldn't surprise him if she was sitting on the bright sofa, phone in hand, with her legs pulled up under her, waiting impatiently for his call. He had better call and say goodbye as promised. He tried three times in a row, but Majken didn't answer. He felt disappointed. So she wasn't waiting for him. But then he became restless. Could something have happened? Apparently, not much happened here in Jutland. He tried to call one last time. Then he grabbed the jacket lying over a chair next to the packed suitcase and ran out to his Opel Vectra. He began to sweat in the hot, humid evening air. It had rained most of the afternoon again, with temperatures well above twenty degrees Celsius.

His unrest increased when he turned the car into Majken's driveway. A squad car was parked with its front wheels turned sharply to the left, so the white gravel had settled in a small heap by a tyre.

Majken looked confused and dazed when she opened the door. "Danny. Oh, good, you came!" She heaved him into the hall and quickly closed the door, as if she wanted to keep other people out.

"What happened?"

"A break-in. There's been a burglary!"

The officer in the living room cast a brief glance at Danny and continued to take notes on a pad. "And who do we have here?" he said without looking up again.

"Danny Cramer. A close friend of mine," Majken replied.

"Was anything stolen?" asked Danny, looking around. The living room didn't look like it had been burgled.

"It's the clinic. They broke in through the window. I don't understand how I didn't hear it. Unfortunately, the alarm wasn't set. I don't usually set it until I'm going to bed. I just went in to get my diary. Suppose I'd gone in when they were there, then . . . ?" She put a hand to her head, confused.

"You checked the medicine, didn't you?" the officer interrupted her.

"Yeah. I've checked everywhere, and it all seems to be there. Computers, valuables. I don't have any money there, and the medicine's there, too. The medicine cabinet's locked and wasn't broken open."

The officer made a few notes and put the pen in his pocket. "I'll head back, then. Unfortunately, we rarely find the burglar in these kinds of cases. He was probably surprised. A drug addict perhaps. But we will, of course, do what we can," he said.

"Were there no fingerprints?"

"Not any we can use. Nothing was rummaged through or touched. It's like the thief knew exactly what he was looking for and knew the place to find it. Just call if anything turns up. I'll let myself out," said the officer to Majken, taking his leave. The wheels of the police car crunched in the driveway as it turned onto the road.

"I don't understand how I didn't hear anything!" Majken exclaimed in despair, plopping down heavily onto the sofa. Danny sat down next to her.

"Are you sure nothing's missing?"

"Absolutely! I need a drink! Will you have one with me?"

He nodded.

<h1 style="text-align:center">43</h1>

It was one of the better ones, even though it had been on special offer in føtex supermarket. Like a wine connoisseur, she sniffed the scent over the edge of the glass. The bottle was small and plump. Italian, like the inspector. She smiled at the comparison. It had a faint scent of blackcurrants. She took a small mouthful and tasted it. Not the worst she had tried. The label was nice, too. That was always how she chose wine, because she didn't know much about the precious drops, despite learning a nice label didn't always mean a nice wine. The label boasted 14 per cent alcohol. "Lucky it's Friday!"

Kamilla got comfortable on the sofa, feeling the hygge. A little cosiness on a Friday evening. It felt extra comfortable now that she was working again. Last year, all the days had flowed into each other in one long month, where she couldn't distinguish the weekdays from the weekends.

The TV was on, but the volume was turned down. Tarzan lay asleep in the chair. The dishes were still in the kitchen sink, but she just wanted to relax. She could do them tomorrow if she didn't get to them this evening. She took a mouthful of the powerful wine. *And I probably won't*, she thought, looking at the red glow through the glass. The evening sun shining through the curtains turned the colour of the wine to a burgundy hue. *Blood*, she thought. *It looks like blood.*

Anne had managed to get hold of the inspector after the press conference, even though he had done everything he could to escape. Anne had told her about their conversation on the way home in the car. Having car-pooled, Kamilla had to wait until Anne had come back. She hadn't wanted to intrude when no photos were to be taken, so she looked at the police station's art collection in the meantime. Forensics found the blood by the latch on the edge of the skip, Anne had explained as she pushed her bristly hair back and steered the car through the traffic.

"But couldn't it be from anyone?" Kamilla asked.

Anne nodded and stuffed a piece of V6 chewing gum into her mouth. Kamilla accepted one, too.

"Yeah," Anne had muttered as she shifted gears. "I asked that, too. But the blood was also found on Gitte's clothes. So the police suspect the killer scratched himself on the skip door or gave himself enough of a cut that it bled profusely. That'll catch him—a cut like that is a wound."

A teenager with developmental disabilities has been released in connection to the Aarhus murder case, the news anchor's voice came from the TV. She turned up the volume. Tarzan looked up, annoyed at her for disturbing his sleep.

There were pictures from the press conference. She spotted the car with the TV 2 East Jutland logo in the car park in front of the police station but hadn't noticed them in the commotion of the press conference. Superintendent Kurt Olsen was announcing the boy's release due to lack of evidence. Then the newscaster took over, sharing what the TV 2 editorial staff thought people should know. They also showed pictures of the skip where people had laid flowers, teddy bears, written thoughts and prayers on little notes fluttering in the wind, flickering tea lights. Her gaze slid over to the photo of Rasmus on the bookshelf, but a picture of a girl with dark curls quickly pulled her eyes back to the TV screen.

Ten-year-old Gitte Mikkelsen disappeared on Monday afternoon at two o'clock when she left her home to attend a classmate's birthday party a few metres away. She never reached her friend's house. No one knows her where-abouts from two o'clock on Monday afternoon, when she was seen at Bazar Vest, until one o'clock Tuesday afternoon, when she was found dead. Police are looking for the driver of a dark car seen stopping at the waste container on Edwin Rahrs Vej on Monday evening at six o'clock, the news anchor summed up.

Kamilla stared paralysed at the girl's face. Her eyes were full of life and joy. As a ten-year-old girl's should be. It was the first time she had "seen" Gitte despite the television networks probably showing her picture in every newscast. It moved her to see the person behind the assignment. Put a face on it. She had always avoided the idea that it was all about a person. A little girl who had once been full of life. Just like Rasmus.

A dark car is also wanted in connection with the abduction of Gitte Mikkelsen's classmate, Louise Poulsen, who disappeared on Wednesday afternoon. Police suspect it may be the same car. Unfortunately, no witnesses have been able to give the make of the car, the newsreader continued, and a new image appeared on the screen. Louise Poulsen was a pale, skinny girl with thin blond hair and blue eyes. The photo was a private one of Louise sitting on a black leather sofa. She smiled crookedly and shyly.

Louise Poulsen disappeared on Wednesday afternoon between four and half past six after leaving a friend's home. She was wearing a yellow raincoat, red T-shirt, dark blue jeans, and white runners. Please contact East Jutland Police with any information . . .

Kamilla pulled a blanket around her. She was freezing despite the living room being warm. Again, she looked up at the picture of Rasmus with the football in his arms. It was so unfair when life was interrupted so abruptly and meaninglessly.

An American sitcom began on the TV. The artificial canned laughter came in short bursts. The mechanical response seemed so out of place after the images of the two girls and their fates. As if life shouldn't go on after such a tragedy. But it did. It had done so after Rasmus, too. Though it was not life as before.

There wasn't much on the TV that interested her. The wine had made her drowsy, and she must have fallen asleep. It was almost dark outside when she woke up instinctively, thinking a sound had awakened her. Tarzan sat up on the couch, his ears pointed tense and stiff at the hall. Kamilla became aware of his behaviour. *Cats hear everything—even a tiny spider crawling across the floor, the wind, or the woodwork creaking.* She muted the TV with the remote control and listened. One of the cat's ears turned towards her at the movement, but he continued staring at the hall. He grew restless and jumped down from the couch. Tarzan walked slowly, vigilantly, and furtively towards the hall. He made himself as low as possible. *Mouse? Rats? Did I remember to lock the front door?* Thoughts whirled around her head, groggy from sleep and wine.

"What's up, Tarzan?" Her voice revealed she was nervous. As she got up, the cat ducked quickly, turning his head towards her as if he were going to hiss at her. His eyes were black; the pupils filled them. But he continued stealthily towards the hall. Kamilla still couldn't hear anything but the muffled bass of the music from a street party somewhere nearby.

All at once, the lights went out. Her heart raced in what seemed like a brief cardiac arrest. *It's just a blown fuse*, she reassured herself, but it didn't alleviate the panic. She could make out the furniture in the semi-darkness and quickly found her way to the hall and the cupboard with the fuse-box. She couldn't see Tarzan. She turned abruptly as she sensed a movement behind her, but there was no one there.

"Is there somebody there?" she whispered hoarsely. It sounded like a line from a bad thriller—she now felt like she was starring in one. As she approached the door to the hall, which stood ajar, she could feel the evening air. The front door had to be open. Had she had forgotten to lock it? Had it blown open? It wasn't windy. With a quick movement, she pushed open the door to the hall and was greeted by the wide-open front door. The leaves rustled on the trees. The music from the street party became clearer. She hurried to slam the door and lock it, then she opened the cupboard with the fuse-box and picked up the torch that lay inside.

To her surprise, she saw the fuse supplying power to the living room, kitchen, hall, and toilet was loose. She dropped the torch with a gasp as a sound in the living room made her flinch. As she stepped backwards, she heard Tarzan's heart-rending yowl and hiss. The cat's dark shadow dashed into the living room, into the light from the torch on the floor, and it dawned on her that she had stepped on him. She picked up the torch with a breath more reminiscent of a sob. Her hands shook, so it was difficult to both hold the light and screw in the fuse. She felt like an eternity had passed before the lights finally came back on.

Carefully, she went back to the living room. The curtain fluttered. The patio door was open. Had she not closed that, either? As she stared out into the garden, she saw the red taillights of a car slowly disappearing up the road. Usually only those who visited her were on that part of the road. Someone who had taken a wrong turn, she thought, but things weren't making sense. She could still feel panic in her body. She shook. The dark garden made her more uneasy. The trees were silhouetted against the bright evening sky. A breeze rustled the leaves, so it sounded as if someone or something was moving in them. She hurried to close the patio door and draw the curtains.

She jumped when her mobile phone rang as she was pouring a new glass of wine. She spilled it on the table, and the red liquid ran like blood towards the edge. She had almost no voice when she answered, but Anne was too eager to notice.

"I'm on my way to pick you up. There's been another murder," she said feverishly.

"Now? It's so late!" Kamilla managed to stammer as she tried to keep the spilled wine from the edge of the coffee table so it didn't run down to the floor.

"Murderers don't exactly work nine to five," Anne replied with an inappropriate, restrained laugh. "I'll be there soon. The murder was committed on your street."

44

Anne turned from Grenåvej onto Mejlbyvej. She hated the country, with all the smells and fields and the Morten Korch–novel atmosphere. Her grandparents had lived in the countryside in North Zealand. She had spent a lot of time with them, but the memories weren't of the good kind, and the visits hadn't been voluntary. She wasn't her grandparents' favourite. Whenever she had spent weeks on end with them in the small, dilapidated farmhouse, where she was forced to help in the stinking pigsty and driven to school by her grumpy grandad who smelled of chewing tobacco, they had called it a holiday. She had learned as she got older that it was when her stepfather was in jail that she'd been placed in care there. Her mother hadn't been able to have all the children on her own, so as the eldest, Anne had been sent to North Zealand.

Thankfully she couldn't see much of the landscape in the dusk, and it wasn't really out in the country, either. But she could smell the fields, and that was enough.

She parked in Kamilla's yard, put her palm on the steering wheel, and honked three times. Kamilla came running out with the camera bag over her shoulder and sat down next to her in the passenger seat. She smelled of wine and looked exhausted, as if Anne had woken her.

"Hi," Kamilla said, trying to sound cheerful. "What happened?" Her anxiety shone through.

"An old lady was found dead in her house here on this road." She looked at Kamilla's face in the semi-darkness. "You look a little pale, Kamilla. It's not too much for you, is it?"

Kamilla shook her head and fastened her seat belt. "No, I just had an unpleasant experience tonight. The lights went out, and I felt like someone was in the house." She gestured uncomfortably with her hand. "But it was probably just a loose fuse. I've always been afraid of the dark."

Anne put the car in gear and was about to turn out onto the road when she heard police sirens approaching. She let the cars with the blue flashes pass, then quickly followed.

"We'll let them show us the way." She laughed.

"How did you find out something had happened out here so late at night—even before the police?" Kamilla asked curiously.

"I have my contacts," Anne replied secretively, winking.

"But not that Roland Benito, right?"

"The inspector? No, you have to pull everything out of him," Anne replied grimly.

"I'm guessing you don't like the police?" Kamilla asked with a crooked smile.

"The police have never done me any good," Anne said dryly. Her face showed Kamilla shouldn't probe any further.

The squad cars turned off the road and stopped in front of a little yellow house hidden between tall trees. Anne parked on the roadside a little further ahead. The lights on top of the cars cast an eerie blue glow in the twilight. The blue flashes evoked mixed feelings. Anne had hated law enforcement authorities when she had lived in Nørrebro. The police didn't always act tactfully during a demonstration. They often made it much worse. There was always an element among the protesters who weren't there to demonstrate for a good cause, but who had a score to settle with the police and enjoyed watching them go straight into the trap and help escalate the unrest. But she also remembered the blue lights from when they had last arrested her stepfather. She had woken up in her bed to the sound of sirens and blue flashes flickering across the walls of her room. When she had looked out of the window, she saw them put him in the back seat of the police car with a hand on his head so he wouldn't hit it as they pushed him in. He had been handcuffed, and for a moment, she'd had the feeling he was looking up at her face in the gable window. Mum had shouted and screamed the police were pigs, and her siblings had yelled at each other. She left home that night. Gone into the city centre and met other teenagers who weren't happy with life, either. They all agreed the police were shits. Only when she got into the realities of crime, did she realise they did some good, too. Both in terms of information for her work and solving crimes. Her stepfather hadn't been innocent, either.

They got out of the car and went up to the house. The neighbours had begun to flock. Due to the late hour and the location of the house, there weren't many passers-by. Some of the neighbours were in their night-clothes, but curiosity was greater than the need for sleep. Anne rigged her equipment and introduced herself to an elderly man in a dressing gown. No other journalists had arrived yet, so she took advantage of being the first to catch the story. Thygesen would be delighted.

"Do you know what happened? Did you see anything?" she asked in a voice encouraging the man to share something terrifying. He didn't take his eyes off the house as he replied he hadn't heard or seen anything. He only knew the old lady who had died had just returned home from the hospital after breaking her leg.

"It was her, there, who found her—the home help," he said, pointing with a shaky, wrinkled index finger to a middle-aged round-shouldered woman standing hunched by a car. She was white in the face. Anne went over to her, but she wouldn't comment on anything; she was too shocked, she said. So not a sensationalist who would have loved to talk at length about her find to the media, Anne concluded.

Kamilla hurried to take pictures of the house with the squad cars parked in the yard. Anne waved her over to the house. They went in, both knowing they were doing something wrong again. The police hadn't cordoned it off yet.

The inspector, who had shown up with a team of technicians and a forensic pathologist, paled before entering the house.

"Did you touch anything?" he asked in a sharp voice, which didn't match his tired appearance, when he spotted Anne and Kamilla. They hadn't. The forensics team and the medical examiner, who resembled a noble count, asked for space and peace and quiet to do their work.

"Get out!" said Roland Benito sharply, pointing to the door. But Kamilla managed to take a picture of the bedroom and the bed as Anne had ordered.

She smiled contentedly when they were standing in the garden again. It smelled of freshly cut grass and privet hedges. Only the drunken voices of the stragglers at the summer street party could be faintly heard through the hedges. Anne kept an eye on the house.

"This time, we need a picture of the dead woman. As soon as they carry the body out, be ready," she whispered to Kamilla, who nodded as though hypnotised.

Roland was the first out of the house, walking in front of the stretcher as soon as the initial examination of the body had been completed. Kamilla captured a series of images just before the stretcher was placed in the ambulance with its tinted windows. The woman was covered by a white bag and was fastened to the stretcher with two straps, so only the contours of her person could be seen. Roland did nothing to chase Kamilla away. After the ambulance had driven away, while forensics were still working at and in the house, he went over to Anne. She was standing out on the road behind the barrier tape some distance away from the nosey neighbours.

"Hope you're taking some pictures we can use," he said.

Anne immediately picked up the sarcasm in his voice. "Of course, just contact us if you need anything forensics missed." She smiled. "Was it murder?"

Roland nodded bitterly. "You'll probably find out anyway, so I might as well tell you—the woman was suffocated with her own pillow."

Anne took a cigarette from the packet he offered her and let him light it with his lighter.

"Are we allowed to smoke at a crime scene?" she asked, blowing the smoke out into the darkness.

"As long as we stay here outside the tape," he said, looking like someone who couldn't do without the cigarette much longer. She looked at his face in the flame of the lighter. She liked his features. They were rough and ready, yet he was charming for his age. It was something in the eyes.

"Where in Italy do you come from?" she asked, wanting to know.

"Naples," he replied shortly.

"Ah, the mafia." She laughed.

Yes, and olives, orange and lemon groves, the white beaches and the blue Gulf of Naples with Mount Vesuvius in the background, the scent of oregano, basil, and espresso in the narrow streets of cosy restaurants and cafés, and the sun shining almost luminescent in red bougainvillea vines," Roland replied, firmly establishing he loved his homeland.

Anne fell silent, sensing she shouldn't say more on that subject.

"Do you think this murder could have anything to do with the murder of Gitte Mikkelsen?" she asked instead after a short pause, while they followed the technicians' examinations of the house's doors and windows. A crisis psychologist who had been called in was talking to the home helper in her car.

Roland shook his head and removed a piece of tobacco from his lower lip.

"I strongly doubt it, but nothing can be ruled out at present."

"How old was she?" asked Kamilla, who had come over to them.

"Didn't you know her? You live on the same road," Anne said a tad reproachfully.

"No. I never knew who lived here. The house always looked uninhabited."

"She was a little into her nineties," Roland interrupted. It wasn't a nice case to get into on top of a child murder and a kidnapping. He looked at his watch. "There's nothing more to do here tonight, so I guess we should see about getting home?"

Anne knew he was saying it considering the work that still lay ahead of him in the house, along with forensics, and interviewing the home helper if she could face it tonight. But Anne didn't protest. Something told her she was tuning into the brusque inspector's wavelength, and he would certainly benefit from her more as a friend than a foe.

45

The water lay still in the summer night, evocative of liquid oil. His thoughts were the only thing disturbing the quiet evening. Danny inhaled the clean sea air and the smell of seaweed. The lights from the towns along the bay shone like a brilliant string of pearls.

Majken hadn't realised he wasn't interested in the kind of relationship she wanted. He had said it was because of the divorce. Not the full truth, but it had been all he could come up with when she had hinted at ending the evening in her bedroom. Her legs had been twisted around his on the sofa. Her lips had whispered enticing offerings close to his ear. It had certainly affected him. She was an attractive woman, and he wasn't made of stone, but she didn't turn him on sexually. That's just the way it was. She had, naturally, been in shock from the burglary at the surgery. They hadn't talked about anything else. But as the drinks had slid down, the atmosphere had changed. He had even held back a bit with the drinks. Coffee had chased the last of the alcohol from his blood before he had decided to say goodbye and leave.

He sighed, got out of the car, and sat down on the grass. The ground was cool, and the moisture seeped through his thin canvas trousers. Only the lapping of the water broke the silence. Occasionally, a car drove past on the road, destroying the illusion of nature without human intervention. His thoughts were allowed to flow with the splashing of the sea. Tomorrow, he would be back in Zealand. Should he start working again? Was he ready to move on now? He missed the hubbub of the advertising agency, he had to admit. The vitality of the design studio, where creative people radiated a pulsating energy. The excitement of seeing a project turn into something. In print. On film. Whatever. He even missed his visits to his elderly, senile mother who didn't recognise him.

He tapped a cigarette out of the packet but didn't bother to light it in the fresh sea air.

But he was leaving something here, too. An urge made him get up and go back to the car. He glanced quickly at his watch and up at the rear-view mirror before putting the car in reverse. Past midnight. Was it too late? No, he had to try; he couldn't leave Jutland without seeing her again. Whatever the cost.

Kamilla poured a new glass of wine as soon as she was home again. The bottle was almost empty. Usually, a bottle saw her through most of the weekend. Tarzan still hadn't come back.

She had accompanied Anne back to the newspaper office to transfer the photos to her computer so Anne could choose the best ones for the article herself. Otherwise, she wouldn't make the deadline. Thygesen had still been at work, despite the late time, so not much had changed in editorial.

She went into the study and turned on the computer. A large question mark was flashing on the screen. The Mac hadn't been able to cope with the power outage, of course. *As long as it's not the hard drive that's gone.* She took the memory card out of the camera and stored it in her safe. Those kinds of images couldn't be retaken.

A wet sensation under her bare foot made her squat and take a closer look at what she had stepped in. She picked it up and rubbed it between her fingers. Soil. There was earth on the floor. She never wore shoes inside. The discovery made her stand up with a jerk as she looked around. Someone had been in here. Someone who had come from outside. Feverishly, she rummaged through her things to see if anything was missing. Then she opened the cupboards, her heart thumping with fear that the burglar had hidden in there. Then she smiled. "Tarzan," she said aloud. The cat must have dragged the soil in. The relief calmed her tense muscles a little.

When the doorbell rang, she initially thought it was her confused brain playing a trick on her. She looked at the clock hanging over the cupboard. It rang again. She stood stock still, wanting to give the impression she had gone to bed, but then she remembered candles were lit throughout the house. The doorbell rang again. The sound cut through the silence, making her flinch. The night the two officers had called, she hadn't wanted to open the door, either. As if something in her knew she was about to get terrible news that would ruin her life. Despite it being the last thing she could have imagined at the time. But not now. The innate sense of "that won't happen to me" had disappeared. It was replaced by fear and insecurity.

"Who is it?" Her voice sounded hoarse and uncertain.

"It's Danny!" The voice that answered sounded firm and decisive. She wished she hadn't revealed she was home. Her thoughts whirred. The embarrassing situation when they had been together last. The dishes she still hadn't washed.

"Open the door, Kamilla. I won't stay long. I just want to say goodbye!"

Still, she hesitated. Then she opened the door, and when she saw him, he suddenly seemed like the only one who could protect her.

"I'm sorry for coming over so late. But I saw the light." He smiled.

"How did you find my address?" Kamilla looked at him sceptically, despite the obvious answers. There were phone books and contact information and Google maps on the internet.

"I asked at the paper," he admitted. *The paper!* Was it really that easy? She let him in.

Danny looked around the room. *The wine bottle!* What would he think of her for drinking by herself?

"I had to talk to you again. And then, fortunately, I met you by chance in Den Gamle By." He looked at her. She looked away quickly.

"I was actually on my way to bed," she lied, suddenly noticing she was shaking from the evening's many eerie experiences.

"I know it's late, but . . . Is there any more wine?" Danny sat down in the armchair.

She shook the wine bottle. "A glass, maybe."

"Should we share a glass?"

She fetched a glass for him from the cupboard.

"I was just at Majken's," he said cautiously.

His words stopped her in her tracks. *Of course he was.*

"There'd been a burglary," he continued.

"Burglary?" Kamilla put the glass in front of him and plonked onto the sofa opposite. He took the bottle and poured for her first, then himself. There was enough for just one glass each.

"Nothing was stolen. Very mysterious, really."

"When did it happen?" She thought of the open front door, the murder further up the road, and the soil on the floor of the study.

"Majken had gone into the surgery to get her diary, and she discovered the window had been smashed."

"Didn't she hear anything at all?"

Danny sipped his wine and shook his head.

"No. It makes you think someone was watching her and knew exactly when she wasn't going to be in the clinic," he said pensively.

She felt the tingling sensation of unease and again saw the car head-lights, which had appeared like the glowing eyes of an animal between the dark shadows of the trees before disappearing. She considered whether she should tell him about her own experience and fears. She was verging on tears from the panic.

He took his glass over to the other side of the coffee table. As if he could feel her anxiety, he sat down beside her on the couch.

"I'm sure the burglary's nothing. A drug addict looking for something," he comforted.

She felt his closeness as a warmth that spread throughout her entire body. He put his arm around the back of the sofa by her shoulder. His warm fingers stroked her neck, and he turned her face towards his. She smelled his aftershave and willingly followed as his hand slid behind her neck, bringing her face closer to his. His earnest eyes filled her entire field of vision. She fell into their deep brown and drowned. His kisses became more demanding and his breathing faster. She gasped for breath. Gentle, warm hands slowly unbuttoned her blouse and slid onto her stomach, up along the lace edge of her bra and behind it, where they expertly snapped open the hooks. Every touch felt like little hot shocks. But she didn't protest. Not even when he gently pulled the blouse down over her shoulders as he kissed them and she sat practically naked in front of him.

"I don't usually move so fast . . ." she stammered as he kissed her neck, and she felt desire taking over. She heard how faint and unconvincing her voice sounded.

"Neither do I," he whispered hoarsely.

All her embarrassment disappeared. She just wanted to enjoy it. Merge with him and forget everything else. She was vaguely aware of him carrying her into the bedroom. A lamp overturned along the way, but neither really registered it.

"Was it *that* good?" He smiled as he wiped the tears from her cheeks with his thumb. His cheeks flushed, as did hers. And then the tears flowed. A redemptive and silent cry that came from deep inside, and over which she had no control. She had once read about it in an advice column in a women's magazine at the hairdressers. *Why do I always cry afterwards?* the woman had asked. And the psychologist replied that sexual satisfaction hits our inner emotions, so emotions lying just below the surface emerge.

She lay close to him with his arms around her. Their bodies glued together with sweat, as one person, unable to move without the other following. Her body was light. She felt a pleasant drowsiness.

She hid her face in his chest. The dark hair smelled faintly of sweat and soap. He stroked her hair. This was different than with Jan. He had always lain on top of her, writhing with his eyes closed, like a blind worm, breathing hard through his nose to prevent himself groaning. Afterwards, he would turn his back to her.

"What are you so sad about?" He whispered it into her hair.

Should she tell him? She knew he wanted to understand her. He wouldn't rebuke her the way Jan had.

"It was over a year ago," she began after a short pause.

He waited anxiously and held her closer to him.

"What was?" he asked when she didn't continue.

She ran her hand up over his back and shoulder and further down over his tense arm muscles.

"My son," she began.

"Your son?" he repeated. "So are you married?"

She felt the little jolt it produced in his body and looked up quickly into his chin.

"Not anymore. We're divorced."

"What happened?"

Again, she hid her face in his chest.

"His name was Rasmus."

She fell silent and closed her eyes.

"He was run down and killed. A drunk driver."

46

———

Something she felt she had overlooked or forgotten shook Majken awake every time she was about to slip into slumber throughout the night. But when she woke up, she couldn't remember what it had been. She sat down wearily at the edge of the bed in the morning. Then she remembered it was Saturday and she could stay under the covers a little longer. She rolled back into bed with a blissful smile and pulled the duvet up over her head.

The trip to the bakery to buy rolls, as was her custom at the weekend, didn't give her the sense she had forgotten anything. It was a lovely morning. The wind rustled her hair, and the blackbird sang its soft song from the rooftops. The gardens she passed were fragrant with newly bloomed flowers. They were beautiful now, the gardens. Not her own, she had to admit as she walked in through the door with the bag from the bakery and a litre of skim-milk in her arms. A sheet of chipboard had been placed in front of the broken window in the surgery. The glazier couldn't come until Monday morning, so she had to settle for the chipboard all weekend. It did nothing to make her feel less insecure.

The aroma of the coffee beans and the freshly baked bread rolls, which lay bare like small round bellies in the ripped paper bag on the kitchen table, put her in a weekend mood. It was only at the weekends that she allowed herself the luxury of eating warm bread rolls with cold butter.

You had to mind your figure at her age, and in her profession—as a doctor. Despite advising her patients to exercise for at least thirty minutes a day, she wasn't too good at doing it herself.

The sun fell on the kitchen counter, making the coffee pot glint as the light hit the glass. She put it on the table in the dining nook. An odour that didn't belong to her usual pleasant Saturday morning "smell" bothered her nostrils. The ashtray from last night was still full. When she threw Danny's cigarette butt into the bin, she thought of him again. He was going home today. It pained her inside. That and the fact he had rejected her. He still loved his wife in Zealand, even though they were divorced. The jealousy gnawed at her. A familiar feeling that she hated and hadn't felt for a long time. Because she hadn't been able to form a lasting relationship with a man. She began to feel the hatred again, too. Now it was aimed at Danny's wife. If it weren't for her, she was sure Danny would have slept with her last night. Then they would be sitting here together now, eating bread rolls. Her sister also came to mind. It was all her fault. Then she pulled herself together and reminded herself she was a doctor—and a psychologist. But they were also often the ones who couldn't look after themselves and their own emotions, just like the smith's horse and the shoemaker's wife always having the worst shoes.

She took a bite of the roll and stared out into the garden. The neighbours had hoisted the Danish flag, as tradition warranted on birthdays. *Must be one of the kids' birthdays.* It fluttered lightly in the wind between the treetops. There was a birthday soon in her own family, too. The nice family of doctors, who held birthday celebrations in groups because of the skeletons of the past, which weren't allowed to fall out of the closet. But she wouldn't be able to be in their company anymore. Never.

The egg-timer rang, pulling her back to the present with a startled jerk. The soft-boiled eggs were done. She took the pot off the stove, fished up an egg with a tablespoon, and placed it in a wooden egg cup decorated with hand-painted daffodils. She cracked it with a teaspoon. The blow was too hard, and the runny egg yolk trickled out onto the table. "Shit!" She wiped the yellow sticky mass up with a piece of kitchen roll. "Why am I thinking about that again now?" she muttered bitterly. Now she had got her life together, given up hope, and got used to the idea of living alone.

She flicked quickly through the newspaper and tried to concentrate on the articles while she ate breakfast. Nothing caught her interest, until she saw the image of the girl. A tragedy greater than her own. Gitte Mikkelsen. She read the article, but it didn't tell her anything she didn't already know. Something clicked in her brain, but like last night, she couldn't quite reach it. It remained a black undeveloped strip of negatives with silhouettes she could glimpse but not see clearly. She stared at the girl's happy face. It seemed so familiar. Then it struck like lightning. She got up so forcefully that the chair almost tipped backwards.

The first sight that met her in the surgery was the dark chipboard. It made her jump a little with surprise; she had completely forgotten it was there and initially perceived it as a dark shadow. She had put duct tape around the windowsill so the rain wouldn't get in.

Being in the clinic was uncomfortable. Knowing a stranger had broken in. Had rummaged through her personal belongings. Seen something so private. She still felt the presence of something alien.

She noticed the filing cabinet had been broken open and closed again so as not to be immediately detected. Apparently, the police officer from last night hadn't discovered it, either. She quickly pulled out the drawer with the folders, searching with growing desperation. Why hadn't she thought of it before? That was what her subconscious had been trying to tell her all night.

47

The door to her room was closed. She should be happy. It was Saturday. The summer holidays had just begun. School and homework lay far in the future, and in a week, they were to travel to Hungary. It was a new destination Mum and Dad wanted to experience. Sofie, Line, and Sebastian weren't going there; they were going to Bulgaria for the holidays. They were too big to want to go on holiday with their parents now, Mum explained. Amalie felt she was, too, but she had to go. When you're only ten years old, you're too young to be home alone, Dad said. She sulked even more. She wouldn't be treated like a little baby.

She tried to concentrate on reading, but she couldn't. Her thoughts kept wandering off, and she forgot what she had just read.

Her computer pinged a new email alert, making her put down the book. She sat for a long time looking angrily at the computer. If it were an email from him, she wouldn't reply, she decided. He was weird. All the things she'd had to do to be allowed to see the horse. She had begun to doubt there was a horse, even though he had shown her the saddle and stirrups. But she couldn't be bothered anymore, even if he looked at her and said she was beautiful, and even if he was nice to talk to. The only one who didn't treat her like a child. But if she wasn't allowed to go horse riding, it didn't matter anyway.

The email *was* from him. She was sitting right on the edge of the chair. Unconsciously, she grew nervous as she read. She clenched her hands, which were damp with sweat. The email started, as usual, with how beautiful she was, and how she would become a beautiful girl with perfect curves. She didn't quite understand what he meant by that, but it sounded like a compliment coming from an adult, so she took it as the truth. Most children today were too fat, he wrote. He had found a new day they could meet, and he promised the horse would be saddled up, ready for her, in the yard when she arrived. She hurried to close the email tab when there was a knock at her bedroom door, and her mum entered soon after.

"What are you doing, Amalie?"

Tove Bang sat down on the sofa bed and looked seriously at her daughter.

"Nothing."

"We need to have a talk, honey. I can feel something's wrong. What is it? You're not sick, are you?"

She shook her head.

"Is it the summer holiday in Hungary?" She waited for the answer, but Amalie sat looking down at her bare knees. She had gone no further than putting on her underwear.

"I know it's boring for you that your siblings aren't coming with us. But that's how it is when children are nearly adults. At that age, they'd rather go on holiday on their own. I'm sure we'll have fun anyway." Mum smiled, but Amalie didn't look at her.

She wanted to tell her everything but wasn't sure how mad her mum would be. "Mum, why can't we move to the country?" she pleaded instead.

"Oh, not the horse again! You have to understand we can't . . ."

Amalie had heard it so often that she couldn't be bothered hearing it again. She turned her back and pretended to do something on the computer. Her mum sighed loudly behind her and didn't say anything for a while.

"Have you made a new friend we don't know about?" she asked suddenly.

Amalie turned towards her abruptly. "Why?"

Her mum had a severe frown on her forehead, though she didn't have many wrinkles. Not like the mums of her classmates. She thought Mum was attractive. She was wearing a little bit of lightly coloured lipstick and some mascara on her lashes, the same way Sofie and Line always did. Amalie was too young for that, too, she was told. She hoped she would look like her mother when she grew up. Her blond hair was gathered in a ponytail, making her look even younger.

"Well, it's just I've noticed your clothes are often very dirty. You never play outside, so I thought . . . Where were you yesterday afternoon?"

She looked away. "I was with Nanna; I told you."

"Yes, that's what you said. But Nanna says something else. What are you up to, Amalie?" Her mum sounded angry, and Amalie realised she had been caught lying. "I've also noticed you're taking a lot of showers at the moment—several times a day. You don't usually do that, either," her mum continued, then she suddenly smiled.

"Have you fallen in love? Do you have a boyfriend?" There was something teasing in her voice that offended Amalie. She felt the tears welling in her throat. He had asked her that, too. Whether she had done *that* and whether she had a boyfriend. Her lower lip began to tremble.

"Why can't we just move far away? Near Grandma, where I can have my own horse." She was becoming weepy now.

"What do you mean *your own horse*? Do you know someone who has a horse?"

Her mum squatted down in front of her and took her face between her hands. She looked deep into her eyes. She saw the tears clearly now.

"Oh, honey, you're crying." She hugged her, and when Amalie smelled the safe scent of her mum and felt her protective arms, she suddenly didn't feel quite so grown-up. She started to cry. Without really wanting them to, the words spilled out of her, interspersed with sobbing and sniffing as her mum held her, listening and stroking her hair.

48

Anne couldn't lie in, despite it being Saturday. It wasn't that she didn't want to. She had felt as heavy as a boulder when the alarm clock had rung at eight o'clock, and she had almost fallen over a moving box when, sleep-drunk, she had tried to find her way to the bathroom. She hadn't even unpacked in her new apartment before having to move again. It annoyed her this time because she actually liked this apartment, even though it was old, and the kitchen and bathroom were the epitome of seventies perfection. The bathroom had olive-green tiles with a floral motif and matching olive-green sanitary ware, of course. The floor was grey-striped terrazzo, and cold; there was no underfloor heating. From the windows in the living room, she had a view of the City Hall tower, the famous landmark of Aarhus, which she didn't consider particularly beautiful. But the sound from the bells of City Hall and the cars on Frederiks Allé made her feel at home—as though she were in Copenhagen.

Now she enjoyed the cold floor and being cooled down at night after the heatwaves. It was balmy in the small bedroom, where the sun baked on the façade until it set on the horizon. When it did actually make an appearance, it was unfortunately often in the evening. She had slept in only a pair of little knickers, yet she had sweated so much that the bedding was damp. It had been difficult to fall asleep after covering the murder of the woman in Gammel Egå. There was something spooky about that house. Something that reminded her of something, she just didn't know what. Probably a horror film she had once seen in the cinema with Esben. There had also been something very contradictory in the house's decor. She had noticed a little room with a modern computer on an oak desk. What did a ninety-year-old want a computer for? It seemed so out of place compared to the rest of the house's old-fashioned decor. Maybe it wasn't hers. A son or daughter perhaps? Anne took off her knickers and slipped into the shower.

After a quick shower, she put on some clothes and looked at her watch. She was due to be in the new apartment to meet the landlord in two hours. She lit a cigarette and looked around at the mess. Where was she supposed to start? Luckily, there wasn't much to pack, given she had never *un*packed. Just the laptop on the table, some clothes lying around, and her toiletries in the bathroom. She had rented the apartment furnished, as she didn't own a bed, a table, or even a single chair. It was old and worn furniture. Not pretty. But she wouldn't be able to thrive in an *Ideal Home* house. The new apartment she was moving into was for rent for a year, the quickest she had been able to find. It was furnished, too, and lay outside the city centre. A longer commute to the newspaper.

She found an empty cardboard box and started stuffing it, cigarette dangling from her lips, while she thought about Thygesen's enthusiasm for her work last night. It was late when she had left the office, but Thygesen had still been at work, and he was completely different when it was only the two of them. He had praised her quick efforts, completely embarrassing her. Praise wasn't something she was accustomed to. But she had also been the first on the scene. The other journalists had only started to show up when she and Kamilla had left, and the party was almost over. Today, the article *Mysterious Murder in Gammel Egå* would be on the front page together with Kamilla's photo of the white body bag fastened with straps to the gurney. All thanks to the good source she had made, despite it not being entirely legal. A friend by the name of Nordic, who had come into possession of a system, a kind of scanner, that could access the police radio frequency and intercept conversations between squad cars and the police station. She had even listened to it herself. For her, it had mostly been crackle, but Nordic could distinguish the words. He contacted her whenever something interesting came up. Like the murder last night.

When everything was loose in the cardboard box, she took the vacuum cleaner and went through the apartment. She had to stop for a moment to tap the ash off the cigarette. As she leaned over the table to reach the ashtray, she saw a private email had arrived in her inbox. Rolling the ciga-rette against the edge of the ashtray to get rid of the excess ash, she thought about who it might be. Not many people had her private email address.

The carpets were once again in the same condition as she had received them—evenly stained. She made a cup of coffee and sat down at the com-puter. Her hand shook as she opened the email. She breathed a sigh of relief. It was just an email from a colleague at the newspaper in Copen-hagen who wanted to hear how things were going in the provinces. Anne read it but waited to reply until she had more time. That wasn't going to be a short one. A lot more went on here in the sticks than they realised in the Big Smoke.

With the cardboard box containing her essentials, and the laptop under her arm, she went out into the hall. The other moving boxes were stacked up here, waiting to be dragged to the car. There was a small stack of adver-tisements under the letterbox, but as she gathered them up to throw them in the bin, a letter fell to the floor. Although it had been a long time since she had seen his handwriting, she recognised it immediately, even from a distance. She picked up the letter. Her name and address were written on the front, and as if he knew she wouldn't open the letter, he had written something on the back of the envelope. There was no sender, only: *I know where you live!* She gasped with fear. She furiously ripped the envelope and its contents in two, then once more in quarters. She tossed the pieces of paper in the bin and ran down the stairs with the first cardboard box.

As she put the last box into the back seat of the car, she glanced up at the window on the fourth floor. She smiled. Never again. Never again would he find her. She was moving again, and this time no one would know where.

49

Dennis woke up at a friend's. His mouth was as dry as sandpaper and tasted like sewage. His breath had to stink, too. He held a cupped hand up in front of his mouth and breathed into it to smell, grimacing at the result. Gently, he opened his eyes to narrow cracks, but immediately closed them again when the sunlight penetrating the thin curtains nearly blinded him. He turned to the other side and heard an empty beer bottle rolling across the wooden floor.

Torben had made up an old mattress on the floor for him—one he used for overnight guests. Torben's arm with the snake tattoo on the bicep hung limply down from the bed next to him. His fingers were yellow with nicotine stains. Dennis envied his buddy. They had met in primary school. Neither had amounted to much since then, but at least Torben had his own apartment and worked in a warehouse at one of the supermarket chains in the city.

Dennis's eyes slowly got used to the sunlight. The apartment wasn't very big and, quite frankly, it was shit. Yellow water stains had penetrated the ceiling tiles and spread over most of the ceiling. A bucket stood under the worst stain. The wet summer was doing its part to make the stains grow bigger. But better this than living at home with his parents, Dennis thought. He spotted his jeans tossed on the floor next to the mattress and fished a packet of cigarettes out of the pocket. Freedom, that was what having your own place meant. Freedom to do as he pleased. He lit the cigarette and smiled as he laid his head back on the pillow and blew the smoke up towards the ceiling. His parents were probably beside themselves now, given he hadn't come home last night. Or they didn't give a shit. The cigarette smoke reached Torben in bed; he began to move.

"What the hell! Are you lying here smoking? Put that bloody thing out!" Torben sat up in bed and rubbed his eyes. They were red and narrow, with yellowish sleep in the corners. He looked around and found the ashtray on the windowsill, reached for it, and threw it on Dennis's mattress. It nearly hit him in the head.

"Put the fucking thing out!"

"Yeah, yeah, yeah! Why the fuck can't I smoke in here?" Dennis twisted around and threw the cigarette into the ashtray.

"Look at this dump. It's a fucking fire hazard."

"Not with the fucking wet ceiling." Dennis laughed.

Torben pulled on his worn jeans and went out to the cramped toilet, his upper body bare, while he messed up his bristly blond hair. His urine splashed loudly in the toilet bowl. "For fuck's sake! What do I look like? What the hell were we doing last night?" he roared as he caught sight of himself in the dirty mirror over the sink with its dripping tap and rust stains.

From the mattress, Dennis sniggered. "I can't remember, but it was fun. God, is it almost one o'clock?" He struggled to sit up and put on his watch. His head felt like it was expanding from within. "You don't have any aspirin, do you?"

He took the aspirin with a sparse breakfast consisting of a slice of toast with butter and a cup of tea.

"Do you not have any sliced ham or anything, man?"

"You're not at your mum's house now. If you want ham, the butcher's just around the corner," his friend retorted.

Dennis only sought him out when things were bad at home. Really, the chair in front of the computer in his room was the only place he liked to be. If only the old fogies weren't there, too. His mother was driving him round the twist with her rebukes and her coldness. But hitting him with a wet tea towel was the last straw. The limit.

"I have to be at work by two; should you not be getting home to Mother now?" said Torben viciously, throwing the cups in the kitchen sink.

That's how they were, his drinking buddies. When there were no more beers or hash on the table and the party was over, they weren't friends. If only they knew what he had done. His member throbbed, hardening at the thought so it hurt. Then they might look up to him a little and show a little respect. Still, he didn't dare brag about it. Not even to them.

He got off the bus on the main road and slunk home with an empty feeling in his gut and a full feeling in his head. He hated the little shithole of a city where everyone knew each other. Every now and then, he saw faces behind the curtains in the houses along the main road. *Look, there's Hansen's lad. He was probably out drinking himself into a stupor again. Did he steal something this time?* he imagined them whispering to each other. He wished he lived in a big city, where no one cared about each other, and he could do whatever he wanted.

The three steps up to the front door were the worst. The hall stank of something fried that made him heave, thanks to his hangover. Then her voice cut through the smell and intensified the nausea: "Dennis! Is that you, dear?"

50

Of course the sun wasn't shining now that it was Saturday and he had time off to enjoy it. But it wasn't raining, either. It was rather balmy, so he had lured Irene into having a late breakfast on the garden table under the copper beech. The towels were ready on one of the garden chairs. He was going down to Ballehage sea baths later to take a dip. He let go of his thoughts so easily when he was floating around in the water.

He was dressed in khaki shorts and a white T-shirt with a small black Kappa logo on the chest. It had been a late night, after the murder in Egå, so he didn't feel quite on top. A long day. He hadn't made it in time for Irene's dinner, either, and he had completely forgotten to call her. Still, she smiled warmly as she set a glass of freshly squeezed orange juice in front of him and sat down in the chair opposite. He was watching Marianna, who was wearing a warm jumper and playing with her doll's pram. They looked like little dolls themselves at the age of five. The thought made his hairs stand on end. Doll child. God forbid Marianna ever calling herself that.

"What is it, Rolando?" asked Irene. She never changed his name to Roland. She had married an Italian—and so it should be. "Are you thinking about the murder of the girl?"

He didn't need to answer; she could usually tell what he was thinking. Twenty-eight years of marriage accounted for a lot, but Irene's ability to understand other people's problems was probably also a contributing factor.

He nodded. They had talked about it late into the night—how the case was affecting him, and how he was desperate to find the perp. More than ever. His gaze fell on the newspaper. The image the photographer had taken really captured the sober tone. The mood he had felt in the house last night. The mood of death. The flash had lit up the white body bag, so it was in full focus. The trees behind the gurney were almost black in the dark, yet with the depth that let you know someone could be hiding in the shadows. Had the murderer been watching? That was the feeling he'd had since. He peered several times into the dense trees and sensed there was someone in there watching him. He didn't link the murder of Olga Halgren to the murder of Gitte Mikkelsen, so he had passed the case on to his colleague Inspector Morten Holsted. He had enough to do with a child's murder and a kidnapping. There was still no trace of Louise. They were completely high and dry.

"Marianna's much better. Cold isn't as bad anymore," said Irene, placing a thin slice of cheese on half a bread roll without butter. The words tore Roland back to everyday life.

"That's good. She looks better, too." He waved back to the little girl who had spotted her grandad and was waving at him with both hands. She continued to dress her doll. "Is Rikke going to collect her today?" he asked.

"She's coming late afternoon. You're staying home, aren't you?" Irene replied hopefully, her mouth full of bread. The wind blew her hair down over her dark brown eyes. She pushed it behind her ear with an elegant motion that ended up sliding down her neck. He always had loved her elegance. All her movements reminded him of caresses. Italians had a reputation for preferring blonds, but that wasn't true at all. It was Irene's dark, entrancing appearance he had fallen for.

"Yes, I have the day off. It's Saturday." He smiled. "My only plan is to look into Brabrand Cemetery a little this afternoon. Gitte Mikkelsen's being buried today. But I'll hurry back." But just as the words were out, the mobile phone he had placed on the garden table rang. He took it and listened.

"It's the station," he whispered to Irene, who looked at him questioningly. She sighed. The conversation was short. Roland nodded a few times and ended up promising to go in. He looked at her apologetically and gave her a quick kiss on the forehead when he got up. She was obviously disappointed, but she didn't say anything.

"I have to, Irene," he said with regret in his voice. "A mother called. Her daughter's been sexually abused by a man she met on the internet. She can give a detailed description of him. I'm sure we have him now!"

51

Kamilla opened the door to the young man shyly ringing the doorbell. Thygesen had immediately sent his nephew, a computer genius, over when he had heard her computer had crashed after the electricity had gone down.

It wasn't hard to see he was Ivan Thygesen's nephew. They had the same plump facial features, and eyes that almost disappeared in their high cheeks. But the eyes looking through the lenses of the Björn Borg thick, black-framed glasses were attentive. The rest of his body bore evidence to his sedentary occupation and meals of a Coca-Cola and a burger between crisps and coffee. His complexion lacked fresh air and sun, and he smelled of garlic salami when he spoke.

"Asbjørn," he offered summarily, holding out his hand. It was like clutching a lump of dough.

"Kamilla," she replied just as briefly, directing him into the study.

"That's the one." She pointed to the computer as though it were guilty of a crime.

"Ah, a Mac," he exclaimed with awe in his voice. "I know more about PCs, but . . ."

He sat down in Kamilla's office chair, which at once seemed like a high-chair. His buttocks spread out over the seat, which looked far too small.

She left him in peace to look at the computer while she made a new pot of coffee. There was still some left of the morning coffee Danny had brewed for her. When had he gotten up? Why hadn't she heard it? He should have woken her. She had woken with the feeling of having had a good dream. An intimate dream. At first, she thought it had been a dream, until she saw the imprint of his head on the pillow next to her, the crumpled sheet, and she faintly smelled the scent of him and of herself. But he had left and promised to call her as soon as he was home in Klampenborg. It was on the note he had placed under the insulated coffee pot.

She had just finished breakfast and was in the middle of reading Anne's article when Asbjørn had rung the bell. It was lucky he could come so quickly, and on a Saturday.

When the coffee was ready, she poured it into a mug and went in and set it next to him on the desk. He nodded thankfully and immediately took a large sip.

"The flashing question mark means the computer can't find the operating system. Everything's been deleted from your computer," he said. "Hopefully you still have all the system and program discs?"

"Deleted! Can a power outage do that?" mumbled Kamilla, thinking momentarily about where she had stored those discs. She knew they had to be somewhere; she would never throw out something like that. There were floppy discs and CDs somewhere, including all the old versions of Photoshop—all the way back to version 1.0.

"This wasn't caused by the electricity going out," said Asbjørn, taking another gulp of coffee from the mug. "The contents were deleted using the uninstall program by someone who knew what they were doing."

Kamilla staggered a little and sat down on the edge of the desk.

"That doesn't make any sense, it's only me who . . ."

She remembered the fuses for the two bedrooms hadn't been loose in the box. Only now did it dawn on her the living room fuse must have been deliberately loosened by whoever had been inside the house. The power hadn't gone in the two smaller rooms—one of which was her office, the other her bedroom. She remembered the feeling of someone being in the living room. The soil on the floor she had blamed Tarzan for. She hugged her arms to herself, like she had to stop them from shaking.

"I'd be happy to install it all for you again if you get me the discs," Asbjørn continued as if he hadn't noticed her panic.

She got up slowly and opened the safe, where she remembered everything of value was hidden. She found the right discs and handed them to him. She didn't know what else to do. Should that kind of thing be reported to the police?

Asbjørn looked busy, so she went back to the kitchen and sat down. Someone had loosened the fuse so the light had disappeared in half the house, and had gone into her office and deleted everything on her computer. The office couldn't be seen from the hall, so she hadn't been able to tell what was going on in there. The door was usually closed, too. Who would do that kind of thing? Who would want to delete the contents of her computer?

Not long after, Asbjørn appeared in the kitchen. She hadn't heard him sneaking in, in stockinged feet. Beads of sweat were on his forehead, and his hands were stuck awkwardly in his trouser pockets.

"That's all done," he said in his clipped style. "I hope you didn't have anything of value on it. And you remembered to make a backup—most people forget to do that." Kamilla gloated that she wasn't "most people." She backed up the most important files regularly.

"Only my emails, but they're not that important." She smiled. "Could this have been a bug—a system error, I mean?" she asked in a fresh attempt to eradicate the idea someone else had been inside her house.

"I doubt it. But like I said, I mainly know PCs. I'm not exactly sure how Macs behave, but I can look into it," he said, hitching up his trousers.

"No, don't worry about it. Thanks, Asbjørn. You'll send me an invoice, won't you?"

He shook his head and explained to her Ivan had already taken care of it. Employee service, he had said.

Asbjørn was barely out the door before the doorbell rang again. Initially, she thought he had forgotten something. But it was Majken, who entered the hall and looked completely beside herself.

"Good, you're home, Kamilla. I've discovered something terrible," she gasped, as though she had run all the way to Mejlbyvej.

"Come in. What happened?" She got an extra cup and poured some coffee for Majken when she sat down at the table.

"I had a break-in last night," she said, adding two spoons of sugar to her coffee.

Kamilla hadn't seen her use sugar before, so wondered whether she had made the coffee too strong. She was about to reply that Danny had told her about the burglary, but for some reason, she didn't want to tell Majken

Danny had been here. That he had spent the night. Feeling like a traitor, she discreetly looked around to see whether he had left any belongings she should have removed.

"Was anything stolen?" she asked, trying to seem like she didn't know anything.

"I didn't think so, at first, but then I discovered a file's gone." She drank the coffee, seeming restless.

"Which file?" Kamilla asked, sitting down.

"Gitte Mikkelsen's file. I remembered she was a patient of mine last summer, but her medical records have been stolen."

"Shouldn't you go to the police?" asked Kamilla, wondering whether she should do the same.

Majken gestured with her hand. "I can do it on Monday," she said.

"But isn't it a little strange Gitte Mikkelsen's file was stolen?"

"Yeah, I was thinking the same thing. I panicked. Maybe other files are missing, too. I haven't gone through all the medical records yet. Maybe I should do that before talking to the police. Best not to make a mountain out of a molehill, I mean. It might be random."

"How come you only remembered Gitte was a patient now?" Kamilla asked, fearing it sounded accusatory.

"It was a coincidence really. I remembered seeing Gitte Mikkelsen's name in my filing cabinet the other day, but the name didn't register with me at the time."

"Don't you remember her at all?"

"I have so many patients, especially children. Unfortunately. It was only when I saw the photo in the newspaper that it began to dawn on me why the name was familiar."

"Didn't you see her picture on the TV? They showed it again last night. And a picture of Louise, too," said Kamilla, remembering she herself hadn't seen the picture of Gitte before last night. Ida and Allan Mikkelsen hadn't wanted to give any of their photos to the newspaper. They had told Anne they thought it pointless to put her on show. But another reporter must have persuaded them.

"No. And I completely forgot about it last night. What with the break-in and all . . ." She paused as she stared down at her coffee cup. "And then Danny came by," Majken said, her eyes turning sad.

Guilt gave Kamilla a cramp in her stomach.

"It was a pity you didn't get to say goodbye to him. He went back to Copenhagen this morning," she continued and looked at Kamilla.

"Klampenborg," Kamilla corrected with a little smile.

"Oh yes, Klampenborg." Majken gestured indifferently.

"Unfortunately, he couldn't stay the night." She blew on the cup to cool the coffee before drinking with narrowed eyes, as if she had burned herself anyway. "Apparently, he had to hurry home to his wife. Good riddance. I don't care!" she continued, rolling her eyes in indignation. Then she caught sight of Kamilla's face. "What's up, Kamilla?"

"Nothing."

"I know you. There's something wrong! What is it?" Then, slowly it began to dawn on her.

"You *did* say goodbye to him! Didn't you?"

She nodded. Not saying anything was one thing; lying when asked directly was something else entirely.

"When?"

"He came by last night." Her voice sounded hesitant and a little distant.

"But, he was with me . . ." Majken put the cup down so hard that it clinked against the saucer. "So quite late then!"

"Yes, it was quite late, but I was still up. I'd had a really unpleasant experience . . ."

"When did he leave?" Majken's voice grated like metal. Hard and as sharp as a blade that cut across Kamilla's words with a slash.

"I don't know. Sometime this morning. I wasn't up. Majken . . . ?"

She reached for Majken, who pulled back her arm with a quick jerk and got up. The expression in her eyes made Kamilla feel even more like a traitor.

"Don't be angry with me. It just happened. Danny said there was nothing between the two of you," she said in an unhappy voice.

Majken didn't answer. She got up and left without deigning to glance at her.

52

Jesper Ingemann was sitting in Roland's office again. It was otherwise rare for Roland to be in the police station on a Saturday. But after Tove Bang had reported her daughter Amalie had been subjected to sexual abuse, the situation required it.

The girl had pointed out Jesper without hesitation from the album of mugshots of all the paedophiles East Jutland Police knew about. Roland had to form a small team to deal with some of the overtime, despite it practically being a forbidden word after the EU summit, which had consequences for a long time afterwards regarding time in lieu. That was not to happen again, so overtime was closely monitored, which, on the order of the police commissioner, had to be regularly counterbalanced with time off.

These cases needed to be solved soon. After all the rapes, women felt unsafe walking the streets alone in the evenings. Were they now supposed to be afraid of sending their children out to play and to birthday parties, too? And a new murder on top of it all. The elderly, who felt unsafe already about walking the streets, now didn't dare to be by themselves in their own homes, either. So better to sacrifice a Saturday morning, even if Rikke was coming to collect Marianna, probably with a box of chocolates or a bottle of Italian wine, as was her habit whenever they looked after their grand-daughter. She didn't need to do so. It was enjoyment enough to watch the little girl, even though he hadn't been home much this time. He hoped to make it to Gitte Mikkelsen's funeral and be back in the house in Højbjerg before Rikke arrived.

"So here we are again," he announced unnecessarily to Jesper Ingemann, who didn't look at all nervous. But they hadn't told him about the overwhelming evidence they had this time.

He lit a cigarette, despite deciding to give them up several times during the week. Quitting them had become so popular. Smokers were becoming an unpopular group, and politicians were threatening a smoking ban more and more in the debate. The smell of smoke rose in his nostrils. He inhaled greedily. He couldn't do without cigarettes when working on solving a case. Jesper took one from the packet, too, when he pushed it towards him.

Roland looked at the glow of the cigarette, then at Jesper. After all his years in the police, questioning the guilty *and* the innocent, he had gradually learned what to look for. He had always sensed Jesper was guilty. But was he guilty of Gitte Mikkelsen's murder and Louise Poulsen's abduction, too?

"I don't really understand what you want with me," Jesper said confidently. "I know you've spoken to my colleagues and my dentist, verifying what I told you last time. My wife and kids can confirm it all, too. Haven't you spoken to Sussi?"

Roland got up and walked over to the window, his back to Jesper—a technique he often used. An attitude that could be interpreted by the interrogatee in several ways. Experience had shown him some people began to speak as soon as he wasn't sitting, staring them in the face. He ignored Jesper's comment but knew well why he was saying it. He was an ordinary man with a wife, children, a job. A profile that didn't match that of a man who murders a little girl, throws her in a skip, then abducts her classmate who might be able to identify him. But Roland knew better. There wasn't necessarily a profile to fit that. When he sat opposite Kristoffer Kjær, he had no doubt he was facing an unlucky teenager whose brain didn't function as it should. It was far worse with those where you couldn't tell. Psychopaths, for example. Their traits could so easily be confused with those of a neurotypical human being. A person who was exceptionally popular, good at making friends, ambitious, confident, and self-assured. It could be any ambitious businessperson or politician. Even himself, some people would probably think. Was Jesper the type who could identify other people's weaknesses and exploit them to his own advantage? Cold and calculating?

He remained by the window, letting him sweat. Jesper moved uneasily in the chair behind Roland, and it delighted him. He looked at the cars in the police station car park. When the window was open, he could hear the noise from the Port of Aarhus if the wind was coming from that direction. The stench from the oil mill used to send a nauseating odour into the station, but that had changed after new owners had taken over. And then, for a while, there had been the unbearable noise of the renovations of the police station's ground floor, including a new main entrance. The old familiar revolving door was no more. Permission hadn't been granted for the desired copper canopy over the new entrance, to everyone's great disappointment.

"You could at least tell me why you've brought me in on a Saturday! We were about to visit family." Jesper broke the silence that had obviously become too overbearing for him.

Roland turned and looked at him with narrowed eyes. "Do you spend a lot of time talking to children on the internet?" he asked loudly and directly.

"No, not at all." The hand with the cigarette shook slightly. He tapped ashes into the ashtray to hide it.

"So you don't have a Hotmail account called Teddy Bear, then?"

Jesper laughed, his mouth crooked. "What rubbish! Of course I don't. That's childish!"

Roland sat down noisily in the chair opposite him and opened the folder lying on the table. He found a picture of Amalie and laid it in front of Jesper.

"And you haven't seen her before, either, have you? Her name's Amalie Bang."

All the colour drained from his face. He shook his head as he stared at the picture of the blond girl.

"And you don't have a horse, do you?"

The question tipped Jesper over the edge. Furious, he got up with a jerk and snorted the words out. "What did she say? You don't believe her, do you? Children have active imaginations. It's the parents' fault. Maybe she's so desperate for a horse that she . . ."

"Cycled all the way out to your late mother's house at True Forest to see it?" interrupted Roland angrily. "Sit down, Ingemann. You've always underestimated the work of the police. Do you think we can't easily check who owns the house you lured the girl to? Do you think we're stupid?" The latter he shouted so loudly that Jesper jumped, landing down in the chair again like stone.

"Your mother died a few months ago, and you're trying to sell the house. Practically everyone can find that information. Obviously, you have my condolences for your mother," said Roland in a calmer voice. "One of my officers is talking to your wife in another interview room here at the station right now, but I'd still like you to tell me, once again, where you were on Monday and Wednesday. I want to hear it minute by minute."

Jesper shook his head. He had completely clammed up, and Roland began to fear they weren't going to get anything out of him for the time being. Then came the words he had been waiting for: "I'm not saying anything until my solicitor gets here."

Once again, the trees were his shelter from being discovered. Through dark sunglasses, he followed the procession slowly, walking after the coffin carried by male members of the family. He couldn't see who it was clearly. His moist eyes and the sunglasses blurred his vision, and the distance was too great, too, but he dared not go nearer. The pressure in his chest grew. She was lying there, his little doll child, who he loved so much it hurt. But there had been no other way. She had asked for it. Like he had asked for it, too—his father.

Of course his little sister had tattled about the toads. Father had been mad, had shouted and screamed that all the toads were protected and how what he had done to them was a criminal offence. He had slapped him so it stung and left the imprint of five fingers on his cheek for several days afterwards. But he hadn't cried. Not even when he had stood at his grave, his little sister by the hand, as Grandmother had ordered while she held an umbrella over their heads. It had been raining heavily that day, and the hole had quickly filled with water. He had stared hatefully at the wooden box and felt nothing as it lowered into the black pit in the ground. He hadn't even felt the hatred anymore. He had never forgotten the splashing sound as the coffin plonked down. He had rejoiced. It had sounded like when the toads jumped into the algae-green water of the garden pond. In the end, it had all gone up to a higher entity. He had won. It was after the funeral that he had lost the desire to kill the toads. Not because his father had scolded and beaten him; he just didn't feel like it anymore. It was also after the funeral that it had all started to go wrong, as though his father's evil spirit had possessed him.

The trees overshadowed his view as the small coffin was lowered into the ground. He stood on his toes to get a better look. The coffin was white and adorned with flowers. He had sent a bouquet himself. He sobbed silently. He'd had no idea she was so loved. There were children in the procession. Her class-mates for sure. But one was missing. The thought made him look at his watch, then he took one last look at the graveyard before quickly walking away.

53

Kamilla moved a few tufts of grass around the marble stone and touched the gold letters of her son's name. She needed some fresh air and to calm her mind after Majken's visit. She hadn't imagined Majken would react so violently to Danny spending the night with her. She hadn't even been able to tell her *she'd* had a break-in, too. There were so many thoughts whirring around that soon she wouldn't know what was worse. Was it a coincidence they had both had burglaries that night? Did it have anything to do with the murder? The photos maybe. Was it someone trying to cover their tracks, or prevent them from moving on in the case?

A butterfly fluttered past confused, as though off course, and continued up over the bushes and on past the other graves. Kamilla got up and pulled her jumper tighter around her. It was cool, even though it was supposed to be summer.

She had just sat down on the bench when she saw Nina walking down the path between the graves. She saw her squat down and lay a bouquet on Rasmus's grave, then she got up and stood looking at the headstone for a long time. Kamilla thought she could just make out a little round belly under the summer jacket.

"Congratulations. Jan told me the happy news," she said as Nina sat down on the bench next to her. She walked and sat as if she were already heavily pregnant.

"It'll be good for Jan. He needs to get his mind off Rasmus."

"What's he doing?" Kamilla asked, trying not to express how she felt.

Nina lit a cigarette. "Jan's at home. He's cleaning. I'm not to exert myself physically in my condition," she said, sending her a tired smile.

Kamilla wondered at her smoking given her "condition." She tried to imagine Jan with a vacuum cleaner, but she couldn't. Apparently, there had been a change in his behaviour since she had been pregnant. They sat in silence for a while. She contemplated whether Nina was enjoying the silence, too. How different were they actually, when it came down to it? Nina had to be different—Jan had chosen her over his family.

"Was giving birth to Rasmus bad?" Nina asked, her voice anxious.

"Very, very painful," Kamilla said emphatically, seeing the corners of Nina's mouth pull as she took another drag of the cigarette. Kamilla felt a little sorry for her. She obviously loved Jan so much that she would do anything to make him happy, even this. Subject herself to the pain she feared and destroy her otherwise perfect model body. For a while, at least.

"But it'll all be worth it!" She looked at Rasmus's grave as she said it.

Nina laid her hand on Kamilla's. It felt awkward and she quickly pulled it back again. "You know my heart goes out to both of you—what happened to Rasmus," she said quietly.

Kamilla knew it well, but still, Nina had no idea what it was like to first lose her husband to a much younger woman and then to lose her son. She got up. The calm she had come here to find had evaporated.

"Jan found the guy who did it." Nina's words made her sit down again.

"He has? Where?"

"It turns out he's here in Jutland at the moment. I'm sure Jan will take him down," Nina replied triumphantly.

"What's he going to do?"

Nina shrugged indifferently. She took one last big puff of the cigarette, tossed the butt into the gravel, and stubbed it out with a pointed black shoe.

"But I can tell you this: the man to blame for his son's death isn't going to escape so easily." She searched for a new cigarette in the crumpled package.

"He didn't do it on purpose," Kamilla said meekly. She had never seen revenge as the answer.

"Are you defending your son's killer?" Nina looked at her with eyes full of contempt.

"No, of course not, but . . ."

"He was drunk, Kamilla. If he hadn't driven a car, it'd never have happened. Because of that, he's a killer. Not premeditated murder like with the little girl in the case you're working on. But still."

Kamilla stared ahead without thinking. She smelled the cypresses. A scent she hadn't cared for since her father's funeral, where the fragrance had set in as another sad reminder of him. But she had begun to like it again after many peaceful hours on the bench. Then the stench of smoke from Nina's cigarette took over. Kamilla got up and coughed.

"I think Jan should forget about revenge. What good is it?" she said, waving her hand in front of her nose. Nina didn't seem to notice the gesture. Or she did. Either way, she suddenly stubbed out the cigarette on the bench and threw it into the bushes.

"The idiot will get what he deserves—that's the benefit," Nina replied, fired up.

"Say hi to Jan and tell him to reconsider. After all, there's another child on the way," said Kamilla before leaving. Of course, Nina didn't get the irony of those words, either.

Kamilla went into her home office when she returned. Asbjørn hadn't turned off the computer, and the stench of garlic salami still hung in the air along with an irritating smell of his underarm sweat. She opened a window and sat down at the computer. Opening programs without anything stored in the many folders she had created was weird, but luckily she had backed everything up and was able to install it all again. She wished there was just one little glass of red wine left. She felt like opening a new bottle from the wine rack and submerging herself in the soothing effect as the alcohol made its way into her blood, but she decided to brew a pot of strong coffee instead.

There was a different atmosphere in the house now that she knew for sure someone had been inside and it wasn't Tarzan who had left soil on the floor. Had she really forgotten to lock the door? She felt silly as she walked out into the hall and tried the door handle. She had remembered this time.

Despite it being a little chilly, she sat out on the patio while she waited for the coffee to brew. The garden chairs were wet. She dried one with a tea towel. As if by magic, Tarzan stood in the middle of the lawn like he owned it all. She stroked him along his back as he affectionately rubbed against her trouser leg. He had apparently forgotten she had stepped on him last night.

"Oh, there you are, Tarzan. Where have you been all night?" she said.

Tarzan heard the car in the driveway before she did. The blue-black car practically glided into the yard. Danny stepped out.

"Danny!" she cried happily, waving to him through the bushes. He caught sight of her and waved back. He had a bouquet of red roses in one hand.

"You have to go through the house. I'll come through and open the door!" she shouted, running inside. When she opened the door, he pulled her into him and gave her a kiss on the mouth. Without letting go of her, he put the bouquet of roses up in front of her face so she could smell their sweet scent.

"For you," he said solemnly.

Kamilla found a vase in the corner cupboard in the hall, put the roses in water, and spread them out so the bouquet filled out more. Twenty red roses.

"Thank you, Danny. They're beautiful. But how come you're not in Zealand?" She set the vase on the coffee table and thought about how much flowers spruced the place up. It was rare she bought flowers for herself.

"I changed my mind and drove down to the marina instead, where I sat to think about things," he said as he took off his windbreaker and hung it up on a free arm of the coat stand. He rubbed his hands together as if he were freezing.

"What about a cup of coffee?" He heard the coffee machine spluttering as it finished in the kitchen. Kamilla got some cups.

"Let's go outside," she said, nodding at the patio door.

"Why didn't you wake me this morning?" she asked when they had sat down.

He helped her put the cups on the table.

"I couldn't wake you. You were sleeping so sweetly." He stroked her cheek with his hand and smiled.

"When are you going back?"

"Later this afternoon. I just missed you, and there's something I need to tell you."

Sparrows chirped in the treetops. A bumblebee buzzed heavily across the table. Kamilla poured the coffee and sat for a while looking at him. He didn't say anything as he stirred sugar into the coffee with slow, controlled movements.

"Were you and your wife married for a long time?" She suddenly felt like knowing more about him, and she listened quietly as he told her. She loved hearing him speak. A breeze rounded the nook, blowing his hair down onto his forehead. She smelled his aftershave. A pleasant masculine scent that reminded her of their night together.

Suddenly, he froze. She followed his eyes. Tarzan had stopped in the middle of the terrace. The cat stared at Danny with wide-open eyes and a hostile posture, as if wanting to hiss at him. The bright light turned his pupils into narrow streaks in his green eyes.

"Is that your cat?" He shuddered.

"Don't you like cats?" She laughed. "This is Tarzan. He's a runner. Seems to live a little everywhere around here. But one day he turned up at my door, looking like he wanted to tell me something." She looked lovingly at the cat.

"Tarzan," he repeated, laughing uncertainly as he followed the cat with his eyes until it disappeared under a bush in the garden.

"Yes, that's what Rasmus wanted to call his cat—if he'd had one." She tried to smile.

"I'm sorry about your son, Kamilla. I'd also like . . ."

She laid a finger on his lips to quieten him. She didn't want to talk about it. Right now, she only wanted to enjoy the safe feeling he gave her.

54

———————

Dark clouds climbed the horizon, giving everything below a grey and gloomy expression.

What's wrong with me? Majken had asked herself several times after she had left Kamilla in anger. *Why do I feel so angry and hateful again?* she thought as she rinsed the tablets down with a glass of cold water and stared out into the garden, where the bed of pink foxgloves blossomed in front of the conifers. She was ashamed of how she felt, but it wasn't something she could control. She leaned against the edge of the kitchen table as she tried to regain her common sense.

Images flickered like a quick film before her eyes. In front of the kitchen window, she fleetingly registered the postwoman in her red jacket at the letterbox. She was back in time. When she had first seen them together. Elizabeth's naked body, which she hadn't seen since she had bathed it when her little sister was much younger. Martin's, which she knew so well after all those years. A body she had thought belonged to her. The paralysing feeling. Her own shrill voice. *How long has this been going on?* Her sister's startled eyes. Martin's apologetic ones. Maybe she had known deep down inside that there had been something going on between them, but she had refused to believe it. The looks they sent each other. The random lingering touches. Their deep conversations. They had been married for a year, she and Martin. He had said they should have children. Move to a new house. Everything she had dreamed of when she had finished medical school. Their shared house with her medical clinic at one end and his accounting firm at the other. The kids in the middle. Their idyll. Seeing them together like that had made everything come crashing down around her. If she hadn't gone back for her purse, she might never have discovered their affair. Though, of course, she would have guessed it when they later got married, she thought ironically, letting out a sharp scornful laugh. And now Kamilla and Danny had done the same to her. They were no better than Elizabeth and Martin.

The phone in the living room had rung a few times, but she didn't feel like talking to anyone. When her mobile phone started playing its tune on the kitchen table, she answered it anyway.

"Oh, hi, Mum." She drank the last drop of water in the glass in one mouthful.

"No, I've just walked in the door." She sat down at the kitchen table so she could look out the window. The neighbour pushed a lawn mower. The scent of freshly cut grass reached her nostrils through the open window.

"Yes, Mum, of course I'll come. Is Tobias coming?"

Her mother fell silent. "No, he won't come, your brother's—you know . . ." She didn't finish the sentence. Majken had hoped he would come. They got on so well. But the hostility was so great not even their father's seventieth birthday could make him come home. Their father had never forgiven Tobias for choosing a path other than the medical profession, despite him having a good position in IT in Hamburg. Rumours he was "on the wrong side" and living with Jürgen in a fashionable apartment on Große Elbstraße hadn't helped the situation.

"How are you, Mum?" Majken knew they had to talk about something else. She settled herself in the chair. Her mother always had plenty to say about the family's achievements. Though she omitted Elizabeth and Martin's, of course, because she knew that would only bring stiff monosyllabic replies from Majken. That's how it was. But today was different. Today was the exception.

"Majken. I have great news for you." Her mother breathed nervously.

Majken imagined her grey hair that smelled of hairspray, the new perm for the coming family birthday celebration. A celebration Majken wouldn't attend until the following week, so as not to bump into Elizabeth and Martin. She knew her mum was sitting in the high-backed black leather chair by the phone with her legs crossed, nervously twisting the phone's cord around her ring finger with the large gold ring, while she stared at the view of Holbæk Fjord through the panoramic windows of the living room.

"Now promise me you won't get angry. But you need to hear this from family."

Majken held her breath, preparing for the worst.

"You're going to be an aunt in January!" Her mother exhaled once she had dropped the bomb. "Isn't that great?" The excitement of being a grand-mother shone so brightly in her voice that she couldn't possibly conceal it. Majken knew her mum feared her reaction, but none came. She felt noth-ing at all, neither joy nor anger. *The tablets. It must be the pills I just took.*

"Majken, isn't it time you made peace with them? My God, it's your sister!"

Not that again. She couldn't bear it. Not today.

"Forget it, Mum!" Majken wanted to hang up, but she didn't. Her mother wasn't to blame for what had happened then.

"But, honey. You're going to be the auntie of a new little person. You have to forgive them!"

No, the only fault of her mother's was that she always took her young-est daughter's side. *But what mother wouldn't take the side of the daughter who was about to present her with her first grandchild,* Majken thought ironi-cally. She slid slowly down from the kitchen counter and sat on the floor, her back against the cupboard doors. She wanted to answer that it wasn't about forgiveness. That she had forgiven them long ago. It was about losing trust and building that trust back up again. About not feeling like a victim whenever she saw Elizabeth and Martin.

"Majken? Are you still there?" Her mother's voice sounded worried.

Majken nodded until it dawned on her that her mum couldn't see her on the phone. "Yes, Mum. I'm still here."

She tried to imagine what their child would look like. Would it get Eliz-abeth's slightly curved nose, a little turned up, and Martin's cheeky hazel eyes? She saw the child in front of her. An innocent little child. Should it never know its aunt? She swallowed a lump.

"Would you like her phone number? You could call and say congratula-tions. Reach out, I mean." Her mother tried again.

Majken felt the anger. Why should *she* reach out? Had *she* done some-thing wrong? Was *she* the one who should apologise?

"See you next Saturday, Mum. Say hi to Dad. I'll call him on the big day." She didn't hear the answer before she hung up the phone. She sat on the kitchen floor for a long time, feeling nothing. Only emptiness. An emptiness that frightened her. She looked up at the ceiling and began to laugh quietly as the tears came. Imagine if her patients could see her now.

She got up and took a deep breath. *Aunt. I'm going to be an aunt.* It surprised her that she felt something. As if the word *aunt* sounded like something significant. She imagined a child reaching out to her and saying *aunt*. Auntie Majken. She tasted the words. They sounded good. But then the destructive thoughts returned. She should be the mother of Martin's child. The child shouldn't say *aunt*, but *mum*.

The fantasy image of the child brought her thoughts back to Gitte Mikkelsen. She tried to recreate the image of the girl sitting in the big chair opposite her last summer. Why had Gitte come to her?

There was more coffee left. She poured it into her cup and took it into the clinic. She looked for her reading glasses and found them on the windowsill next to the roll of tape. Again, her heart skipped a beat at the sight of the chipboard in the window. "Well, the glazier's coming tomorrow," she said loudly, setting the cup down next to the computer.

She had to admit again that she would soon need a new computer. It was taking too long to access the system. Maybe that's why she was still holding on to the filing cabinet with its hanging folders. She put on her reading glasses and typed in Gitte Mikkelsen's name.

The file opened with the girl's name, address, date of birth, and other personal information. Then came the text Majken had written up after the consultations. She had diagnosed her with stress. She vaguely remembered her conversations with Gitte as she started reading the notes on the screen. She remembered thinking she would be beautiful when she grew up. Back then, she hadn't known Gitte would never get that far because of a psychopath who should have been sitting in the chair instead.

Majken scrolled down the page. Gitte had only had three consultations. Her mother had stopped the treatment as, according to her, they weren't helping. Ida Mikkelsen worked as a nurse at Aarhus Hospital, where Majken was occasionally called in to talk to a child in the paediatric ward. It had been easy for Ida to get Majken's details, which is why she had come to her. It was Ida who had decided Gitte needed to see a psychologist. Her husband didn't know anything about it. He didn't believe children could develop stress, she had noted. The little girl's hands had been clammy, and she had seemed very tense during the first consultation.

Unfortunately, it wasn't uncommon for children to be diagnosed with stress nowadays. She had seen many children with different causes of stress—often down to adults' expectations of them. Weekdays, when both parents worked outside the home, meant children were very much on their own, and often had to make decisions they were not yet old enough to make. That alone could cause stress. Many of her young patients had only been praised and loved for what they could *do*, not for who they *were*. Many had been hospitalised with chronic headaches and stomach problems, due to their digestive systems stalling from stress.

Majken drank the coffee, which had become cold and bitter, and read on in the file.

Gitte had been plagued by anxiety attacks. A man who had come into their home had lifted her up onto his lap during dinner. He had touched her thighs under the table and brought his hand even further up. Majken straightened up on the chair as she read on. It had happened several times, even when Gitte was younger. She had been terrified of that man and hid whenever he came, but he had always found her under the pretext he was playing hide-and-seek with her. Majken had asked Gitte if the man had harmed her. Gitte had just shaken her head, her eyes dark and scared. Majken never got any further with the sessions because the treatment stopped, so she never found out how far this man had gone. It could take a long time before kids started to open up about that kind of thing. Especially a nine-year-old girl, as Gitte had been at the time. Ida Mikkelsen had rejected Gitte's revelations by saying it was the girl's active imagination. Their friends weren't like that.

Majken scrolled down the page in search of a name but found none. Only that it was one of Gitte's father's friends. Children tended not to register such names. *They remember better how we treat them.*

Preoccupied, she slowly took off her glasses. According to Section 152 of the Danish Penal Code, as a psychologist, she wouldn't be punished for sharing patient information if it were for the investigation of a serious crime, such as manslaughter, sexual assault, or grievous bodily harm. She put down her glasses before going back to the kitchen and making a call from her mobile.

55

Danny was on his way out to the car, a suitcase in each hand, when a red-haired man in a light windbreaker appeared in front of him, saying he wanted to talk to him. He was standing on the other side of a large puddle of water the violent storm, which had just passed, had made in the car park at Danhostel Aarhus.

He was already feeling very down. His conscience was gnawing at him. He reproached himself for not telling her, neither that night nor when he had visited her that morning. What could he say? I was the one who did it. I was the one who killed your son. He hadn't slept last night. Just lay there staring out into the darkness, holding her close to him. He was nearly about to fall asleep when he woke with a familiar start and caught sight of the shadow outside the window of her bedroom. Someone had been looking in. The cat? In the moonlight, he saw its silhouette through the curtain. Then it was gone again.

Ironically, he had rejected the psychologist's advice of seeking out the boy's parents. He had only come to Jutland again in an attempt to gain control of his mental imbalance by visiting the site of the accident and facing his discomfort. It seemed too incredible to be true.

"I have to catch a ferry," he replied curtly to the unknown man, throwing a suitcase in the boot. The man stood looking at him from a distance. The sun made his red hair look like a flaming fire.

"Can I help you with something?" he asked more accommodatingly, scowling at his watch. He didn't have time for this if he was to make the next ferry.

"Is that your car?" said the man, looking with sheer hatred at Danny's navy blue Opel Vectra.

"What do you mean?" Danny smiled, now putting the other case in the boot. When he slammed the door down, the man was standing right next to him. His face contorted with loathing.

"I think you're confusing me with someone else," Danny said calmly, taking the car keys out his pocket. But as he was about to get into the car, the man grabbed his collar.

"No, I'm fucking not. You're Danny Cramer, aren't you?" he hissed.

Danny didn't know whether to confirm it. He didn't seem to be very popular at the moment.

"Child killer," the man continued, shoving him hard against the car. Danny could easily have taken the relatively slender man with a single blow, but the tormented expression in his eyes made Danny think again.

"Did you come here to Jutland to murder children! You have a large dark car. A person fitting that description's wanted in connection with the murder of a little girl—have you reported yourself to the police?" He snarled. The pent-up anger in the man's voice stemmed all the way from his stomach and didn't fit with the man's stature at all.

Danny began to relax his muscles a little. The deranged man apparently thought he had something to do with the murdered girl in the skip. He wanted to find a scapegoat to punish.

"Are you the girl's father?" He tried to make his voice sound as understanding as possible. The man tightened his grip even more, and Danny noticed he would soon have to retaliate to avoid being hurt.

"No, he probably would have spat on you, you fucker. But I am a dad, too. Why did he have to die?" There was something tearful in the man's voice. Carefully, Danny tried to loosen the man's grip on his jacket collar.

"Wh-who?" Danny stammered, feeling the panic of having been delayed meaninglessly. He would have to drive fast now to make the ferry.

"Did you have that car a year ago, too?" asked the man. Some of the words were almost incomprehensible because his voice was mixed with tears. His nose had started to run. "Was that the car you were driving when you murdered my son?"

It finally dawned on Danny who the stranger was. He was just about to say something when the man loosened his grip and landed the first blow. It struck with much greater force than Danny had expected, sending him sliding down the car and toppling to the ground. The hard blows and kicks that followed non-stop sent him deeper and deeper into a hazy world, where all sound disappeared, and the fog was eventually replaced by darkness.

56

The smell of freshly baked bread rolls mixed with the smell of bad coffee, cigarettes, and Mac Baren tobacco.

The stragglers had found their seats, and the morning briefing had just begun. It was early Monday morning, and everyone had a little of the Monday blues, tired after the weekend.

The call from Majken Thorup meant Roland was seeing light at the end of the tunnel. And if those lights weren't the headlights of the oncoming freight train, he and his team could be on to an important lead in the murder case.

Jesper Ingemann had received help from his solicitor. There was sufficient evidence of sexual assault, but they couldn't pin murder and kidnapping on him. His alibi checked out, and the DNA didn't match. Roland had begun to fear the blood might not have anything to do with the killer. That the only way they would be able to convict Jesper would be to find the crime scene and obtain incriminating evidence. For now, he was remanded in custody.

Fortunately, answers had finally come from the analysis of the mud. The technical explanations didn't tell him much. The analysis showed it was heavy clay soil and, to cut a long story short, involved microorganisms, hydrogen, nutrients, and so on, which he intended to explain to his people in two words: "forest floor." Finally, a crime scene was in sight. Now the task was to comb every forest area in the vicinity of Brabrand with the hope of finding something. First, it concerned those with the same forest growth the samples had shown traces of—oak.

Time was of the essence. Crimes against children concerned the population, and police work was mocked from almost every side, even politically. The mayor had spoken personally to Superintendent Olsen about the matter. This was one of the worst cases Roland had investigated. At least, the one he had the hardest time letting go of in his spare time. But that was life as an inspector.

A police officer's brain worked around the clock to solve crimes, whether they wanted it to or not. A journalist's brain did the same. Anne Larsen kept the case alive with daily articles on the investigation, or the lack thereof, no doubt helping to emphasise how incompetent the police seemed.

"Progress Stalls in Gitte Murder and Missing Louise Probe" read the latest headline in bold type on the front page of the newspaper that had caught his eye over morning coffee. But at the same time, he had to reluctantly admit it was because of the press that people in the area had become aware of what was believed to be the killer's car. Despite the poor description, several people had confirmed they had seen what was apparently the same dark car, at the same time as the murder. Of course, they could also have read the appeal for the car on the East Jutland Police website, but people probably read newspapers more than police websites.

It was undoubtedly the same car seen in connection with Louise's disappearance. Roland was convinced the two crimes were related.

Mikkel Jensen had visited a woman in Brabrand who thought she would recognise the make and model if she saw a picture, but when he showed her pictures of the possible cars, she had still been confused and pointed out an Opel, a Honda, and a Mercedes.

Louise had been missing for five days. As time elapsed, the trail became colder. And what was the nature of the person she was with? Would the perpetrator panic and hurt her? It was a ticking time bomb. Was she already dead? Neither Gitte's bike, helmet, backpack, nor tights had been found. They had disappeared, just like Louise.

Kim Ansager had questioned Simon Agger, who had sobbingly convinced them he had simply found Louise's mobile phone. Simon had replaced the cover, but thankfully he hadn't managed to get hold of a new SIM card—that would have made tracking the phone even more complicated. Gitte's phone still hadn't been found.

Roland observed his trusted officers in the case. They were sitting around the table chatting to each other about their experiences over the weekend. It was different for the younger generation; they have so much else in their lives that a murder or two doesn't stand in the way of having fun at the weekend, which is how it should be.

Roland cleared his throat. There was immediate silence as everyone's attention turned to him. He reached across the table and grabbed the insulated coffee pot.

"Let's get started. We have a busy day ahead of us," he said, pouring coffee into the white plastic cup and passing the pot to Mikkel, who was sitting to his right.

"Did you go to the funeral on Saturday?" he asked, looking at Roland with tired eyes, revealing he must have had a little too much fun on his date at the weekend.

"I only made it for the end of the service. They'd just lowered the coffin into the ground when I arrived, then most people headed off. There was coffee and cake afterwards in the Mikkelsen's home, but I didn't think it appropriate to attend. It was only for immediate family."

The men at the table nodded knowingly, their faces serious. It was a difficult subject to swallow after a happy weekend. Roland had made it home to Højbjerg just as Rikke had been reversing the car out of the driveway with Marianna in the back seat, though he had managed to get a hug from his granddaughter and his daughter before they left. Tim was waiting for them. Some could fulfil their familial obligations. Others couldn't. Roland felt guilty when he saw the disappointment in the eyes of Rikke, Marianna, and Irene.

"What's new?" Morten Toft asked curiously as he poured coffee into his mug and passed the pot on to Kim.

"Majken Thorup, the doctor who had a break-in last Friday. She specialises in child psychiatry and remembered Gitte Mikkelsen was a patient of hers last summer. The file seems to have been taken during the burglary," Roland announced.

Toft whistled tellingly. "How did she only notice it now?"

Roland shrugged. He had asked himself the same question.

"She has so many patients, she can't remember them all." Those were Majken's own words. He sank his teeth into the crispy bread roll from the canteen and enjoyed the taste of the thick layer of butter that melted on his tongue and mixed with the taste of poppy seeds. He rinsed it all down with the coffee. Irene would have asked him to scrape off some of the butter. He could almost hear her reprimand.

"I thought medical records were kept digitally nowadays. On the computer, I mean." Toft was up to speed with most things.

Roland nodded. "Exactly! Luckily, Majken Thorup keeps both. Therefore, she was able to tell us Gitte was afraid of a man who came to the family home. The theft may have been committed to remove that lead."

"Isn't she breaking her oath of confidentiality by telling us?" Mikkel looked surprised at the remainder of the butter-scraped roll. Roland had followed Irene's reprimand. Mikkel, like most others at the table, looked at Roland and felt slightly ashamed.

"She can't be punished when it's in relation to solving a crime, as I'm sure you remember," Toft quickly answered.

"But she isn't obliged to tell us?" Mikkel got the last word.

Roland was pleased to hear his officers had a good grasp of the law. He wiped his mouth with a paper napkin from the canteen.

"Jensen, you take Majken Thorup. Review everything she can remember from her conversations with Gitte. Every single word. And, if you can, get a printout of the file. Unfortunately, no names are mentioned, according to Majken. Only that the man in question is a friend of the family who occasionally came into the house," he continued, feeling uncomfortable. Could one of his own family friends try to harm Marianna? The job could make him completely paranoid at times. If he couldn't even trust his friends . . .

"Jesper Ingemann's not a friend of the Mikkelsens. He only knows Gitte from the short period she attended the Søvejen After-School Centre in Brabrand, and he said a passing hello to her parents. But maybe the man Gitte mentioned doesn't have anything to do with the case. That's what we need to clarify now," Roland informed them.

"I'd still wager he has a Hotmail address called Teddy Bear," said Mikkel confidently. "Have Ingemann's emails been reviewed?"

"Cyber's on it."

"How do we find him—the friend?" Kim wanted to know, pushing his glasses into place with his index finger.

He hadn't said anything all morning, despite not usually being the quiet type. His skin was extra pale under his dark curls. The case was affecting him, too. He had a daughter only a few years older than Gitte and Louise, who had been in the same chat forum as the two girls. The Amalie Bang case also bothered him.

"First we have to ask the Mikkelsens about their circle of friends. I'll take that. Then we must go through the friends and interview them one by one," said Roland.

"Do you think the murder of the woman on Mejlbyvej has anything to do with it? Isn't it weird she was murdered days after Gitte?" asked Superintendent Kurt Olsen, unscrupulously taking the last half of bread roll on the platter.

Roland shook his head as he turned his plastic mug, deep in thought.

"Inspector Holsted will keep us informed, of course, but I don't see a connection." He looked resolutely at his officers and raised his voice. "The result of the analysis of the mud on Gitte's clothes and hair has finally arrived. Now we can start looking for the crime scene. The analysis shows the mud originates from a forest area."

"Aarhus municipality owns most of the forest in Denmark," Kim said resignedly.

"I've been on to the Danish Nature Agency and received some pertinent information," said Olsen, stuffing his pipe with delicate fingers that practically caressed its highly polished surface. "Most Aarhus forests are comprised of deciduous trees, predominantly beech trees, of course. But that's mainly along the coast, so we're ignoring those areas for the time being."

Roland lit a cigarette. A cigarette was perfect after the bread rolls and coffee. "We assume it's one of the new forests we need to concentrate on, given the results were from an oak forest. That limits it to about five hundred hectares of forest. That's significantly less than the thirteen hundred hectares of old forests out there," he offered, blowing cigarette smoke out of the corner of his mouth. "First we take the oak forests around Brabrand. They're closest. And it further narrows the area. The superintendent has a map." Roland nodded towards Olsen, who confirmed with a nod.

Roland shared more about the analysis of the mud, after which he allocated assignments. He stacked his papers by slamming the edges against the tabletop, then emptied his mug. They knew the routine and that the morning briefing was now over. Chairs scraped, and the chat gradually began to buzz again.

"Any questions?" shouted Roland above the noise, but the group was already out of the room, eager to get on with the day's duties. Olsen gave Roland a complimentary pat on the back.

"There's a visitor coming this afternoon," he said.

Roland looked at him questioningly.

"Her name's Julie Hermansen and she's from the Special Operations Unit. She's a specialist in criminal profiling. An order has come from on high. I expect you to be here to meet with her and fill her in on the cases. I'm heading out to a meeting," he continued before returning to his own office, puffing his pipe, clearly relieved he had other things to do.

57

It was a little after noon. Kamilla was in Aarhus taking some scenic pictures by Aarhus River. Thygesen had given her the assignment so he could get pictures for an article entitled "New Harbour Atmosphere in Aarhus" in which he had written about the attractive café environment and the history around Aarhus River from the time Viking trading ships had sailed all the way up to Immervad. Even then, it was a place where people met and shopped. Thygesen obviously thought it was time to show the newspaper's readers Aarhus wasn't just crimes and unsolved murders.

Afterwards, she window-shopped along Strøget and enjoyed city life. She had again ended up down at Vadestedet opposite Magasin department store. She sat down at a vacant table outside Café Sidewalk and ordered a cappuccino even though the air was a little cold and damp. It looked like it would start to rain soon. The mobile phone in her camera bag rang. She took it out and waved to the waiter. He was standing confused on the doorstep of the café, looking around for her with a large cappuccino on a tray with tall glasses. He was a very young man, a student with a summer job perhaps.

"Finally, there's news!" Anne said excitedly over the phone. "My contact says the police are apparently on the trail of the killer. He's supposedly a friend of the family."

Anne was chewing gum and rummaging noisily in some cardboard boxes. She continued eagerly, "It was a child psychologist in Risskov who made the discovery. She treated Gitte last summer. The girl's medical records were stolen from her clinic last Friday."

So Majken had checked her computer and found something important. Kamilla accepted the large cup and nodded her thanks to the waiter, who disappeared again with an apologetic smile when he discovered she was in the middle of a phone conversation.

"I was thinking we should pay the psychologist a visit?" suggested Anne.

"I know her. The child psychologist. She's a friend of mine. I think we should leave her be. The police will deal with it," said Kamilla firmly. She wouldn't be party to intruding on Majken with a camera and a pushy reporter. Especially not after their quarrel on Saturday. A press photographer who didn't want to intrude—it sounded completely wrong. But that was also why she had become a commercial photographer. She often thought journalists and press photographers must feel they are being invasive and thoughtless when intruding in people's lives at the most inconvenient of times. Especially nowadays, when journalism was no longer just about disseminating information and news, but more about creating sensation and displaying the misfortune of others. There were even websites where accidents and violence were exhibited with photos taken on mobile phones. Images and stories put before human understanding and consideration. The worse, the better.

"You know her?" Anne's voice reflected the great opportunity she had just seen. "Well then, let's take the other one first." She carried on chewing.

"What other one?" Kamilla only wanted a day of peace and quiet. She stirred the white milk foam and cocoa powder into the hot aromatic coffee so it became creamy and golden.

"I found out something about the doll," Anne said eagerly.

"The doll?" Kamilla took a mouthful of cappuccino as she watched the other patrons at the tables outside the café. Those sitting closest to the river were starting to move indoors. Drips were beginning to fall from menacing black clouds.

"I got hold of Kristoffer Kjær—the developmentally disabled boy. My gut keeps telling me there's something about that doll. He confirmed my suspicion. I've been allowed to do an interview with him this afternoon. Do you want to come along so we can get a few pictures?" asked Anne.

Kamilla looked at her watch. "When?"

"Can we meet in Brabrand at three o'clock?"

Kamilla reluctantly confirmed, hung up, then moved inside with the other café guests when the rain broke through with a force that threatened the parasols' ability to withstand. She balanced her cup and the heavy camera bag and got a seat by the window. In front of her sat a young couple in love, French kissing. To her surprise, she didn't feel the usual discomfort that probably came from sheer envy. She smiled instead and thought of Danny. Her gaze shifted to the rain behind the window, where umbrellas had been unfurled. Wet domes of various colours and with assorted logos paraded past. On the tables, the heavy rain plopped in the used cups and glasses the waiter hadn't yet managed to collect. A boy in yellow rain gear jumped in a puddle between the tables. The water sent a dirty splash up on the window where Kamilla was sitting. His mother grabbed him by the arm and pulled him with her. *Same age as Rasmus*, Kamilla thought, emptying the cup and paying. Then she threw the camera bag over her shoulder and walked with her yellow umbrella over her head back to the car parked in the Magasin department store. She should make it home in time to email the photos to Thygesen before she had to meet Anne.

It was still raining heavily when she drove past the water tower on Randersvej and turned onto Hasle Ringvej. The wipers threw cascades of water from side to side on the windshield. *Dazzling summer,* she thought. On the whole, it had been a terrible summer so far. Danny was the only good thing that had happened. He had repeatedly wanted to talk to her about Rasmus. But she wouldn't talk to him about her son. Not yet.

She braked hard at a red light she had almost overlooked. The cars thundered ahead from the opposite side. She told herself to be more attentive for the rest of the journey.

The boy's foster family wasn't home. Kamilla was surprised to see him in real life. The picture she had accidentally taken of him behind the skip was blurred because of the distance. Now she could clearly see the crossed eyes under the heavy eyelids that gave him a tired look. His face was small and flat, his nose short. It pointed up over his very thin upper lip. The proportions were completely off. There was too much distance between his nose and mouth. *This boy would have been born healthy if he hadn't been fed drugs and alcohol right from the fetal stage,* she thought and shuddered.

Anne was already there, as usual, and had probably been sitting talking to the boy for a long time to gain his confidence.

"I'm so glad you want to talk to us, Kristoffer. Here comes Kamilla; she's going to take a few photos of you for the paper. Is that okay?" She spoke slowly and pedagogically as though to a small child. His development was also no further advanced, despite his fifteen years. He laughed with such intensity that his eyes almost disappeared in the short eye sockets. Was he capable of a serious interview, and did the foster parents even know about this?

"Have you been here long?" she whispered to Anne.

"I live out here. I've just moved."

"Again! Didn't you just move into your apartment?"

Kristoffer sat, following their conversation with his crossed eyes. Anne nodded and concentrated again on the boy.

"We chatted a little about the doll before. Why did you take it from the skip after the police had taken Gitte?" Anne started her interview.

Kristoffer grew serious. His lips became narrower and formed the beginning of words. "It wa-wa-was Gitte's doll," he stammered. His face writhed with exertion at uttering the words.

"Yes, it was Gitte's doll, wasn't it?" encouraged Anne. The voice recorder was on the table. He nodded violently, and saliva began to dribble from the corner of his mouth, but he realised it himself and wiped it on his sleeve.

"Were you going to give it, the doll, back to Gitte?" asked Anne.

He nodded again and pointed to the bookshelf. "Yes, hid it up there."

"Are you hiding the doll in the bookshelf?" Anne asked, sending Kamilla a sideways glance as the boy nodded, apparently forgetting again that the police had retrieved the doll.

"Did you give the doll to Gitte, Kristoffer?"

The boy shook his head and fiddled with his sleeve, which now had a dark stain from his saliva.

"Do you know who gave the doll to Gitte?"

"A man!" It erupted from his mouth.

"A man? Do you know the man?"

Again, he shook his head quite violently. His hair was thin and cut short. "A st-st-strange man," he replied with exaggerated mouth movements. He bit his lower lip afterwards.

"Can you tell us anything about the strange man, Kristoffer?" Anne continued with an eager expression in her eyes. At the police station, the boy had clammed up.

Again, Kristoffer shook his head. He tried to get some words out but gave up.

"Did you see when Gitte got the doll?"

Kamilla didn't want to disturb them by using the flash, so she sat waiting in a chair next to Anne. She looked around the room. It was messy and looked more like a little girl's room than the room of a fifteen-year-old boy.

Kristoffer thought for a while, then nodded.

"Where did she get the doll?"

"At the p-playground. Gitte was scared." He sniffled.

"Was Gitte afraid of the man at the playground?"

He nodded again and began to look around the room nervously.

"Did you see what he looked like? Can you describe him?" Anne became too eager, and the questions were too difficult. He began to get restless. Kamilla feared he would refuse to keep going. She spotted the row of toy cars on the windowsill and thought of Jonas's and Rasmus's interest in cars, and how Kristoffer loved to ride in his foster father's lorry. She had read it in one of Anne's articles.

"Should we take a picture now, Kristoffer?" she asked cautiously, hoping it might help him regain his concentration. He nodded and looked expectantly at her.

"Which car's your favourite?" she asked with a nod to the row of toy cars on the windowsill, getting the camera ready.

"That one!" Not surprisingly, he pointed to the truck.

"Did you see the man's car?" Kamilla dared to ask, trying to sound as teacher-like as Anne. Kristoffer nodded again.

"Do you have a car that looks like the man's car?" Anne followed up on Kamilla's idea.

He searched among the cars and picked up a black passenger car.

"This one!" He offered it proudly to Kamilla and her camera. She pressed the shutter button. He was dazzled by the flash and blinked.

"You go to the playground often, don't you, Kristoffer?" asked Anne to keep him concentrated.

"Yeeaahhh." He laughed, clapping his hands once to show his excitement.

"Do you also know Gitte's friend, Louise? The one who disappeared?"

Kristoffer thought again, then he nodded. Wasn't it unusual for him to remember names like that? Kamilla considered his face. Saliva had begun to dribble from the corner of his mouth again, but now he was too busy to notice it. Who knew what was going on inside that head of his?

"Was the car there the day Louise disappeared?" Anne continued.

Kristoffer remained silent. He bit his lower lip again, then he started laughing with a rattling sound that came from his throat.

"It has a funny animal ding-ling at the back." He laughed and jumped in the chair.

"Does the car have a funny animal dangling at the back? Where? In the rear window?" said Anne, meeting Kamilla's eyes over his head.

Kristoffer nodded eagerly, the grin stuck on his face.

"What colour was the car? Did you see? Was it black?"

He thought hard; his eyes became even narrower.

"Black," he said clearly. "No, blue."

58

On the stairs, at the door of the house in Brabrand, Roland felt a kind of stomach cramp. He had called beforehand, so his visit wasn't a surprise. He hadn't done that the first time he had spoken to them in this house. Of course, you must consider the grieving family. The situation was different with criminals; there, it was an advantage to come unannounced.

Inside the house, the dog barked. Ida Mikkelsen was clearly nervous when she opened the door. On the phone, he had only said something new had come up in the case and he would like to discuss it with her and her husband, but she had probably already decided what it was. Allan Mikkelsen wasn't home. He was out at a bricklaying job. They were busy at the moment, Ida had said on the phone. He could have waited until later to visit, but for some reason, he wanted to talk to Ida on her own. After all, she was the one who had taken her daughter to see a psychologist without her husband's knowledge. He hadn't really heard her voice the last time, either. Allan had done all the talking.

"Come in."

Ida pointed towards the living room with one hand as she held her big, pregnant belly with the other. It had to be any day now. Roland went in, getting the smell of dog again. It had struck him the first time he had been there, too. The dog's basket was in the hall. Now it aroused curiosity in him. A kind of hunting dog, he judged without knowing much about dogs.

The dog sniffed Roland's crotch, and he dutifully patted it on the head. Ida took it by the collar.

"My husband hunts," she said almost apologetically, banishing the dog to the utility room.

Roland took off his jacket and pulled the sleeves of his jumper back down.

"I made coffee," she said; it sounded like a question.

"Thank you." He sat down on the bottle-green velvet-like sofa where he had also sat last time. He heard her pottering about in the kitchen with cups and a tray, which she set down with difficulty on the coffee table a short while after. He immediately got up to help. She sat opposite, then waited for him with eyes that betrayed the grief she was carrying and the nervousness of what was about to come.

"I don't want to waste your time, so I'm going straight to the point. He poured coffee for both of them. She had a hard time leaning forwards because of the way she was holding her stomach, as though afraid of losing that child, too.

"We've spoken to a doctor—Majken Thorup." He didn't need to say more. Ida Mikkelsen put the cup down hard, despite having just lifted it up.

"Oh, I hadn't thought of that. Everything that happened last summer . . ."

"It may be important. Do you know the content of the conversations Dr. Thorup had with Gitte?" he asked seriously.

Ida started laughing nervously. "It was nonsense. Gitte went through a period where she felt persecuted by everyone. Even my husband. She was afraid of her own father," she laid extra emphasis on the word *father*. "It must have been something she'd heard at school. Or seen on TV. A film maybe. I don't know." She tried with the cup again.

"You're sure there's nothing to what Gitte said? Could someone in your circle of friends have molested Gitte?"

Her eyes went dark, as if she hadn't ever followed that thought through to its end before.

"No, that's impossible!" she said firmly after a brief pause. She drank from the cup and put it back on the saucer. "We only have good, genuine friends. They wouldn't do that sort of thing," she assured him. Still, there was a touch of uncertainty in her voice.

"Your husband said on the phone that he doesn't know Jesper Inge-mann—a youth leader at the after-school centre Gitte attended for a short while. Do you know him?"

She thought about it and shook her head. "Was it him? Is he the one who . . . ?"

"Did you know Gitte had a profile on an internet chat forum with her picture?" Roland interrupted her.

Nervous, Ida pushed her hair behind her ears. It was dark and shoulder-length. The purple in the blue of her eyes was enhanced by her lightly flowered purple maternity top with a ribbon just below her large bosom. Her eyes were red from crying.

"Not until you took her computer. Was she lonely maybe?" The question sounded like it was being asked of herself.

"Gitte didn't need to have been lonely to chat on the internet. Most children have *chatted*," he replied with a little smile.

"But the police now think it's her own fault? When she posted there, I mean?" Ida looked at him worriedly.

"Of course not," he said quickly.

She sighed and straightened her coffee cup. It seemed as if she herself had thought that.

"Gitte called herself Doll Child in the chat group," Roland said tenta-tively. "Could there be a specific reason for that?"

She smiled and her eyes welled up again. "He always calls her that. Allan. My husband. She's his little doll child. Did she really call herself that?" she said, obviously touched.

Roland considered it a somewhat derogatory name for a girl, but Gitte's father apparently didn't see it like that.

"Did Louise come here often?"

Ida shook her head. "They were mostly at Louise's. She has a bigger room than Gitte, and then there was Louise's little brother. Gitte was crazy about the little boy." Her lower lip began to tremble.

"Did Gitte have any other friends we can talk to? Did she see anyone other than Louise?"

Ida shook her head a little. "Gitte didn't have many friends. She had a hard time fitting in on the whole. That was why we had to take her out of the after-school club. Gitte and Louise were thick as thieves. She also hung out with Berit. They played badminton together. She's a few years older than Gitte. Would you like her address?"

Roland nodded. She got up awkwardly, stretched with both hands on her lower back. She stood like that for a while before going over to a dresser and getting an address book. She sat down on the sofa again and flipped through the book.

"Here it is. Berit Bjerre. She lives with her parents on Emmasvej." She made a note of it and handed it to him. He thanked her and put it in his trouser pocket.

"I'll speak to her. And you haven't thought of anything else since I was last here?"

She shook her head.

"I have to ask for a list of your male friends who come here regularly," Roland said cautiously.

The tears filled her eyes. It would be a difficult task. Hanging friends out to dry and maybe losing them forever.

"I can't. My husband . . ."

"Is it mainly your husband's friends who come here?" Roland was familiar with families where the circle of friends consisted mainly of the husband's friends. "I hope your husband's just as interested in finding Gitte's murderer?" The words were a little harsh, but he had to make her understand it was important for solving the case.

"He'll be angry. He didn't know I was taking Gitte to see a child psychologist. But her obsessive thoughts couldn't continue." She began to cry quietly. Roland handed her the handkerchief he always had in his pocket for such occasions. She wiped her eyes.

"Listen, we'll be discreet about it. It'll be between us. You give me the names. I'll make a note. And your husband will never know," he said confidingly.

Ida nodded silently.

59

Berit Bjerre was fourteen years old but looked like a young woman of twenty. When Roland sat down opposite her, he rejoiced that his daughters weren't that age today, when reaching maturity dictated that girls show both cleavage and a bare belly. He would never have allowed his own girls to dress like this young lady, even though he knew well he probably wouldn't have had much say on the subject. Berit's father probably didn't have much say, either. He imagined the quarrels there had to be on the subject in their home. She was a beautiful girl and looked like the thin young models from the flyers that came through his letterbox. It probably wasn't a coincidence. But she was very upset by the murder of her friend and by Louise's disappearance. She moistened her lips with the tip of her tongue, despite them already shining with a thick layer of lip gloss.

"What happened to Gitte is awful," she said, her eyes filling with tears under her very long mascara-black lashes that curved unnaturally upwards.

"When was the last time you saw her?"

"The day before she disappeared—Sunday." Berit looked down at her hands and peeled off some flaking pink nail varnish. It was similar to what he had seen on Gitte's bitten fingernails at the autopsy. But Berit's nails were long and well-manicured.

"Had Gitte disappeared then?" Roland tried to catch her eye, but she avoided his gaze.

"I tried to call her mobile on Monday, but she didn't answer. I tried a few times."

"When was that, Berit?"

"From when she finished school on Monday afternoon."

"Was it unusual for Gitte not to answer the phone?"

"Yeah. Gitte could easily decide not to answer if it didn't suit her. But she usually always answered when it was me. I just wanted to hear how her date went." Berit nervously turned a plastic red Speak Up wristband that had become popular in support of some cause.

"Did Gitte have a date?" He raised an eyebrow and felt his heart skip a beat.

Berit's fringe fell in front of her eyes as she nodded seriously. She flicked it away with a quick toss of her head. It looked like a clip from a shampoo ad on TV.

"She'd met someone online."

Roland moved uneasily. They were sitting in Berit's room. There was only room for him on a pink beanbag chair. It made him sink very low and sit in an awkward and humiliating position. Her computer was on, and the rotating screensaver in his field of vision was making him dizzy.

"Was she supposed to meet someone she'd chatted with online?"

Berit nodded again and looked at him with large, scared eyes. "Do you think it was him? I haven't been online since all this happened. It just makes you think twice. You don't know who you're talking to."

"We can neither rule out nor confirm it may be someone from the chat group," Roland replied honestly. He had no qualms about making the girl more scared. It wouldn't hurt for her to learn to think twice.

"Then it's all my fault. It was me who taught her to use that website."

"It could never be your fault. But do you know who he is? It's very important we talk to him so we can rule him out. Has she ever mentioned a guy from Søvejen After-School Centre named Jesper?" he asked, trying to use young people's jargon; he didn't usually say *guy*. He knew it meant a rope or cord to guide something with.

"She never talked about a Jesper, but everyone's anonymous online. That's what makes it so cool." She smiled uncertainly. "We only know each other's usernames. A kind of nickname," she elaborated, as if she didn't expect a man of Roland's age to know what a username was. She probably thought him ancient.

"Her date wouldn't be called Teddy Bear, would he?"

Berit laughed, revealing she didn't have completely straight front teeth.

"Yeah, in his email address. We talked about how funny it was because Gitte calls herself Doll Child. They suited each other." Then she grew serious, as if it had suddenly dawned on her that Gitte was dead and she shouldn't speak about her in the present tense.

"But that's not his username? Do you know what it is?"

Berit thought about it. "No, we've never talked about that. He didn't have a picture, either. That was why I was so excited to hear about what he looked like from Gitte. Maybe he was ugly."

"Do you know if he's an older man?"

"No! That's gross!" Berit made an unpleasant grimace. "He may be older than Gitte, but not much. Fifteen—sixteen, I think."

"Why do you think that?"

She shrugged.

"Do you know anything about a gift he gave Gitte? A doll perhaps?"

Berit shook her head, making the shampoo-toss with her head again to get her hair in place.

"No. But Gitte played with dolls. She was a bit geeky like that. I taught her to be more grown-up. You don't play with dolls when you're ten. At least, I didn't." She studied her nails.

"So you have no idea who he is?"

Berit shook her head and looked bored.

"No. I don't know more."

60

His body ached as if he had been run over by a steam train. It had been a struggle to lug the suitcases up to his apartment, where the slope of the steps had taken his breath away before he had reached the second floor.

A few of the guests from Danhostel Aarhus, who were from Fyn, had also been packing their cars for the journey home. They had found him lying by his car in the car park. But he had begun to regain consciousness by then. They had wanted to drive him to A&E and call the police, but he had waved away their offers as persuasively as he could while making a huge effort to get back on his feet. Fortunately, he had only received one blow to the face—the one that had sent him to the ground. The other punches and kicks had hit him in places that couldn't be immediately seen. But they could be felt.

He hadn't made the next ferry. The people from Fyn had persuaded him to sit on a bench for a while before driving on. They had agreed it was good he hadn't been beaten too much in the face, though they were sure his jaw was broken.

On the ferry, he had sat huddled out on the deck in the wind and rain, away from the reproachful glances of others. He had got some toilet paper from the ferry's toilet and sat and dabbed blood from his nose and mouth.

* * *

He looked at his face in the bathroom mirror and wiped the clotted blood from the corner of his mouth with a wet cloth, then he wrung it out in cold water and placed it on the left side of his head, which was swollen after the man's direct right hook. A black eye couldn't be ruled out. The man had to be Kamilla's ex-husband. *So I got to meet them both anyway.* The whole trip to Jutland had been one huge fiasco. Still, he couldn't get her out his head.

He opened the window to get some air into the apartment. After being empty for a whole week, the air was so dead and stagnant he could hardly breathe. There were planks leaning along the walls. He wasn't quite done with the kitchen yet. It all suddenly seemed so unmanageable.

The open window created a draught and made the door in the hall slam shut with a bang. He hadn't thought to close it after he had finally made it up all the stairs with the two suitcases. A picture fell over on the bookshelf. When he lifted it up, he saw it was the photo Sanne had taken of him and her together one sunny day in May. Sanne's green eyes shone under her dark bob. *They did back then,* he thought bitterly. He had taken that from her, too. He looked at himself in the photo. Six years younger. Six years happier. He put the picture back and slumped heavily onto a chair at the dining table, hiding his face in his hands. He let them slide up into his hair, so the dark tufts protruded between his fingers. He sat like that for a long time, until the loud ringing of his mobile phone tore him out of despair.

"Hi, Danny! Where am I catching you? How are things in Jutland?"

He immediately recognised the voice of his managing director and friend and straightened up in the chair. The voice sounded like it came from a distant past, where everything had been completely different.

"Rainy, Tonny. Dark and rainy," he replied, pulling himself together.

"Ah, so dark and rainy Jutland isn't just an old wives' tale." On the other end of the phone, Tonny Langdahl let out his deep, hollow laugh. He was ringing from the agency. Danny recognised the clattering sounds of the DT publishers' keyboards and the muffled hum of voices speaking softly in the background. He missed work suddenly. Or maybe just the past. He didn't really know which.

"But I've left dark Jutland now. Is something wrong, Tonny?"

"Are you back again already?" Langdahl sounded disappointed.

The sound of a lighter clicked. Danny guessed he was lighting a large Cuban cigar, bought on one of the countless trips to the Caribbean with the family. *It has to be a real Havana!* he would insist.

"I'd actually hoped I'd catch you before you got back to Zealand," he said, blowing cigar smoke into Danny's ear. "We have a potential client over there, and I was going to ask you to pay them a visit. That's a pity."

Danny looked at the picture of himself with Sanne. The family that had slowly disintegrated. An wild thought began to take shape.

"I'll go back," he said resolutely, feeling in his entire aching body that this was what he wanted. There was something he needed to resolve. However difficult it may be, Kamilla needed to hear the truth from him. She needed to know who he was and how he felt. Kamilla's ex-husband knew. How much contact did they have?

"You're going back to Jutland? Do you mean that?" His manager's voice sounded both puzzled and uplifted.

Danny looked at the photo again. What did he have to stay here for? Everything that made him belong here was gone.

"I've never been more serious about anything," he replied.

"That's great. Come by the agency before you leave so we can lay out a strategy."

61

Roland threw the notebook down hard on his desk. What had he overlooked? Officers had been ringing the doorbells and visiting the Mikkelsen family's circle of friends since yesterday. Even those who lived on Funen and Zealand. Morten Toft and Kim Ansager had volunteered to drive there. But everyone they had interviewed had an alibi, and some were ruled out as the perpetrator for other reasons.

Majken Thorup refused to hand over Gitte Mikkelsen's medical records. She had already cooperated, she insisted, stubbornly adhering to the Psychology Act, Paragraph 21, Section 2 on the statutory duty of confidentiality of psychologists. Maybe the episode with the family friend had nothing to do with the murder. What was going on? What was he missing? Berit hadn't been of much help, either. It had only made the matter more complicated. Could a boy of fifteen or sixteen commit such a cruel murder? He doubted it. Were there two perps?

After his conversation with Berit, he had driven back to the station for the meeting with Julie Hermansen from the Special Operations Unit. She was older than the ones they usually sent, but it didn't matter to him. You needed several years of experience to gain the level of knowledge of criminal profiles this woman possessed. She was one of Denmark's best. She was probably in her late fifties, but it was very difficult to judge due to her short, modern hairstyle with its red-blond colouring. Her figure wasn't young, either. She wasn't solid, but she had Irene's round hips. She wore a dark single-breasted suit jacket with matching trousers, a red blouse, and a white marble pearl necklace. From her handshake, Roland immediately liked her, despite the SOU not usually being among his favourites. But it was about time they drew up a profile on the perp. He had given her the information she needed and shown her to the office she could use while she was working at the police station.

He let out a loud sigh and watched a flock of seagulls against the blue sky outside the window. They let themselves float on the upward thrust. He wished that were him. That this was all over. That he could feel free like the birds. But he felt bound by his hands and feet. He watched one of the gulls make a quick dive. They caught insects up there. They were better than him at that, too. He had caught nothing, despite working hard for over a week, and again he felt there was something important they had overlooked. Time was against them and could be crucial for Louise's uncertain fate. Jesper Ingemann still hadn't been ruled out, but it didn't look like he was a murderer or kidnapper.

And then there was the article about the developmentally disabled boy and the doll—the cover story of the day's paper. "Doll child," he mumbled. Was there a connection to that doll? Was that what he had overlooked? It was a short article featuring a picture of the boy with a black toy car in his hand. That journalist was always one step ahead. Was it him? The boy they had overlooked? He had put Toft on the case. He would have to wait and see what it brought. Would Kristoffer even talk to them now? After all, they had just been given a vital new detail that could identify the car. Hopefully the murderer didn't read the papers, so he would know to remove evidence. If it were true, that is. Luckily, they had the tyre prints, so if they found the car, it could be easily identified—if the perpetrator wasn't cunning enough to change the tyres, too. But Roland doubted it. Criminals generally make some mistake that gets them caught. He comforted himself with the thought, and that new forensic technology certainly didn't make it any easier for them.

DI Holsted opened the door and knocked gently on the doorframe. It interrupted Roland's gloomy thoughts.

"I thought I'd find you here. Am I disturbing you?"

"No, not at all. Come in." He straightened up in his chair and hoped that, given everything, things were going better with his colleague's murder investigation. Holsted sat down in the chair in front of him and crossed his legs elegantly. The trousers had sharp creases. A massive gold chain appeared under the cuff of his right shirt sleeve as he casually placed it on the armrest. He was, as always, immaculately dressed in the latest fashion. His features seemed too attractive for a man. His lips were large and full, and his eyes clear and unnaturally blue surrounded by long black eyelashes. And he was happily married with three children. So you really couldn't judge a book by its cover. In any case, despite his young age, he was a skilled detective. Roland predicted he had a great future ahead of him in the Criminal Investigation Department.

"I just saw Angela Merkel out in the hall." He smiled.

Roland looked at him, confused, and raised an eyebrow questioningly.

"The woman from the SOU. She looks like the German Chancellor," said Holsted, adjusting his shirt cuff.

Roland smiled. Something about her had reminded him of someone.

"I just came by to hear how your cases are going, run a few theories by each other," Holsted continued before Roland had time to comment.

Roland didn't offer him coffee as he knew he preferred tea. Understandably so.

"May I help you?" Roland was ashamed to feel a small sense of joy. Holsted scratched his chin, which was never unshaven or with traces of black stubble—unlike Roland's.

"We're trying to find Olga Halgren's grandchild. But apparently, she doesn't exist. Neighbours say she often mentioned a grandchild, but there's no lead in the house. No pictures, no phone calls or letters. Nothing."

"What about the rest of the family? The grandchild must have parents," Roland offered helpfully.

"We're working on it. But how the hell do you find someone when you don't have a name or a sex?" Holsted sighed, rattling his bracelet.

"If it's a grandchild, it has to be a son or daughter of one of Olga Halgren's children. Are they so difficult to find?"

"Apparently. Olga Halgren married twice and had children in both marriages. Two sons and a daughter from her first marriage, and a daughter and a son from her second, but the dead son took his own life over thirty years ago. He left behind two children. The sons from the first marriage have several children between them. It could be one of them. Unfortunately, finding them is taking time. The girls could have married and changed their surnames. But as I said, we're working on it."

"Are you sure the grandchild exists? Maybe it was wishful thinking. Have the neighbours ever seen anyone?"

"No, they haven't, oddly enough. But the house is well hidden between tall trees," replied Holsted.

Roland remembered the garden of tall trees that would make it impossible for the neighbours to keep an eye on what was going on inside the yellow-painted house.

"The only evidence of the grandchild's existence is a computer he or she, according to a neighbour, used during their visits. I mean, what would a ninety-year-old want with a computer?" Holsted aired his thoughts.

"You never know," muttered Roland, thinking grandmothers were no longer old women who knitted and wore their hair in braids twisted into buns, like the memories he had of his own grandmother. Older ladies nowadays were globetrotters and members of all sorts of clubs and associations—and used computers.

"Did you not find anything on the computer?"

"Clean as a whistle. Not a fingerprint. The hard drive was cleaned recently—there's nothing there. Do you believe Olga Halgren was capable of doing that?" Holsted looked doubtfully at Roland, who responded with another indistinct murmur. It was hard to know these days. Maybe she had taken an IT course.

"Why's it so important to find that grandchild?" Roland wanted to know.

"He's apparently the only one who visited the old woman. Except for the home help, of course. A neighbouring couple saw a car parked in the driveway on Friday night. But they don't know the make or model and they didn't see it drive away. It could only be the grandchild. But how's it going with your case?" inquired Holsted, interested.

"Yeah, we're struggling to clear up a few details, too. A forest, an IP address, a bike and bike helmet, a backpack, a mobile phone, a pair of white tights—and a motive, to name just a few."

"Do you think a criminal profile could help?"

"Maybe." Roland sighed. "If nothing else, it might help us rule people out."

"Do you mean Jesper Ingemann?"

He nodded.

"We can also rule out that our cases are connected, can't we?" Holsted's gold chain rattled again as he undid the top button of his striped shirt. The sun made its entrance to announce the Danish summer, warming the small office.

"Yes, I think so. One's the murder of a ten-year-old girl in Brabrand, and the other's a ninety-year-old woman in Gammel Egå. What's the connection supposed to be?" Roland replied.

Holsted got up and shot him a crooked smile. "You're right. I better be getting a move on, too. Good luck." He politely closed the door behind him.

Roland resumed watching the blue sky and the seagulls. He reached absently for the phone without taking his eyes off them when a buzzing tone told him someone had been put through.

"It's the reporter," said Mikkel Jensen.

"Oh no! Not now!" Annoyed, he put his hand to his head.

"It's apparently very important. I think you should talk to her. She has something . . ."

Roland sighed, knowing she wasn't going to give him anything without getting something in return. And he had nothing to give.

"So has the murderer been identified from among the friends of the family?" was the first thing Anne Larsen said. Roland didn't respond immediately.

"No, of course he hasn't!" She moved on quickly. He couldn't tell whether she sounded relieved or disappointed.

"Do you have anything new to tell us?" he asked sarcastically.

"I need to know what you have first," she continued. She chewed a piece of gum loudly. He found it a little rude, but young people were so free and easy nowadays.

"We have nothing," he replied honestly. His own words made him feel the panic. He still wasn't going to tell her about the girls' chat on the internet. A review of the website's database hadn't led them anywhere because they didn't know the username. He had been amazed at the number of members—over a hundred thousand names. A database that could be misused, not only by sex offenders, but also by extreme political organisations to recruit young, susceptible members. But the Cyber Unit was close to tracking an IP address, they said. It would be a disaster if that was leaked to the press now.

"I have something you could dig a little further into." Anne took an artful pause as if to evaluate whether it had piqued his interest. It had.

"A little birdy told me Gitte Mikkelsen wasn't born a Mikkelsen. She was adopted," Anne continued in a whisper.

"Where do you know that from?" It burst out of him. He straightened up in the chair and leaned forward as if she were sitting in front of him and he had difficulty hearing.

"I inquired among friends. Well, not the *real* friends," she replied. There was an undertone of reproach in her voice that the police had only interviewed the real friends.

"Gossip, then?" he stated, annoyed they hadn't discovered that information for themselves, if it were true.

"Maybe," she replied, sounding indifferent, which she probably was. For a journalist, a story was probably just a story, whether true or not. They could always just issue a retraction and apologise for the mistake. It was different for the police. There had to be evidence, otherwise it wouldn't hold in court.

"So Gitte Mikkelsen was adopted?"

"As a baby, apparently." Anne sounded like she was enjoying the situation. "But I want exclusive rights to the story." *There it is.*

Roland had been waiting for it. "Okay. If there's anything to it," he agreed reluctantly.

"And you should probably look into the doll again, too," she continued.

He squeezed his temples between his thumb and middle finger and closed his eyes as he nodded. He was starting to feel the lack of sleep.

"Yes, I saw your article. We're working on the case," he mumbled. He should have thanked her but didn't.

As soon as he had finished the conversation, he picked up the phone again and dialled DS Kim Ansager's extension.

"Kim, will you check to see if the Adoption Board in the Ministry of Justice has anything on Gitte Mikkelsen? Or whatever the hell her name was back then."

It was late afternoon when Ansager came into his office and sat down.

"There's nothing on Gitte Mikkelsen," he said. "The Adoption Board doesn't have anything."

"Nothing? So who's Gitte Mikkelsen?"

"She's down as Ida and Allan Mikkelsen's biological child. But strangely enough, there's no birth certificate. Maybe an error in the system?"

Roland decided to pay the Mikkelsen family another visit. At this time, Gitte's father—or perhaps adoptive father—should be home from work, so he could have a serious conversation with both of them. Why hadn't they mentioned anything about Gitte's adoption? And what else had they "forgotten" to tell him?

62

The roses bloomed on the coffee table. They had opened up more now, so you could really see each flower's complex design of blood-red petals winding around each other. She sat watching them as she thought of their visit to Kristoffer and his talk about the doll and the man in the dark car at the playground. Maybe he didn't have anything to do with the murder and the kidnapping. But why would he give a girl he didn't know a doll at a playground? Would Kristoffer's explanation hold up in a court of law? Maybe he had made it all up. Anne was going to drive to Gitte's parents to ask them if they knew who had given Gitte the doll. They didn't want to be photographed, so Kamilla had decided to drive home to get to the supermarket before it closed.

Kamilla took a bite of the chocolate-covered marzipan she had bought. The urge for chocolate had overwhelmed her, so she had succumbed to buying it. It had been Rasmus's favourite, too. Anthon Berg's marzipan in the fine light purple metallic paper she remembered from her own childhood, and that they used to roll into little balls and fire at each other afterwards. She realised she was unconsciously rolling the paper. She was removing her mobile phone from her camera bag when she heard its ringtone. Unsurprisingly, it was Anne, who had promised to get back to her about the doll.

"Unfortunately, it was a hoax." Anne's mournful voice was full of annoyance. "Gitte's mother says Gitte got the doll from a friend."

"Is she sure?"

"Yes. Unless that's only what Gitte told her mother. But why would she do that?" Anne wondered out loud. "According to her mother, Gitte had wanted that doll for a long time, then one day she came home with it and said she'd got it from a friend." Anne sighed.

"Don't you think it's more likely it's Kristoffer we can't trust?" Kamilla asked.

"Maybe. I also asked her about the adoption. But Ida denies Gitte was adopted, so maybe that's all gossip, too." Anne sounded completely resigned.

"Or rumour," said Kamilla. She heard a car door slamming and, shortly afterwards, the doorbell ringing. "I have to go, Anne. There's someone at the door," she said. They said a quick goodbye.

Jan pushed the door inward before Kamilla had even managed to open it completely. With long, resolute steps, he strode into the living room and looked around as if searching for someone. Then he marched into the bedroom, where he hadn't been since she had moved here with Rasmus.

"What happened, Jan?"

"Is he gone?" he asked through clenched teeth.

"Who?" She was surprised by and afraid of Jan's appearance. She had only seen him like this when he was furious.

"Is it Nina?" She tried to sound as compassionate as possible to calm him down.

"No! Nina isn't the one doing anything wrong! It's fucking YOU!" he hissed. He turned towards her abruptly with saliva in the corners of his mouth; he was angry.

"Me? What have I done?" Kamilla retreated a few steps from him, but he reached out and grabbed her hard by her upper arm. He shook her so violently her arm nearly dislocated.

"Ow, Jan. That hurts! What's wrong with you!" She moaned with tears of pain in her voice.

He pushed her so hard she fell backwards onto the couch. Before she could register she had landed on her back, he was over her. His clenched hand was just above her face, as if it had stopped in the middle of preparing for a hard blow. His eyes had a wild expression she had never seen in him before. She held her breath and stared into them. Knew one wrong word from her could cause him to explode and let the blow fall.

He lowered his fist and took a firm grip of her collar with both hands instead, lifting her up brutally towards him. Her blouse ripped under one arm, and she felt like she was being suffocated.

"How could you fuck him?" he shouted into her face, splashes of his saliva hitting her. "Your son's killer!"

He pushed her back into the cushions of the sofa, so the feeling of being suffocated intensified. She gasped for air. Then he let go of her, got up, and looked down at her with deep contempt.

Kamilla struggled to get air back as she reached for her throat. She stared at him with frightened eyes, and unstoppable tears running down her face. No sound came out her mouth, despite her wanting to say something and moving her lips.

"I saw his car parked here two days in a row," he said harshly.

"Who?" she repeated, trying to fight her way up to a seated position, still feeling his hands around her neck, which hurt.

"Danny Cramer, for fuck's sake! Rasmus's killer!" He spat with anger, but his words didn't seem to penetrate through the fog and the thick cotton wool inside her head.

"I didn't need to look for him when he was here with my . . ." He turned towards her again with his clenched hand raised. She feared he was going to strike her now. But his fist didn't fall. Instead, he struck out hard into the air and snorted loudly. All the muscles in his body were tense. They raised up on his arms, bulging under his skin, and the thought of how hard his blow would hit her was one of the many confused thoughts tumbling over each other inside her head.

"Ex-wife!" He finished the sentence harshly, with disgust and contempt in his voice. He stuck his face right down into hers again. She felt his breath and the heat of his rage.

"Maybe he hasn't told you? You're not exactly quick enough to figure it out for yourself, are you?" He sneered. "If I see him here again, I'll fucking kill him. Do you understand?"

The sound of the door closing with a loud bang after him made her body jerk with fright, then she let the tears and the thoughts run free. *Oh God, is it true? Has Jan found the man who killed Rasmus—and is it Danny? No, it can't be.* She straightened up and wiped her eyes with the back of her hand. Dizziness overwhelmed her as she made to stand up. A headache was on its way. Then she remembered Jonas had said he had seen the car. That was the day they had met Danny at the restaurant. An Opel Vectra, Jonas had said. He wouldn't make that mistake. Danny drove a dark blue Opel Vectra.

63

The red Ford Transit was parked in front of the house in Brabrand. MASTER BUILDER ALLAN MIKKELSEN stood in large white curved letters across the side of the van, and in small print below: MIKKELSEN MASONS WITH FINE JOINTS. A little contrived for Roland's taste, but everyone had their slogan. What was theirs—the police's slogan? He couldn't immediately think of anything that would sell.

The dog had heard him before he reached the steps and pressed the doorbell. The ringing mingled with the dog's aggressive barking inside the house. Ida Mikkelsen shushed it.

"Who can it be at this time?" she asked, probably to her husband. A quick glance at his watch told Roland it was six o'clock, the time most people usually ate dinner.

When she finally opened the door with a firm grip on the dog's collar, the smell of homemade meatballs hit him. The dog threw itself towards him with such force that Ida's large, pregnant body jerked.

"Inspector!" She sounded surprised; he hadn't called ahead this time. Not because he considered them criminals; he had quite simply forgotten to. Allan Mikkelsen sat bent over his plate at the dining table in the kitchen, cutting a meatball with a knife. Ida's almost full plate sat next to her husband's.

"Sorry, I'm disturbing you in the middle of dinner," he said. He didn't take off his jacket but sat down uninvited on the chair opposite Allan.

"Would you like a beer?" he asked, already gesturing to his wife to get one from the fridge. Roland didn't protest. It could well be described as an after-work beer. He needed it.

"I'm here about Gitte," he said, accepting a cold Ceres Top. Ida handed him a clean glass.

"We've learned she isn't your biological daughter," he lied. "Why didn't you mention that?" It was a method Kurt Olsen had admonished him for using, but it had often worked.

He poured frothy beer into the glass and enjoyed the scent that reached his nostrils. He kept an eye on Allan's expression. He had protruding blue-grey eyes under bushy light blond eyebrows with a reddish tinge, and a ruddy, weather-beaten face that showed he spent a lot of time outdoors. He was in his work clothes—a white shirt and white Kansas overalls. The stubble drew a light contour around his mouth.

He stopped chewing and put down his knife and fork. His wife sat on her chair, confused, holding her round belly.

"Yeah, but is it important? We . . ."

Ida made to say something. But a quick glance from her husband immediately made her fall quiet. She looked down at her plate, where the food likely had grown cold. Allan wiped his mouth with a cloth napkin and fixed Roland with his gaze.

"We adopted Gitte as an infant. Is it important?"

"It's not insignificant information. The murderer might be someone from her past."

Ida started sobbing. Her husband looked at her quickly, then turned his gaze back to Roland.

"Impossible. She was a baby. Practically a newborn. She was ours." He pushed the half-empty plate away from him, as if he had lost his appetite.

Roland sniffed the aroma of the homemade meatballs and missed Irene's cooking. Even if it was often made according to Anne Larsen's diet recipes, it was still better than the burgers and pizzas he had been living off the last week.

"Do you know Gitte's biological parents?"

Again, Allan glanced at his wife, who responded this time after wiping her eyes. "Not personally."

"It was the parents—Gitte's grandparents—who took care of the adoption. That poor girl was under fifteen years old," Allan spoke again and placed a soothing hand on top of his wife's. She looked at him lovingly with shining eyes.

"You didn't get Gitte through the adoption board?"

"Nah. Some acquaintances told us the family wanted the child adopted. Gitte's mother was five months pregnant at the time. It happened very privately."

"An illegal adoption, then?" said Roland harshly. The case kept leading to more and more crimes. That was the reason the Mikkelsens hadn't revealed the adoption, and why the police hadn't been able to find any information on it.

"So you're not Gitte's legal adoptive parents. That's against the law; do you know that?"

"All that bureaucracy. Application forms, approvals, and shit and paper. We'd still be waiting on an answer. Not that we'd have been able to afford it, either." Allan snorted angrily.

Many childless couples who desperately wanted a baby were in the same situation. In vitro fertilisation or adoption were the only resorts. But it could be a struggle to get through the eye of the needle. Roland sighed; another officer would have to deal with it. He already had a murder case and a kidnapping to think about.

"Do you still have contact with the family?" he asked, drinking from the glass. The cool liquid ran down his throat. He enjoyed the taste of bitter hops, and it also sated his empty stomach.

Ida shook her head.

"Did Gitte know she was adopted?"

Ida and Allan again exchanged knowing glances.

"We chose not to say anything, but it was weird—she'd started to ask questions." Ida looked at him as if something had suddenly dawned on her.

"What questions? As if someone had told her she wasn't yours?" he asked, a new theory forming.

"Maybe someone was bullying her about it. Children can be so mean to each other. But if she'd asked us directly, she would, of course, have been told the truth." Allan squeezed his wife's hand and continued. "We tried to have a child for so long. But we didn't succeed. Gitte saved us. Since then, we succeeded." He cast a grateful glance at his wife's round belly. "But now Gitte's no longer here." His chin began to tremble, and he took a sip from the beer bottle to hide it.

Roland got up and went to the shelf at the end of the kitchen. He had noticed the hobby-related books from his chair at the dining table. He read the spines of the books. *Politiken's Hunting Book; Politiken's Angling Book; The Hunter in Nature.*

"You're a hunter?"

Allan nodded. "For years." It was clear by his face that he didn't understand the turn in the conversation. Ida, who had probably seen *Columbo* on TV, understood a little better, or the change of subject suited her fine. She began to clear the table, even though neither had finished eating.

"Allan's always hunted—and fished. A bunch of them go off together once in a while. Men-only trips," she said.

Roland sat down again and drank the last of the beer in his glass. So there were also hunting friends they had to talk to.

"If you'd have told Gitte about her biological parents, you must know their names?" he said when he could see Allan had regained his equilibrium.

"We might have the mother's name in some papers," Ida said.

Allan capitulated. "They don't know who the dad was," he mumbled.

The James Bond theme ringtone coming from the phone in Roland's pocket interrupted them. He smiled, embarrassed, and apologised. The tune had been his daughter's idea. How she had done it, he didn't know. He himself was all fingers and thumbs when it came to using mobile phones.

"Hello! Roland? It's Mikkel. The dog unit found the crime scene in Gellerup Forest. Forensics are already out there."

He let out a sigh of relief. He had feared it was going to take much longer. He frowned at Ida and Allan, who were looking at him anxiously, unaware he was about to give them terrible news. He would also have to report them for their participation in an illegal adoption and ask for the names and addresses of Allan's hunting buddies.

64

Roland parked the car by the woods, next to the cars from the forensics department. An area in front of the forest, a little inside the bushes by the Swedish-red wooden barrier, was cordoned off with the police's red-and-white tape, so he guessed they had found something.

As he stepped out of the car, his foot twisted in the grass. He cursed and leaned against a green rubbish bin before hobbling past the almost hidden barrier and onto the path between the trees.

A few metres along the path by the clearing, Mikkel Jensen had said on the phone. He stopped and rubbed his ankle as he orientated himself. Water dripped from the trees after the recent rainstorm, and there was that pleasant smell of fresh oak and musty wet forest floor. A jay's warning cry sounded like a machine gun in the distance. By the clearing, he repeated, thinking it had to be the one he could sense ahead. Then he caught sight of them. The forensic technicians were easy to spot in white suits that glowed between the tree trunks. They were rummaging around on the forest floor, picking things up with their white gloves. The samples were put in small bags, which were carefully closed. Roland fought his way through the trees. He walked through damp grass and scrub and noticed his socks were getting wet.

"Have you found anything?" he asked breathlessly after his hike across the uneven terrain.

"We've taken casts of some tyre prints at the edge of the forest," said one of the forensic technicians who was squatting and looking up. "There's been a lot of rain, but I think we'll get something out of it."

Roland nodded contentedly and stood next to another technician who was in the process of making a new casting of the forest floor. "Shoe footprint—from a dress shoe with smooth soles. Size forty-six," he informed Roland, who again nodded contentedly. *A dress shoe in a forest? Curious.* But then he looked at his own wet shoes. What if going into the woods hadn't been the plan.

He spotted Mikkel, who was talking to another forensic technician, and went over to them.

"The tannic acid in acorns is released and converted into a toxic substance when the horse absorbs it into its body. The horse gets colic and can die if that's not detected," the forensic technician said.

"Are we absolutely sure the crime scene's here?" Roland asked, interrupting them in the middle of a conversation about acorns that had made the technician's horse sick.

"The Dog Unit found the site, and both tyre and shoe prints have been found here, too," Mikkel replied.

Roland nodded. "But isn't it a busy area? There's a shelter somewhere around here, isn't there?"

"That's further in. No one comes here. People tend to follow the paths," said Mikkel.

He looked around. Mikkel was probably right. What did people want here between the trees when nice passable paths had been laid out.

"But nothing else of importance?"

Mikkel threw his head towards the clearing. "Angela Merkel's here," he said.

Roland couldn't contain his smile. Mikkel had seen the similarity, too—or he had spoken to Morten Holsted. Envoys from the Special Operations Unit were always in for friendly teasing. Mikkel and the forensic technician continued to search the forest floor.

Roland walked towards the clearing as he looked around. *Why would a perp choose this exact place? How would you lure a little girl here?* The oak trees were of Dutch descent. Beautiful and upright, but quite uniform. Since the twenty-two-hectare forest had been laid out in 1989, it had already been thinned out several times. Still, he found it somewhat impassable. He stepped in something soft. *Dog shit.* Luckily, it was in a plastic bag. Roland shook his head disapprovingly. He knew well some dog owners dutifully picked up their best friend's leftovers in a plastic bag only to throw it in the nearest bush. They were in his neighbourhood in Højbjerg, too. *Does shit in nature degrade faster than shit in a plastic bag?* Misunderstood consideration.

He made it over to Julie Hermansen, who was sitting in her own thoughts on a weather-dried wooden bench by the clearing, looking at the bushes and the wildflowers. Purple rosebay willowherb was dominant, blooming in large clusters between tall species of grass, thistles, and yellow tansy. The bench she was sitting on was surrounded by grass with an abundance of white clover flowers. The grass was worn down to the bare earth under the bench, proof of the many people who stole quiet moments there. The forest was a lovely spot in the middle of Gellerup's built-up area, he had to admit. Out on the horizon, he glimpsed the concrete buildings on the other side of Silkeborgvej.

"Can you picture him?" asked Roland.

Julie looked up at him in surprise, as if startled.

"I'm not psychic." She smiled. "But there's been a little breakthrough, hasn't there?"

Roland nodded, wanting a cigarette, but as this was also part of the crime scene, it was strictly forbidden to even have the thought.

"Do you already have a criminal profile drawn up?" he asked, sticking both hands in his trouser pockets instead. The sun shone down into the clearing, where the wildflowers stretched to get the only bit of sun they could in the wet summer. May had been a hot month, but June had been the rainiest and had broken one of the many weather records. Something was wrong with the weather gods' planning. Or was it global warming?

"It's not a given that you're looking for a male paedophile," Julie said after a pause. "Only about five per cent of people who sexually abuse children are actually paedophiles, according to experts." Interested, Roland looked at her face. She kept staring beyond the clearing.

"So you mean it could be anyone?"

"No, not anyone. It's someone who's lived under psychological pressure for a long time. He isn't necessarily driven by sex, but he's certainly been the victim of gross neglect."

"You say *he*. Can we rule out a woman?" Roland asked cautiously.

"No, definitely not. It's purely incidental I'm using the masculine. According to the autopsy report, the girl wasn't raped." She looked questioningly at him with very blue eyes that seemed to have their colour enhanced by a pair of coloured lenses. The edge of the lenses could just be sensed in the light. She was obviously a woman full of surprises. Her attire had also changed from neat business to a pair of worn jeans, runners, and a cotton blouse. She must have gone back to her room at the Hotel Atlantic before leaving for the crime scene.

"We can't rule out that the perp may have used a condom, but the forensic pathologist found no semen or signs of violence," he replied.

"Was virginity intact?" asked Julie.

Roland looked at her in surprise.

"The hymen, I mean." She smiled. Roland got annoyed; he knew well what she was talking about, it just surprised him those words had come out her mouth.

"I haven't heard it in so many words from Henry Leander," he admitted.

"It probably doesn't matter much, either. A girl's hymen can break from so many things—gymnastics, cycling, falling, and what have you. And not even all girls are born with one. Anyway, I'm due to review the autopsy report with Henry later."

Julie began to walk back towards the crime scene. Roland followed after her. They walked side by side when there was room between the thin tree trunks and little bushes.

"Perhaps you can give me a little clue as to what kind of person we're looking for—if it's not a paedophile?" he asked.

Julie lifted an oak leaf from a branch and twisted it between her fingers as she walked and spoke. "Perps are divided into three groups: those who are *sadistic*, those who are *angry*, and those who feel *powerless*."

He looked at her with an expression that showed he was none the wiser. She continued: "About five per cent are sadistic offenders—mentally ill people who act perversely and violently when carrying out their abuse of children. You can ignore that category as Gitte wasn't violently abused. About forty-five per cent are angry perps. They're usually friendly and sociable. They suppress their anger towards others, and it comes out as impulsive abuse. Your perp could belong to this category." They stopped when they reached the others.

"What about the last category?"

Only a few technicians remained at the crime scene. There probably wasn't much to find now.

"The last group's the largest. About half of all criminals fall into the category of powerless perps. They try to regain power and control over their situation through planned assaults."

"So we can only rule out sadistic perps?" muttered Roland.

Julie nodded. She stood peeling some small bumps off the back of the oak leaf.

"They're gall wasps," she explained, a little embarrassed when she discovered he was looking at her curiously. "They lay eggs on the back of the oak leaves, whose tissue then grows over the eggs and develops into these little nodules as the leaf grows. They're called *galls*."

He rolled his eyes behind her. She and Henry would probably have a lot to talk about.

Mikkel's loud shouts pulled him away from the show. Mikkel was waving a small bag in the air. Roland and Julie walked over to him.

"I think we can well assume we've found the crime scene. We found this there." Mikkel pointed to an area further away as he handed Roland the small bag.

Roland turned it in the sparse light and nodded, then handed it to Julie. In the bag was a small hand in skin-coloured plastic. The doll's right hand.

65

Darkness was falling when Danny drove into the car park of Danhostel Aarhus. He parked, got out of the car, and took the two suitcases out of the boot. He was staying longer this time. Tonny had given him a couple of assignments in Jutland, delighted to have him "back in business."

It felt good. Being back in Jutland, too. The sight of the car park made his stomach clench. He cast a sideways glance at the site of the assault. But he could understand Rasmus's dad's anger. He had seen the boy's photo the morning he had got up early to make coffee for Kamilla after their night together. But his courage had failed him. He couldn't sit there, drinking coffee with her, and, at the same time, look at the picture of Rasmus on her bookshelf. He had to leave. Needed to think. So he had left a note for her, even though he hadn't wanted to leave her. But he couldn't stay away. He had to tell her what had happened, but again his courage failed him. He knew he would lose something good that hadn't even begun yet. But this time, his courage wouldn't let him down. Kamilla would hear the truth from him.

As he dragged the suitcases in, he thought of how strange fate was. He threw himself on the bed with an unexpected feeling of freedom inside. Suddenly, he felt it would all work out. Optimism had grown on the ferry on the way to Jutland. Despite the rain, he had stood on deck, watching the wake foaming behind the express ferry, and Zealand disappearing into the hazy grey horizon. The smell of seawater was in the air; it sent cool salty splashes up into his face. He hoped Kamilla would understand. Forgive him. Could she? He lay there for a long time looking up at the ceiling as his thoughts whirled. He could also refrain from saying anything about it. Pretend it was nothing. But he knew that wouldn't work in the long run. The truth always came out. *Justice will prevail,* it was said. He considered calling her and telling her he was back, but he decided to wait. It was getting late. He got up and closed the curtains. Even though it was raining quietly, he could hear a blackbird singing somewhere out in the dusk. He opened the suitcase and found the newspaper someone had left on the ferry. He had taken it because he had spotted an article with one of Kamilla's photos on the front page, but he hadn't managed to read it on the boat. It was a picture of the developmentally disabled boy who had been a suspect. He was holding a black toy car in his hand and squinting at the camera lens. Danny read the article.

66

Kamilla hadn't slept that night. Troubled dreams woke her hour after hour. In one, her mother had appeared as a death-like creature promising doomsday was upon her. When the blackbird began to sing along with the rest of the dawn chorus in the garden, she gave up trying to sleep and got up.

Tarzan was already waiting to be let in. The cat stood by the patio door and put wet paw prints on the glass. She let him in and felt the coolness of the morning and the cat's damp fur brush her bare legs. She went into the bathroom and took a hot shower.

As she sat over her coffee cup in her dressing gown, she felt tired, but it was too late to go to bed again now. She looked enviously at Tarzan, who curled up in the chair and immediately fell into a deep sleep after emptying his food bowl.

The headache hadn't let up, even though she had taken two Panadol. After Jan's visit, she had wanted to call Majken, but the memory of the hate in her eyes when she had left in anger on Saturday held her back. But there was so much she needed to talk to her about. Majken needed to know it was Danny who had taken Rasmus from them. Maybe her infatuation would disappear then, too. Had he come here to seek her out and exploit her vulnerability? What did he want?

It was eight o'clock. She got dressed and packed her camera bag, which accompanied her now like it always had before. Some things were starting to get back to normal again. Just a week ago, she would have sworn nothing would ever be the same. She had even felt the first throes of a love affair. The longing was still there, but she had to forget about it. Could she? She asked herself the question as she locked the front door, after putting Tarzan outside strongly against his will, legs squirming. Yeah, she could easily live without sex and love. She had learned to live without them. *Being alone isn't necessarily the same as being lonely.* As long as she had her job, she would manage. She felt determined as she got behind the wheel of her silver Ford Ka.

She was going to drive past Rasmus first. Then she was going to drive as far away as she possibly could and think. Find somewhere quiet—a place of natural beauty—and take some pictures, if the sun stayed in the sky.

The graveyard was even more peaceful this early in the morning. According to summertime, it was eight o'clock, but in reality, it was seven. She could feel it in the coolness of the air. The bench was damp, so she didn't sit down. The sun penetrated a thin layer of white cloud, sending a gentle golden morning glow over the graves and hedges, where the cobwebs had collected dew. They became apparent when the faint rays of the sun hit them. She felt like taking a picture but found it inappropriate to photograph in a cemetery. The silence closed in on her. She slipped into another world. Hers and Rasmus's world, with all their memories, laughter, and joy.

She didn't hear anyone hobbling across the gravel but instead felt the presence of another person behind her. He stepped forwards and stood next to her. She saw a small bouquet of marguerites in his hand but avoided looking at him.

"I picked them at the side of the road," he said quietly, offering his hand, so a few white petals fell to the ground. Kamilla didn't respond. Her breathing was rapid. There wasn't enough air to get the words out. Not that she could find them. He laid the flowers by the headstone. She wanted to go. Run away. But her legs didn't obey her. The tears, which she had otherwise sworn would not appear in her eyes today, blurred her vision.

He tried to take her hand, but she tore it away with a jerk and folded her arms over her chest in a defensive protective position. She still avoided looking at him. She didn't want to see his eyes.

"Is it inappropriate that I've come, Kamilla? I'm sorry. I didn't think there'd be anyone here so early." Danny's voice sounded husky.

"How did you find out where Rasmus is buried?" There was no friendliness or kindness in her voice. It was as cold as the morning air.

"It was easy enough to figure out. And then, when I saw you, I . . ."

"Why have you come back? I don't want to see you here! You're not to come near Rasmus again!" Tears sat in her throat, making it difficult to speak. Her legs started to listen. She ran down the path towards the exit, through the grey gravel that crunched under her shoes.

The car's wheels spun in the gravel as she turned onto Mejlbyvej and continued at too fast a speed towards Grenåvej.

The bench was wet and made the thin canvas trousers stick to his skin, but he didn't feel it. He only registered one thing: Kamilla knew. There was no doubt about it. She hated him. She really hated him. The round marble stone stood before him, blurred through the tears, as a symbol of her hatred. He put his hand on his head, feeling the pain in his left side. His eye was almost closed in its blue-black swollen socket. Luckily, Kamilla hadn't seen it.

"Can't you forgive me, either, Rasmus?" he asked into the air, feeling foolish. It was so important for him to be forgiven for the sin that had destroyed him, but he didn't know where to find it. Certainly not within himself. He rubbed his face. He had hardly slept. At two o'clock, he had appointments in Aarhus. First, a potential new client who wanted to hear more about the advertising agency's work. Then a meeting with another advertising agency interested in selling its premises. He wondered how to explain his appearance, but he would come up with something. Tonny had said a little white lie was probably best and suggested a sports injury. Afterwards, he had entrusted Danny with his plans to open a subsidiary in Aarhus and asked whether Danny would be interested in running it. That kept him awake at night, too. Moving from familiar surroundings to start as a managing director in an advertising agency with its own employees was a major decision. But did he have anything to stay in Klampenborg for? Did he have anything here? He stood for a moment in silence at the boy's grave, his head bowed as if in prayer.

67

Roland glanced at Mikkel Jensen, who was sitting in the passenger seat next to him. They had just listened to Niels Nyborg's scratchy voice on the police radio. Ida Mikkelsen had called and given the name of Gitte's biological mother. Nanette Pedersen. There was only one address listed for the girl's mother, Gunda Pedersen, who lived in Vejle. Nyborg assumed the daughter lived there with her mother.

Roland checked the rear-view mirror before overtaking. "Bloody summer," he grumbled. The rain hit the windshield as they drove up Dronning Margrethes Vej.

Mikkel nodded in agreement. "The weather's forecast for even more rain in the coming weeks," he complained.

It wasn't just the weather Roland had been alluding to. The sun could still come, couldn't it? He would set out in the first week of August for a much-needed holiday in his home country. He visited his family in southern Italy every summer. What was left of it. For a brief second, he was back on the dirty streets of Naples, where rubbish lay scattered in heaps around the bins, attracting rats by the droves in the heat. Such a shame for the otherwise beautiful city. But even the waste collection was controlled by the Camorra, a name that turned his blood to ice. After his mother's death three years ago, he had kept up the tradition. And despite him not remembering his father, he couldn't give up the visits to the graveyard in Naples, either. Standing there, by the white headstone with his father's cast portrait, he felt such intense hatred that he wanted to return and complete his father's work of fighting the mafia, but he felt it was useless; a far bigger and more dangerous task than fighting crime in Aarhus, even though that was bad enough at times. Italy has the mafia, Denmark has the gangs and the new immigrant gangs, which were far more bloody and dangerous than the original groups.

A cyclist fought his way up the hill on Dronning Margrethes Vej, the hood of his raincoat pulled far down over his forehead. Heavy drops dripped from the leaves of Riis Forest. Fortunately, forensics had casts of the footprints and tyres in Gellerup Forest. But how much was ruined? It had rained almost non-stop for the last week. The technical department was busy working overtime to analyse all the traces found. Thank God for forensics in that regard. The net was starting to tighten around the murderer. Roland felt it as a slight tingle in his neck.

The morning briefing had been sluggish, despite the positive turn in the case. Everyone was tired after yesterday's work, which, after finding the crime scene, had ended late with a review of Allan Mikkelsen's hunting buddies. Were they the ones they had overlooked? Would they find Gitte's killer among that group? Jesper Ingemann had been ruled out as a hunting buddy. It was beginning to look like they would have to settle for jailing him for sexual violations. The police's specially trained staff were conducting video interviews of other children from the after-school centres where he had worked as a youth leader, so more cases could lead to a heavier sentence. Jesper's email address hadn't tallied, either. It was proving impossible to find the person behind Teddy Bear. They could only wait for the IP address to be tracked. Sometimes Roland feared they were on a wild goose chase—maybe the email address and hunting buddies didn't play a role at all.

There was so much weighing on him. Louise Poulsen's parents had blamed him for the investigation into the murder of Gitte taking precedence over finding their little girl, who could still be alive. But that wasn't true. They were doing what they could to find Louise, but there weren't many leads to follow. There was only the car. The technical department had found a match between the tyre impression in front of the skip and the one from the playground. They were from the same car. If they could find that car, he was sure both cases could be cleared up in one fell swoop. They hadn't got the results of the tyre prints from the crime scene yet, but it wouldn't surprise him if they originated from the same car. He hoped so.

The phone interrupted his thoughts.

"Hi, Morten! Is there anything new in your case?" he asked when DI Holsted made himself known on the phone. He was breathing heavily.

"No, in fact, it's your case. Cyber tracked the Hotmail account. They found an IP address."

"Why didn't they contact me about it directly?" he said curtly. Mikkel stared at him curiously from the passenger seat, but Roland didn't take his eyes off the road.

"Because it concerns my case as well. The email was sent from the old woman's computer."

"From Olga Halgren's computer? But there's no way she was sending emails to little girls! Was she Teddy Bear?"

Roland braked hard at Mikkel's command to turn as he pointed to the next traffic light.

"Maybe our cases do have something to do with each other. We're still in the process of locating that grandchild. We need to have a talk at some point."

"Thanks, Morten." He hung up and, with a shake of his head, focused all his attention on the traffic again, turned gently onto Egå Havvej, and followed Mikkel's directions. He had found the address.

"Egå Angling Shop! There!" he shouted, pointing to the left. "What's the story with the email address?" he asked curiously a little while later.

"I don't know what the fuck's going on." Roland only cursed when something really bothered him. "The email to Gitte Mikkelsen was sent from Olga Halgren's computer."

He parked the car in the car park in front of the shop. There were the last of the hunting buddies to talk to. If there was nothing here, they would have to rule out the killer being among the Mikkelsens' circle of friends.

"From the old woman's computer? That's unbelievable. It's like something you'd see on TV." Mikkel shook his head as he opened the car door.

A little bell over the door to the angling shop chimed as they entered. There was no one behind the counter, and there were no customers. *Not the weather for anglers, either,* Roland told himself, despite not having a clue about fishing.

A tall, thin, pale man emerged from a curtain behind the counter.

"CID—Criminal Investigation Department," Roland informed him, showing his ID.

The man's small eyes grew slightly larger.

"So the police go fishing as well?" The voice was calm with a touch of sarcasm.

"Yeah, and we may have found ourselves a big catch. Are you Troels Mortensen?"

Mikkel always went straight to the point. Sometimes a little too direct for Roland's liking. He stood looking at a Vertex distance fishing rod.

"How much does a rod like this cost?" he asked politely. He always went for innocent until proven otherwise. Troels edged over to him between boxes of wellies and tents, suddenly eager to serve someone who might be a customer.

"Two thousand six hundred and ninety-nine kroner," he replied without looking at a price list.

Mikkel whistled. "That's nothing to shake a stick at."

Offended, Troels looked at him. "It's also ESP. When only the best is good enough!"

"What do you fish for with a rod at that price?" Roland asked curiously. He had a notion a fishing rod cost no more than a few hundred kroner.

"It's for carp fishing actually. One of the best rods on the market from British carp guru Terry Hearn," said Troels professionally.

"For a *gold carp*, at least," Mikkel stated dryly.

Roland smiled a little at his comment.

Mikkel stood turning an all-round knife he had pulled out its holster, looking at the sharp blade.

"Perfect for a murder," he said, deep in thought.

Troels began to show signs of nervousness. He withdrew behind the counter. "Why are you here, if it's not to buy something?" he said, his voice turning hostile.

"We're investigating the murder of Gitte Mikkelsen. I'm sure you've heard about it?" Roland put his hands in his pockets and walked towards the counter.

"Is there somewhere we can talk privately?" Troels asked.

He followed the tall, thin man into the room behind the curtain and, from the corner of his eye, saw Mikkel sneak out the door to look around the garage and the warehouse. The door's chime sounded again, but the pale man didn't seem to hear it. He moved a stack of papers and a box of lines lying on a chair so Roland could sit down. Troels sat down on a worn office chair at a low desk. The little room was almost as cluttered as Roland's office. In the corner was an old computer with a dusty screen. The keyboard was tucked under stacks of paper that looked like old invoices.

"Of course I heard about the murder. I know the family," Troels said calmly. There was a sad expression in his eyes. He wiped his palms on the thighs of his jeans. For a brief second, Roland doubted the insecure man could be the perp. He had immediately admitted knowing the family of the murdered girl.

"Do you know her friend Louise Poulsen, too?"

"I heard about her on TV. But no, I don't know her."

"Where were you on Monday and Wednesday afternoon last week?"

The man thought, with a wrinkle between his almost imperceptible eyebrows. "That was a long time ago, but I think I was here in the shop. I nearly always am."

"Are there any witnesses? Customers, for example?" asked Roland.

The pale face sent him an equally pale smile. He gestured towards the curtain out to the shop floor. "As you can see, Inspector, it's not exactly the busiest shop on earth. But what's all this about? Am I being arrested?"

"No, no, this is just routine. We're interviewing the family's circle of friends. Any employees?"

Troels shook his head.

"So no alibi," Roland stated dryly.

"Do you suspect me of something?" There was a slight uncertainty in his voice, Roland noticed.

"How well did you know Gitte Mikkelsen?" He calmly maintained contact with the pale eyes, letting him sweat a little.

"I fish with her father, Allan, so I visit them from time to time. It's tragic for the family."

"When was your last visit?"

"Hmm, last month, I think. Allan probably remembers better than me," he replied cagily.

Roland didn't respond to the comment. Troels didn't need to know they had talked to Allan Mikkelsen if he hadn't already guessed that.

"Did you know Gitte was adopted?" The question made the man look away. He absently moved a box of hooks that looked like small fish in fluorescent colours.

"No, I had no idea. Was she?" He looked at Roland again.

"If you think of anything, give me a call." Roland got up and laid his business card on the table. "Though I have to ask you to come down to the station to have a blood sample taken for DNA analysis. But you don't mind that, do you?"

"Of course not." Troels got up, too, and held out a freckled hand in goodbye. Roland took it and felt the weak, greasy handshake.

The curtain was roughly torn aside. Mikkel stuck his head out. There were raindrops.

"Where's your car?"

Troels looked at him calmly, without being able to hide his contempt for the young officer.

"My wife has it."

68

The TomTom was set to the address on the outskirts of Vejle, where Gunda Pedersen lived. Anne gloated to herself over her contact's helpfulness with the police radio. It paid to have acquaintances in crime.

She lit a cigarette and listened to a Guns N' Roses hit on the car radio. The music made her feel both on a high and on the right track. Maybe she should have invited Kamilla along, but the article about Gitte's biological mother, Nanette Pedersen, didn't need any supporting photos. Not at first, at least.

In a monotonous computer voice, the GPS announced she should continue straight ahead, and after eight hundred metres, turn right. After the Vejle Bridge. An angler was standing with a line in the water. Ibæk Strandvej was long, offering a beautiful view of Vejle Fjord.

Suddenly, the TomTom announced she should turn right; she had arrived at her destination. It was a gravel driveway on a slight slope. The house was partway up the slope in the woods. An expensive location, it seemed, with a beautiful view of the fjord. It was a redbrick house from the fifties.

Her stomach feeling a little uneasy, Anne rang the doorbell. Roland Benito would be angry if he knew about this. She knew they were in the process of investigating the family's hunting friends. Maybe they had sent someone to Vejle, and she was about to bump into them. She shouldn't go anywhere before the police but impressing both Thygesen and Benito had become a sport, even if it didn't make her popular with the police.

It was hard to put an age on the woman who finally answered the door. Anne sensed she looked older than she was. She had a wrinkled slender face and matte brown eyes that seemed too dark for her pale complexion. They looked at her questioningly. Her hair was short, grey, and permed. Her white blouse emphasised her pale expression even more. She said nothing but continued looking at Anne, who asked if she could come in. Gunda Pedersen opened the door, still without saying anything.

Anne entered a living room where time seemed to have stood still since the sixties. It was pure retro—wallpaper, rugs, and furniture of the time were looking a little dilapidated and faded, but she could see they had been once modern and beautiful. Atop a circular white runner on a small round teak table stood a teapot, teacup, and cream-and-sugar set from Fanny Garde's famous Danish seagull collection.

"Are you expecting guests?" asked Anne considerately.

Gunda shook her head. "No, I was just making tea. Who are you and what do you want?" She was a small woman. Despite Anne herself not being so tall, she looked down at her.

"I'd like to talk to your daughter. Nanette. Is she home?"

Gunda shook her head and went to a teak cabinet with glass doors to get another teacup. Anne took it as an invitation to sit down, and she sank into a deep beige velour armchair with fringes standing on the other side of the round table. There was just room for one more cup on the table. From the window, she could look out onto the fjord.

"This is a lovely place to live," said Anne as tea was poured into her cup with a slightly trembling hand. She noticed the gold ring and the fine gold chain around Gunda's slender wrist. She wasn't used to older people and felt insecure. Her memories were of old ladies from Nørrebro who had looked degradingly at her attire and piercings and threatened her with their canes. There was no need for that anymore. She was wearing white capris and a denim jacket over a blue-striped blouse bought at H&M. She tried to relax.

"It'll do. The only noise is from the train." Gunda sighed as she sat down in the chair opposite Anne. "What do you want with my daughter?"

Anne didn't know whether she should tell Gunda everything. Mrs. Pedersen was Gitte Mikkelsen's grandmother, despite not knowing her—Gitte having been given up for adoption as an infant. But hearing her granddaughter had been murdered might still come as a shock. Anne had no training on how to deal with that, so she thought it best to leave it to the police.

"I'm a journalist," she admitted, throwing herself into it. She took a mouthful of the hot tea and burned herself. Gunda didn't seem to mind journalists. Her neutral facial expression didn't change.

"Oh, I forgot the biscuits. I was on my way out to get them when you called," she stated, getting up. She walked slowly, leaning against the doorframe on her way out to the kitchen. While she was away, Anne looked at the many pictures on the dresser opposite. Most, she guessed, were of Gunda and her husband. It was a young version of Gunda. Three children smiled and had their arms around each other. Grandchildren, definitely. There were pictures of two other girls. One, who was probably around twenty, had dark curls, the other was much older, and short-haired like Anne.

Gunda returned with a bowl of biscuits and set it in the middle of the table. Anne quickly took her eyes off the pictures.

"How do you know Nanette?" Gunda sat down again.

Anne explained she didn't know the woman's daughter, but she was writing an article about adoption from ten years before and had discovered Nanette had given up a child for adoption at that time. Anne hoped the cover story would work, though it didn't sound very convincing. Gunda paled.

"Where did you get that information from?" she asked suspiciously.

Anne hesitated. "I'm afraid I can't tell you that. My source is anonymous," she lied.

Gunda looked out over the fjord and was quiet for a long time. As if she had disappeared into another era. Then she began to speak monotonously, like it was something she did every day during afternoon tea.

"We lived in Zealand at the time. Nanette was only fourteen. I don't know if that brute raped her, but she was a licentious child. Maybe we were too old. Nanette was an afterthought. When I became pregnant, I didn't think I was able to have more children. We agreed her child needed to go. We had big plans for Nanette. Despite her being wild and difficult to control, she was so talented." Her dull brown eyes began to shine in the light from the window.

"Who did you give the child to—to adopt?" Anne dared to ask, even though she knew the answer.

"A family here in Jutland." Gunda returned to the present and looked directly at her. "I don't remember who they are anymore. I didn't want to know, either. It all happened so fast. But it was the best thing we could do for Nanette."

"Why didn't you choose an abortion?"

Gunda looked at her sternly. "Both my husband and I have always been faithful Christian Democrats. Abortion's a sin. It's murder!"

Anne shuddered at those words, given Gitte had been murdered. What would it have spared both her and Nanette if an abortion had occurred ten years earlier?

"Do you know who the child's father was?" she hurried to ask to rid herself of the unpleasant controversial thought and the woman's accusing gaze.

A muscle on Gunda's face twitched. She quickly took a sip from her cup. "He was a beast. He was. My husband and I moved here to Vejle five years ago. I've always been afraid he would seek us out. He wasn't normal. But he probably thinks we still live in Zealand."

Anne felt the knot in her stomach tighten. She knew well what that was like. "Where's your husband? Is he not home, either?" she asked, taking a bite of a biscuit.

"Anders lives in Rosengården—the nursing home. He couldn't cope with the pressure and has had two blood clots. The last one was in his brain." Gunda looked out over the fjord again, back in her own world.

Anne sat quietly eating the biscuit, not wanting to disturb her peace. She emptied her cup and got up. Gunda looked up at her. Her eyes showed a pain that hadn't been there when Anne had arrived. She wondered whether she had stirred up old memories and felt a tad guilty.

"Which of the girls is Nanette?" she asked with a nod to the pictures, smiling.

Gunda turned around and took the picture of the dark-haired girl with shoulder-length curls and smiling brown eyes. Anne had guessed she had to be Gitte's mother. They had the same dark curly hair and the same eyes. Gunda looked at it lovingly, but she didn't say anything. There was a glimmer of anger in her eyes, too, but it disappeared again quickly.

"When can I meet Nanette? I would very much like to talk to her," said Anne gently.

Gunda looked directly at her again with her dark eyes. The anger had returned.

"Then you'll have to dig her up from her grave. She died five years ago."

69

———

$\mathbf{S}$he had moved out into the garden in front of the house. From here, she had a view of the bay. You could just sense the Mols Mountains, which lay bluish in the haze on the other side of the water. She leaned her head against the back of the deckchair and closed her eyes, about to enjoy the rays of sunshine that had graciously appeared this summer. They had talked about buying tickets to Mallorca or Tenerife, she and her husband, if the bad weather persisted.

She pushed the sunglasses up into her hair so her forehead was free. The sun burned her face, which reflected her fondness for sunbathing; her skin resembled dark leather because, even in winter, she used the solarium that hung over the bed in the guest room. She didn't notice her husband coming until she felt him stroke her cheek and caught the scent of his aftershave.

"Have you finished already, honey?" She didn't look up at him but sensed him lying down on the other deck chair. She guessed he had changed into his shorts but didn't bother looking.

"Yeah, I left early today. There's a meeting in the district court tonight that I have to get ready for."

She contented herself with nodding. She didn't know much about his work—didn't understand it, either. *Land shall by law be built*, she tended to say roguishly.

They lay in silence for a long time. She could hear him flipping through some papers and was about to doze off when a cloud passed in front of the sun. At least that was what she thought had happened, but then she heard her husband's shocked voice. "Oh my God! What happened, child?" She heard a bang and sat up with a start. In the middle of the deckchairs lay a girl, who had overturned the small garden table. Her glass of water had shattered on the Italian terrace tiles. The girl lay on her stomach and wasn't moving. The man squatted down and gently turned her over so they could see her face. She looked starved and neglected. A girl of about ten with thin blond hair and an emaciated body.

"Is she dead?" The woman's voice went up to a falsetto.

"She's breathing," her husband replied calmly, grasping the situation.

"What does she have on her wrist? Her other wrist looks awful, too!" The woman put her hand over her mouth in horror.

"It's a rope. It looks like she's been tied up and managed to file off the rope." The husband's voice shook a little, but he was more hardened than his wife from his many years of work with criminals, having seen every-thing under the sun.

"Where in the world did she come from?" Appalled, she looked out over the manicured garden with the huge well-mown green lawn that had enjoyed all the rain of the summer. It was the only access to the terrace if you didn't come through the house. The girl must have come stumbling across it. That was what the woman had perceived as the shade passing in front of the sun.

"Did you see her coming?" she asked her husband, frightened.

"No, not before she fell. But she must have come across the lawn—from the residential street perhaps." He held the girl's head up and tried to shake her into consciousness.

"Dear God, a child. What happened to her? She looks like the girl they've been searching for—on the TV—doesn't she?"

Her husband was on his way into the house at a run.

"Watch her; I'm going to call for an ambulance," he shouted over his shoulder.

70

———

The call came just as they were parking the car at the police station.

"Louise Poulsen's been found. She turned up in Judge Johansen's garden in Risskov."

"Turned up how?" Roland wasn't in the mood for smartness. Something gnawed at him, as if he should be thinking of something his brain just wouldn't reveal to him.

"She's very hungry; she doesn't seem to have had anything to eat or drink for some time. She must have escaped and found her way through the hedge to the judge's garden. She was tied up like Gitte and still had some of the rope around one of her wrists. It's been sent to forensics. The kidnapper has to be in that area," DS Dan Vang continued in a less joking tone.

"Has she been interviewed?" asked Roland, feeling the tingling sensation in his neck again.

"She's been admitted to Aarhus Hospital. We don't have access until they've stabilised her. She's on a feeding tube."

"Shit. So when?"

"I don't know; I'll keep you informed. Where are you, by the way?"

"We're on our way up," Roland replied.

Mikkel Jensen sat down on the corner of Roland's desk.

"We're making progress now," he said.

Roland painstakingly hung his jacket over the back of the chair. It wouldn't come as a surprise to him if they were called out to an emergency again soon.

"Yes, but it's only loose ends. How are we to tie them together?" He sat down heavily on the chair so the gas-assisted height adjustment gave way under him and lit a cigarette.

"When we get Louise Poulsen's statement, we'll have him." Mikkel grew optimistic.

"And when might that be? We don't know when Louise will be ready to talk to us. She must be in shock. My hunch is it all has something to do with Gitte Mikkelsen's unknown father."

Roland rubbed his eyes; they were running from fatigue and cigarette smoke. Still, he felt a certain degree of relief. Louise was in good hands and apparently out of danger, despite the ticking time bomb being triggered.

DS Kim Ansager knocked on the doorframe and stepped inside. He announced he had news on Gitte Mikkelsen's mother.

"Nanette Pedersen died five years ago. She was only nineteen," Kim said with a sad look in his eyes.

"How did she die?" asked Roland, fearing a new crime. But Kim explained it had been a traffic accident. Nanette had been riding a bike when she was hit by a truck turning right in inner Copenhagen, where the family lived at the time. Gunda and Anders Pedersen had moved to Vejle after that, where their eldest daughter lives with her own family and three children. Later, Anders Pedersen had entered a nursing home in Vejle.

"We can't question him. He's paralysed due to a brain haemorrhage," Kim finished his report.

"We sent somebody over there, didn't we?" Roland asked, hoping a trip to Vejle wasn't on the cards. He was exhausted from too much overtime and too little sleep. Strong coffee was the only thing that kept him going. Kim nodded.

"How did she take the news her granddaughter's dead?" Roland asked worriedly.

"It didn't come as a complete surprise. A journalist was there before us," Kim replied, leaning against the doorframe with his arms crossed. "Anne Larsen," he said dryly.

"Bloody hell!" shouted Roland, whacking the table. "Does that mean it'll be in the paper tomorrow?"

"Most likely. Unless you can stop her?" Kim inquired, and Mikkel sent Roland a look that encouraged him to give it a try. They left both his office and him alone.

Roland leaned back in his chair and tried to get an overview of the case. The crime scene had been found—they were just waiting on the results from forensics. Louise was safe, but he wasn't going to get anything out of her for the time being. Gitte Mikkelsen's biological mother had died in an accident, and they still had to find her father. That had to be their priority. He looked at his watch and stubbed out the cigarette. Then he made good on an idea he had been toying with for most of the day. Irene had been so patient. A guilty conscience gnawed at him. He would call and invite her out to dinner tonight, so they could eat together for once. He would book a table at Italia, which was close to the police station, so he could easily head out if something important came up. But first he needed to have a few serious words with Anne Larsen.

71

Anne was satisfied with her article by the time she emailed it to Thygesen. She thoroughly enjoyed those days when she could work from home, and she needed the freedom it gave her to move. Working from home also meant no noise from Britt's transistor radio with its annoying pop music, other people's loud private conversations, or disturbing phone calls, so she got a lot more done. Of course, the trip to Vejle did mean a pause in her unpacking, but it was worth it.

Discovering Gitte Mikkelsen had been adopted as a baby had been a scoop. Even Roland Benito had seemed impressed. He had called her mobile and given her the green light to write the story with exclusive rights. She smiled. Although it was normal for the police to help reporters, it had been a great pleasure for her to be able to help them. It wasn't like her. The shock that Nanette had died at only nineteen hadn't quite subsided yet. Neither had the shock from the phone conversation she had just had with Roland. It hadn't been as pleasant as the first conversation. He had been very angry. He had cursed and reprimanded her worse than her stepfather had ever done. But contrary to her stepfather's loud shouts and punches, which didn't get to her, Roland's words had affected her. She didn't want to be in his bad books. He had threatened to stop all cooperation with her and the newspaper if she didn't learn to stay in the background a little. It would affect her relationship with both him and Thygesen. That must not happen. So she had reviewed the article about Gitte's mother with him and written nothing other than what he had approved.

She stretched, leaned back in her chair, and looked around. It was an okay apartment. Better than the other one in fact. This time, she had unpacked most of her belongings and decided she was going to live here for the next year. Her phone number was unlisted, so only those she personally gave the number to could ring her. It made her a lot harder to track. Only Kamilla knew she had moved, but not where she had moved to. For the first time since she had come to Jutland, she felt safe.

It was hot, so she pulled her jumper off and threw it on the couch. The furniture was okay, too. Maybe a little too modern for her liking, but it worked. She looked at the tattoo of the little fish on her right upper arm, which she had rubbed with salt for several years to make it go away. It had been done in a tiny, dingy, poorly lit room somewhere in a basement on Istedgade in Copenhagen, when she had been under eighteen. Back then, she had been a member of a Christian sect, which a small group of young people from Nørrebro had formed. Nothing serious, more for the sake of togetherness. Some may well have been Christians, and the fish tattoo was obligatory. She had often regretted it. The sect didn't last long and had dis- integrated. Many people confused the tattoo with the logo of the Danish Evangelical Lutheran Church's Charity. Not that it meant much, but she would rather not send signals of any sort nowadays. The tattoo had gradu- ally become so faded and damaged one could no longer tell it had once resembled a fish.

Her eyes slid further over to the picture of her father on the sideboard. The only family photo she always displayed. Everything had started to go to hell after his death. How her mother had found a shit like Torsten, she didn't understand. She had no idea her mother was involved in that sort of environment. She couldn't remember her father very well; she had been very young when he died. But she did remember he had been good. Not like Torsten. She often asked herself what had become of her mother. Her four siblings were Torsten's offspring from a previous marriage. Anne had never been close to them. She hadn't seen them for years, neither had they contacted her. She had been ostracised the night it happened, and when she had chosen life on the streets and in Ungdomshuset—"The Juvey," as they had called it. It was gone now, and she hadn't taken part in the dem- onstrations herself because she'd had to flee to Jutland. But she probably wouldn't have joined the protests anyway. This was a different era. She had become kind of, as the others from Juvey would call her, middle class. She smiled. Other cases held her interest now.

The case with the little girl was affecting her more than she realised. Gitte Mikkelsen had an adoptive father. Was he like Torsten? When she had interviewed the parents with Kamilla, she had sensed they were hiding a secret. Was it just Gitte's secret adoption they were hiding, or was it something else?

She looked at the clock. Nearly dinnertime. The only thing she hadn't unpacked was all the kitchen stuff, and she had nothing in the fridge. She quickly put her jumper back on, grabbed her purse from her bag, and ran down the stairs. Out on the street, she heard the train pass noisily on the tracks. She stuffed her purse in her pocket. There had to be a pizzeria or a restaurant somewhere nearby.

72

Irene wore a nice red dress that complemented her tanned skin and dark hair perfectly. It wasn't often they went out for dinner. Too rare, Roland thought when he watched her come walking back from the toilets, apologising with a smile when she had to push in someone's chair to get by. After Italia had been renovated, the tables were so close it was difficult to move back and forth. Roland was a little disappointed he hadn't been here since the original Italia. It was certainly nicer than before, but it wasn't as cosy and intimate. Now you couldn't sit and talk without the people at adjacent tables listening.

Irene sat down opposite him and smiled happily. The crowd didn't seem to bother her. The scent of Estée Lauder Beyond Paradise, which he had given her as a birthday present, reached his nose. He felt "beyond paradise" as he reciprocated her smile and lifted his wine glass in a toast. For a moment, he was able to forget about all the crimes and evil in the world.

Irene leaned over to him and sent a discreet nod towards a table some distance behind him. "Isn't that the forensic pathologist—Leander—sitting over there? Who's he with?"

Roland was about to turn around to see when the waiter arrived with their main course. When he had gone, after pouring more wine into their glasses, Roland turned and saw Henry Leander sitting at a table further down the room. He smiled when he saw who he was with.

"That's Angela Merkel," he replied with a mischievous laugh.

"Why do you call her that? Do you know her?" Irene tucked into her tournedos portobello and nodded contentedly over the first mouthful.

"Good?" he asked, and she nodded again. "We call her Angela Merkel because she resembles her a little. Can't you see it?"

Irene looked for a long time but shook her head. "Not at this distance. Who is she?"

"Julie Hermansen from the Special Operations Unit. She's doing some criminal profiling for us to help us with the murder investigation of the little girl. Like I told you on the phone, we had a breakthrough today."

Irene smiled. She was probably looking forward to it all being over, too. They continued eating. Roland sat content, looking forward to dessert. It was great to see Irene enjoying real, non-diet, dishes—she even agreed to a tiramisu.

While waiting for dessert, they were interrupted in the middle of a conversation by Henry and Julie, who were leaving.

"Ah, you needed to get away from it all, too," Henry said, sending the white moustache up to his ears as he smiled. Julie stood next to him, her cheeks flushed. She was wearing a tight black dress with wide shoulder straps and carried a gold clutch bag. Henry was also unusually nicely dressed in a suit and white shirt. It was rare for Roland to see him in anything other than the smock he wore at the morgue.

"Are you gallivanting?" he asked, unable to resist sending Julie a wink. She blushed even more, and only now did Roland notice the wedding ring on her right hand clutching the gold bag. They probably didn't want to have bumped into them.

"We ended our meeting this afternoon with dinner. I think it'll soon be a bloody week since I've eaten proper food." Henry sent Julie a reassuring smile. Roland wondered how many insect species they had covered in their conversation. Whether Julie had seen Henry's collection of creepy-crawlies in his basement, or whether they'd had anything else to talk about. They said goodbye with an assurance they would see each other the next day. Roland followed them with his eyes as they walked, and, through the window, saw Henry put his arm around Julie's back when he thought they could no longer be seen.

"That was awkward," he grunted quietly, smiling again when he saw the tiramisu in front of him. He hadn't noticed the waiter.

"They make a sweet couple," Irene said happily. "Is she the one who helped you with your breakthrough?"

Roland cleared his throat and sank the spoon into the creamy dessert. "No, it was actually mostly the journalist—Anne Larsen." He sighed. He couldn't help but smile when he thought about how silent Anne had been when he had scolded her on the phone.

"You've never cared for the press, Rolando, but now you can see what I've always said. They can be of use, too." She winked at him and went to war with their dessert.

He had just ordered two espressos when his mobile played its familiar tune in his pocket. It took a while for the sound to get through to him in the din. The screen indicated the call was from a private number. He put the phone to his ear and squeezed his eyebrows together, as though that would make him hear better. Even covering his other ear with his hand, he still had a hard time hearing the voice on the phone. Only fragments escaped the noise and reached his ear.

"Help me, Roland. You have to help me!" Then the sound disappeared.

73

Anne let herself into the apartment as she balanced a pizza box from Super Star Pizza and a one-and-a-half-litre bottle of Coca-Cola. She had dropped the key twice as she was about to unlock the door, cursing because she had almost dropped the pizza each time she bent down for the key.

She'd had to drive all the way to Louisevej to find a pizzeria. On the way up the stairs, she scolded herself for not ordering dinner from Just Eat and having it brought straight to the door instead.

Using her elbow, she flicked on the light switch in the kitchen and set the pizza box down. The moving boxes with kitchen stuff took up most of the space. She had to move one to be able to open the fridge. The smell that hit her immediately told her it hadn't been used for a long time, but she put the bottle on the shelf anyway. It wasn't cold enough. The lone bottle in the big fridge looked silly. She smiled slightly and slammed the door shut.

The melted cheese stuck to the cardboard lid when she opened the pizza box. The scent of oregano filled the kitchen, intensifying her hunger. She was rummaging around for cutlery and a plate in one of the moving boxes when she caught sight of movement in the semi-darkness of the living room. As she squinted to see better, the dark shadow formed into a silhouette by the window facing the railway. He was sitting in the armchair. She straightened up quickly as she felt her heart pounding hard in her chest.

"Is there anybody there?" she said, restraining the urge to turn on the light in the living room. She feared what she would see, for now she could smell him.

"You little bitch," came the familiar hissing voice. Torsten gasped when he was nervous or agitated.

Anne's hand automatically searched for the scar above her eye. She backed away until her back bumped against the kitchen table.

"How did you get in?" Her voice was full of anxiety and rising sobs, which must have pleased him to hear.

His dry laughter came from the darkness, followed by a fit of coughing, which he quickly gained control of.

"You get sick from being in prison for fifteen years. Did you know that?"

She didn't answer. She opened the kitchen drawer behind her and felt around in it with her hands behind her back. If only she had unpacked the kitchen things.

"You also get sick from knowing your own daughter stabbed you in the back!"

His words made her quickly withdraw her hands from the drawer and discreetly push it in. It was empty, so it wasn't of any use anyway. She had hoped the owner had forgotten to empty it and had left a knife or scissors or a knitting needle or better yet—a gun. She was aware she was standing fully illuminated under the light in the ceiling, but she also knew if he couldn't see her, he would emerge from the darkness, and she hoped he would stay there. A quick glance at the door told her she had locked it behind her. She had fooled herself. To keep him out, she had locked herself inside with him.

"I have to say, you've changed since the last time." He grumbled in dissatisfaction. "Where are all the piercings, the heavy make-up, and the patched clothes? What happened to my little girl? But it was a long time ago. What were you then—thirteen?"

Anne didn't know if she should answer him or if it was best to stay quiet.

"I know it was you who reported me to the police. You know that, don't you? Don't you?" When he said it a second time, he shouted so loud her body shook, but it also set her adrenaline in motion. Maybe the neighbours would hear him and call the police.

"I saw you do it!" she yelled. "What do you think it does to a child to see that kind of thing? And by the way—I'm not *your* little girl!"

He laughed. His laughter gave her more goosebumps than his cries.

"You didn't understand that world, my darling. That man owed Dad money for drugs. How was I supposed to support your mother and you and all your siblings if my customers cheated me of my money?"

"He didn't deserve to die for it!" She felt the old, rebellious Anne emerging again, despite the fear. He hated it when someone opposed him, and she had done nothing but ever since her mother had dragged him into their safe home. Despite them being on their own for years after her father died, they had done well. But it had been her rebellious streak that was dangerous. It had landed her in hospital several times, but the authorities hadn't done anything. *The girl was probably asking for it—that type always were*, they would say. And her mother had always covered up for him, saying she had fallen or been in a fight with her siblings or some teenagers in Nørrebro. No one had believed her. Certainly not the police who knew her from the riots. The clashes with her stepfather had left many scars, on the outside and the inside, but she felt better equipped to deal with them now.

"Rats have to die. And you're a rat, Anne." The calmness of his voice made her courage falter.

Inside the living room, the silhouette rose. Suddenly, he stood in front of her in the light, so she once again saw the face she had tried to forget and escape from. His gaze wandered down her body and rested for a moment on her small breasts, then it slid back to her face.

"You've got a scar," he said, wanting to touch it. But she slapped his hand away before he reached it. He still had that bleary-eyed look from his heavy drugs habit. Maybe he was under the influence now; the nauseating smell sat in his clothes. His skin was older and looked rawer than she remembered, his eyes more evil, but more insecure, too, as if he had experienced things in prison that had broken him.

"You've grown into quite a pretty girl, Anne. A little boyish, perhaps—and flat-chested. But who would have thought your ugly mother could give birth to someone like you? You must take after your father." He coughed again. Anne wanted to hit him, but her arms seemed paralysed.

"You have a boyfriend, I assume?" he continued, glancing at the pizza that had gone cold with its wrinkled cheese. "Only one pizza!" He shook his head, following with a disapproving tutting sound. "Did Esben never come back, then?"

Anger boiled up inside her, overshadowing the anxiety. She began to attack him with all her might. But he only laughed, and she quickly noticed he was still stronger than her. When his blow struck her, the ceiling light became a shining sun in her field of vision. The next thing she saw was his face over hers as she lay on the floor next to the kitchen table. His eyes revealed he was enjoying the turn in events. His smile showed he hadn't been to the prison dentist.

"No boyfriend," he said slowly, laughing lewdly. "So you must need something." He tried to pull her skirt off, but his attempt caused her to regain her strength. She kicked and hit him in the stomach; it floored him long enough to allow her the chance to sit up and wipe the blood off her face with her sleeve. When he sat up, she scratched his face. If he was going to succeed in murdering her this time, she would make sure to have plenty of his DNA under her nails. That would trap him when forensics found it. When he collected himself, his anger was stronger than before, and she knew she had made a mistake again.

The knife in his hand flashed in the light from the kitchen lamp. In slow motion, she watched him, just as she had done back then, when she had followed him and witnessed the murder. His knife had stabbed the man in the chest so many times that she had been about to shout for him to stop from where she had been hiding. Instead, she had fled. That night, she had wandered the streets not knowing what to do or where she belonged. Then she had called the police anonymously from a telephone box in Nørrebro. But she had been so shocked and scared that she hadn't given them all the details, so it was a long time before the police turned up at her address. She had long gone to bed and didn't wake up until the blue flashes and sirens disturbed her.

Anne closed her eyes and waited for the inevitable. But she didn't feel the sting, only the cold metal of the knife against her skin as her jumper was ripped open, as his howling voice told her from a distance that traitors had to die. She kicked her feet into the doors of the kitchen cupboards, so the noise could be heard in all the neighbouring apartments. Far out in the fog, she heard a knock on the door and an unknown voice ask if anything was wrong. She screamed. Then came the liberating blow that sent her into oblivion.

Slowly, reality came back. The tap was dripping; otherwise, everything was quiet. Eerily quiet. She tried to open her eyes. They were stuck together.

She raised a hand, which didn't want to do as she wanted, and tried to feel. Her whole face was sticky with blood, and she could barely move her lips. Nausea came in waves, but she held it back and slowly turned her head to look down at herself. She was lying in her own blood with her jumper torn to shreds around her. To her relief, she saw she was wearing both her skirt and knickers. She was about to lose consciousness again, but that could be fatal. She caught sight of her shoulder bag on the floor and managed to reach the handle with her fingertips as she moaned in pain at stretching her arm forwards. After a tortuous period of groping around, struggling to stay conscious and keep the nausea down, she grabbed her phone and dialled Roland Benito's number. She heard him shout hello in a din of voices and laughter.

74

W ho was it, Rolando?" Irene asked anxiously.

"Anne Larsen—the journalist," he mumbled, already dialling the 118 Danish Information service to get her mobile number. The number had come up as private, so maybe she wasn't calling from her mobile at all. Despite her voice being faint and distant in the noise of the restaurant, he could hear it was her. The Nørrebro dialect was easy to recognise. But something was wrong.

The female voice at Information said good evening and asked what she could help him with. It took a long time to search, given the snippets of information Roland had—Anne's name and job. He knew no more. Still, after a while, the female voice informed him there were many Anne Larsens but only one was a journalist. And, unfortunately, her number couldn't be disclosed as it was ex-directory. Roland explained he was a police inspector and needed the number promptly but was told anyone could say that. He asked for the photographer's information and got that instead.

"Has something happened?" Irene asked, looking worriedly at him in the light from the candle on the table. He nodded with his phone at one ear and his hand over the other trying to shut out the noise.

An age passed before he was connected. It was also after eleven o'clock when he looked at his watch. Kamilla was probably in bed. The voice sounded sleepy when she finally answered. Roland explained he needed Anne Larsen's mobile number and address. Kamilla gave him the number.

"Anne just moved. I don't have her new address. Has something happened?"

"That's it—I'm afraid something has. Anne just rang me asking for help, but she was gone again before she told me where she was. I assume she's at home given the late hour. Has she really not told you anything about where she's moved to?"

There was a long pause as Kamilla thought. "She mentioned there was noise from a train, but that she'd probably get used to it. So it must be near a railway—somewhere in Brabrand. I'll drive out to look for her." There was a sudden panic in Kamilla's voice. Roland regretted ringing her and making her uneasy. He persuaded her to stay at home, promising he would let her know as soon as he knew what had happened. Once he hung up, he tried Anne's mobile, but it rang out and switched to voicemail, where Anne's happy voice told him to leave a short message after the tone. He took the chance and rang the police station. After a short while, the phone was answered, and he asked for a free officer to check an address for him. Thank God for the officers who worked overtime in the Criminal Investigation Department. After a few minutes, he had the address and thanked the helpful sergeant.

Irene stood next to him and handed him his jacket. He hadn't even noticed her leave the table. She had her own jacket on and her handbag under her arm. "The restaurant's closing soon and you seem to be busy now," she said with a tired smile.

The feeling of guilt rolled over him. After a kiss on the cheek and his assurance he would be home soon, he watched her get into her own silver Hyundai Getz, in which she had also arrived, to head back to Højbjerg. But he didn't watch the car for long; shortly afterwards, he was on the way to Brabrand and J. P. Larsens Vej—where he had been informed Anne Larsen lived—at full speed. He hoped he hadn't wasted too much time calling Information and Kamilla.

There was light in a window on the third floor of the stairwell where Anne Larsen lived. Roland stormed up the stairs and knocked on the door of the apartment. There was no name tag, but it had to be here. A door behind him opened slightly. It couldn't open any further due to a security chain.

"Does Anne Larsen live here?" asked Roland into the crack.

He put all his strength into pushing in the door to Anne's apartment with his shoulder, which, after three attempts, gave at the hinges and sprang open. He collapsed into a small narrow kitchen filled with moving boxes, almost stepping on a lifeless figure on the floor. Had she been a little further up, the door would have hit her in the head. Anne had her phone in one hand. Roland squatted down next to her and took her pulse. It was very weak; he didn't hesitate for a second before calling an ambulance. He took off his windbreaker and laid it over her naked upper body. He wouldn't have done so to an unknown victim. He had learned long ago not to touch too much for the sake of forensic evidence, but he didn't like seeing her lying there exposed. He took the phone out of her hand, which was sticky with blood. It looked as if she had put up a good fight. He took her thin hand and gave it a gentle squeeze.

"Can you hear me, Anne? I'm here and I've called an ambulance. Who did this to you?" His practised gaze photographed the surroundings. At the door, he saw parts of a bloody shoe print—the perp had stepped in the blood before leaving the apartment. Could this have something to do with the murder of Gitte Mikkelsen or Olga Halgren? Had Anne got too close? These were questions he couldn't ignore as he sat there, hoping the ambulance would soon arrive. Suddenly, he regretted scolding her on the phone earlier in the day. She was just doing her job, too.

His eyes returned to Anne's face as he felt her hand move with small jerks in his, as if regaining consciousness. She tried to open her eyes. He smiled encouragingly at her bloody face.

"The ambulance is on its way. Who did this, Anne?" He heard the fatherly tone that lay in his words. He leaned all the way down to her and listened as she tried to say something. She said it several times before he was able to grasp the words.

"My stepfather, Torsten Lund," she whispered faintly. Then he heard the ambulance sirens and nodded to her.

"We'll find him. I promise you we'll find him," he said.

75

Inspector Morten Holsted passed the village church and looked at the car's GPS. He was definitely driving on small country roads now.

He rolled up the driver's window as he drove past yet another farm and got the strong smell of being in the country. The landscape spread out around him, with large green and golden fields of grass and cornfields as far as the eye could see. He could feel how far it was to the blue sky. The compact farms lay in all their Danishness, dotted around the landscape. At one farm, the Danish flag was hoisted, waving red and white between the treetops in the light wind. Morten smiled. *Just like a picture postcard for tourists.*

He parked in a small yard in front of a derelict farm. The roof looked in need of renovation. Green moss had found fertile ground between the roof tiles. The whitewash on the walls needed repainting, and the blue paint on the window frames was peeling off. He glimpsed a garden with old fruit trees behind the house. The yard and garden needed a loving hand, too. But it could be a cosy place. And if you could afford to renovate such a house, it could be worth a lot of money. *It was a shame smaller older farms were falling into disrepair like that,* he thought as he stepped out of the car and put his nice shoes onto the muddy yard. The rain had gathered in large puddles in the many uneven holes. The rural stench from the surrounding farms dominated. It stank of cowsheds and wet straw. The garage was empty. Karl Hansen worked at a factory in Grenå, Morten had noted in his pad, but he was also interested in meeting Vivi Hansen and her son, Dennis.

He had spent the last few days visiting Olga Halgren's many grand-children from both marriages, to find the grandchild who had used her computer. He drew a thick line through the grandchildren from her first marriage. None of them could be the mysterious grandchild. Now he needed to interview the grandchildren from Olga's second marriage. Their father had hanged himself over thirty years before. His divorced wife was dead ten years, so there were only the two children left, now that Olga was dead, too. If it were at all true a grandchild had visited her, it had to be one of those two.

He looked around for a doorbell. There wasn't one. The woman who opened the door, after he had knocked a few times, looked confused at seeing such a finely dressed gentleman standing on her steps. She automatically pulled down the stained top of her tracksuit and shyly straightened her hair. It was shoulder-length, unkempt, and greying from the scalp and several inches down, where an unnatural red colour took over, making it look like her hair started there, because the grey hair blended into her white scalp. *She needs to be renovated, too*, he thought ironically.

"We don't buy from door-to-door salesmen," she said.

He showed her his police badge. "Morten Holsted, Criminal Investigation Department," he stated with authority. "Are you Vivi Hansen?"

She nodded and let him into a hallway where mud and water had been dragged in on the brown tiles. A row of dirty wellies lay on top of each other under a row of hooks with heavy jackets and rainwear, but there was a nice aroma of freshly baked bread.

"Is it Dennis? What's he done now?" she said nervously, showing him into the living room, which, to his surprise, was neat and tidy with reason-ably modern furniture.

"No, it's not Dennis. It's about your grandmother, Olga Halgren."

Vivi Hansen's face didn't reveal anything. "Gran? I haven't seen her in years. Is she still alive?"

"So you haven't seen her recently?" asked Morten, standing in the doorway to the living room as he hadn't been invited to sit down. In the silence before she answered, he heard the clatter of a keyboard from a room behind a closed door.

"No. So much happened in our family that we don't see each other anymore." She looked away, peeling a withered leaf off a red geranium on the windowsill.

"What happened in your family?"

"What happens in most families, I suppose." She evaded the question.

"Does it have anything to do with your father taking his own life?" asked Morten directly.

A flinch passed over her face. She looked up at him, scowling, as if to assess how much he knew. "Gran never forgave us," she said tamely.

Morten caught a glimpse of something that might be a guilty conscience in her eyes.

"May I sit down?" he asked, pointing to the nearest chair.

"Yes. Yes, of course," replied Vivi, as if waking up from a trance. She stood by the window, looking out at the rolling cornfields of the neighbouring farm.

"Who did she never forgive? You and your brother?"

"Mostly me. She never cared about me," she said absently. "But what about Gran?" She looked at him with eyes that still showed no interest.

"Olga's dead," he replied tentatively. "She was murdered," he continued, still not seeing any reaction.

Vivi Hansen sat down. Morten thought it was lucky there was a chair behind her.

"Murdered," she repeated in horror, but she didn't ask who, how, when, or why. She stared down at the carpet and fell into a sort of trance again.

Morten knew she'd had mental health issues and had been hospitalised often. Maybe it ran in the family and was the reason for the father's suicide—that kind of gene could be hereditary.

"Olga mentioned a grandchild who visited her and used her computer. It's not you?"

A crooked smile appeared on her grey face. "I don't understand computers at all. But she was married before her wedding to Grandad. It could be a grandchild from her first marriage," she suggested.

Morten shook his head and felt the hollowness in his stomach as it rumbled with hunger. He squinted at the freshly baked bread, which he could see was cooling on a rack in the kitchen. The aroma was making his hunger worse.

"We've spoken to all of them. It's not any of them. What about your brother?" He focused his attention on the thin woman in front of him.

"My brother? I haven't seen or talked to him in over twelve years. We keep to ourselves out here." She laughed nervously.

"And it couldn't be your son who Olga called her grandchild?" he asked, suddenly thinking of it.

"Dennis? He doesn't move out that room." She nodded towards the closed door and rolled the withered geranium leaf into a tiny ball.

"But you can ask him yourself—Dennis!" She shouted the name out so loud that it grated on his ears. It took a while before the door opened, and a young man in his twenties stood in the opening with an annoyed, questioning look on his face. He swept a greasy tuft of hair away from his pimpled forehead with a limp hand and looked at Morten with eyes that revealed an alcohol and hashish addiction. Morten knew the signs. Dennis didn't ask who he was. He only looked condescendingly at the nice trousers with the crease and the gold chain around Morten's wrist. A stark contrast to his own washed-out tracksuit.

"What?" he said, looking at his mother with the same disgust in his eyes.

"It's the police. Your great-grandmother's dead. Did you ever visit her?"

"Who?" he said, and it seemed genuine enough.

"There—you see," said Vivi Hansen with a telling look at Morten. "We don't have anything to do with that side of the family."

Morten got up and noticed a sleek computer with a large flat monitor on a desk behind Dennis. *Why would he travel all the way from Mols to Egå when he had a much more modern computer at home*, he thought. And Vivi Hansen certainly didn't look like someone with that kind of ability. He apologised for the inconvenience and politely took his leave.

When he was sitting in his car, he took out the notebook and drew a bold line over Vivi Hansen's name. He sighed and felt hungry again. He hadn't even been offered so much as a glass of water.

He had just started the engine when an old woman on a black far-too-big women's bike turned into the yard with a tray of eggs in the basket. The bike swerved when she spotted the car and had to brake, so she almost fell off. Morten jumped out to help her and just managed to grab the handlebars before it all went wrong.

"Oh, thank you. Thank you. I have eggs for the Hansens," she said breathlessly. Her face was wrinkled and her teeth, no doubt her own, were tinged yellow. Periodontitis could be seen clearly when she smiled. But her eyes were full of life and curiosity. The Woman with the Eggs— the village gossip, Morten thought immediately with a little smile at the opportunity.

"Those eggs look lovely," he said, engaging in conversation. "Are they from your own chickens?"

The woman nodded proudly. "I have good chickens. Thank God there was no bird flu again this year. My chickens are all free-range. It produces the best eggs with orange yolks. Who are you?" She blinked, her eyes running in the strong sunlight as she looked him up and down with an appraising eye. She clearly wasn't used to seeing his type in Vivi Hansen's driveway.

"Morten Holsted. Criminal Investigation Department."

Her eyes widened. "Has Dennis done something wrong again? He's a bad apple!" The latter she whispered confidentially with a glance towards the house. But Vivi hadn't opened the door, nor could she be seen in the window.

"No, it wasn't Dennis this time. I came to let Vivi know her grandmother's dead," Morten replied honestly, hoping to find out more.

"Her grandmother. Oh, that poor thing. She must have had a sad life. Losing your son like that." She shook her old head, which, just like in *The Woman with the Eggs*, was wrapped with a patterned scarf to protect her from the sun.

"How did she lose him?" asked Morten, playing ignorant.

Again, the woman leaned in confidingly towards him, holding the bike by the handlebars, and squinting towards the house to keep an eye on whether Vivi would show up.

"It's said he took his own life. It was the boy who got him convicted."

"What boy? For what?"

She looked up at him with eyes shining triumphantly at being the one in the know.

"Vivi's brother. He had his father convicted of incest. Said he'd abused Vivi, his own daughter—just think. Later it turned out he hadn't, but by then, it was too late. Not so strange Dennis has turned out the way he has." She shook her head slightly and sent Morten a wise look.

"Do you have eggs for me, Mrs. Møller?" Vivi's voice sounded abruptly from the steps. It startled the woman so much she nearly dropped her eggs again.

76

It had been a busy morning at the police station. He had retired to his office to think and to try to figure out the big picture. Copenhagen Police Station had been involved in the search for Gitte Mikkelsen's unknown father. They were in the process of questioning friends and acquaintances of Gunda and Anders Pedersen and investigating the circumstances surrounding the illegal adoption. Roland had sent another officer to Vejle to talk to Nanette's sister. He hoped it would pay off because he couldn't let go of the feeling Gitte Mikkelsen's father had played a major role in all of this. That feeling had only intensified.

He called Aarhus Hospital and asked about Anne. Again, he had to explain he wasn't a relative and elaborate on who he was before he was told she was fine. He sent her his best wishes. Her stepfather still hadn't been found. He could have returned to Copenhagen. The Copenhagen police were working on that case now, too. Torsten Lund had been released on probation only, so the episode could put him behind bars for another few years, in addition to the years he still had to serve for the murder back in 1991. Roland had ordered security on Anne's door at the hospital in case Lund should seek her out there. He realised it was lunchtime and went up to the canteen to get himself a smørrebrød.

He wasn't quite done with his open-faced salami sandwich and Ramlösa water when a call came for him. There was news from the capital—it was important, and he needed to hurry. On the way down to the lift, he wondered in which case there had been a development. Although he hoped it was about Gitte's biological father, he had to admit the arrest of Anne Larsen's stepfather would make him calmer.

Fifteen minutes later, he was sitting with Mikkel Jensen in his car in the police station car park. An aunt in Copenhagen, who had been Nanette's support during the long and difficult pregnancy, knew the name of the man who had defiled her niece. She had called him a devil and made the sign of the cross when she referred to him.

"We should have taken him in," Roland muttered bitterly as he made a quick turn from the car park out onto Sønder Allé. Mikkel clung to his seat belt.

"He probably won't show up for the blood test," he commented, sliding in the seat due to the sharp turn. "But the fact he's Gitte Mikkelsen's biological father doesn't automatically make him her killer. Quite the opposite, I'd say!"

Roland didn't look at him. "I have a strong hunch. He doesn't have an alibi, and why didn't he mention he's Gitte's father?" he replied angrily.

"Maybe he doesn't know."

Mikkel's words made Roland's strong hunch falter. Maybe he was right. Maybe Troels Mortensen didn't know he was the father of the murdered girl at all.

A call came through on his phone.

"Roland?" It was DS Niels Nyborg's voice. "I investigated this Troels Mortensen in more detail. He's not all he seems."

"Go ahead, Niels." Roland concentrated on both the traffic and the conversation.

"Do you remember the case from Næstved back in 1976, where two siblings accused their father of incest?" began Niels.

"Hmm, that was a long time ago," Roland grumbled, glancing at the rear-view mirror and overtaking a blue bus, after which they ended up behind a tractor, causing him to swear quietly and light a cigarette.

"The two siblings were alone with the father after the parents' divorce. He was convicted in the incest case. It was too much for the law-abiding office manager. He took his life by throwing himself in front of a train at Næstved station," offered Niels. "The mother didn't want anything to do with the children because of the new man in her life." He paused. Roland could hear him drinking from his cup before continuing: "After her father's suicide, the girl was placed with a foster family, while the boy went to live with his grandmother. Why the grandmother couldn't take both of them isn't clear in the report," he continued. "When the sister was sixteen, she revealed there had never been any incest. Their father was a good and exemplary man who had tried to do everything for them, but the brother hated his father and blamed him for his parents' divorce. The sister's been admitted to psychiatric wards several times. The brother joined the military and was later stationed in Iraq. Guess who the brother and sister are?" But Niels answered his own question without waiting for a reply: "Troels Mortensen and Vivi Hansen." There was silence again while Niels waited for Roland's reaction.

"Great job, lad, but that doesn't make him a killer," Roland finally said in a tired voice.

"No, but he's not mentally balanced. Then there's his time as a soldier in Iraq," continued Niels. "He became friends with an American soldier who was killed by a roadside bomb. It made him unleash his military weapon on Iraqi civilians."

"We never heard of that in the press." Roland stopped the car in front of Egå Angling Shop.

"Do you think we hear everything? No one was seriously injured, and Troels was immediately discharged from the army. It says PTSD in his file."

Roland played with his car keys as he watched Mikkel run up to the shop door and shake it. He turned to Roland on the steps and shrugged with both arms resignedly, his expression saying they had driven in vain.

"Well, the family's past isn't exactly as white as snow. Let's take a closer look at Troels. We just need to find him first. Do you have his home address?"

Roland got the address and turned off the phone.

Mikkel climbed into the passenger seat.

"The shop's closed. The bird's flown the coop. What was that?" He pointed to the phone.

Roland quickly filled him in on what Niels had told him, then he made a U-turn and drove back.

Roland turned off on Grenåvej and parked in the yard in front of a nice, detached house with a new tile roof. *Remortgaged*, he thought involuntarily.

There didn't seem to be anyone at home, but as he rang the doorbell, he heard footsteps from high heels on a wooden floor. The door was soon opened by a fair-haired woman with masculine features. Her face looked bare and fresh without make-up. She looked at him curiously with tired green-grey eyes.

"Is Troels Mortensen at home?" he asked. Mikkel Jensen came up the steps and stood behind him; they both showed her their IDs.

"Vera Mortensen. I'm his wife," she said, inviting them inside. She was dressed like a businesswoman on her way to a meeting. "He's not home. Maybe he's down in the fishing hut," she said kindly.

"Fishing hut? Is he at the harbour?" asked Roland.

"No, he built a shed for all his fishing gear down in the back garden. I can't stand the stench of fish and don't want it in the house. Has something happened?" She suddenly looked worried.

"We just want to talk to your husband about a case we're investigating," he replied, giving Mikkel a look that told him to keep his mouth shut and let his boss do the talking.

Roland looked around the living room, while Vera walked out onto the tiled terrace with its beautiful flowerpots and looked out into the large garden, using her hand to shield her eyes from the sun. She was a solicitor, he just knew. That explained the expensive furniture and the exclusive home decor. Apparently, the angling business wasn't such a goldmine, given the number of customers he had counted during his visit, so she had to be the majority breadwinner. The shiny brown leather sofa with accompanying deep armchairs was a Chesterfield. Though whether original, he couldn't tell. Nor whether the large abstract paintings on the walls were genuine. An imposing dark oak bookcase matching the sofa arrangement in colour and style took up one entire end wall. It was filled with books, foreign souvenirs, and family photos. Roland glanced over at them. Vera had a more feminine face in her wedding photo. Her make-up was elegantly done, and she wore a white veil. Troels stood next to her, smiling, a white carnation in his buttonhole.

"I can't see him down there," she said apologetically, walking over to them silently, the soft carpet absorbing the sound of her high heels. Roland smelled her perfume; a heavy sweet smell that gave him the same headache as his father-in-law's cigar did.

"Is it something I can help you with?" she smiled, telling them in the same breath she was on her way to a meeting at City Hall. She was a city councillor, she explained with pride in her voice.

"We'll find him," Roland assured her, not seeing any immediate reason to involve Vera yet. She smiled and showed them to the front door through the hall, which had an antique dresser and a mirror set in a gold frame.

"You can check whether his car's in the garage. If it is, he's probably in the hut. Just walk through the gate here and all the way down to the bottom of the garden. I have to go now." She shut the door with an apologetic smile.

The modern detached house was built on a large hilly site. Roland noted the garage was empty. A huge lawn spread out as far as the eye could see. A medium-size garden pond with goldfish, water lilies, and other aquatic plants, surrounded by ferns and flower beds, had been laid out on a small terrace.

He didn't make it all the way down to the hut. His phone played the James Bond theme in his pocket. It was Holsted.

"Morten! Have you found the grandchild?" said Roland, stopping in the middle of the lawn.

"No. We've driven around the entire country to talk to all of Olga Halgren's grandchildren, but to no avail. I'm just back from Mols after visiting the granddaughter from the second marriage. Pretty interesting stuff. We need to talk as soon as possible."

"Interesting how?" Roland looked at the little shed. It was painted a greenish colour, blending in with the foliage of the trees that completely enclosed it. It was well hidden, at the very bottom of the garden. It looked empty. Mikkel studied the garden pool with interest.

"Information regarding an old case—which I've checked out. I think we need to sit down together. Our two murders might be linked more than we think after all. Where are you?"

"We're on our way back," Roland said resolutely as he waved Mikkel to come with him.

"Shouldn't we go down to that shed?" Mikkel asked with an expression of disgust on his face as he sat down in the passenger seat.

"It looks empty. He's not there. The garage is empty, too. Morten Holsted has something important we need to talk about." Roland looked at Mikkel questioningly. "What's wrong?"

"Some of the toads in their garden have some disease," he said. "They're lying dead, belly up, in the garden pond." He made a muffled gagging sound and fastened his seat belt.

77

Morten Holsted had set up the briefing room with coffee and cakes. Roland sat down in front of him. He couldn't prevent his eyes from being drawn to the pictures of Gitte on the board this time, either. Julie Hermansen sat down, too. She watched them reflectively as she turned a ballpoint pen. A notebook was ready in front of her. She sent Roland a shy smile and blushed a little. He returned the smile and briefly wondered how the rest of her evening with Henry Leander had gone. He wished his old friend the joy of rediscovering love. Mary Leander had been an amazing woman; he would never find another like her. Involuntarily, Roland looked at Julie's wedding ring. Could Leander settle for a summer fling? His thoughts were interrupted by Kurt Olsen, who came stamping in, disturbing the peace.

"Ah, the aroma of good coffee. And strawberry cakes! We must have made great progress!" He sat down next to Roland and poured coffee. Roland looked curiously at Morten, who was in the process of sorting out some photographs.

"I think it's all falling into place now," Morten said, placing a picture of Olga Halgren on the board with all the others that had been hung up as the investigation had slowly progressed. There were images of the skip, Louise, Kristoffer Kjær, Gellerup Forest, and the doll, too.

"I visited Olga Halgren's granddaughter in Mols today. Vivi Hansen, married to Karl Hansen, a factory worker in Grenå. Together they have a twenty-year-old son, Dennis, who lives at home."

Morten took an artful pause and poured coffee. He sat down and put a strawberry cake on a paper plate. He carefully wiped his fingers on a paper serviette before moving on.

Roland looked down embarrassed at his own cake. He had just wiped his fingers on his trouser leg.

"When I was driving back, I stumbled across a Woman with the Eggs," he continued, smiling when Julie, Roland, and Kurt all looked at him questioningly. "The village gossip who was delivering eggs," he explained. "She was pretty eager to share the family's gloomy secrets." Morten took a plastic teaspoon and stuck it into his cake. Again, Roland felt the blush on his cheeks. He had eaten half his with his fingers, but now he wiped them on a serviette as he looked at Morten.

"Are you sure it's not just gossip?" Roland asked.

Morten finished chewing before answering. "No, it's true. I've checked her information. Vivi Hansen's father took his own life by throwing himself in front of a train after he was convicted of incest. Reported by his own son. In other words, Vivi's brother."

"Niels Nyborg just told me about it on the phone!" exclaimed Roland in astonishment.

"Exactly." Morten smiled, his gold chain rattling as he pushed back his wavy hair.

"Who wants to fill me in me here?" Kurt broke in abruptly. Morten quickly brought him up to date. He had already briefed Julie when he had asked her to attend the meeting.

"So I only need to talk to one grandchild now—who I'm sure is the missing grandchild. Vivi's brother. But I'll let you take that, Roland, because this is where our two cases meet."

Roland stared in disbelief at Morten. "Troels Mortensen," he said, shaking his head in wonder. "Troels Mortensen is Olga Halgren's mysterious grandchild! The grandmother he lived with as a child?"

"Yes, but back then she lived in Korsør in Zealand. Both of her marriages ended in divorce. After her last marriage to Egon Mortensen, she took her maiden name again, so she was no longer Olga Mortensen. She moved to Jutland ten years ago. Troels Mortensen broke contact with his family many years ago. The sister hasn't spoken to him for over twelve years."

Kurt looked at Julie. "How does such a profile fit our perpetrator?"

"There's no doubt we have someone here who falls into our second category." She nodded at Roland, who knew she was referring to the categories of offenders she mentioned at their first meeting. In her words: sadistic perps, angry perps, powerless perps.

"Angry offenders suppress their anger and take it out on anyone they know they can handle—such as children. Troels Mortensen carries a lot of anger—towards his father, his mother and, not least, himself. Maybe even at the sister, too. Perhaps because she couldn't defend herself against her father, and because her father preferred her to Troels."

"So pure jealousy?" commented Morten.

Julie nodded and stared at the picture of Gitte Mikkelsen's dead body for a long time.

"But he could also easily fall under the category of powerless offender. Now we don't know whether the children really were sexually abused, but the sister may have lied when she stated the father was innocent. It happens—children start to feel guilty about their parents being punished for something they reported. That the father took his own life may have triggered such a reaction in her."

"So it seems we have our man," muttered Kurt. "What about Vivi's son—do we know more about him?" he asked, looking at Morten again.

"The son, Dennis, isn't what you'd describe as a good kid, either. He's been arrested twice for attempted rape in Grenå, but he was released both times due to a lack of evidence," said Morten.

"Troels's wife?" Roland asked, thinking of her masculine face.

"Vera's a stand-up example of her flesh and blood. Comes from a nice family. An educated solicitor and a city councillor. We can't find anything on her."

"Do we have enough for a search warrant for Troels's home?" Roland asked, looking hopefully at the superintendent.

"Shouldn't we pay him a visit first? That he's related to Olga Halgren and maybe used her computer doesn't make him her killer," Kurt replied as he searched for his pipe.

"There's more," said Roland, fishing for his packet of cigarettes, having seen Kurt about to light up. He had to enjoy it before politicians' threats became serious.

"He's not only Olga Halgren's grandson, who sent emails to Gitte Mikkelsen from his grandmother's computer . . ." Roland lit the cigarette, took a breath, and exhaled the smoke through his nostrils. "He's also Gitte's father."

Kurt stopped abruptly in the middle of carefully stuffing his pipe. Julie looked up from her papers surprised, her jaw almost dropping.

"So you mean this Troels Mortensen murdered both his grandmother and his own daughter?" Kurt lit the pipe and shook his head as if he didn't believe that story. The smell of Mac Baren tobacco fought with the smell of smoke from Roland's Cecil cigarette.

"We don't yet know if he has anything to do with any of it, but he certainly knew Olga Halgren, and he's Gitte Mikkelsen's biological father. Maybe he doesn't know he is." Roland reused Mikkel's words, for it was a fact he had thought of since.

"Let's find Troels and bring him in!" said Kurt in a firm voice.

"Can't we get a search warrant now? Troels may have held Louise at his residence. He doesn't live far from Judge Johansen's house, which she stumbled across when she escaped from her captivity. She couldn't have made it far in the condition she was in," said Morten.

"With a politician in the house! I doubt he held her at home," the superintendent mumbled over the mouthpiece of the pipe.

"Troels is wanted; we'll find him," Roland said convincingly, looking at Kurt when the phone rang. "Maybe that's the call now."

But it was the hospital. They had promised to ring when Louise Poulsen was stable enough to talk. She could now, the nurse said, if it didn't take too long. Roland promised it wouldn't.

He didn't like hospital wards, despite coming here often as part of work. The sight of sick people always made him think of a side of life where everyone, especially himself, could end up at any second.

Louise was even paler than he remembered from the picture on the bulletin board in the briefing room. Gerda and Peter Poulsen were sitting by their daughter's sickbed when he entered. Both had red eyes full of tears. Relief surrounded them like a halo. Roland thought, for a brief moment, of their accusations the police weren't doing enough to find their daughter alive. He was quietly annoyed the police hadn't found her. But the main thing was she was safe and well. He would have to let his pride go.

"I'm happy and relieved on your behalf," he said, shaking hands with both parents. They got up but were clearly having a hard time walking away from their rediscovered daughter. Gerda kept holding her daughter's thin white hand in hers and seemed to never want to let go of it again.

"Unfortunately, I have to talk to Louise on her own. It's very important we get the culprit."

The parents reluctantly left the hospital room. Roland pulled an uncomfortable wooden chair over to the bed and sat down. Louise looked up at him nervously with dull eyes.

"I'm from the police. We must catch the person who did this to you. And I'll make sure to do it quickly, okay?"

The girl nodded silently. She had a clear oxygen tube in her nose that restricted her movements.

"How were you abducted? Was it in a car? Do you remember the car?" he asked.

"It was a big black car. He pulled me into it suddenly. I lost my phone." Louise's voice was weak. Roland leaned forward towards the bed to hear her better. He could smell the hospital in the bedding.

"Was it him?" Roland showed her a picture of Jesper Ingemann. She shook her head. He slowly flipped through the album of all the pictures Amalie Bang had seen, too, giving her plenty of time to look at them before moving on to the next page. But she shook her head at every picture she looked at. Roland put the book away and looked at the girl for a long time.

"Do you know where you were held captive, Louise?"

She began to speak faintly. "When I woke up, I was tied up and couldn't move." Her chin trembled slightly from the tears that were welling up. "I saw Gitte's bike and her backpack, and then I knew . . ." Tears began to run down her cheeks under the plastic tube.

"Do you know where she was?" repeated Roland. "Do you remember any sounds—church bells, a train, sounds from a farm, anything else?"

Suddenly, she was crying so much her body trembled and a machine started howling heartbreakingly next to Roland. He got up quickly from the wooden chair and was almost knocked over by a couple of nurses, who appeared to have been keeping guard at the door. Gerda and Peter stood in the doorway, too. They looked at him angrily.

"I have to ask you to leave. Louise is unable to talk any more today," said a nurse to Roland, while another tried to stabilise Louise again. "We probably allowed it too early," the nurse continued almost apologetically, placing a hand on his shoulder as she showed him out. She was a sweet, young, fair-haired girl who had probably unbuttoned her white tunic a little too much in the stifling heat for the hospital rules. Roland caught himself lingering a little too long at a hint of a tanned breast.

"Was this necessary?" he heard Peter's voice behind him as he began to walk down the long hospital corridor. He chose to ignore it. He still needed to find a murderer. The Poulsens probably hadn't thought of that. They had their daughter back in good condition. He owed another family the answer of finding their daughter's murderer.

78

Kamilla walked along the long corridor of Skejby Hospital. The oppressive sensation in her stomach now went all the way up to her chest. Her father had been very ill and hospitalised in Horsens long before he died. At the time, she hadn't understood what was wrong with him. It had sounded like something he gained more strength from, yet he had become weaker and weaker, eventually fading to a skeleton with a transparent layer of skin on the outside. Since then, she had discovered the disease was cancer. He had died slowly and painfully and was eventually so full of painkillers he didn't recognise them when she and her mother stood by his sickbed. *This is what God's punishment looks like,* her mother had said as they left. *That's how we will all die.* From then on, Kamilla had stayed far away from hospitals.

Roland Benito had called her late last night and informed her of what had happened. But she still couldn't sleep after his first call and the thought of what might have happened to Anne. She should have been tired after the trip to Mols, which she had completed as planned after meeting Danny in the graveyard. She had taken off her jumper and walked around in a camisole top to get some sun on her body. It had been a freeing feeling to walk around the water's edge at Sletterhage on Mols with rolled-up trouser legs and her bare toes in the cold water, which certainly hadn't been inviting enough for a full dip. She had filled the digital camera's memory card with pictures of the beautiful landscape and the sea. Sletterhage Lighthouse, flowers, insects—everything beautiful she had seen. She had been torn by her mixed feelings for Danny, which were all conflicting with each other. Hate and love, forgiveness and revenge. She hadn't got home again until darkness was falling, and she had fallen asleep after eating. Shortly afterwards, Roland had called and woken her up. She had tried Anne's mobile several times without getting an answer, and her unrest had grown. Only when Roland called the second time, telling her Anne was in the hospital and would make it through, had she taken a sleeping tablet and got some dreamless sleep. But now her head felt heavy, and she didn't feel at all rested.

At last, she found the ward number Roland had given her. An officer was sitting on a sofa just outside Anne's door. He got up immediately when Kamilla took the door handle.

"Are you allowed to be here?" he asked, assessing her.

Kamilla nodded and explained she worked with Anne Larsen and had been given permission to visit her by Roland Benito. The officer nodded and sat down again with his book.

Anne's face was completely unrecognisable. Her upper lip was split. The left eye was completely closed and swollen in shades of black and purple. Kamilla wondered whether Anne would have a new scar and was in no doubt she had received her old scar in the same way, probably from the same man. *Better to be without a father than to have someone like him in her life,* she thought briefly before sitting down on the chair next to the bed. Anne's thin arms lay on top of the duvet; they were bruised and so were her hands. They looked like Jan's hands had. She never found out what had happened to him. But Anne had undoubtedly defended herself as best she could. Tears welled up in Kamilla's eyes. She took Anne's hand gently and sat holding it in hers without saying anything. She didn't want to wake her as she had probably been given something to help her sleep.

Kamilla had been sitting and holding Anne's hand for a very long time when Anne began to move and slowly opened her eyes. She tried to smile when she caught sight of Kamilla.

"Hi. Thanks for coming," she said weakly. It dawned on Kamilla that Anne probably didn't have anyone else.

"Such an ordeal. Did your stepfather really do this?"

Anne nodded and told her it wasn't the first time, and that she had fled Copenhagen when she had heard he had been released on parole. Slowly, and in a weak voice, she began to tell Kamilla about her childhood, in a home where everyday life meant violence towards the children and her mother. One day she had fled, becoming one of the squatters in Nørrebro. Kamilla only knew them from the TV, where they threw bricks at the police. She hadn't had much sympathy for them. But the hand of fate always lay behind human behaviour. Young people clearly had anger they needed to get out. Whether against themselves or others was secondary. Anger finds a way to come out. Quite automatically, Kamilla began to share details of her own childhood. Although it wasn't gruesome in the same way as Anne's, they did have one thing in common. Anne had been oppressed by violence that had left its mark both inside and out. Kamilla by a strict religious upbringing and assurances life wouldn't be easy, that she would lose all those she loved, and that she was to blame for it.

Kamilla went out into the corridor and got some coffee. She smiled at the officer, who nodded back at her, an insulated coffee pot in front of him.

"You're being well looked after," she said, smiling, as she entered Anne's room with two cups of coffee.

"Yeah, it's incredible how nice they are. Roland's afraid Torsten will contact me here." The horror Kamilla had seen in Anne's eyes the day she had visited her returned briefly, then she smiled and edged herself up to sit in bed. Kamilla helped her raise the headboard of the bed. Anne only sipped her coffee. Every muscle and her cracked upper lip hurt when she drank the hot liquid.

"Who's Esben?" Kamilla asked cautiously after they had sat in silence for a while, thinking about each other's fates.

"He was my boyfriend," Anne said quietly, looking down into the coffee cup with a sad expression in her eyes. "Torsten chased him away. He once beat him so badly that he looked like me." She tried to smile but was unsuccessful.

"Did he never come back? Could you not have run away together?"

"Esben wasn't very old, either. I don't know where he went. In fact, I think he moved away from Nørrebro with his parents." She set the cup down and seemed to have given up on getting rest.

"But to think Danny Cramer's the drunk driver who killed Rasmus. It's completely unbelievable!"

Kamilla nodded and again felt the hatred mingle with other emotions that were coming to the surface. But she couldn't forgive a man who had killed her son. If she could, that would make her a bad mother.

"Do you know how the murder cases are going?" asked Anne, as if she could tell by looking at Kamilla that she needed to talk about something other than Danny.

"The last I heard, they found Olga Halgren's grandson. They think he has something to do with the murder. I haven't heard anything about Gitte's murderer, but Louise has been found, so maybe she can identify him," Kamilla said, relieved by the change of subject.

"Thank God Louise was found. Is she okay?"

Kamilla didn't have time to answer. She was interrupted by the officer who entered the room and closed the door behind him. He watched Anne and smiled broadly. "I have a message for you from Roland Benito. Torsten Lund has been arrested in Copenhagen. You can relax now."

Anne took Kamilla's hand. Her eyes shone with joy as tears of relief flowed down her cheeks.

"Say hi to Roland and tell him—tell him I love him." The mischief in her eyes was back.

The officer laughed and said goodbye to them both. He didn't need to be there any longer.

79

In the fishing hut in the back garden, behind the stylish detached house in Risskov, they found Gitte's bike, helmet, and backpack during the search of Troels Mortensen's home. There was no doubt Louise had been held captive in the shed. The remnants of the rope left around her wrist when she had stumbled into the judge's garden corresponded in structure to the rope that had caused the marks on Gitte's wrist. Forensics determined it was the same type of rope. In a drawer, they found Gitte's mobile phone, the white tights stained with mud, and pairs of children's knickers hidden as little trophies. Roland could see Troels sitting and sniffing at them in the sinister shed. It obviously wasn't the first time he had been successful catfishing on children's chat sites on the internet. But it was the first time it had led to murder. Hopefully. He felt nauseous.

The girls probably hadn't dared tell their parents about their experiences. The parents probably didn't know the girls were chatting online. But maybe more girls would come forward now. That often happened when a case like this came to light—all the other reports followed in its wake.

There had been a couple of episodes recently of date-rape drugs being used. Rape and attempted rape, where perps at various nightclubs had spiked their victims' drinks with drugs. It was a difficult crime to investigate, as it was crucial the trace took place no later than four days after the incident in the form of a urine or blood sample. But usually the victim couldn't remember what had happened, so the urine trace test didn't take place within the optimal timeframe. But when one episode popped up, more followed. The girls were made aware of the danger. Roland sighed, happy again his girls were now adults and not vulnerable as children and young people were today.

He looked at the pictures on the board, which he now soon hoped to be able to take down and thought of Anne's involvement in the investigation. He smiled at the thought of Dan Vang's greeting from her, where she had said she loved him. He shook his head a little. Who would have thought that would come from someone like her? In the investigation of the case of Torsten Lund, he had discovered information on her past in Nørrebro. She wasn't exactly a favourite of the Copenhagen police, but that was the past, and just as he believed you shouldn't convict a suspect until the evidence was laid out, he equally believed you should never judge people on their past sins. We all have them.

It had been with great relief when he received the message from Copenhagen that Torsten Lund had been arrested. At first, Lund had pleaded not guilty and claimed he had never been to Aarhus. But when the evidence was presented to him, like the trail of blood originating from his shoes—which he was still wearing—his fingerprints all over Anne's apartment, and the scrapings with his DNA from under her nails, he had broken down and confessed. Forensic science had come a long way in the years he had been behind bars.

The phone interrupted his rejoicing thoughts. It was forensics. They were investigating Troels Mortensen's car. In the rear window, they had found the funny animal mentioned by Kristoffer Kjær. The tyre prints matched, too, but they needed to find more evidence if a conviction was to be certain.

"We've finished investigating the Honda," said Gert Schmidt.

"Did you find anything?"

"We did. The girls were definitely kept on the back seat of the car. We found both light and dark curly hair, as well as some artificial hairs—probably from the doll. We also found a strange object on the back seat."

"What kind of object?" Roland asked curiously.

"I had no idea what it was. It kind of looks like a large screwdriver with a blade-shaped tip at one end and a half-hollow plastic tube at the other. But one of the technicians is an angler and told me it's a rod holder for when you're out fishing. The blade's inserted into the sand, and the fishing rod's placed in the hollow tube, so you're free to hold the fishing rod your-self while waiting for a fish to bite."

Roland thought for a moment to ascertain the importance of the rod holder for the case. He thought of it before Gert could remind him of it.

"I have a picture of the mark on the girl's back in front of me. Without doubt, it's the same object that made the imprint. She must have been lying on top of it on the back seat of the car."

Roland lit a cigarette. His hand shook a little.

"Probably when he drove the dead girl to the skip," he mumbled.

"The way the blood collected in the imprint shows it happened while she was still alive," Gert replied.

"I wonder how long he was driving around with her in the car?" said Roland absent-mindedly.

"Everything found has, of course, been sent for further technical inves-tigation, so I'll be in touch again," concluded Gert.

Roland thanked her and hung up. They had him now. The long search and sleepless nights were at an end. They only needed to find him, and it couldn't be that difficult. Troels Mortensen couldn't be far away. They only had to find him before he panicked and did more harm.

80

She was locking the door when her arm was twisted behind her back and a weight pressed against her body, pushing her in towards the door of the surgery. Her jaw hurt from being forced against the door. A pointed object went through the thin fabric of her blouse and coldly touched the skin on her right side.

"Unlock the door," he said softly in her ear. She smelled alcohol on his breath.

She obeyed and unlocked the clinic again. He pushed her in, closed the door, and turned the lock.

"Troels! What are you doing?" Majken saw the knife in his hand. She wanted to say something but couldn't make another sound.

Troels pointed the knife at her while he went to the window and looked out through the blinds. "They're looking for me," he said, as though to himself.

"Troels, sit down. Tell me what happened." Majken realised she needed to summon everything she had learned about psychiatry. This was a clearly desperate and sick man. Something quite different to the children who sat and confided in her with big innocent eyes. The thought made her unsure whether she could handle the situation.

"Stop your psychological shit. Sit down, Miss Thorup." He twisted around, walking along the wall towards the medicine cabinet, still with the tip of his knife pointed at her.

"Give me something soothing." He waved her to him with the knife and pointed with it towards the cupboard. "Open it! You have to have something in there!"

She dared not do anything other than obey, first taking out a jar of Alprazolam sleeping tablets. He snatched the glass out her hand and read the label.

"Very clever!" He raised a finger and waved it warningly in front of her nose as if she were a naughty child. "I'm not going to sleep that fast. And what would you do, then? Call the police again?"

He pushed her so she fell back into the chair. He rummaged in the medicine cabinet himself, read the labels, and found a couple of jars, then stuffed them in his jacket pockets. But she couldn't see what they were. He sat down opposite her and looked intensely at the sharp blade of the knife.

"Would you believe it, a police officer told me this knife would be perfect for a murder."

Majken swallowed a few times as she saw the savagery in his eyes. The doctor in her wanted to diagnose acute psychosis, but she suddenly didn't feel like a doctor. Was that why he had come? Did he know he needed help?

"You didn't ring to get the result of your blood test. Everything's fine," she said calmly. An attempt to get things back to normal.

"Fine!" He snorted. "I don't give a damn about that blood test. I know how I feel."

She straightened up and took a deep breath.

"Are you and Vera not doing any better?" She tried again to get a normal conversation going.

He leaned back in his chair and put the knife into its sheath with a smile she couldn't decipher. He didn't respond immediately.

"Things are never going to get better between us. I can't give her a baby, can I?" He sat with his eyes closed. Then he opened them quickly and looked directly at her. His eyes were pale and dull, and his face had an expression she had never seen before.

"You don't need to have children to have a good marriage," she said, trying to smile encouragingly.

He got up abruptly and wandered restlessly around the surgery, slamming the knife against his thigh with each step he took. It was still in its sheath. That reassured her.

"Children." He snorted with his back to her. She couldn't work out what was in that comment.

"You like children, don't you?" She said it gently, knowing the calm that had come over him now could quickly turn. But she had to get him to open up about his problem. If he had come to her for help, he was going to get it.

"I'm not a paedophile," he said quietly, still with his back to her. She was amazed by that answer and felt all the alarm bells starting to ring. There was more going on here than she realised.

"I didn't say that."

He quickly turned around and laid both hands hard on the table in front of her. The blood vessels appeared bluish under the transparent skin on his thin arms.

"Why's it so important for women to have children? After all, they don't want to know them once they're born!"

"Is that something you've experienced? Did your mother turn her back on you?" Majken suddenly saw an opportunity to get him to talk.

"They're all the fucking same!" he said savagely.

"Who? Women?"

He sat down on the edge of her computer desk and let a finger wander along the rim of the screen.

"Only children are good company. Little girls who don't expect you to . . ."

He stopped and sat staring at the new window put in after the burglary.

"Expect you to get it up?" Majken dared, hoping her boldness would overpower him.

"Only you know my problem," he snarled. "And Vera, of course, who has to go to someone else to feel like a woman." He began wandering again.

"Tell me what happened. You won't get rid of the pain until you let it out."

"The pain!" He turned angrily to her. "I don't feel any pain. Psychological drivel. But if you want to know, she offered it herself. It's her own fault. She looked like her mother."

Majken froze. What was he talking about? Her mouth was dry; she couldn't swallow.

"Her own fault how? Who are you talking about?" she asked hoarsely as he sat down opposite her again. He had drawn the knife again and was lovingly drawing circles on the tabletop without leaving scratches.

"Little girls in tops cropped at the navel, and thigh-high dresses so you can see their little round buttocks. That's what she was like—Gitte." He looked at her defiantly.

Majken froze and thought of the description of Gitte's clothing in the newspaper. There had been no mention of a thigh-high dress or a crop top.

"Do you mean Gitte Mikkelsen?" she asked in a voice that barely answered.

He nodded silently and kept staring at her.

"Did you see her like that?" She wanted to get up to have a glass of water, but he pointed at her with the knife angrily.

"Sit! You must write something in my file. Write it like it is—that I don't know what I'm doing because of my mental state."

She sat down again and tried to think clearly. Tried to be the psychologist she was. But the desire to clarify things intruded more than the desire to help her patient.

"Unfortunately, I can't. I had a break-in last Friday. My records were stolen." She looked at him tentatively as she said this. His eyes flickered.

"Not mine. Mine wasn't stolen."

"Was it you? Why did you take Gitte's file? Did you see it when you were here for an examination, or how else did you know Gitte was my patient?"

Troels didn't answer; he didn't even look at her.

"You were afraid of what she'd said? The police discovered Gitte was afraid of one of her father's friends—are you one of her father's friends?" She felt her courage slowly return.

"Her *adopted* father!" he screamed angrily, so his saliva hit Majken in the face.

He got up quickly. A blood vessel protruded clearly on his forehead. Majken knew she had surprised him again. She had read in the paper that Gitte Mikkelsen had been adopted by Ida and Allan Mikkelsen. Now she was sure it was her he was talking about.

"How did you find her?"

He turned to her and smiled broadly. "Piece of cake. I fish with Allan Mikkelsen! When you've had a crate of beers on a fishing trip filled with locker-room talk, you start to reveal a little about yourself. We're very close, Allan and me." He winked provocatively at her.

"Do you know who Gitte's biological father is?" She couldn't believe the suspicion that had begun to sprout. He had to confirm it.

"You should have been a police officer." He laughed.

She figured she wouldn't get an answer.

"You abducted Louise, too? Where is she?"

Troels grew serious and started pacing the floor again. "The little bitch, she saw me. She wanted to go running to the police."

"So you killed her, too?" Majken's voice trembled.

"No! I didn't murder anyone!" he yelled. He sat down and put both feet up on Majken's desk. He waved the black Lloyd shoes as he looked at them.

"Do you know how grown up ten-year-olds are today? They put it all out on the internet, their hairless little bodies, and even ask for it. They got their first screw!"

Majken shook her head and smiled indulgently. "You're wrong. That's just how you think it is."

He shook his head, too. "She wanted it herself; she offered it to me."

Majken got up without him protesting. "She had a doll with her. She was just a child," she said, shakily pouring a glass of water from the jug she always had on the table.

"I gave her that doll," he said. It surprised Majken.

"Because she was a child, right?" She leaned against the cool wall and drank the tepid water. It moistened her throat and gave her new courage. He didn't answer.

"But why did she end up in a skip?" She felt the tears in her throat. It dawned on her how close she had been to Gitte without being able to help. Troels sat staring petrified in front of her.

"She made me want to, but I still couldn't. She started screaming. Then I got angry. I hate that whingeing! She should have done as I said!" He began to sob and hid his face in his clenched hands.

"She looked at me, Majken." He sobbed into his hands and bit his knuckles. "Her eyes stared up at me, dead in the rain. And they keep staring."

He curled up in the chair like an unhappy child. His body shook as he cried silently.

81

Kamilla was relieved Anne was doing well after everything, and that her stepfather was no longer a threat. The warm wind blew in through the car's open driver's window, causing her hair to fly around her ears as she drove back along Grenåvej. She felt free inside after telling Anne about the things that had always weighed heavily on her chest. And about Danny, too. Fate sometimes intervened in the most unusual of ways. Her mother would probably say it was God's punishment. Kamilla believed more in an evil destiny.

Had Jan completed his mission? She quickly shooed the thought away. She wasn't going to think of either Jan or Danny. Never again.

She turned on the radio and let the notes from Shu-bi-dua's "Midsommersangen" fill the car and her head. Since leaving the hospital, she had planned to visit Majken. She wished she'd had the long talk with her. Suddenly, she felt she knew Anne better than she knew Majken, despite them knowing each other for years. Only when you know another person's innermost feelings, sorrows, and joys do you truly know who they are. *Then you know more than just the outer shell,* Kamilla thought. Majken had never opened up to her like Anne had done today, and so she hadn't told Majken much about herself, either. Your private life was intimate and not something to be talked about. But something lay behind Majken's strange behaviour on Saturday. They hadn't talked to each other since. They needed to.

* * *

No one opened the door when she rang Majken's doorbell. The house was strangely quiet. Kamilla looked at her watch. Surgery hours should be over. Maybe Majken was still at the clinic. She put on her jumper and walked around the house. The door was locked. The new window with the clear glass and neat frame looked out of place on the older wall.

Majken's car was parked in the garage. She should be in the garden. Majken was always in the garden when the weather lent itself to it. The blinds of the surgery were pulled down, but when Kamilla stretched up on her toes, she was able to look through a narrow crack. She leaned gently against the windowsill, keeping her balance on the stone edge of the flower bed. There was nothing to see, only the corner of Majken's computer and a hint of the medicine cupboard. A cramp began in one leg. She was about to jump down from the rock when she caught a glimpse of someone entering her field of vision and disappearing again. She suddenly felt ashamed of peering inside. What exactly was she doing? What if the neighbours saw her! Kamilla jumped down from the rock and tried to shake off the cramp in her leg. Then she heard a sound from the clinic, as if something had overturned and shattered. Glass?

"Majken?" she called outside the window. "Is everything okay?" When no answer came, she ran to the door and knocked hard on it.

"Majken, open the door. What's going on? I know you're in there. Open the door!"

Majken looked absolutely awful when she finally opened the door. She was unusually pale, and her eyes were red as if she had been crying.

"Thank God, Majken, I heard glass being shattered. I thought something had happened to you." Kamilla laughed, relieved, and went inside. Then she caught sight of the knife against Majken's neck and of him as he stepped out from his hiding place behind the door.

"Welcome," he said slimily, heaving her into the surgery so violently she lost her footing and fell onto the floor in front of the medicine cupboard.

Troels slammed the door by giving it a hard kick with his foot. Without taking his eyes off them, he turned the lock.

Kamilla sat up and rubbed her elbow, which had hit the corner of the cupboard.

"Are you injured? Are you okay?" Majken asked worriedly, wanting to run to her, but Troels held her back with a firm grip on her arm.

"Drop that bullshit; she's fine." He put the knife back in its sheath. "You were in the process of writing I'm of unsound mind in my file; I'm sure you remember. It was stupid to throw the glass at me when my back was turned, but I know where I have you now." He sat down heavily in the chair and looked malevolently at her.

Kamilla sat on the floor and looked at his shoes. They were black and polished. Above the black ankle sock on his right foot, she spotted a large wound. It looked like a shin bone wound, but suddenly Anne's words after the press conference echoed in her head: *The police suspect the killer scratched himself on the skip door or gave himself enough of a cut that it bled profusely. That'll catch him—a cut like that is a wound.* She also saw the small lumps of earth stuck under his fine shoes by the slightly raised heels.

"You murdered Gitte and threw her in the skip?" Kamilla mustered the courage to say the words. At this point, it didn't matter anyway. They were going to die. Troels would never let them go now. "You cut your leg on the hatch of the skip when you crawled in with her. And it was you who broke into my home office and deleted the contents of my computer, too."

Troels looked as if he wanted to get up and hit her, but it was only a sense; he remained seated and smiling in a disturbing way. His eyes stared at her like the deadened eyes of a shark. "Wise girl. The police could probably use you," he said, and immediately turned his gaze to Majken again. "Write, Majken. For Vera's sake!"

"Why for Vera's sake?" Majken couldn't hide the anxiety in her voice.

"Write, for fuck's sake!" He slammed a palm hard on Majken's desk, evoking a jerk of terror in both of them. Kamilla looked into Majken's restless eyes and knew she was thinking the same thing as her.

Majken wrote as Troels wanted. They both knew what it meant. He wouldn't receive a long sentence. After some time in treatment in a closed psychiatric ward, he would be able to act stable again and be released. The cold from the linoleum floor crawled under Kamilla's blouse and up her back. Her elbow hurt and had begun to swell.

Troels stood behind Majken's chair with the knife against her neck. His eyes desperately followed her fingers across the keyboard as he silently read every word she typed. *Majken could delete it again afterwards,* Kamilla thought. If there was an afterwards. Was it now? Was it time for them to die? She shuddered.

Troels sat down in the chair again. "Well! Is that digital patient record now available to every doctor and hospital?" he asked. Majken nodded.

He suddenly seemed apathetic and as though he didn't know what was going to happen next. The scowling gaze slid from Kamilla to Majken and back again. Eventually, it landed on the roll of duct tape still lying on the windowsill after Majken had sealed the chipboard.

It hurt as he tightened the tape around her wrists and ankles. She protested until he placed a piece brutally over her mouth. Majken resisted, too. Kamilla struggled to sit up and grunted her protests when Troels gave Majken a blow so she fell back into the chair. Kamilla started to cry. The crying couldn't come out of her mouth. She snorted to get air and felt the mucus accumulating in her throat, almost suffocating her. Troels disappeared without a word.

Majken bled from her nose and the blood ran down the duct tape over her mouth. They tried to communicate with their eyes, but the only thing that came was despair. He had spared their lives. They would certainly be found—if not soon, then tomorrow when the medical secretary came in.

Then Kamilla heard a sound she knew but couldn't place. A crackling. When the smell penetrated under the door, she saw the shared panic in Majken's eyes.

The house was on fire.

82

Roland sat uneasily in his chair. The search for Troels Mortensen was in full swing, and he could do nothing in relation to it. The interrogation of Vera Mortensen had just finished. They had let her go as she didn't appear to have any knowledge of her husband's hobby beyond angling. However, she had confirmed their marriage wasn't among the best, and that Troels was impotent. Julie Hermansen had then elaborated on how that fact put him even more so under the category of powerless offender, but Roland had gradually become uninterested in what kind of offender he was. He just had to be found.

The news a fire had been reported at Majken Thorup's doctor's surgery came later in the afternoon; he was with Henry Leander at the time, reviewing the results of the analyses from Troels's car and from the crime scene in Gammel Egå. They had such concrete evidence that both Olga Halgren's and Gitte Mikkelsen's murderer was one and the same man—Troels Mortensen—even a skilled barrister wouldn't be able to deny them. The tyre prints in Olga's driveway had been almost destroyed by the rain, but they had got enough to confirm they were from the tyres on Troels's blue-black Honda.

"Bloody hell, why didn't we think Troels might go to his doctor?" he said to Henry when the message came in.

"Do you think he was the one who set the clinic on fire?" Henry asked with his bushy white eyebrows raised high. There was a new expression in the blue-green eyes Roland hadn't seen since Mary had been alive.

Shortly afterwards, Roland had Mikkel Jensen on the phone. He said both Majken Thorup and the photographer Kamilla Holm had been in the clinic, but both had been rescued from the burning building. The doctor had been admitted to Aarhus Hospital with smoke poisoning; the photographer had suffered some burns on her right arm but was otherwise unharmed.

"They say it was Troels Mortensen," Mikkel said breathlessly. "He came to get the doctor to write that he's mentally unstable on his medical records. He doesn't need to tell anyone that," he added. Roland cleared his throat like he usually did when Mikkel crossed the line.

"Is the fire under control?"

"It looks like it. It's still smouldering a little, but it was a bloody good job the neighbours called it in so quickly; otherwise, I don't think they'd have survived." The sound disappeared in voices and crunching. Roland shouted hello several times, then Mikkel's voice came back on the line.

"You can't keep those journalists at a distance. They're like vultures."

"They're just doing their job," Roland said.

Henry sent him a surprised look as he twisted his well-groomed white handlebar moustache between two fingers.

He had barely finished the conversation with Mikkel before a new call came in.

"Troels Mortensen has been found." It was Niels Nyborg's voice.

"Thank God!" exclaimed Roland, followed by a loud sigh of relief.

"We found him in the fishing shed. He must have walked the back road through the garden, so Dan didn't see him," Niels explained. Roland nodded without commenting, but he would soon need to have a serious talk with that officer. He had been stationed to watch the house if Troels decided to return home, against expectation.

"Great, Niels. Have you brought him in?"

"Unfortunately, we found him with a couple of empty bottles of tablets."

"Suicide?"

"Definitely an attempt. He left a farewell letter to his sister."

"To his sister? Why not to his wife?" exclaimed Roland in astonishment, lighting a cigarette with his free hand. He really needed one now.

"Hard to know. You write to the person you want to explain your situation to, don't you?" Niels answered pensively.

"Will he survive, or did he succeed?" Roland had to admit, with shame, whether Troels survived or not didn't affect him one bit. Not every case deserved humanity. He had no sympathy for a man who behaved like that towards his own family. Of course, it wouldn't benefit the investigation if he died. A confession and punishment were among the things people were waiting to read about in the news.

"He's been admitted to Skejby Hospital. They say he'll survive," Niels replied.

Dear Vivi,

I hated Dad. I know you hated him, too, deep down inside. It was his fault Mum left us. Do you remember the toads by the garden pond? When I stepped on them and strangled them, it was Dad I was taking life from—but it was you, sister, who I made stop whingeing. I know you're thinking a lot about why I decided to report him. He never hurt me—not in that way. But I heard through the wall when he was in with you at night, and as you wouldn't report him, I had to do something. I love you and just wanted to protect you.

But I know you're suppressing what he did to you and Mum, and now you're suffering from the guilt that things developed the way they did. That's why I've stayed away all these years. I wanted to give you a chance to have a good life with your husband and son. I have no regrets. Dad got what he deserved for what he did to our family. He was worse than the toads. But why have I inherited his sick mind? The mind I loathed so much. I always swore if I ended up like him, I'd put an end to my miserable life.

Forgive me, sister.

Your brother, Troels

83

———

He ended the day by celebrating the successful investigation of the murder cases with the entire team in the cosy basement of the Bryggeriet Sct. Clemens brewery. Candles were lit on the tables, and Roland sat taking in the large, beautiful, hand-beaten copper kettles visible in the room, and listening to the chatter around him. He missed Irene. He was looking forward to returning to normal working hours. In secret, he watched Henry Leander and Julie Hermansen, who were sitting opposite him.

"Are you going back to Copenhagen tonight?" he asked Julie.

She glanced quickly at Henry, who was drinking a large beer and getting foam on his moustache.

"I'm staying here this weekend. I'm going hunting."

"You're going hunting?" he said, discovering the same astonishment in his voice he heard from others when he told them he was a winter swimmer.

"Julie's full of surprises," Henry said, wiping his moustache.

Roland had no doubt they were going hunting together. Julie's wedding ring still shone alarmingly in the glow of the candlelight. But seeing Henry so happy overshadowed Roland's concern. So some joy had come out of the case. But he wished so much hadn't happened. Ida and Allan Mikkelsen had been charged with participating in an illegal adoption along with Gunda Pedersen. Given the circumstances, they were looking at a fine. Roland didn't believe they would get jail time. He felt for them.

Fortunately, he had heard Ida had given birth to a healthy little girl the night before. But he hoped Troels Mortensen got a very long and harsh punishment or was put in treatment.

"It's inconceivable Louise had the strength to saw through the rope on the blade of a shovel in the shed, then to smash the door with the shovel and escape." Mikkel's voice sounded clear through the noise. He was always loud when he'd had a little to drink.

"Even children develop unimaginable strength in pressurised situations," Julie said, so loudly Mikkel could hear it at the end of the table.

"But still, she must have been weakened having not had food and drink for a whole week," Mikkel replied. Kim nodded. "But why did he strangle his grandmother?" he continued with disgust in his voice. Roland looked down at him and made eye contact.

"Olga Halgren had got too close. She knew about his 'chatting' on the internet and his fondness for children. Her son had had the same inclinations. Troels desperately tried to erase all traces of a crime he probably hadn't intended to commit. The burglary at the clinic was also an attempt to prevent the information from getting out that Gitte had been afraid of a friend of the family. And the photographer had had a break-in, too. The contents of her computer were deleted. Probably also to be sure there were no pictures that could identify him."

"Are they both okay?" Niels Nyborg asked worriedly.

Roland smiled. "They're both fine. Kamilla Holm will be discharged tomorrow. They want to keep Majken Thorup in a little longer."

"And the reporter?" Mikkel asked, drinking from the large beer.

"She's recovering, too. Her stepfather gave her a serious beating, but she's a tough girl, and she should be discharged soon—to a safer life—as long as Torsten Lund's in prison."

Everyone was reassured, and the talk moved on merrily to completely different things. Soon, new crimes would come in, and the memory of this horrific case would fade into oblivion. As soon as the press stopped covering the story, people would forget about it and no longer worry about when their children walked to birthday parties or played in the playground on their own.

Roland was tired when he drove up to the front of the house in Højbjerg. But tired in a pleasant way. He smiled, relieved his parking space under the copper beech wasn't occupied. The terrace lights were on. Only now did he realise it was a balmy summer evening. Irene sat with her legs pulled up under her in the sun lounger, with a glass of red wine in her hand resting on one knee. There was a glass for him and a bottle of Barolo on the table. Luciano Pavarotti's powerful voice sounded muffled from the speakers in the darkness of the living room. He poured wine into the glass, smiled, and raised it to her.

"Congratulations," she said, reaching for him.

He took her hand and sat down next to her, so she had to scooch up a little.

"You smell of beer," she commented.

He gave her a kiss and pulled her into him. They sat looking at the stars, and a blissful calm fell over him. The mobile phone played the James Bond theme in his pocket, but he didn't answer it. Tonight was just for him and Irene.

ABOUT THE AUTHOR

Inger Gammelgaard Madsen is a prolific Danish crime writer best known for her Rolando Benito detective series. Ever fascinated by police work and forensics, crime fiction was a natural fit for Madsen when, after working for some time as a graphic designer, she decided to return to her first love: writing. She is also the author of the Mason Teilmann series, which has been published in four languages.

DISCOVER
STORIES UNBOUND

PodiumAudio.com

www.ingramcontent.com/pod-product-compliance
Lightning Source LLC
Chambersburg PA
CBHW021809110726
47902CB00006B/1716